David Malcolm

by

Nelson Lloyd

Double 9 BOOKS

David Malcolm

by Nelson Lloyd

ISBN: 978-93-73408-25-5

Published by

DOUBLE 9 BOOKS
2/13-B, Ansari Road
Daryaganj, New Delhi – 110002
info@double9books.com
www.double9books.com
Tel. 011-40042856

ABOUT THE AUTHOR

Nelson Lloyd crafted a literary career in the early 20th century, known for his insightful exploration of small-town life and human nature. Throughout his writing, he often blended humor, social commentary, and psychological depth, revealing the intricacies of ordinary lives shaped by community dynamics and personal challenges. His works frequently focus on themes of innocence, identity, and social judgment within rural or close-knit settings. Among his notable publications are novels and short stories that capture the complexities of youth and adulthood, often through richly drawn characters facing moral dilemmas and societal expectations. His storytelling balances light hearted adventure with moments of profound reflection, making his narratives both engaging and thought-provoking. Lloyd's literary contributions remain valued for their empathetic portrayal of human struggles and the nuanced depiction of the social environment of his time. He passed away in 1933, leaving behind a legacy as a keen observer and chronicler of early American life.

CONTENTS

CHAPTER I 8
CHAPTER II 18
CHAPTER III 28
CHAPTER IV 37
CHAPTER V 49
CHAPTER VI 57
CHAPTER VII 67
CHAPTER VIII 75
CHAPTER IX 85
CHAPTER X 96
CHAPTER XI 102
CHAPTER XII 111
CHAPTER XIII 119
CHAPTER XIV 123
CHAPTER XV 133
CHAPTER XVI 142
CHAPTER XVII 149
CHAPTER XVIII 159
CHAPTER XIX 168
CHAPTER XX 175
CHAPTER XXI 184
CHAPTER XXII 193

CHAPTER XXIII 198
CHAPTER XXIV 204
CHAPTER XXV 210
CHAPTER XXVI 214
CHAPTER XXVII 225

TO

THE RARE, SWEET MEMORY OF
SUSANNE LIVINGSTON GREEN LLOYD
MY WIFE AND THE DEAR COMPANION
WHO WORKED
WITH ME OVER THESE PAGES

CHAPTER I

"Take care not to tumble into the water, David," said my mother.

She was standing by the gate, and from my perch on the back of the off-wheeler, I smiled down on her with boyish self-assurance. The idea of my tumbling into the water! The idea of my drowning even did I meet with so ludicrous a mishap! But I was accustomed to my mother's anxious care, for as an only child there had fallen to me a double portion of maternal solicitude. In moments of stress and pain it came as a grateful balm; yet more often, as now, it was irritating to my growing sense of self-reliance. To show how little I heeded her admonition, how well able I was to take care of myself, as I smiled loftily from my dangerous perch, with my legs hardly straddling the horse's back, I disdained to secure myself by holding to the harness, but folded my arms with the nonchalance of a circus rider.

"And, David, be careful about rattlesnakes," said my mother.

Had I not seen in her anxious eyes a menace against all my plans for that day I should have laughed outright in scorn, but knowing it never wise to pit my own daring against a mother's prudence, I returned meekly, "Yessem." Then I gave the horse a surreptitious kick, trying thus to set all the ponderous four in motion. The unsympathetic animal would not move in obedience to my command. Instead, he shook himself vigorously, so that I had to seize the harness to save myself from an ignominious tumble into the road.

"You won't let David wander out of your sight, now, will you, James?" my mother said.

James was climbing into the saddle. Being a deliberate man in all his actions, he made no sign that he had heard until he had both feet securely in the stirrups, until he had struck a match on his boot-leg and had lighted his pipe, until he had unhooked the single rein by which he guided the leaders and was ready to give his horses the word to move. Then he spoke in a voice of gentle protest:

"You hadn't otter worry about Davy, ma'am, not when he's with me." His long whip was swinging in the air, but he checked it, that he might turn to me and ask: "Now, Davy, you're sure you have your hook and line?"

I nodded.

"And your can o' worms for bait?"

Again I nodded. The whip cracked. And I was off on the greatest adventure of my life! My charger was a shaggy farm-horse, hitched ignominiously to the pole of a noisy wood-wagon; my squire, the lanky, loose-limbed James; my goal, the mountains to which were set my young eyes, impatiently measuring the miles of rolling valley which I must cross before I reached the land that until now I had seen only in the wizard lights of distance.

Every one lives a story—every man and every woman. A million miles of book-shelves could not hold the romances which are being lived around you and will be unwritten. I am sure that when your own story has been lived, when it is stored in your heart and memory, you will follow the binding thread of it, and find it leading you back, as mine leads me to one day like that day in May when I went fishing. There will be your Chapter I. Before that, you will see, you were but a slip of humanity taking root on earth. My own life began ten years before that May morning, but on that May morning began my story. Then I rode all unconscious of it. I was simply going fishing for trout. Yet, as I clung to my heavy-footed horse and kept my eyes fixed on the distant mountains, my heart beat quick with the spirit of adventure, for to fish for trout in mysterious forests meant a great deal to one who had known only the sluggish waters in the meadow and the martyrlike resignation of the chub and sunny. I might begin my story on that winter morning when I came into the world and bleated my protest against living at all, but I pass by those years when I was only a slip of humanity taking root on earth and come to that May day which is the first to rise distinctly on my inward vision when I turn to retrospect. Even now I mark it as a day of great adventure. Since then I have battled with salmon in northern waters, I have felt my line strain under the tarpon's despair, I have heard my reel sing with the rushes of the bass, yet I do not believe that a whale with my harpoon in his side, as he thrashes the sea, would give me the same exulting thrill that came with a tiny trout's first tug at my hook. Filled with so exciting a prospect, I did not look back as we swung down the hill from the farmhouse. I dared not, lest I should see my too solicitous mother beckoning me home to the protection of her eyes. Though I clutched the harness and bounced about on my uncomfortable seat, the horse's rough gait had no terrors for me when every clumsy stride was carrying me nearer to the woods. As we rattled into the long street of the village, it seemed to me that all the people must have come out just to see us pass. The fresh beauty of the spring morning might have called them forth, but from the proud height where I sat looking down on them they had all the appearance of having heard in some mysterious way that David Malcolm was going fishing. They hailed me from every side. Even the Reverend Mr. Pound added to the glory of my progress, leaving his desk and his profound studies of Ahasuerus to stand at the open window as we passed.

> With boyish exultation I called to him: "I'm goin' a-fishin', Mr. Pound—fishin' for trout."

In Mr. Pound's personal catechism his own chief end was to utter trenchant and useful warnings to all who came within reach of his voice. Even to a lad riding forth under careful guidance to fish in a little mountain stream he had to sound his alarm. The soft fragrance of the May-day air, and the restful green and white of the May-day coloring had brought to the minister's face a smile of contentment in spite of his melancholy ponderings over the weaknesses of Ahasuerus; he looked on me benignly from his window until I spoke, and then his face clouded with concern.

"David, David," he cried, stretching out his hand with fingers wide-spread, "don't fall into the water."

There was a mysterious note in his reverberating tones, which expressed a profound conviction that not only should I fall into the water, but that I should be drowned, and looking at his solemn face I could feel the cold pool closing over my head. I tried to laugh away the fear which seized me, but chill, damp currents seemed to sweep the shaded street. Not till we reached the open sunlit square did my sluggish blood start again. There I came under the genial influence of Squire Crumple's radiating smile, and Mr. Pound and his lugubrious warning were forgotten. The squire was trimming his lilac-bush, and from the green shrubbery his round face lifted slowly, as the sun rises from its night's rest in the eastward ridges and spreads its welcome light over the valley.

"Well, Davy, where are you bound?" he shouted, so pleasantly that I could well believe my small wanderings of interest to so great a man.

"Fishin'," I answered, drawing myself up to a dignity far above the chub and sunny—"fishin' for trout."

"Fishin', eh? Well, look out for rattlers." His voice was so cheery that one might have thought these snakes well worth meeting for their companionship. "This is the season for 'em, Davy—real rattler season, and you're sure to see some." To make his warning more impressive, the squire gave a leap backward which could not have been more sudden or violent had he heard the dreaded serpent stirring in the heart of his lilac. "Watch out, Davy; watch sharp, and when you meet 'em be sure to go backward and sideways like that."

He gave a second extraordinary leap, which was altogether too realistic to be pleasant for the boy who saw the mountains, sombre and black, beyond the long street's end, yet very near him. I forced a laugh at his antics, but I rode on more thoughtfully, my hands clutching the harness, my eyes fixed on my horse's bobbing mane. I feared to look up lest I should meet more of these disturbing warnings, and yet enough of pride still held in me to lift my head at the store. I had always looked toward the store instinctively when I passed that important centre of the village life, and now, as always, I saw Stacy Shunk on the bench.

He was alone, but alone or in the company of half a score, in silence or in the heat of debate, Stacy had a single attitude, and this was one of distortion in repose. Now, as always, he was sitting with legs crossed, his hands hugging a knee, his eyes contemplating his left foot. In the first warm days of spring, Stacy's feet burst out with the buds, casting off their husks of leather. So this morning his foot had a new interest for him, and he was absorbed in the study of it, as though it were something he had just discovered, a classic fragment recently unearthed, at the beauty of whose lines he marvelled. He did not even look up when he heard the rumble of our wagon. Stacy Shunk never troubled to look up if he could avoid it. He seemed to have a third eye which peered through the ragged hole in the top of his hat, and swept the street, and bored through walls, a tiny search-light, but one of peculiarly penetrating power. I saw his head move a little as we drew near, and his body shifted nervously as would a mollusk at the approach of some hostile substance. Yet sitting thus, eying me only through the top of his hat, he saw right into my mind, he saw right into my pockets, he saw the mustard can full of worms, he saw the line, and the fish-hooks which my mother had thoughtfully wrapped in a pill-box. How else could he have divined all that he did?

"Well, Davy," he said in a wiry voice, which cut through the din of rattling harness and creaking wagon, "I see you're goin' a-fishin' for trout?"

"Yes, sir, Mr. Shunk," I returned, with a politeness that told my respect for his occult powers.

"Well, mind," he said, intently studying his foot as though he were reading some mystic signals wigwagged from the gods, "mind, Davy, that you don't fall into the hands of the Professor. If the Professor catches you, Davy—" The foot stopped wiggling. The oracle was silent. Did it fear to reveal to me so dreadful a fate as mine if I fell into the Professor's clutches? I waved a hand defiantly to the seer and I rode on. Rode on? I was dragged on by four stout horses through the village to the mountains, for in my heart I was calling to my mother, wishing that her gentle warnings had turned me back before I heard the voice of doom sounding from the depths of Mr. Pound; before I had seen the comic tragedy enacted by Squire Crumple; above all, before the man who saw through the top of his hat had uttered his enigmas about the Professor.

There is something innately repugnant to man in the word "professor." It makes the flesh creep almost as does the thought of the toad or snake. Though when a boy of ten I had never seen a "professor," the word alone was so full of portent that the prospect of seeing one, even without being caught by him, would have frightened me. I suppose that the chill which reverberated through my spine and legs echoed the horror of many generations of my ancestors who had known professors of all kinds, from those who trimmed their hair and dosed them with nostrums to those who sat over them with textbook and rod. Being myself thus perturbed, it was astonishing that James should show no sign of fear, but should keep his horses in their collars, pulling straight for the mountains where the dreaded creature lived. He smoked his pipe nonchalantly, as though a hundred professors could not daunt him. I was sure that there was something of bravado in his conduct until he began to sing, and his voice rang out without a tremor, so full and strong that it fanned a spark of courage into my cowering heart. James had a wonderfully inspiring way of singing. He tuned his voice to the day and to the time of the day. This morning the sky was clear blue above us, and about us the orchards blossomed pink and white, and the fresh green fields were all awave under the breeze, not the grim wind of winter, but the soft yet buoyant wind of spring. So his song was cheery. The words of it were doleful, like the words of all his songs, but under the touch of his magic baton, his swinging whip, a requiem could become a hymn of rejoicing. Now the birds in the meadows seemed to accompany him, and our heavy-footed four to step with a livelier gait in time to his rattling air, all unconscious that he sang of "the old gray horse that died in the wilderness." It was a boast of his that he could sing "any tune there was," and I believed him, for I had a profound admiration of his musical ability. Indeed, I hold it to this day, and often as I sit in the dark corner of an opera-box and listen to the swelling harmonies of a great orchestra, I close my eyes and fancy myself squatting on the grassy barn-bridge at James's side when the shadows are creeping over the valley and he weeps for Nellie Grey and Annie Laurie in a voice so mighty that the very hills echo his sorrow.

This May morning, as James sang, my spirits rose with his soaring melody from the depths into which they had been cast in the passage of the village, and when the last note had died away and he was debating whether to light his pipe or sing another song, I asked him with quite a show of courage:

"Is it very dangerous in the mountains?"

James looked down at me. A smile flickered around the corners of his mouth, but he suppressed it quickly.

"Yes—and no," he drawled.

Inured as I was to his cautious ways, I was not taken aback by this non-committal reply, but pursued my inquiry, hoping that in spite of his vigilance I might elicit some encouraging opinion.

"Am I likely to tumble into the water while I'm fishing, James?"

"That depends, Davy." James looked profoundly at the sky.

"And what's the chance of my being bit by a rattlesnake, James?"

"I wouldn't say they was absolutely none, nor yet would I say they was any chance at all." At every word of this sage opinion James wagged his head.

We rode some distance in silence, and then I came to the real point of my examination. "James, what kind of a man is a professor?"

James looked down at me gravely. "I s'pose, Davy, you have in mind what Stacy Shunk said about him catchin' you."

"Oh, dear, no," I protested. "I was just wondering what kind of a man he was."

"Well, Davy," James said, in a voice of mockery which silenced as well as encouraged me, "if you can fall into the creek, be bit by a rattler, and catched by the Professor all in the one-half hour we will be in the mountains while I loaden this wagon with wood, I'll give you a medal for being the liveliest young un I ever heard tell of. Mind, Davy, I'll give you a medal."

With that he checked further questioning by breaking into a song, and had he once descended from the heights to which he soared and shown any sign that he was aware of my presence, pride would have restrained me from pressing my trembling inquiry.

So, singing as we rode, we crossed the ridge, the mountain's guarding bulwark; we left the open valley behind us and descended into the wooded gut. We passed a few scattered houses with little clearings around them, and then the trees drew in closer to us until the green of their leafy masonry arched over our heads. At last I was in the mountains! This was the mysterious topsy-turvy land, the land of strange light and shadow to which I had so often gazed with wondering eyes. In the excitement of its unfolding, in the interest with which I followed the windings of the narrow road, I forgot the dangers which threatened me in these quiet, friendly woods; and when I cast my line into the tumbling brook I should have laughed at Mr. Pound, at Squire Crumple, and Stacy Shunk, had I given them a thought. But even James's kindly warnings were now uncalled for. That he should admonish me at all I accepted as merely a formal compliance with his promise to my mother that he would keep an eye on me. For him to keep an eye on me was a physical impossibility, as the road plunged deeper into the woods, bending just beyond the little bridge where he had fixed me for my fishing. He was soon out of my sight, and his warning to me to stay in that spot went out of my mind before the rumble of his wagon had died away. Had he turned at the bend he would have seen me lying flat on my back on the bridge, unbalanced by the eagerness with which I had answered the first tug at the hook.

I could have landed a shark with the strength which I put into that wild jerk, but I saw only the worm bait dangling above my astonished face. With my second cast I lifted a trout clear of the water; then caught my line in an overhanging branch and saw my erstwhile prisoner shoot away up-stream. The tangled line led me from my post of safety. Had I returned to it; had I remembered the admonition of the cautious James, and held to the station to which he had assigned me—my life might have run its course in another channel. Now, as I look back, it seems as though my story became entangled with my line in that overhanging branch, as though there I picked up the strong, holding thread of it, and followed its tortuous windings to this day.

My blood was running quick with excitement. I had no fear. A wonderful catch, a game fish six inches long filled me with the pride of achievement, and with pride came self-confidence. The stream lured me on. The rapids snapped up my hook, and with many a deceitful tug enticed me farther and farther into the woods. The brush shut the bridge from my view, but I knew that it was not far away, and that a voice so mighty as James could raise would easily overtake my slow course along the bank. So I went from rock to rock with one hand guiding my precious rod, and the other clutching overhanging limbs and bushes.

What sport this was for a lad of ten who had known only the placid brook in the open meadow and the amiable moods of its people! How many a boyish shout I muffled as I made my cautious way along that boisterous stream and pitted my wits against its wary dwellers! I wormed through an abatis of laurel; I scampered over the bared and tangled roots of a great oak; I reached a shelf of pebbly beach. Around it the water swept over moss-clad rocks into a deep pool; above it the arched limbs broke and let in the warm sunlight, making it a grateful spot to one chilled by the dampness of the thicker woods. Eager to try my luck in that enticing pool, I leaped from the massed roots to the little beach without troubling to see what others might have come here to enjoy with me a bit of open day. My hook touched the stream; my line ran taut; my rod almost snapped from my hands. I clutched it with all my strength. Every muscle of arms, legs, and body was bent to land that gigantic fish. That it was gigantic I was sure, from the power of its rush. I pitted my weight against his and felt him give way. Then, shouting in exultation, I fell over backward. I saw him leave the water, not quite the leviathan I had fancied; I saw him fly over my head and heard him flopping behind me. Getting to my feet, I turned to rush at my prize and capture him. I was checked—first by my ears, for in them rang the sharp whir of a rattle. Cold blood shot from my heart to the tips of my toes and the top of my head. I needed nothing more to hold me back, but there before my eyes was the other visitor to this pleasant sunny spot, his head rising from his coiled body, his tail erect and lashing in fury.

Since that day I have learned that the rattler when disturbed by man will seek refuge in flight, and fights only when cornered. This particular snake, I think, must have been told that a boy will glide away into the bushes if a chance is given him, for he seemed determined to stand his ground and let me flee. But where was I to escape when he held the narrow way to the bank, and behind me roared the stream, grown suddenly to mighty width and depth? How was I to move at all when every nerve was numbed by the icy currents which swept through my veins? Could I escape? Was it not foreordained that I should meet my end in these woods? Had I not spurned the chance of life given me through the prophecies of good Mr. Pound and the warning of the squire?

The snake before me grew to the size of a boa-constrictor. The brook behind me roared in my ears like Niagara. The snake began to drive his head toward me, showing his fangs as though he were making a reconnoissance of the air before his spring. He was so terrible that I knew that when he did hurl himself at me I must go backward and fulfil the prophecy of Mr. Pound. I had forgotten the man who saw through the top of his hat. I awaited helplessly the triumph of Mr. Pound.

From out of the bush, from out of the air, as though impelled by a spirit hand, a long stick swung. It fell upon my enemy's head and drove it to the ground. He lifted his head and turned from me, striking madly, but the rod fell again upon his back. He uncoiled and tried to run; he twisted and turned in his dying agony and lashed the air in futile fury. The merciless rod broke him and stretched him to his full length. But even though dead he was terrible to me, for had I not heard that a snake never dies until sunset; could I not see the body still quivering; might not the bruised head dart at me in dying madness!

I took a step backward, and hurtled into the water. For a long time I groped in the depths of the pool. To me it seemed that I struggled there for hours in the blackness; that serpents drew their slimy lengths across my face; that fishes poked their noses with bold inquisitiveness about me and dared to nibble at my hands; that Mr. Pound looked up at me from the abyss, benignly in his triumph, and that his solemn voice joined with the roaring of the torrent. Knowing well that my end had come and that the prophecy was being fulfilled, I struggled without hope, but my fingers clutching at the water at last met some solid substance and closed on it. I felt myself turn, and suddenly opening my eyes saw the sunlight pouring through the green window in the tree-tops. My legs straightened; my feet touched the stony bottom; my shoulders lifted from the stream, and I looked into a small girl's face, while my hand was tightly clasped in hers.

Since that day the sun's soft brown has faded from her cheeks, uncovering their radiance; since then she has grown to fairest womanhood, and I have seen her adorning the art of Paris and Vienna; but to me she has given no fairer picture than on that May morning when, shamefaced, I climbed from the mountain stream and looked down from my ten years of height on the little girl in a patched blue frock. Nature had coiffed her hair that day and tumbled it over her shoulders in wanton brightness, but she had caught the crowning wisp of it in a faded blue ribbon which bobbed majestically with every movement of her head. Had some woodland Mr. Pound told her that I was coming? Since then I have seen her more daintily shod than when her bare brown legs hurried from view into broken shoes of twice her size. Since then the hard little hand has turned white and thin and tapering, to such a hand as women are wont to let dawdle over the arms of chairs. Then I was a boy, with a boy's haughty way of regarding girlish softness. I was haughtier that day because I sought in my pride to cover up my debt to her. Now I am a man, but the boy's picture of Penelope Blight, the little girl in the patched blue frock and broken shoes, standing by the mountain stream, holds in the memory with clear and softening colors.

She leaned, a tiny Amazon, on the stick which towered to twice her height, and she said to me: "Boy, you hadn't otter be afraid of snakes."

In my shame I answered nothing and my teeth chattered, for I was very cold from fright and the ducking.

Then she said to me: "Boy, you had otter come over to our house and get warm."

I remembered my dignity, and, in a tone of patronage assumed by right of the one year of difference in our ages, I asked: "Where is your house, young un?"

She pointed over her shoulder, over the quivering body of the snake, across the bushes, and through the green light of the woods. There I saw a bit of blue sky, cut by a thin spire of smoke.

"Yonder's our patch," she said, "and father will give you something to warm you up."

I asked: "Who is your father, little un?"

She drew herself up very straight, and even the blue ribbon in her hair rose in majesty as she answered. Then I almost tumbled into the pool again, for she said: "Some call him the Professor."

CHAPTER II

The words of Penelope Blight fell on my ears as chillingly as the rattler's whir. That the prophecies of Mr. Pound and Squire Crumple had come to nothing was little consolation for me. So near had they been to fulfilment that it seemed that I must have been spared only for a harder fate, and the figure of Stacy Shunk peering at me through the top of his hat, uttering his ominous warning, rose before my startled eyes. I should have run, but my retreat was barred, the girl blocking the way over the shelving beach. I took a backward step and for an instant the Prophet Pound's star was in the ascendant, for the foot touched the water. So great was my dread of the Professor that had I been in a position to choose my course I should have taken my chances in the stream, but I lost my self-control with my balance and made a desperate clutch at the air.

Again the brown hand caught mine, and this time it did not release me.

"Come with me," my small captor said in a tone of command.

I did not resist, but I went with fear. To resist would have been a confession of cowardice, and there is no pride of courage like that of a boy of ten in a girl's presence. I might have made excuses, but with that little spire of smoke so close at hand, promising a fire, I, dripping and shivering as I was, could think of nothing to say in protest. I did declare feebly that I was not cold. My teeth chattered, and my body shook, and the girl looked up at me and laughed, and led me on.

James, a man of a superstitious and imaginative mind, in the quiet evenings on the barn-bridge had often told me strange stories in which giants and dwarfs, witches and fairies, entangled men in their spells. One of these tales, a favorite of his, came to me now and caused my feet to lag and my eyes to study my guide with growing distrust. It was of a lady called "Laura Lee," who, James said, sat on the bank of the big river combing her hair and singing, the beauty of her face and voice luring too curious sailormen to their destruction. It was a far cry from the big river to the mountain brook, from the lovely "Laura Lee" to this tiny girl, about whom all my careful scrutiny could discover no sign of a comb. Yet it did seem to me that there was a resemblance between the creature of the story, "the beautiful lady with blue eyes and golden hair who hung around the water," and this child of the woods who had no fear of snakes and boasted a professor for a father. She felt the tug of my resisting hand.

"You're not afraid of me, are you, boy?" she asked, turning to me sharply.

I, a boy of ten, afraid of this mite! Had she really been what I was beginning to suspect, a decoy sent out by the Professor to lure me to his den, she could not have used more cunning than to put to me such a question. I afraid? Though the blood still waved through me, I squared my shoulders, dissembled a laugh, and stepped before her, and it was I who led the way along the path into the open day of the clearing. There I came face to face with the Professor.

First I saw that he was human in shape and attire. Indeed, both his appearance and his occupation were exceedingly commonplace. When we came upon him he was leaning on a hoe and watching a passing cloud. Had he smiled at me, I think I must have fallen to my knees and lifted my hands in pleading, but he gave no sign of pleasure that another victim had fallen into his toils. In fact, there was something reassuring in the perfect indifference with which he regarded me. When the crackling of the bushes called his eyes to us, he threw one glance our way as though a trifle annoyed at being disturbed in his study. Then he returned to the contemplation of the sky. So I stood on the edge of the woods my hand holding the girl's, and watched him, and as the seconds passed and he did not change his form, but remained a lazy man leaning on a hoe in a patch of riotous weeds, fear left me and wonder took its place.

There was nothing about this man to merit the opprobrium of his name, and from appearances Stacy Shunk had as well warned me against being caught by Mr. Pound. In the village Mr. Pound was the mould of respectability. He always wore a short frock-coat of glossy black material, which strained itself to reach across his chest. So did the Professor. But his black had turned to green in spots, and he was so thin and the tails were so short and the coat so broad that it seemed as though its length and breadth had become transposed. It was a marvellously shabby coat, but even in its poverty there was no mistaking its blue blood. It was a decayed sartorial aristocrat, ill nourished and sad, but flaunting still the chiselled nose and high, white brow of noble lineage. Here it was all out of place. Mr. Pound wore a great derby which swelled up from his head like a black ominous cloud, and so dominated him that it seemed to be in him the centre of thought and action, and likely at any moment to catch a slant on the wind and carry him from earth. The Professor wore a great derby, too, but one without the buoyant, cloud-like character of Mr. Pound's. It was a burden to him. Only his ears kept it from dragging him to earth and smothering him, and now as he looked up at the sky I saw clear cut against its blackness a thin quixotic visage, shaded by a growth of stubble beard. I marvelled at a man working in such attire, for the sun baked the clearing, but watching, I saw how little he swung his hoe and how much he studied the sky. The whole place spoke of one who kept his coat on while he worked, and gazed at the clouds more than he hoed. It was wretched and dismal. It hid itself away in the woods from very shame of its thriftlessness. Age had twisted the house askew, so that the mud daubing crumbled from between the logs, and the chimney was ready to tumble through the roof with the next puff of wind. The shanty barn was aslant and leaned heavily for support on long props. The hay burst through every side of it, and the sole occupant, an ancient white mule, had burst through too, and with his head projecting from an opening and his ears tilted forward, he was regarding me critically. Everywhere the weeds were rampant. Everywhere there were signs of a feeble battle against them, bare spots where the Professor had charged, cut his way into their massed ranks, only to retreat wearied and beaten by their numbers.

Over this wretchedness the girl waved her hand and said: "Here is our farm." The blue ribbon in her hair bobbed majestically as she pointed across the stretch of weeds to the cabin. "And yonder is our house." She pinched my arm as a sign of caution. "And there is father," she added in a voice of muffled pride. "He's studying. Father's always studying."

She would have led me on in silence, not to disturb his labors with either mind or hoe, but he looked down and asked in a tone of yawning interest: "Who's the lad, Penelope?"

"I don't know," she answered. "He fell into the creek, and I pulled him out. I've brought him in to warm him up."

Wet, shivering boys emerging suddenly from the woods might have been a common sight about the Professor's home, did one judge from the way he received his daughter's explanation. He merely nodded and fell upon the weeds with newly acquired vigor. As we walked on we heard the spasmodic crunching of his hoe. But the noise stopped before we reached the house door, and the silence caused us to turn. He was standing erect looking at us.

"I think you'd better have something, lad," he cried, and, dropping the hoe, he hurried after us.

So it came that the Professor did me the honors of his home, and with such kindness that all my fear of him was soon gone. He stirred the fire to a roaring blaze and placed me in front of it. He spread my coat before the stove and drew my boots, and quickly my clothes began to steam, and I was as uncomfortably warm as before I had been uncomfortably cold. The shy politeness of my age forbade my protesting against this over-indulgence in heat, and not until the Professor declared that he must give me a dose to ward off sickness did I raise a feeble voice in remonstrance.

My protest was in vain. From the cupboard he brought a large black bottle. Had I seen my mother approaching me with a bottle as ominous as that, even her favorite remedy that I knew so well, the Seven Seals of Health and Happiness, I should have fled far away, but now the girl had my coat, and was turning it before the fire, while her father stood between me and my boots. He smiled so benignly that had he offered me our family nostrum I should have taken it without a grimace. I accepted the proffered glass and drank. Never had anything more horrible than that liquid fire passed my lips. In a moment I seemed to be turned inside out and toasting at a roaring blaze, and to increase my discomfort the Professor poured another dose, many times larger than the first. Had he held it toward me I should have abandoned my coat and boots, but to my relief he raised it to his lips and drained it off with a smile of keen appreciation of its merits.

"Now I feel better," he said, putting the bottle and glass on the table, and dropping into a chair.

It was strange to me that he, who was perfectly dry, should prescribe for himself exactly the same remedy that he had given to me for my wringing wetness. Yet there was no denying the beneficence of the dose, for I was most uncomfortably warm, and had he been feeling badly he was certainly now in fine spirits.

Drawing his daughter between his knees, he enfolded her in his arms protectingly. "Well, boy, I warrant you feel better," he said.

I replied that I did, and if he did not mind I should like to sit a little farther from the stove.

> He consented, laughing. "And now we should introduce ourselves—formally," he went on. "You have met my daughter, Miss Blight—Miss Penelope Blight. I am Mr. Blight—Mr. Henderson Blight—in full, Andrew Henderson Blight. And you?"

"I am David Malcolm, sir," I answered.

> "Ah!" He lifted his eyebrows. "You are one of those bumptious Malcolms."

"Yes, sir," I returned proudly, for the word "bumptious" had a ring of importance in it, and I had every reason to believe that the Malcolms were persons of quite large importance.

Why Mr. Blight laughed so loud at my reply I could not understand, but I supposed that in spite of his saturnine appearance he was a man of jovial temperament and I liked him all the more.

The wave of merriment past, he regarded me gravely. "Then you must be the son of the distinguished Judge Malcolm."

"Yes, sir," I said, pride rising triumphant over my polite humility.

"Penelope," he said, as though addressing only his daughter, "we are greatly honored. Our guest is a Malcolm—a sop of the celebrated Judge Malcolm."

By this adroit flattery my host won my heart, and in the comfort he had given me I lost all care for passing time. When I recalled James, it was with the thought that I was safe and he would find me, and I was troubled by no obligation to save him worry. This strange man interested me, he held my family in high regard, and I was well satisfied to see more of him. So I fixed my heels on the rung of my chair, folded my hands in my lap, sat up very straight, and watched him gravely. In this was the one grudge that I long bore against the Professor—that he baited me as he did, played with my child's pride, and with my innocent connivance vented his contempt on all that I held most dear. I did not understand the covert sneer against my father. Years have given me a broader view of life than was my father's, and at times I can smile with Henderson Blight at the solemnity with which he invested his judgeship, but mine is the smile of affection. With no knowledge of the law, with a power restricted to county contracts, when he sat on the bench in court week with his learned confrère, drew his chin into his pointed collar, and furrowed his brow, Blackstone beside him would have appeared a tyro in legal lore. The distinguished Judge Malcolm! So Henderson Blight spoke of him in raillery and so he was in truth, distinguished in his village and his valley, and as I have come to know men of fame in larger villages and broader valleys I can still look back to him with loving pride. Yet that day I sat complacently with my feet on the chair-rung, regarding the Professor with growing friendliness.

"You know my father?" I asked, seeking to draw forth more of this agreeable flattery.

"I have not the honor," he replied. "You see I am comparatively new in these parts—driven here, as you may suspect, by temporary adversity.

But a man with ideas, David, must some day rise above adversity. All he needs is a field of action." He looked across the bare room and out of the door, where the weeds were charging in masses against the very threshold; he looked beyond them, above the wall of woods, to a small white cloud drifting in the blue. Young as I was, I saw that in his eyes which told me that could he reach the cloud he might set the heavens afire, but under his hand there lay no task quite worthy of him. "A field of action—an opportunity," he repeated meditatively. "It's hard, David, to have all kinds of ideas and no place to use them. When a man knows that he has it in him and—"

"Is that why Mr. Shunk calls you the Professor?" I interrupted.

Henderson Blight turned toward me a melancholy smile. "Yes," he said. "They all call me that, David, down in the village. Ask them who the Professor is. They will tell you, a vagrant, a lazy fellow with a gift of talking, a ne'er-do-well with a little learning. Ask Stacy Shunk. Ask Mr. Pound—wise and good Mr. Pound. He will tell you that ideas such as mine are a danger to the community, that I speak out of ignorance and sin. As if in every mountain wind I could not hear a better sermon than he can give me and find in every passing cloud a text to ponder over. They don't understand me at all."

The Professor drew his little daughter close to him and regarded me fixedly, as though to see if I understood.

"Yes, sir," I said. "I will ask them."

At this matter-of-fact reply his mouth twitched humorously. "And perhaps you will find that they are right," he said. "That's the worst of it. Even dull minds can generate a certain amount of unpleasant truth; that's what sets me on edge against them—when they ask me why I don't carry out some of my fine ideas instead of criticising others."

"Why don't you?" The question was from no desire to drive my host into a corner, but came from an innocent interest in him and a wish to get at something concrete.

He took no offence at my presumption, but rose slowly, lifted his arms above his head, and stretched himself. Unconsciously he answered my question.

"Had I the last ten years to live over again I would," he said as he paced slowly up and down the room. "Perhaps I shall yet. Long ago, when I was home on a little farm with the mountains tumbling down over it, I used to plan getting out in the world and doing something more than to earn three meals a day. It is stupid—the way men make meals the aim of their lives. I wanted something better, but to find it I had to have the means, and means could only be had by the most uncongenial work. So here I find myself on a still smaller farm with the mountains coming down on my very head. It was different with Rufus."

"Rufus who?" I demanded with the abruptness of an inquisitive youth who was getting at the facts at last.

The Professor halted by my chair. "My brother Rufus. You see, David, I taught school because it was easy work and gave me time to think. Rufus was a blockhead. He never had a real idea of any kind, but he could work. When he owned a cross-road store he was as proud as though he had written 'Paradise Lost.' He went to conquer the county town and did it by giving a prize with every pound of tea. He wrote me about it and you might have supposed that he had won a Waterloo. Yet he had his good points. Now if Rufus and I could have been combined, his physical energy with my mental, we should have done something really worth while."

"Yes, sir—yes, indeed, sir," I said politely. My conception of the Professor's meaning was very faulty, but I found him engrossing because he talked so fluently and made so many expressive gestures. He, I suspect, was pleased with a sympathetic listener, though one so small.

Laying a hand on my shoulder, he asked: "David, what are you going to do when you grow up?"

"I am going to be like my father," I replied.

"Like the distinguished Judge Malcolm?" he exclaimed. "That's a high ambition—for the valley." He was standing over me pulling his chin, and from the manner in which he eyed me I believe that he quite approved my choice of a model. Suddenly his arms shot out. "Try to be more, David. Try to be what Rufus and I combined would have been. Try to work for something better than three meals a day. Wake up, David, before you fall asleep in a land where everybody dozes like the very dogs."

To enforce his admonition his hands closed on my shoulders; he lifted me from my chair and began to shake me. Being so much in earnest he was rather violent, so that James, now in the doorway, saw me wincing and looking up with a grimace of fright and eyes of pleading.

"Steady there, man," he cried. He thought that he was just in time to rescue me from torture, and came forward with his whip raised.

"I beg your pardon," said the Professor, dropping me gently into my chair. "I didn't mean to hurt you, David. Did I hurt you?"

"Not at all, sir," I answered, and feeling more at ease with James near I made a dive for my coat and hat.

"Well," said James, glaring at my host. "I advise you to keep your hands off anyway, for if I catch you a-hurting of him again—" There was a terrible threat in the eyes and in the upraised butt of the whip, but suddenly the manner changed, for James was looking at the bottle on the table and it had a strangely quieting influence on his temper. The blaze died away from his eyes; his voice became soft to meekness; the whip fell limply. "I might think you'd done it a-purpose, Professor, and you know I allus tries to be friendly."

"I hardly believe David will complain of my treatment," returned the Professor. "You see he came to us all wet and cold from a tumble into the creek."

James turned to me with wide-opened eyes. "And I suppose you met a rattler," he cried.

"Oh, yes," I answered, as though this was but a petty incident of my day.

"Well, you are a boy!" From me his eyes moved to the bottle again, and as he looked at it he began to tremble and his legs lost their strength and he sank to a chair by the table. "You'll be the death of me yet, Davy. Why, my nerves has all gone from just thinking of what might have happened."

His hand was groping toward the bottle, and he gave the Professor a glance that asked for his permission.

"Penelope," the Professor said quietly, "the gentleman would like a glass of water."

Evidently the gentleman did not think that water would quiet his nerves, for he did not hear the command and was contented with the healing power nearer at hand. He poured the tumbler almost full of the fiery liquid and raised it to his lips. He winked gravely at Mr. Blight, threw back his head, and drained the glass without taking breath. The Professor failed to see the humor of the act, and, seizing the bottle, drove the cork in hard, while the unabashed James beamed on him, on Penelope, and on me.

"Thank you," he said, rising, and slowly drawing his sleeve across his mouth; "I feel better—much better. Another drop would set me up all right, but, as you say—" He looked hopefully from the bottle in the Professor's hands to the Professor's face, but finding there no promise of more of the sovereign remedy, he took my arm and led me to the door. "Davy, you must thank Mr. Blight and the young lady."

"You'll come again, Davy," Penelope cried.

"And all by yourself, Davy," the Professor added.

To me this remark was of the kindest, but it irritated James. He picked up his whip and fumbled with it while he stared at our host, who stood by the table, with one hand on the bottle and the other pointing the way over the clearing. "You're a good talker, Professor," James drawled. "You can argue down Stacy Shunk and make Mr. Pound tremble, but when it comes to manners—the manners of a gentleman—I never see such a lack of them."

With this parting shot he strode away so fast that I could hardly keep pace with him. At the edge of the woods, I looked back and saw the father and child in the slanting doorway waving their hands to me. From his window in the barn the white mule was watching with ears pricked, and now he brayed a hostile note, as though he divined the trouble which could come at the heels of a wandering boy. I waved my hat and plunged into the bush.

"Now, Davy, tell me how it all happened," said James, drawing himself up very straight in the saddle as he started the horses toward home.

I began to tell him. He broke into a song. When I tried to make myself heard, his voice swelled up louder. Never before had James sung as he was singing now, and I watched him first with wonder and then with increasing terror. As we dragged our way up the ridge, out of the narrow gut, he droned his music in maudlin fashion in time to the slow motion of the beasts. When the valley stretched before us he fairly thundered, striving to make himself heard across the broad land. I hoped that before we entered the village exhaustion would silence him, but in answer to my appeals he raised his voice to a pitch and volume that brought the people running out of their houses, and he seemed to find great pleasure in the attention that he was attracting. The high throne from which I had looked down so proudly that morning as I rode to my fishing became a pillory of shame. I could not escape from it, for the whip was swinging in time to the music, and the horses, confused by the riot, were rearing and plunging. I had to cling to the harness with all my strength. We halted at the store. It was quite unintentional and made the climax of a boisterous progress. James, lurching back in his saddle, would have fallen but for the support of the rein. The horses stopped suddenly. He shot forward, clutching at the air, and hurtled into the road. From my height and from my shame, I saw the whole world running to witness our plight—men, women, and children, it seemed to me hundreds of them, who must have been lying in wait for this very thing to happen. Through them Mr. Pound forced his way, waving back the press until he reached the side of the fallen man.

"James," he said, looking down and speaking not unkindly, "how often have I warned you!"

The answer was a look of childish wonder.

"Come, come," said Mr. Pound, taking a limp, sprawling arm and lifting the culprit to his feet. "Tell me, who was the tempter who brought you to this?"

James gazed stupidly at the minister. Then a devil must have seized him, for in his nature he was a gentle soul, as I knew, who had heard him so often crooning over his horses or sitting on the barn-bridge of an evening sorrowing for Annie Laurie and Nellie Grey, women whom he had never seen. Before all the town he raised his hand and brought it crashing down on Mr. Pound's cloud-like hat.

CHAPTER III

My mother was a McLaurin of Tuckapo Valley. In the mid-part of the eighteenth century, when that valley was a wild forest, her great-grandfather, Angus McLaurin, came out of the air, out of the nothingness of a hiatus in our genealogy, and settled along the banks of the Juniata. His worldly goods were strapped on the back of a cow; his sole companion was his wife; his sole defence his rifle. To the dusky citizens of the valley he seemed a harmless person, and they sold him some thousands of acres for a few pounds of powder and beads. They must have smiled when he attacked the wilderness with an axe, as we should smile at the old woman who tried to ladle up the sea. With what chagrin must they look down now from the Happy Hunting Ground to see McLaurinville the busy metropolis of McLaurin township, and McLaurins rich and poor, McLaurins in brick mansions and McLaurins in log cabins where they once chased the deer and bear! My mother was one of *the* McLaurins, which is to say that she was born on the very spot where Angus felled the first tree in Tuckapo. These McLaurins were naturally the proudest of all their wide-spread family, some of whom had gone down to the poor-house, and some up and over the mountains to be lost and snubbed among the great ones of other valleys. There was a tradition in our family, which grew stronger as the years covered the roots of our family tree, that Angus was really *The* McLaurin, chief of the clan, and had fled over the sea to save his head after Prince Charlie's futile struggle for a crown. With my mother tradition had become history. She had one grudge against Walter Scott, whose novels, with the Bible, made her sole reading, and this was that he never mentioned "our chief," as she called him. More than once I can remember her looking up from the pages of "Redgauntlet," and declaring that had the Prince been a more capable man we should be living in a castle in Scotland. From the incompetence of Prince Charlie, then, it came that my mother entered life in a red brick house in McLaurinville instead of in a highland keep, and as it is just six miles as the crow flies over the ridges to Malcolmville in Windy Valley, she met my father in the course of time, and in the course of time the two great families were united in my small self. The Malcolms were a great family, too. They were a proud people, though not in the same way as my McLaurin kin. They had no fine traditions based on the fragments of a Scotchman's kilt. Quite to the contrary, my father used to boast that they had been just simple, God-fearing folk, Presbyterians in every branch for generations, and sometimes he delighted in the idea that he was a self-made man. As he always chose a large company to make this boast in, it was to my mother a constant source of irritation, and she would contradict him with heat, and point out that his father before him had farmed three hundred acres of land, while his grandfather on his mother's side had been for fifty years the pastor of the Happy Hollow church.

Knowing this little of our family history, it is possible to realize the consternation which prevailed when in the middle of a formal dinner-party, in the presence of Mr. Pound, Squire Crumple, and that most critical of women, Miss Agnes Spinner, in the presence of these and a half-dozen others of the most important persons in the neighborhood, in the silence which followed the appearance of the first asparagus of spring, I, a small boy, suddenly projected my head from the shadow of the good minister and asked: "Mother, what is a bumptious Malcolm?"

Mr. Pound lowered his fork, turned half around, and looked at me. Miss Agnes Spinner began to choke and had to cover her face with her napkin, while Squire Crumple with great solicitude fell to patting her very hard between the shoulders. Mrs. Pound glanced at my father, and then found a sudden interest in her coffee, pouring it from her cup into her saucer, and from her saucer into her cup, so often that she seemed to be reducing it to a freezing mixture. Mrs. Crumple discovered something awry with the lace of her gown, for she drew in her chin, and one eye examined her vertical front while the other covertly circled the table. Old Mr. Smiley, never an adroit man in society, crossed his knife and fork on his plate, lifted his napkin half across his face like a curtain, and over the top of it stared at my mother as though he were waiting with me to learn just what a bumptious Malcolm could be.

My father never lost his self-command. He seemed not to have heard me, for he leaned over the table, and in a voice designed to smother any further interruptions from my quarter, said: "Mrs. Malcolm, my dear, Mr. Pound's coffee is all." As a matter of fact Mr. Pound's coffee was not "all." My mother, never niggardly, had just filled it for the third time to overflowing, and a full cup rose from a full saucer; but she had an opportunity, while turning solicitously to her guest, to give me a frown, which in private would have found fuller expression in a slipper. As Miss Spinner was still choking, my father proposed dropping a brass door-key down her back as the most efficacious of cures. Had she consented to this heroic treatment I might have been shunted into silence, but her prompt refusal to allow any one to do anything for her left diplomacy at its wit's end. In the portentous silence which followed I was able to repeat my question with more incisive force.

"Yes, but, mother, what is a bumptious Malcolm?"

"David," said my father sternly, "children should be seen and not heard!"

"But, father," I exclaimed, being aroused by this injustice to defend myself, "Professor Blight said that I must be one of those bumptious Malcolms. Those were his exact words—bumptious Malcolms."

As the horse saith among the trumpets, ha! ha! and smelleth the battle afar off—the thunder of the captains and the shouting—so Mr. Pound lifted his great mane at the mention of the Professor and swept the table with eyes full of fire.

"Ha! Judge Malcolm, what have I not told you of this man? Don't you recall that I warned you we should have to deal with him? When I found him making trouble in my flock, setting the sheep against the shepherd, I told you the time would come when he would strive to set the son against the father."

While I could not understand in what way I had turned against my father, it was plain to me that the term which the Professor had applied to my family was one of opprobrium. It was clear, too, that it had considerable explosive power, for after the first frightened hush it stirred the whole company into a terrific outburst against my friend of yesterday. Even Miss Spinner stopped choking, and announced that she "declared." What she declared was not imparted, but as the general trend of exclamation was against the Professor I knew that did she continue her statement it must be aimed at him.

My father leaned back and grasped the knobs of his chair-arms. "David," he said slowly, "when did Henderson Blight speak in terms so disrespectful—no, that is not the word I want—in this sarcastic—that is hardly correct—when did he speak thus of us?"

"Yesterday, sir," I answered, "when I was in his house getting warm. But he didn't mean anything bad, father. Why, he told me that you were the celebrated Judge Malcolm."

I expected that such gentle flattery would propitiate my
father.
Instead, his brows knitted, and he shot forward his head
and asked:
"The what kind of a judge, David?"

Before I could reply Mr. Pound injected himself into the examination.

> "Pardon me, Judge, but I should like to ask my young friend if Henderson Blight smiled as he said it."

"No, sir," I answered promptly. "He was just as solemn as you are now."

Miss Spinner fell to choking again. My mother gave vent to a long-drawn "Dav-id!" an exclamation which I had come to fear as much as the Seven Seals, and her use of it now so unjustly made me feel as if every man's hand were against me, for Mr. Pound was solemn, and in using the best comparison at hand I meant no ill.

"Dav-id!" said my mother again, lifting an admonishing finger.

The good minister saw nothing offensive in my remark, but even repeated it with a nod of understanding. "As solemn as I am now. Judge Malcolm, your son has quite accurately described this man Blight's way of speaking—of saying one thing when he means quite another. I should hardly dare repeat some of the terms which have come to my ears as having been applied by him to me. Just the other day, as we were walking through town, I overheard him talking to Stacy Shunk, and he referred to my wife as the lovely Mrs. Pound. Now I have no objections to persons speaking of my wife as lovely, but I want them to mean it and not to infer quite the opposite."

It was Mrs. Pound's turn to "declare," but she was clearer in the meaning than Miss Spinner. She would have told us some of the things Mr. Blight had said of Mr. Pound with a meaning quite as inverted. My mother, seeing the tempest rising, sought to still it by protesting that she was sure that in this instance the Professor was quite sincere.

"I know he meant it," she said over and over again, until Mrs. Pound was unable to make herself heard and retired to silence and coffee.

But Mr. Pound, a believer in truth at all hazards, would not admit that the Professor did mean it. "A person of such an insinuating character is a danger to the community," he said. "I have repeatedly warned the judge against him, Mrs. Malcolm, and now my warning has come home. Yesterday's deplorable incident has been forgotten by me; I have blotted it from my memory because I realized that you were in spirit struck down as I was, though not so publicly. I have forgiven James. Since he has come to me sober and penitent, and confessed where he got the liquor, I have passed his part in the affair by with a kindly warning. But I cannot pass by the real culprit, the man who struck at me through the weak James, and almost felled me before the town, the man who furnished James with the sources of his intoxication. His punishment I leave to you." Mr. Pound drove his fork into an asparagus stalk to show that he had said all that could be said and all that he would say. That he had said enough to bring others to his way of thinking was evident from the gravity with which my father shook his head.

"David, when I questioned you as to yesterday's unfortunate occurrence you confessed that this man Blight gave James the liquor."

"No, sir," I returned quickly. "I didn't say that."

"How was it, then?" my father asked.

I had pleaded with my mother to allow me to be one of this great dinner-party, that I might partake, first-hand, of the good things which I had seen preparing. I was to enjoy the feast in a silence proper to my years. So I had promised. And now one of those dangerous questions which rise like a rocket from a boy's lips had transformed me from a small guest whose part was to sit silently in the shadow of the mighty clergyman, and there only to even up the side of the table, into a person of unpleasant importance. Had my father rapped for order, risen, and announced that we had the good fortune to have with us Master David Malcolm, who would tell us where James found the source of his intoxication, he could not have made me more dreadfully conspicuous. I wanted to run, but, if nothing else, my father's eyes would have held me. I wanted, above all, to keep silent because I loved James, who from the day when I had first toddled out of the house into the broad world of hay and wheat fields had been almost my sole playfellow. As yet I did not know what a bumptious Malcolm was; I did not understand the man who always said what he did not mean; I remembered him only as the kindly host who had found me dripping and cold and had made me gloriously warm. And more than that, I remembered the little girl who had dragged me from the creek. Something in the gaunt man who lived among the clouds, something in the ragged creature who lifted a smiling face and ribboned head above the weeds of that lonely clearing, had touched me strangely. It seemed that I must be their only friend, and for them I would tell the truth. I should have told the truth but for Mr. Pound.

"I said, sir," I answered my father, "that James just took the bottle and"

"The bottle was Blight's, was it not?" broke in Mr. Pound.

"Yes, sir," I said.

It had dawned on me the afternoon before, as James and I rode home, just what was the medicine I had taken. It was hard for me to believe that the vilely tasting stuff was whiskey, which I had heard men drank for pleasure, but when all doubt was removed by the exclamations of the crowd who hovered about the prostrate man I was overwhelmed by a sense of my own sin. Yet I had feared to confess to my mother the dose which I had taken. It would only make her unhappy, I had told myself, and I had tried to still my turbulent conscience with the plea that my silence was saving others. Now simple justice demanded that I tell everything, even to the admission of my own fault.

"Father," I cried, "the Professor didn't want James—"

"It is high time the community were rid of this man," Mr. Pound interrupted.

"David!" said my father, and I shrank into the minister's shadow.

"And it seems to me, Squire Crumple," Mr. Pound went on, "it is clearly your duty as a justice of the peace to act."

"Act how?" cried the astonished squire.

"Have him arrested!" replied Mr. Pound, making the dishes rattle under the impact of his fist on the table.

At this suggestion every one forgot the dinner and sat up very straight, staring in amazement at the bold propounder of it.

"Arrest him," exclaimed the squire, "and for what?"

"For anything that will rid the community of him,"
snapped Mr. Pound.
"Do you not agree with me, Judge?"

The Judge quite agreed with Mr. Pound. He admitted that until the unfortunate occurrence of yesterday he had opposed any proceedings which were not altogether regular in law. "And yet," he said gravely, "it is incumbent on us to rid the community of him. We all know that from the porch of Snyder's store he has been preaching doctrines that are not only revolutionary but, if the ladies will pardon me, I will call damnable. What good is it for us to have Mr. Pound in the pulpit for one day of the week, and this glib-tongued man contradicting him for seven. Yet no statute forbids him to do this. What can you suggest, Mr. Pound?"

Mr. Pound sought an inspiration in the ceiling. "The man has no visible means of support," he said after a moment. "His child is badly clothed, and, I presume, badly fed. Right there is an indictment. Vagrancy."

This bold suggestion was greeted with general approval save by the squire, who protested that a man could not be called a vagrant who had paid seventy dollars in cash for his clearing and was never known to beg or steal.

"But I tell you he is a moral vagrant," argued Mr. Pound, "and I will make such a charge against him. It will be your duty then, Squire Crumple, to offer him his choice between six weeks in jail and leaving the valley and taking his bottle with him."

Still the squire was unconvinced, but he saw himself being overawed by my father and the minister, and his efforts to combat them evolved futile excuses.

"Who will arrest him?" he pleaded.

"Haven't we a constable?" retorted my father. "What did we elect Byron Lukens for?"

"Precisely!" cried Mr. Pound.

"The one arrest he has made was a source of endless trouble," returned Squire Crumple. "He had to lock the prisoner overnight in his best room, and his wife has since said distinctly and repeatedly that—"

"You can avoid trouble with Mrs. Lukens by arresting him in the morning," said Mr. Pound.

"And the chances are he will leave the valley rather than go to jail," my father added.

"But suppose he is cantankerous and chooses jail, what will we do with the girl?" argued the reluctant magistrate.

"The girl?" Mr. Pound waved his great hands about the table. "Surely we can find her a better home and better parents than she has now. Surely there are among us good women who will esteem it a privilege to care for an orphaned child."

My mother said "surely," too, and so did all the other good women at the board. Even Miss Spinner, while not prepared to receive the child into her home, was ready to teach her "as she should be taught."

"And she should be taught," my mother broke in. "Her father has been the stumbling-block. I heard him say myself to a committee of our Ladies' Aid that he would gladly place her in Miss Spinner's Sunday-school class if Miss Spinner could convince him that she had any knowledge worth imparting. I never liked to tell you that before, Miss Spinner; I feared it might hurt your feelings."

Miss Spinner's feelings were decidedly hurt, and she began to vie with Mr. Pound in urging that the valley be rid of the obnoxious Professor. So drastic were the measures which she called for, and so vigorous her demands on the gentle squire, that he retreated on Mr. Pound for aid, advocating all that the minister had proposed as the most humanitarian method of dealing with the case.

"A warrant will issue to-night, but to avoid trouble with the constable's wife I shall order it served in the morning," he said at last as he stood by his chair, folding his napkin. Thus he eased his conscience by making the warrant responsible for its own existence, and his words struck deeper into my heart for their impressive legal form.

A warrant will issue! As I slipped out by the kitchen this rang in my ears with the insistence of a refrain. Because I had disobeyed, left my post of safety, and plunged into the woods in pursuit of a few small trout, a warrant would issue, a ghoulish offspring of my reckless spirit, seize the gentle Professor in its claws and drag him to ignominy. A warrant would issue! And the blue ribbon would no longer bob majestically in Penelope's hair, but would droop with her father's shame. The picture of them standing in the cabin door, waving their farewell and calling to me to come again, was very clear in my mind, and made sharper the sense of the trouble which I had brought to them. Three times I ran around the house wildly, as though I would blur the picture by merely travelling in a circle; but instead it grew clearer, and the Professor seemed to regard me with eyes more kindly and Penelope to call to me in a more friendly voice. So became clearer my obligation to help them, and intent on making my plea I burst into the parlor. The scene there chilled my ardor. In the dim evening light, like sombre ghosts, the company sat in a wide circle about the borders of the room, erect and uncomfortable as one must sit on slippery horse-hair, listening to Miss Spinner at the piano droning through the first bars of "Sweet Violets."

"Ssh!" exclaimed my father, and even the gloom could not hide his frown.

"But, father, the Professor didn't—"

My mother tiptoed across the room and gently pushed
me out of the door.
"David, go to bed!" she commanded.

To bed I went, but not to sleep. Did I close my eyes I saw the Professor in the clutches of Byron Lukens being dragged along the village street amid the jeers of the people. Swallows fluttered in the chimney, and I heard there the echoes of the struggle when the constable laid his hand on the shoulders of my friend. The wind moaned in the trees, and I fancied Penelope now upbraiding me for the trouble I had brought upon them, now pleading with me to send her father home to her. A faint crowing sounded from the orchard, hailing the shadow of the morning, the gray ghost rising from the dark ridges. I slipped from my bed to the window, and watched the valley as it shook itself from sleep. How slowly came that day! The birds stirred in their nests, but, like me, they dared not venture forth into a world so filled with uncanny shadows. Yet the day did come. Over by the dark, towering wall that hemmed in the valley the gray turned to pink, and I could see the trees on the ridge-top like a fringe against the brightening sky. Louder sounded the crowing in the orchard, and to me it brought a warning that I must hurry. I looked to the northward, and saw only the mists covering the land, and in my fancy beyond them the mountains where bear and wildcat lurked. There the Professor and Penelope lay unconscious that even now the terrible warrant might be issuing and at any moment would fall upon them. There was only one thing for me to do, and though when I had closed the house door softly behind me and turned my back to the reddening east the mists were tenfold more mysterious and the mountains tenfold more forbidding, I ran straight down the road into the gloom, as though the warrant were racing with me.

CHAPTER IV

When with a last desperate spurt I ran into the clearing, I saw the Professor sitting in the cabin door, smoking his pipe and basking in the sunshine as though life held no trouble for him. I believed that I was in time to warn him of the threatening danger, that I had outsped the warrant, that I had outrun the redoubtable Lukens, and in the luxury of that thought my overtaxed strength ebbed away and I sank down on a stump, hot and panting. I had run a hard race for so small a boy. At times it seemed as though the mountains drew back from me, that every one of the five miles had stretched to ten, but I kept bravely on, going at top speed over the level places, dragging wearily up the steep hills, cutting through fields and woods where I could save distance, following every brief rest with a spasmodic burst of energy, and now I had come to the last stretch, the ragged patch of weeds, exhausted. I tried to call my friend, but my throat was parched and I could not raise my voice above a whisper, and as my head barely lifted over the wild growth of his farm, he smoked on, unconscious of my presence. Something in a distant tree-top engaged his attention, something vastly interesting, it seemed to me, for he never turned my way to see my waving hand. So I struggled to my feet and staggered on. At last he heard me, sprang up, and came striding over the clearing. Then my tired legs crumpled up; I sat down suddenly and, supported by my sprawling hands, waited for him.

"Davy—Davy Malcolm," he cried, "who has been chasing you now?"

"A warrant!" I gasped. "Mr. Lukens, he is coming with a warrant to arrest you!"

The tall form bent over me and I was raised to my feet. Supporting me in his strong grasp, he held me off from him, and for a moment regarded me with grave eyes.

"And you've come to warn me, eh, Davy?" he said.

"Yes, sir," I answered. "Mr. Pound he thinks you are a
dangerous man.
Mr. Pound he wants to get you out of the valley. Mr.
Pound he—"

The Professor seemed to have little fear of Mr. Pound and as little interest in him. "Never mind the learned Doctor Pound," he exclaimed, and his mouth twitched in a smile inspired by the mere thought of the minister. "The point is, Davy, that you left home before daylight to tell me, and you must have run nearly all the way—eh, boy?"

"I had to," I panted. "You see, Mr. Lukens he was to come here early for you, and I thought if I was in time you might run away."

To run away seemed to me the only thing for the Professor to do, and I expected that at the mere mention of the terrible Lukens he would scurry to the mountain-top as fast as his legs would carry him. Yet he held the constable in as little terror as he did Mr. Pound, for instead of fleeing he drew me to him, and held me in an embrace so tight as to make me struggle for breath and freedom.

"Davy, Davy!" he cried; "you understand me, boy. You are a friend, a real friend—my only friend."

Again and again he said it—that I was his only friend—and not until I cried out that I had had no breakfast and would he please not squeeze me so tight did he release me, and then it was to keep fast hold on my arm and lead me to the house. Penelope had heard us and met us half-way, running, halting suddenly before us, and staring wide-eyed at the bedraggled boy who lurched along at her father's side.

"Davy," she cried, "have you come fishin' again?"

My answer was to hold out my hand to her, and together we three went into the house. There, with my breath regained, and my parched throat relieved, and my tired legs dangling from the most luxurious of rocking-chairs, my spirits rose with my returning strength. It nettled me to see the Professor giving so little heed to my warning. I had performed what was for me a herculean task, and yet the precious moments which I had fought so hard to gain for him were being frittered away in preparations for a breakfast for me. He was evidently grateful for what I had done, but he was getting no good from it. Had I run all those miles to tell him that the bogie man was coming he could not have moved about his cooking with less concern. For a time I watched him with growing indignation, yet I hesitated to mention the purpose of my errand before Penelope, who had fixed herself before my chair and, with her hands clasped behind her back and her head lifted high, was gazing at me in admiring silence. My uneasiness increased as the minutes flew by, and when the first sharp demands of appetite had been satisfied I looked at the Professor, now seated at the other side of the table, and nodded my head toward his daughter, and winked with a sageness beyond my years.

"Mr. Blight, hadn't you otter be going?" I asked.

The Professor, in answer, laughed outright. He clasped his hands to his sides and rocked on two legs of his chair in exuberance. "Davy—Davy, you'll be the death of me yet!"

To me this seemed a very hard thing to say, as I had no wish to be the death of the Professor; but, quite to the contrary, had made a great effort and had risked much trouble at home in my desire to help him. Now I was beginning to think that I had done as well to drop a post-card in the mail to warn him of his danger. The disappointment brought tears to my eyes. He saw them. His face turned very gentle and he leaned across the table toward me.

"Davy, I can't thank you enough for what you have done. But don't worry about me—I'm not afraid of Byron Lukens."

At the name of the constable Penelope broke into laughter, and placed a hand on my arm to draw my eyes to her. "Mr. Lukens was here this morning, Davy, just before you came. And, oh, you should have seen father knock him down!"

My fork and knife clattered to the plate as I turned to the girl, and she saw doubt and wonder in my eyes.

"He did!" she cried. "And oh, Davy, you'd have died laughing if you had seen Mr. Lukens tumble over the wood-pile and hit his head against the rain-barrel."

I stared at the Professor. I had liked him for his kindness to me and had pitied him for his misfortune. Now I was filled with admiration for the physical prowess of this man who could whip the intrepid constable, for in Malcolmville there was no one whom I held in so much awe as Byron Lukens. He was mighty in bulk; his voice was proportioned to his size; his words fitted his voice. Often I had sat on the store-porch and listened to his stories of his feats, and I believed that to cross him in any way must be the height of daring. The tale of the men whom he had whipped in the past and promised to whip in the future if they raised a finger against him would almost have made a census of the valley. That this frail man should have resisted him, that those thin hands should have been raised against him, that the intellectual Professor should have knocked down the Hercules of our village, was beyond my comprehension. So my friend across the table saw amazement welling up from my open mouth and eyes.

He shrugged his shoulders. "There was nothing else to do, Davy. He beat you here after all. Probably you missed him in your short cuts over the fields. Why, it was hardly light when I heard him pounding at the door. He said he had come to arrest me." Rising and drawing himself to his full height, the Professor began to tell me of the early morning conflict, forgetting, in his indignation, how small were his two auditors, and throwing out his voice as though to reach a multitude. "He had come to arrest me—me; said that I was a vagrant; spoke to me as you wouldn't speak to a dog, and told me to come along—to come along with him, a hulking, boastful brute. Why, it was all I could do to keep my temper, Davy. I answered him as politely as I could, said that I had done no wrong, and certainly would not allow myself to be arrested. And then—"

"Then father knocked him down," cried Penelope,
clapping her hands.
"Oh, Davy, you'd otter seen it."

"Should have, Penelope, should have seen," said the Professor reprovingly, and having done his duty as a father and a man of education he drove his fist into the air to show with what quickness and force he could use it. "Yes, that's the way I did it, David. He applied an oath to me and laid a hand on my shoulder. What else could I do? I appeal to you—what else could I do but knock him down?"

"And didn't he whip you for it, sir?" I cried, still doubting that the giant could have fallen beneath such a blow.

"Whip me?" The Professor laughed. "Do you think that great bully could whip me? Why, David, you quite hurt my feelings. By the time he had gone over the wood-pile into the rain-barrel there wasn't any fight left in him. He didn't even speak till he was safe across the clearing. Then you should have seen him. He has gone down to the village to get help; he is going to teach me what it means to assault an officer of the law; he is going to send me to jail for life." The Professor glared out of the open doorway as fiercely as though the constable were standing there and he defying him. Then suddenly he leaned over the table to me, and fixing his eyes on mine asked in a hoarse voice: "David, did you ever hear of such injustice?"

"No, sir," I answered. "But Mr. Pound said—"

At the mention of Mr. Pound the Professor sat down and the table reeled under his fist. "Pound—he is at the bottom of it all. He has said that I am a good-for-nothing loafer and the county should be rid of me. Maybe he is right. But he won't have his way. I have done nothing and I will not go—do you hear that, Davy, I will not go. Now tell me what Mr. Pound said."

In a faltering voice I began my story with that fateful home ride with James. As I went on I lost my diffidence in my interest in the tale, and spoke rapidly till the need of breath slowed me down. There were retrogressions to speak of things which I had forgotten, and many corrections where I had slightly misquoted Miss Spinner, Mr. Smiley, or some other equally unimportant person. I told the story as a small boy recites to his elders the details of some book which he has read; so the Professor had to check me frequently with admonitions not to mind what Mrs. Crumple said about my mother's ice-cream and such matters, but to tell him exactly what my father said of him. Still I persisted in my own way, bound that whatever I did should be done thoroughly, even though he might hold in contempt my effort to be of service to him. When at last there was not a word left untold, he leaned back in his chair and gazed at me with a look of utter helplessness.

"Well, what am I to do now?" he cried. His head shot toward me and his hands were held out in appeal. "Davy, can't you suggest something?"

In my pride at being asked for advice by one so old, I sat up very straight as I had seen my father do and allowed a proper interval of silence before I spoke.

> "Yes," I replied slowly. "If you were me I'd run away before Mr. Lukens got back."

This excellent suggestion was met by a frown so fierce that I pushed back from the table in alarm.

"Run away?" he exclaimed. "Why, that's just what they want me to do. What have I done that I should run away? And if I did, what would become of Penelope?"

He drew his little daughter close to his side, while he looked out of the door into the patch of blue sky, seeking there some inspiration. His lips moved, and I knew that he was asking again and again of that little patch of sky what he should do. Then suddenly he rose, as though the answer had been given, for he clapped on his hat, stood erect with shoulders squared and hands clasped behind him, facing the open door with the demeanor of a man whose mind was made up, who was ready to meet the world and defy it. This, to me, was the hero who had knocked down the constable, and I imagined him confronting a dozen like Byron Lukens and piling them one on top of the other, for surely things had come to pass that the man would have to hold the clearing against an army. But as suddenly the shoulders drooped, the back bowed, the head sank, and he turned to me.

"Davy, Davy, what shall I do?" he asked in a hoarse whisper.

As I was silent, he addressed the same appeal to Penelope, and she, in answer, ran to the door and pointed across the clearing.

"Look, father," she shouted; "he has come back."

Byron Lukens had indeed returned and with a heavy reinforcement. Five men climbed out of the wagon which had appeared from the road, and now they began a careful reconnoissance of the house. As they stood on the edge of the woods looking toward us I marked each one of them, and the problem uppermost in my mind concerned what I should do myself, for I was fairly cornered. I could not run away, for they were watching every exit from the cabin, and there was not one of them who would not recognize me did I flee over the open. The presence of James alone meant my undoing, and there he was, standing by the constable, eying the place with a lowering glare which threatened a storm, for here he had fallen and here he would redeem himself by some act of exceptional daring. Caught in this net, I hid behind the door-post and peered around it through a protecting shield made by the Professor's coat-tails. In the silence I could hear my heart beat.

There was one thing for the Professor to do now, and he did that well. He gathered his scattered senses and stood quietly in the doorway, smoking, leaving to the invaders the burden of action. Their indecision gave him strength.

"The idea of my giving in to a crew like that," he said to me in a steady voice. "It's a pity Mr. Pound didn't come, and your father too, David, that they might see how little I cared for their warrants." Then, to show how undisturbed he was by their presence, he called to them pleasantly: "Good morning, gentlemen."

This mild greeting gave courage to our foes and Stacy Shunk advanced. His coming was a sign that reason was to be used before force, and with his first step he began to gesticulate and to protest his friendly purpose. But he could not argue with any acumen while his bare feet were traversing a carpet of briers, and a silence followed, broken by exclamations as he came on slowly but resolutely as though he walked on eggs. Half-way over the clearing he stopped with a cry of pain, and the herald's mission was forgotten in the search for a thorn. The picture of Stacy Shunk balancing on one foot while he nursed the other in his hands made the Professor laugh hilariously and he called to him to hurry.

But Stacy would come no farther. He planted himself firmly on his bleeding feet; his great black hat-brim hid his face, but the voice which came from under it was soft, and he held out his hands as though he offered his dear friend the protection of his arms.

"You know what these other fellows want, Professor, and you know I'd only come along to help you. The whole thing was only a joke first off, but you've gone and assaulted the constable, and there'll be trouble if you don't settle it and be reasonable. Now, my advice is—"

"Thank you for your advice, Stacy Shunk," exclaimed the Professor. "But you know as well as I do that I have done nothing that I can be arrested for."

"Of course I do," returned the herald. "But you hadn't otter upset the preacher so. You'd otter believe what he says, and when he preaches about Noah and the like you hadn't otter produce figures in public to show that Noah and his boys couldn't have matched up all the animals and insects in the time they was allowed, let alone stabling 'em in a building three hundred cupids long and thirty cupids wide and three stories high. Now I allus held—"

"I don't care what you held," said the Professor sharply. "You can't get me into an argument now. I suppose it was unwise of me to try to make you people think, but you can't arrest a man for simply being unpopular. This is my home, and no law of your twopenny village can make me leave it."

"I'm not going to argue about Noah," protested Stacy Shunk. "As your friend, I'm trying—"

"As my friend, you had best go home and take your other friends with you." The Professor's voice was dry and crackling.

He reached behind the door and took up the long rifle which leaned against the wall. There was no threat in his action, for he held it under his arm and looked off to the mountain-top as though he were trying to make up his mind whether or not it was a good day for hunting. Stacy Shunk saw another purpose beneath this careless air, and he abandoned argument. Without heeding the briers, he fled to his friends; he did not even stop there, but plunged into the bushes, and above them I saw his head and hands moving together in an excited colloquy. The ludicrous figure which he cut in his retreat excited the Professor to laughter, in which Penelope joined, clapping her hands with mirth. I, wiser than she as to the danger of firearms, and trusting less to her father's mild intentions, broke into tearful pleading.

"Please don't shoot, Professor," I whimpered, tugging at his coat-tails to drag him back. "They won't hurt you, I know they won't."

"Don't worry, Davy," the Professor said with a reassuring smile. "They wouldn't hurt any one, nor would I. Didn't Shunk run at the mere sight of a gun? Why, if I pointed it at the rest of them they would fly like birds."

It was not fair to judge the courage of the others by the cowardice of Stacy Shunk. The constable's boasts came out of the past to goad him into action, and while Joe Holmes, the blacksmith, might have been very weak in the knees, he was not ready to retreat so early in the action when his helper, Thaddeus Miller, was watching him. As for James, despite the fall his moral qualities had taken in my estimation, I believed him to be a man of unflinching bravery, and he it was that I feared most when at last the advance began across the clearing, the four moving abreast with military precision, while Stacy Shunk hurled at them many admonitions to be cautious. I knew that nothing would stop James; that while his comrades might scatter like birds, he would come on to a deadly hand-to-hand conflict, and I pictured the Professor and him swallowing each other like the two snakes of tradition. I forgot my own safety, and threw both arms about one of the Professor's legs and tried to pull him into the house. Penelope, too, lost her courage when she saw the numbers of the enemy and their bold advance, and she clung, wailing, to her father's waist. He shook us off, and for the first time spoke to us sharply, and so sharply that the child reached her hand to mine and together we slunk into a dark corner.

Of what followed we saw nothing. We heard the voices, nearer and nearer. Then the men seemed to halt and to address the Professor in tones of argument. We are a peaceable folk in our valley and little given to the use of firearms, and I suspect that the constable and his aids really knew the Professor to be a peaceable man or they would not have come thus far with such boldness. To come farther they hesitated until they had made it perfectly clear that they acted in his best interests. Even Byron Lukens was willing to let "bygones be bygones."

"I'm just doing of my duty, Mr. Blight," he said in a wheedling tone, "and if you'll come along quiet-like I'll say nothing about it to the squire."

"You can fix it all up with the squire," I heard Joe Holmes say.

"There's really nothing again you, only you must comply with the law."

Then James spoke—to my astonishment not in a bold demand that the Professor surrender, but softly, asking him to be careful with the gun.

"Nobody has nothing again you, Professor," he said as gently as he would have spoken to me, and hearing this I took heart, for with James in such a temper there seemed no danger of a serious clash.

"No one has nothing against me," the Professor repeated in a tone of irony. "You only want to drag me through the village before the squire. Tell the squire to come here to me and explain."

There was a moment of silence. It was so quiet outside that even the birds seemed to be listening and watching; then came the swish of weeds trampled under foot.

"Be off, the whole crew of you," cried the man in the doorway, and I saw the butt of the gun rise to his shoulder.

> I wanted to cry out, but my throat was parched with fright, and Penelope was clinging to my neck in silent terror.

There was another moment of silence. Then James began to laugh in that vast ebullient way of his, and a bit of dry brush snapped sharply under some foot. The report of the rifle shook the cabin. It must have shaken the mountains too, it seemed to me, for the floor beneath me rocked in time to the echoes of it rattling among the hills, and I heard a wild scream, the cry of a man hurt to death, and the shrill cries of startled birds fleeing to the hiding of the trees. A puff of wind swept a thin veil of smoke into the room, but for me the air was filled with sickening fumes, and I sank to my knees and closed my eyes as a child does at night to shut out the perils of the darkness. I felt Penelope's arms gripped tightly about my neck, her dead weight dragging me down. I heard the last echoes of the shot, faintly, down the narrow valley, and outside the incoherent shouts of men. Then there was a silence, broken only by Penelope's sobs. It seemed to me long hours I was there on my knees before I dared to open my eyes and bring myself into the world again. And when I did it was to see the room darkened and the Professor leaning against the closed door with his hands wide-spread, as though with every muscle braced to hold it against an onslaught. Yet he trembled so that a child might have brushed him aside.

There was no onslaught. I waited the moment when the door would be crashed in. I heard the clock ticking monotonously on the cupboard and the wood crackling in the stove. The birds were singing again, and outside in the clearing it was as peaceful as on that day when I first came upon it, wet and shivering, to find joy in its cheerful sunniness.

I broke from Penelope's embrace and got to my feet. The Professor, hearing me, raised his head from the door and turned to me a face chalky-white, whiter for the dishevelled hair that hung about it.

"Davy," he whispered, "look out of the window and tell me what you see."

I had no care for any trouble that might lie ahead for me. I wanted to be seen. I wanted to be taken from this stifling cabin with its deafening noises and sickening fumes and above all from this mad fellow who looked as I had seen a rat look when cornered in a garner. I ran to the window and peered through the smutted panes, but there was no one outside to see or to help me. The clearing was as quiet as in the earlier morning when I had looked over it at the Professor studying the distant tree-top.

"What do you see, Davy?" he asked in a hoarse voice.

"Nothing," I answered. "They've gone away."

"And isn't Lukens there—out there in the weeds?"

I rubbed the smutted glass and peered through it again into every corner of the clearing. "No," I said, "there's nothing there."

The Professor drew back from the door and stood before me brushing his matted hair from his face.

"I didn't mean it, Davy," he said. "It was all a mistake. They were going away and I was dropping the gun, and somehow I touched the trigger and Lukens fell. They've taken him home, but they'll come back—a hundred of them this time. Oh, Davy, Davy, help me!"

I knew that I could not help him. My thought then was for myself, and I did not answer, but measured the distance to the door and waited my chance to dart to it and get away, for in him before me, driving his long fingers through his hair and staring at me with frightened eyes, I saw the man whom I had pictured in fear that first morning when I came to the mountains. This was the real Professor and I was caught.

"Oh, let me go!" I cried.

"Why, Davy!" He gave a start of surprise. The frightened look passed and he reached out his hands to my shoulders. I shrank back. The scream of Byron Lukens still rang in my ears, and to me there was something very terrible in this man who had dared to kill, this man for whom all the valley would soon be hunting, this man who even now might be standing in the shadow of the gallows. He saw the terror in my face; to his eyes came that same look my dog would give me when I struck him.

"Why, Davy," he said, holding out two trembling hands. "Boy, I thought you were my only friend."

This was the cry of a man worse hurt than Byron Lukens, and in a rush of boyish pity for him I forgot my dread and running to him threw my arms about him, hugged him as I should have hugged my dog in a mute appeal for pardon. So we three stood there in silence, the Professor, Penelope, and I, with arms intertwined and our heads close together. Then after a moment he raised himself and shook us off gently.

"I've been a fool, Davy," he said, speaking quietly. "I've been an idle, worthless fool and now I must pay for it. Soon they'll be coming for me and

I must run. But I'll come back; I'll make it all up—some day Penelope will be proud of me. Until then, Davy, my friend, you'll take care of Penelope, won't you—till I come back?"

Hearing this, Penelope dragged his face down to hers imploring him to take her with him. He kissed her. Then he lifted her high in his arms as though in play and held her off that she might see how gayly he was smiling and take heart from it.

> "I don't know where I am going, child," he said, "but I am coming back for you very soon, and you will see what a man your father really is. I haven't been fair to you, Penelope—but wait—wait till I come back. And Davy will take care of you—won't you, Davy?"

"Yes, sir," I said boldly.

What else could a boy have said in such a case, when every passing moment meant danger to his friend? I had no thought of the full meaning of my promise, for I did not look beyond that day, and that day my goal was home. Home there was safety for me and for Penelope as well. Home all perplexing problems solved themselves. Home was a place of great peace, and my father and mother benign genii who lived only to make others happy. It was easy to lead Penelope home, and I was sure that if I told my father and mother of my promise to take care of her, they would make the way easy for me. So when the Professor had kissed the child and lowered her to the floor, I put out my hand and took hers in a self-reliant grasp.

The Professor picked up the fallen rifle and put it away in its corner; he pushed the kettle to the back of the stove; he seemed to be tidying up the house. He blew the dust from his hat and crushed it down on his head. Then standing in the open doorway, he surveyed the room critically as if to make sure that all was in order before he strolled down to the village.

"Good-by, Penelope," he said in a quiet voice. "Stay with Davy till I come back—I'll come back soon."

For a moment Penelope believed him. "Good-by, father," she called as he turned and walked away.

He had passed the door. Hearing her voice, he gave a start, then broke into a run. He ran as never I had seen a man run. He was not alone a man in flight. Every limb was filled with fear and moving for its life. Even his hat and coat were sensate things, struggling madly to get away to a safe refuge.

Seeing him flying thus across the clearing toward the mountains, Penelope broke from me with a cry, but I caught her and held her in my arms. She called to him wildly, yet he did not turn, and in a moment had plunged into the bush.

Long after he had gone we two stood in the cabin door searching the silent wall of green for some sign of him. None was given. The shadow of the ridge crept away as the sun climbed higher and the clearing was bathed in its brightness. A crow called pleasantly from a tall pine. The birds, back from their hiding, sang as though on such a day there could be no trouble.

I felt the blue ribbon brush my cheek, and two small bare arms about my neck.

I turned to Penelope and said: "Don't cry, little 'un. I'll take care of you."

CHAPTER V

To Nathan, the white mule, I owed it that I was able to take good care of Penelope Blight in the first hours of my guardianship. But for him I should have brought her face to face with the mob that rode out of Malcolmville to storm the clearing. I knew but one road home from the gut, and that was the way James had brought me fishing. Had we followed it, we should have hardly crossed the ridge before we met the van of an ill-organized but determined army, and then to her grief terror must have been added by the wagons filled with men armed as though they were going into battle. The obstinate temperament of the mule served us a good turn. When Penelope and I led him from the barn and climbed to his back, he must have supposed that we were going to the store and should leave him tied for hours in the hot sun, switching flies, while we sat comfortably in the shade of the porch discussing the universe's affairs. Believing this, he protested, stopping in the middle of the clearing to enjoy a few tidbits of sprouting corn. Discovering that the small boy on his back lacked his master's strength and courage, he decided to go on, but as he chose. He chose first a trot. To Penelope and me it seemed a mad gallop, and I clung desperately to his scanty mane while she clutched my waist and pleaded with me to halt him and let her down. In this eternity of suffering—ten minutes really—her greater grief was forgotten, and she was spared the pang of a last look at her deserted home, for when Nathan decided to walk she turned her head to see only a long archway of trees ending in a green wall.

"Davy," she cried, "please let me get off!"

Now I wanted to get off myself, but I suspected her desire to run back to the clearing, and my over-powering thought was to carry her away from that forbidding place. I had promised the Professor to take care of the girl, and responsibility had added years to my age and inches to my stature. I was no longer a shivering, frightened boy clinging to her hand, and, though I was not the master of the mule, while we stayed on his back I was Penelope's master, and that was what I had determined to be.

"Don't be afraid, little 'un," I returned boldly, when I had recovered my breath and balance. "I can handle him all right."

To make good my boast, I even dared to kick Nathan, fearing lest a pause in our journey might allow her to slip from his back.

"I want to find father—to go with him," she pleaded. It was the hundredth time she had told me that.

"He said you were to come with me, Penelope," I argued. "And he told me particular that he wouldn't be home till a week from Monday."

This last was a little fiction of mine, which seemed warranted by the circumstances, and had Penelope pressed me and asked me when her father had made such a definite statement I was ready to go to any extent with like imaginings if only I could keep her with me. She did not, and her cheerier tone quieted my conscience.

"Is he?" she cried. "Do you really think he will come home, Davy?"

"Didn't he tell me so?" I returned haughtily. "And besides, what would he stay away any longer for?"

Still Penelope was inclined to doubt. She knew that the morning's strange events had brought her father into great trouble, and she could not believe that a vain search for him would satisfy his enemies. Two weeks, she thought, would suffice to wear them out, but two weeks in her small mind was an eternity when it was to be faced without him.

> "Oh, Davy, I wish he hadn't done it," she cried. "If he hadn't shot Mr. Lukens, then he wouldn't have to run away, would he?"

"That was just a mistake," I replied, as though shooting constables were quite a favorite sport where I lived. "He told me particular he didn't mean it, but having done it, and they not understanding that he didn't mean it, he kind of had to get out till things blowed over."

"Didn't he do wrong to shoot Mr. Lukens?"

"Wrong?" My tone expressed the greatest astonishment at such an idea. "Why, Penelope, if I was him I'd have done exactly the same thing—exactly."

My approval of her father's act was a great consolation to her. The pressure of her encircling arms made me gasp, and there was a note of gratitude in her voice. "Oh, Davy, I know you would; you are so brave."

"And I'll take care of you, Penelope," I said, quite as though I seconded her approval of my courage and had forgotten that there were such things as rattlesnakes. "As long as you are with me you needn't be afraid of anything."

Nathan's pace was quieter and steadier, and being secure on his back I felt capable of any heroism. We had passed the worst part of the road. It was broader, the trees parted overhead, letting in the sunshine, and danger never seems so near when one moves in the bright day; so my heart grew lighter, and, had I known the words of any rollicking song, I should have sung, like James, but lacking these I had recourse to whistling. Nerves which had been set on edge by the rifle's report, the fumes of smoke, the cries of pain and fright, were quieted first by long-drawn, melancholy notes, and then I swung into a bold trilling, more suited to my adventurous spirit, throwing back my head, extending my lips heavenward, addressing my melody to the sky. Pausing, exhausted, I expected to hear from behind me some expression of astonishment and pleasure at my birdlike song. Instead there was only a muffled sobbing.

"Little 'un," I said in a chiding voice, "you hadn't otter cry when I'm taking care of you. There's nothing to be afraid of. Why, we're going home."

Oh, wise Nathan! Then I thought him obstinate and contradictory. Halting, he planted his feet as though no power on earth could move him, and shot forward his long ears. Then it seemed to me that he was trying to show how futile my boast, and in my anger I dared to kick him. A fly would have moved him as well. His long ears trembled as he watched the road rising to cross the ridge, and he seemed to see over the crest and to hear noises too distant and indistinct for me. Then I thought him obstinate; now I suspect that while the Professor had given Penelope to my care, he must have ordered Nathan to watch over us both. The mule looked right through that hill. He saw the threatening army charging the other slope. He turned. The bushes opened, and we plunged into a narrow path which skirted the base of the ridge. In vain I tried to pull him back. In vain Penelope addressed to him her appeals. He was fixed in his purpose neither to hear nor to obey, and struck into a steady canter. I clung to his mane; Penelope, to me. The earth swung around us. Solid became fluid. The path moved up and down, and flowed beneath us like running water. Great trees broke from their roots and ran at us, and when Nathan dodged them, they swung down their branches to blind us with their leaves, and sometimes almost to lift us in the air like Absalom. The memory of Absalom was very clear in my mind, for just a week before I had seen his picture in our Sunday-school quarterly, and now, confused in my eyes with the dancing trees, I saw him, as I had seen him in the picture, suspended from a limb by his long hair, quietly waiting to be taken down. There was something more than a mere coincidence in that Sunday-school lesson. Here was another warning neglected. With Mr. Pound and Stacy Shunk, Miss Spinner took a place as a prophetess. She had taught me that boys who mocked their respectable elders were eaten by bears, and I believed her. She had demonstrated beyond all doubt that boys who defied their parents and ran away from home must come to a dreadful end in the entangling limbs of trees. With Absalom's example before me I had run away from home, and here I was being carried through the forest on a mad steed, and here were the trees running at me from every side, reaching out their forked limbs to seize my hair. Penelope was forgotten. More than once I tried to avert my impending fate by letting go of Nathan's mane and taking my chances with his heels and the stony path, but as I was about to close my eyes and let myself go he rose in the air, and the distance between me and the earth seemed so stupendous as to become the greater peril. Had the mule kept on his wild career I might at last have gathered courage for the fall, but the path came to an end, our pace slackened, the trees took root again; I was conscious of Penelope's encircling arms, and raising my head saw that we were in a broad road, and, better still, we were climbing the hill; each step was carrying us nearer the clearest and bluest of skies that always held over my home; I knew that from that line where ridge and sky met, I should look down and see home itself.

We reached the top of the ridge, and the valley lay beneath us. It was young and cheerful in its fresh green, with here a brown checkering of fallow, and there a white barn glistening in the sun, and orchards in the full glory of their blossom. Below us a stone mill grumbled over its unending task, and from the meadows came the blithe call of the killdee. It was all home to me from the fringing pines on the ridge-top, across the land to the mountains by the river, for on such a threshold one casts off fear. Danger might lurk about us in the shadows of the woods, but never out there in the broad day under the kindly eye of God. Nathan might gallop through tangled brush, but here even his mood changed and he walked sedately. Even the strange road was friendly to me, for it led into a friendly land. It descended the ridge, passed the mill, rose again over a hill; there at the crest I lost it, but only for a moment while it crossed the hollow and came into view on the easy slope beyond, going straight into the valley's heart and beckoning me on.

"It's all right now, Penelope," I cried, and I pointed to the two steeples of Malcolmville, and then led her eyes to the right to a long stone house, almost hidden in a clump of giant oaks. I could find it by our barn, for our barn would dominate any land. In the distance it seemed a mighty marble pile, lifting its white walls into the blue, and then ambitiously reaching higher with red-tipped cupolas. The Colosseum to-day is not half so large as our barn when placed in memory beside it. So there was pride in my voice as I spoke.

"Yon's our home, little 'un, and yon's our barn, and just the other side is the meadow and the creek where I'll take you fishing."

The splendid promise of fishing had little effect on Penelope's spirits. Such a prospect as I offered, such a home, a Babylonian palace beside the cabin in the clearing, with the added joys of the meadow and the creek, should have compensated in part, at least, for the temporary loss of her father, and I was much surprised that she gave no sign of pleasure. She made no answer even, and I had no evidence of her nearness to me but the two brown hands clasped before me and the brush of the ribbon against my neck. So we rode on in silence, save when I whistled, and I did not whistle very much, for my thoughts were too busy with the morning's adventure and forecasting the days to come. My mind was wonderfully clear about the future; the way seemed very easy. Thereafter I should listen to warnings. I had brought myself to unpleasant passes by a reckless disregard of warnings, and now if Mr. Pound told me to beware, or Stacy Shunk to look out, or Miss Spinner to remember Absalom, I should heed their admonitions, yet those unpleasant passes became in retrospect delightful adventures, and I congratulated myself that I was coming through them with so much credit. That I was conducting myself with credit, I had no doubt. My father could not have accepted the Professor's charge more confidently than I, nor could he have used more adroitness in persuading Penelope to leave the clearing. So I was sure of commendation when I brought her home. Home was such a bountiful place. My mother had impressed that on me very often. She had laid emphasis on my obligation to share my riches with others—generally when I had to carry heavy baskets down to the parsonage. To-day I was mindful of that injunction, and to take care of Penelope was a pleasant task, since for the present it meant simply to share with her from an inexhaustible store. Considering the future, I wandered into hazy and very muddled dreams. Did the Professor never return, I was quite willing to keep my promise and to care for his daughter always. This did not mean that I was contemplating matrimony at some remote time. Matrimony, to my youthful observation, was a prosaic state. It did not seem to me that my father and mother led an interesting life. If they were happy in it, then it was in a very strange way, for they only knew a dull routine of work and worry. Sometimes they laughed, and when they did it was hard to discover the sources of their mirth. How my father could find pleasure in Mr. Pound's sermons was a mystery, and when my mother declared that the meeting of the Ladies' Aid had been most enjoyable I was sure that she was pretending. No; the future held something better for me than such dull days. Somehow, somewhere, when I became a man I should live days like this day, I should live as now I rode, with every sense keyed to the joy of living, and Penelope's arms would encircle me and the blue ribbon would gently brush my neck.

These pleasant dreams were disturbed by realities. I had come to one of those dreadful moments when danger rises like an appalling cloud, through which we can see no gleam of light beyond. This cloud, "at first no larger than a man's hand," arose from a fence in the person of Piney Savercool. I saw him with pleasure, for I knew that I was coming to familiar roads, and then he was such a very small boy that I had not that sense of humiliation which I must have felt had one of my own age seen me riding with a girl.

"Morning, Piney," I said grandly.

For an answer Piney simply opened his mouth very wide, and his eyes started from his head.

My effect upon him was very pleasing to me, and I ventured still more grandly: "Pleasant day, Piney."

> Then he found his voice, "Ma-ma—come quick!" he shrieked. "Davy Malcolm's runnin' away with a lady!"

This announcement brought Mrs. Savercool from the house, and in a few bounds she was before us, checking our further advance with a wide-spread apron.

"Dav-id Malcolm," she cried, "the idea of you lettin' such a little 'un as her set on such a dangerous animal. Stop! Get down, I say, both on you!"

I could not break through that apron, and my heart sank, for, instead of riding grandly home and presenting Penelope to my parents with a proper speech, we were threatened with an ignominious journey in the Savercool buggy. With Mrs. Savercool's charge that we were foolish children, and that she could never forgive herself if she did not stop our wild career at once, years dropped from my age and inches from my stature, and I was at the point of obeying her meekly. But Nathan took offence at her tone. He bolted. Just what happened I could not see, for I had to take myself to his mane again, and he held his terrific pace until we reached the pike, and along the pike to the fork where the road branched off to our farm. When he paused here it was to consider whether he would go on toward Malcolmville or into the quiet, shaded lane. He must have recalled the hitching-rail, the sun, and the flies, and preferred to risk even a road that he did not know, for on he went—quietly.

We crossed the little knoll and the house came into view. The cry of exultation which rose to my lips was checked when I saw, stretching from the gate down the road, a long line of vehicles. The first held the hitching-post. The others took to the fence—buggies, buckboards, phaetons, single horses, and teams, an ominous picture. Not since my grandfather's funeral had I seen quite such a sight before our house, and my heart sank. Could death have come in my absence? On second thought I remembered how brief that absence had been, measured in hours, and I sought another reason for the gathering. I began at the last vehicle and carried my eye along the line, to find that I knew them all. There was Doctor Pearl's buckboard, with his mustang eating a fence post; Squire Crumple's gray mare in his narrow courting buggy; old Mr. Smiley's ponderous black with his comfortable phaeton, speaking the presence of Mr. Pound and Mrs. Pound, who used it as their own; the Buckwalters' rockaway and the Rickabachs' spring-wagon. Even Miss Agnes Spinner's bicycle had a fence panel all to itself, as though it were very skittish and likely to kick and set the whole road in commotion. To my own unimportant self I never attributed this assembly of all the great folk of the valley. There was some more potent reason. As I pondered, hunting for it, we came to the lane. Until I found that reason it seemed wise for me to turn there, and under the cover of the orchard to reach the hiding of the barn, where I could leave Penelope while I scouted and had a peep through the keyhole of the back door. But Nathan saved me from such an ignominious return. He kept right on. My efforts to stop him only made him trot, and in a moment we were at the gate. He seemed to like the house and the shade of the oaks, for he halted, let himself down on three legs complacently and began to switch at flies. And I, with nothing left to do, was measuring the distance to a safe landing when I heard a cry from the door.

"Davy! Davy!" I saw my mother running down the path with her arms outstretched, and after her came a great company.

"Davy—Davy, dear—we thought you had been drowned!" she cried.

Here, then, was the reason for this great gathering. What a commotion for so small a reason—as though a boy's chief end were to tumble into the water, as though he never were to be trusted out of his mother's sight? I dropped the reins; my eyes and my mouth opened wide with astonishment.

"Your father's dragging the mill-dam for you this very minute." She was at the gate. "Where—where have you been?"

She did not let me answer. She lifted her hands and caught me in her embrace, and Penelope's arms were clutching me about the neck as she was swung with me from Nathan's back.

My mother was crying, from gladness I took it, for there certainly was joy in her eyes when she held me off and looked down at me. Then came astonishment, and she lowered her spectacles from the top of her head to make sure that she saw aright.

"But who—who is this?" she said.

For answer I took Penelope's hand and faced the whole company; faced Mr. Pound and the squire, old Mr. Smiley and Miss Spinner, Mrs. Pound, and a score of others of the great folk of the valley. I faced them with defiance in my eyes, for were not they the authors of the Professor's troubles and was I not his only friend?

"It's Penelope Blight," I said, "and I promised the Professor to take care of her."

"What?" cried Mr. Pound. "The Professor's daughter—the man who almost killed Constable Lukens? Dav-id!"

"Yes, sir," I said. Penelope's hand was tightening in mine, and I glanced to my side, to see her standing very straight, and the blue ribbon was tilted as proudly as on that morning when we met by the mountain brook.

"Dav-id!" cried my mother.

> "Yes, sir," I said, looking right at Mr. Pound. "I promised the Professor that I would take care of her—always."

CHAPTER VI

It was well for me that in my hours of absence fear had brought my parents to a just estimate of my character and to a truer appreciation of my essentiality to their happiness. My mother had long been haunted by a conviction that I should meet an early death by drowning or an accidental gunshot, and this very morning she had awakened from a dream in which she saw her only child floating on the murky waters of the mill-dam. Rushing to my room and finding me gone, she had had her worst fears confirmed, and at the moment of my reappearance Mr. Pound was endeavoring to console her for her loss and to bring her to a state of Christian resignation. So all was forgotten in the joy of my unexpected return, and though in the eyes of the minister, Miss Spinner, and the others I was just a small black sheep about whose absence an unnecessary pother had been raised, there was only rejoicing in the home fold. Even my father did not humiliate me with forgiveness, but took me in his arms silently and held me there, as he might have held me had he just rescued me from the depths of the mill-dam. To follow such a greeting with chastisement, however well merited, was quite out of the question. In the seclusion of my own room I did meet with gentle chiding for the anguish I had caused, but my mother remembered her dream, and my father his hours of futile searching, and I knew that the hands which pressed mine would not be raised against me in harsh reproof. Below us, I was sure, ears were strained to hear some real evidence that I was receiving my deserts, for there was a silence there like that outside of the prison wall when the crowd waits for the doleful tidings tolled by the prison bell. Perhaps the listeners were disappointed. I remember that Mr. Pound looked rather nonplussed as he saw us coming down-stairs, my father leading the way, smiling gravely, my mother following, clutching my hand as though she would never release it.

I had told them everything then. The story I had tried in vain to tell them at dinner on the previous day was now listened to with eagerness, and my father, knowing the truth of James's fall from grace, was outspoken in his declaration that an injustice had been done the Professor. In a solemn conference in the parlor, with Mr. Pound and the squire, Doctor Pearl, Mr. Smiley, and all the other important men of the neighborhood, he decried the attack on Henderson Blight as an outrage; he found solace alone in the

fact that the constable had been more frightened than hurt, for it seemed that the bullet had only clipped the flesh of his leg; he took upon himself all the blame for the affair, on the ground that he, at least, should have known better. Squire Crumple heartily agreed with my father, and pointed out that on his part he had only allowed the warrant to issue under protest; henceforth he would rely on his own judgment and would not interpret the law to suit the whims of his friends. Mr. Pound was contrite, but he took comfort in the thought that they had acted for the best in the light of their knowledge of the circumstances, but now, knowing the facts, he advised that the whole matter be allowed to simmer down quietly. He still took issue with his respected friend the squire on the illegality of the means used to rid the community of a most undesirable member. The squire replied with heat, referring to the case of The Commonwealth *versus* Hodgins, and the subsequent action of Hodgins *versus* The Commonwealth for damages. It was very evident that he would be relieved in mind if the case of The Commonwealth *versus* Blight did simmer down. But there was one obstacle to this programme of forgetting. It was not the constable. Lukens could be quieted easily. It was Penelope. Even the gentlest ministrations of Miss Spinner had failed to bring the small girl to a realization of the happy change in her lot. Even Mr. Pound was touched by her grief and so troubled that he offered amends in a home under the parsonage roof. He realized now that the reason he had never been blessed with a child of his own was that when the time came there might be a place at his board and a nook in his heart for this abandoned little girl. On the strength of her husband's offer Mrs. Pound was claiming Penelope as her own, and very soon was complaining that she had a most troublesome child to deal with. Penelope had divined that Mr. Pound was her father's arch-enemy, and she met his most benign approach with her head tilted defiantly and her eyes flashing, so that now, in a quandary, he asked: "What shall we do with the child?"

The question was a sign that he surrendered her. He had shown an honest desire to take her under his roof, and no one could say that if he had fired the train which had wrecked her home, he was not willing to make atonement.

"What shall we do with the child?" my father repeated. He rose to show that the conference was ended and the question settled. "David has already answered that," he said, laying a hand upon my shoulder. "My boy promised Henderson Blight to take care of her until he returned. They have settled it among themselves, and I shall do nothing to interfere with them."

He spoke so firmly that no one dared to remonstrate, and so it came that I kept my promise to the Professor as far as it was in my power. He must have said himself that Penelope had a home better than any he could

have given her. She had a mother's care—a care so loving that I should have grown jealous had I not found a certain compensation in the fact that the watchfulness over me relaxed and I was less hampered in my comings and goings. Before a month had passed my mother was confessing a dread that the Professor might return and claim the child; she was pleading with my father to abandon what she called a useless and an expensive search. Chance had left the door open, and chance had brought me into the hall, so I stopped and stood as silently as I could that I might not disturb their conference. I was frightened by the sternness in my father's voice. He spoke of his duty. To him duty summed up life. He had his duty, even in the matter of so worthless a creature as this Henderson Blight. Declaring this, he stamped the floor in emphasis.

Often in the weeks that followed, when Penelope and I roamed over the fields, when her merriment rang out the highest, and her laughter was so free that it seemed she was forgetting the clearing and the days when her sole companion was the gaunt and bitter-tongued Professor—often then I would hear again the stamp of my father's foot and his stern avowal, and to me it was as though he were conspiring against me in seeking to send away the only comrade I had ever known, and would leave me to pass my days in the wake of James. I abhorred James now. I had come to know the pleasure of real companionship, and looked back to the old days wondering how I had endured them, and with dread to those that seemed to lie ahead. Penelope was a girl, to be sure, but she was not like the insipid creatures of the village who were held in such contempt by boys of my age. Where I dared to go she followed. Did I climb to the highest girder in the barn and balance myself on the dizzy height, she was with me. Did I venture to run the wildest rapids of the creek in the clumsy box which I called my canoe, she trusted her newest frock and ribbons to my seamanship. And better than all was the respect and admiration in which she held me. To her I was no longer the frightened, shivering boy of the mountain brook. I was in a land I knew and followed its familiar ways without fear. One day she saw me tumble from the bridge into the deep swimming-hole, and while she cried out in fright I swam nonchalantly ashore, a full dozen strokes, and as I dried myself in the sun I reproved her for her little faith in me. On another I presented her to old Jerry Schimmel, sitting, a brown, dishevelled heap on his cobbler's bench, and from my accustomed seat by his stove, in a voice cast into the echoing hollows of my chest, I commanded him to tell us how he had fought in the battle of Gettysburg. From my familiarity with the stirring incidents of the fight as Jerry described them, Penelope thought that I must have had a part in it too, and my modest disclaimer hardly convinced her that I had not been a companion-in-arms of this battle-worn veteran.

What days those were! Even the fear that my father would find the missing Professor grew less. They drifted into weeks, and weeks into months, and there was no sign of the fugitive. I found myself looking into the future as though in the quiet evening I were turning my eyes over the valley to the west and the golden clouds hovering there. I dealt only with results. I crossed mountains without climbing them, and always Penelope shared my glory with me. I look back now smiling at that boyish self-reliance. Mountains have been crossed, but with what heart-breaking struggles? Battles have been won, but with what a toll of suffering?

As I recall the day when I first came face to face with real trouble, with a trouble that leaves in the heart a never-healing wound, it was the brightest of all that summer. It was one of those days when there was not the filmiest cloud to veil the sun; you could see the ether shimmering over the land, and the fields of yellow grain looked like lakes of molten metal. Shaded by our wide straw hats, Penelope and I had no thought of the tropic heat. We were engrossed in the reaper as it cut its way through the wheat; we followed it, counting the sheaves as they dropped with mechanical precision; we stepped along untiringly in its wake, as though the rough stubble were the smoothest of paths, and the clatter of the machine the sweetest of music. Above the raucous clacking I heard my mother calling, and, suspecting some needless injunction not to get overheated, I pretended not to hear and looked the other way. But she was insistent. When we had rounded the field again, she crossed the road to the fence; the reaper stopped, and on a day so still that a dog's bark carried a mile there was no escape from her uplifted voice. Reluctantly Penelope and I abandoned our enchanting travel and obeyed the summons.

"Penelope," my mother said, taking the girl by the hand, "come into the house. Your uncle is here."

Penelope stopped and looked up into my mother's face, and there was wonder in her eyes. She had forgotten her uncle, so rarely had she heard her father speak of him, and I was quicker than she to grasp the meaning of his coming, for I remembered that Rufus, who never had had a real idea, who made his first success by giving away a prize with every pound of tea. I believed that he had come to take Penelope from me, and with every step I saw my fears confirmed.

"Your Uncle Rufus," my mother said, and she closed her lips very tightly as she walked on.

The parlor shades were up—an ominous sign, for the parlor would only be opened to a person of importance. Had the Professor visited us, the humbler sitting-room would have been quite good enough to receive

him in, and it seemed a strange commentary on his harsh judgment that his brother should be ushered into the stately chamber where the very air grew old in dignified seclusion. Still more forcibly was this idea impressed on my mind when I stood at the door and saw my father sitting very erect, on a most uncomfortable chair, listening respectfully to the stranger's rapid words.

Rufus Blight spoke in a loud voice; he lolled in the big walnut rocker, with his arm stretched across the centre table, to the peril of my mother's precious Swiss chalet and the glass dome which protected it; on the family Bible his fingers were beating a tattoo as carelessly as they might have done on the counter of his general store. There was nothing in his appearance to suggest kin to the lean and cadaverous Professor. The Professor always seemed to move with effort, but his brother was alive all over. Though short and fat, he had none of the placidity which we associate with corpulence. As he talked his hands moved restlessly; his bristling red mustache accentuated the play of his lips; his heavy gold watch-chain moved up and down with his breathing; even his hair was alert.

"He is a remarkable man—I might say, a very remarkable man," were the words that came to us as we entered the hall. "Of course, you couldn't understand him—few could. He had to go his own way and would take help from no one, not even his brother. Upon my word, Judge—"

Our entrance checked him. He rose, and with arms akimbo stood gazing down at Penelope. She, clinging to my mother, her cheek pressed against her as she half turned from him, looked up at him, abashed and wondering, for to her small mind there was in this stranger something awe-inspiring. The sleek man in spotless, creaseless clothes, with polished boots and close-shaved, powdered, barbered face, was so different from her unkempt father that she could hardly believe him kin. Baal would have seemed as near to her, and had the idol stretched out his arms to take her into his destroying embrace, she could hardly have been more frightened than when she saw Mr. Blight's fat hands reaching toward her. Mr. Blight smiled, and well he might, for this slip of a girl gazing up at him was of his own blood, and all that was good in that blood found expression in her sweetness. He had come prepared to see a slattern, ill-fed, unkempt, the true daughter of shiftless parents and a wretched mountain home; he had found a graceful little body, and he wanted to take her into his possession at once.

"Penelope," he exclaimed, "don't you know your Uncle Rufus?"

There was no particular reason why Penelope should know her Uncle Rufus. She could have submitted herself as easily to the embrace of any well-dressed, smiling stranger, and she shrank back, but my mother pushed her forward within reach of the restless hands.

"It's your dear uncle, child," she said soothingly. "He has come to take you to a nice home."

"And he is going to bring you up," my father added in a wonderfully cheerful voice, born either from his own escape from responsibility or her brightened prospects. "He is going to give you everything."

Penelope was on the verge of tears, but she held them back. "I don't want everything," she said, as she strove to check her forced advance by planting her feet firmly and leaning back against my mother. "I just want to stay here till father comes."

"But your father will come to us—of course, he will come to us, Penelope," Mr. Blight cried. His hands closed on hers, he hooked an arm about her and held her very cautiously, as though he were as afraid of her as she of him. "You mustn't be frightened, my dear," he went on, and, soothed by his kindly tones, she leaned against his knee. "That's better, child." Encouraged by her half-yielding attitude, he stroked her hair. To me, watching them from the hiding of my mother's skirt, she had fallen into a magician's clutches and was being lulled by soft words into an indifference to danger.

"I'm your father's brother, child," he pursued, in his insinuating tone. "Next to him I'm nearer to you than any one else, and to me there is no one as near as he. We will try to find him together—you and I, eh? And we'll all live together in Pittsburgh. You'll like Pittsburgh—it's a very lively, pushing town."

"But I want to stay here with Davy," said Penelope in a low voice.

"With Davy?" Mr. Blight stared at her in surprise. Then he began to laugh as though he were contrasting all he could give her with Davy's humble powers. "Child—child—you don't realize what you are refusing. You don't realize what your Uncle Rufus is going to do for you. I've no one to look after—you will be the joy of a poor old bachelor's heart, won't you, now?"

He spoke as though being a poor old bachelor was quite the pleasantest possible condition, yet he rolled out the phrase twice as if to touch Penelope's heart. Remembering the only other bachelor I had ever seen, I stared at him in wonder. This other was Philip Spangler, who sat all day in the store gazing vacantly at the stove. Once I asked Stacy Shunk why he stayed there, and Stacy, lifting a warning finger, whispered: "He's jest a bachelor, Davy, an old, old bachelor." Contrasting him with Mr. Blight,

I was puzzled. If it was a terrible thing to be an old bachelor, certainly he accepted the condition lightly; he was trying to arouse sympathy when it was plain that he did not need or deserve it, for evidently he was quite well satisfied with a single state, however deplorable it might come to be. Penelope was being enmeshed by unfair means, and it was hard to keep still, but there was nothing that I could do.

Now my father lifted his chin clear of the high points of his collar. "Penelope," he began, "you are fortunate—very fortunate—in having such an uncle. Mr. Blight is a prominent man, and I might say"—glancing apologetically at the guest—"a rich man." Then, meeting no contradiction, he added—"a very rich man, who can give you such advantages as would be far beyond my means, even were you my daughter."

"I don't want advantages," said Penelope, hardly above a whisper, and for want of a better resting-place she dropped her head on her uncle's shoulder and burst into tears.

"There—there—there—" cried Mr. Blight, patting her clumsily on the back. Had she been a full-grown woman, he could hardly have been more embarrassed, yet he was pleased that she clung to him thus, for he was smiling. "I'll not give you any advantages you don't want—I promise you. I just wish to make you happy. What's the use of my working all my life, piling up money, capturing the steel trade, adding mills and mills to my plants, if I have no one to look after. There—there—there—now, child, don't cry. Won't you come with your poor, lonely, old uncle?"

Even to my prejudiced mind, he was playing his part well, for this awkward kindness touched Penelope at last. She did not reply, nor did she demur, but she clung closer to him in silence. I saw my danger and hers, and ran to him and grasped his knees.

> "Oh, Mr. Blight, don't take her away!" I cried. "I promised the Professor I'd look after her. I promised—"

"Dav-id!" exclaimed my father, and he grasped my arm and began to draw me away.

My fear of him even could not restrain me, and I resisted, digging my fingers into the knees, clutching the folds of the trousers where Mr. Blight had so carefully arranged them to prevent them bagging. He intervened, as much, I think, to save his immaculate clothes as me from being torn asunder.

"Dav-id!" cried my father.

"Mr. Blight—Mr. Blight—don't take her away!" I pleaded.

Mr. Blight began to laugh. "Judge—Judge—release him," he said, and freeing me from the paternal grasp, he drew me toward him. When he had ironed out the wrinkled knees with his hand, he patted me on the head. "You are a good boy, David," he went on, "and I understand exactly how you feel. What you have done for Penelope will never be forgotten, will it, my little girl?" The emphasis on the last phrase of possession extinguished the spark of hope in me, and had he stopped there I should have surrendered feebly, but turning to my father, he added: "You have a fine boy, Judge, and I like him. When I get home I shall send him a gun. What kind of a gun do you want, David?"

Young as I was then, I had not yet learned to value the good things of life in terms of dollars, and to the power of the dollar my eyes were just being opened. This man wielded it. He was enticing Penelope behind the barrier of his fat, oily prosperity where I could not reach her. Holding her there, he was magnanimously compensating me with a gun, as though we were making a trade in which the profit were mine, as though he were valuing her in money. My dislike, born of the Professor's contemptuous reference to him, had turned to distrust and aversion as I watched him weaving his toils about Penelope. Now I hated him and drew back from him as though his touch were baneful; I stamped a foot and shook a fist and shouted: "I don't want your old gun; Penelope doesn't want your money. You have no right—"

My father's arms were about me. He lifted me from my feet and carried me to the door, and as I struggled blindly to free myself and return to the attack I looked back at Rufus Blight. It was not to see him sinking under the shame of my anathema. Signs of anger in him would have incensed me far less than his lofty unconcern. He even interceded for me, but this only proved how secure was his victory, and that to his view what fell to me was of little moment.

"Don't be hard on Davy, Judge," he said, interrupting my father's apologies for my rudeness. "He's just a boy. I don't know but what, if I were in his place, I should do exactly the same thing—feel exactly the same way."

This was small consolation to me, for Penelope's head was buried in his shoulder; her face was hidden by her tousled hair, but I could hear her sobbing: "Uncle—uncle—let me stay with Davy."

In the plea alone she acknowledged her kin to him and surrendered. He could well afford to be generous. By every law of custom I had merited severe punishment at my father's hands, and that his hands were stayed by Mr. Blight's intercession was but another evidence of his power. When my father reasoned with me kindly, instead of whipping me, I yielded, not to his sophistry but to that masterful influence before which even he seemed to bend. I realized the hopelessness of my cause, and found myself facing Mr. Blight again, an humble suppliant for his pardon. Humbly I asked him if I might not soon see Penelope again, and she joined in my petition. Humbly I asked that some day he would bring her back to the valley, and she seconded my prayer, standing at my side, clasping my hand and looking up at her uncle from tearful eyes. He promised everything. He took my hand and hers, and for the moment it seemed that this little circle was my real family, and that my father and mother, standing over us, were hardly more than law-given preceptors. Before our guest's expanding smile and the magic of his tongue the clouds fled. Those which hung heaviest he brushed away with his restless hands. Soon, very soon, I was to go to that bustling, pushing town of Pittsburgh and with Penelope explore its wonders. We should ride behind the fastest pair of trotters in the State—his trotters; we should see the greatest mills in the country—his mills—where steel was worked like wax into a thousand giant forms; we should take long excursions on the river in a wonderful new boat—his boat— Why it would make a boy of him just to have us with him!

Under the spell of his words an hour flew by, and then my mother led Penelope away to make her ready for the journey. She brought her back to us decked in a hat and frock born of many days of planning and three trips to the county town. The humble art of Malcolmville had not been intrusted with so important a commission as Penelope's best clothes. For these the shops of Martinsburg, crammed with the latest fashions of Philadelphia, had been ransacked; the smartest modiste in Martinsburg had trimmed the hat with many yards of tulle and freighted it with pink roses; the smartest couturiere in Martinsburg had created that wonderful blue chintz frock, with ribbons woven through mazes of flounces; the last touch was my mother's—the plait of hair, done so masterfully that even the weight of the great blue bow could not bend it.

I looked at Penelope in awe. She was no longer the little girl whom I had met by the mountain stream. I was still an uncouth boy, with face smudged with the dust of the fields and hands blackened in play. Yet she did not see the wide gulf which separated us, and, forgetting the hat, the frock, the chaff that clung to my matted hair and the grime of my shirt, she ran to me, threw her arms about my neck and cried: "Davy—Davy—I don't want to go!"

I knew that she had to go, and though the tears seemed to burst up in a great flood from my heart, I would not show them in my eyes. Tears are unmanly—unboyly rather—and I fought them back, but for them I could not speak. My father took Penelope from me. He lifted her in his arms and carried her out of the house and down the path to the gate, where the carriage was waiting. He placed her on the seat; he straightened out her rumpled frock, and even crossed her hands upon her lap, as though she were quite incapable of doing anything for herself. Then he kissed her. It was the first time I had ever seen him kiss her. When he spoke it was to say good-by to Rufus Blight, who was in his seat, pulling on a pair of yellow gloves.

"We shall all meet again, very soon," said Mr. Blight omnipotently, as though Fate were a henchman of his. "You must all come to Pittsburgh to see us. It's a lively, pushing town, and you'll enjoy it." Leaning from the carriage and holding out his hand to me, he added: "And you, Davy—you will come very, very soon."

I believed him. But the dream that he had conjured for us of the days to come, of his lively, pushing town, the fastest trotters, the wonderful boat, were shattered by contact with the harsh fact of this parting.

I looked past him at Penelope, sitting very straight, with her hands in her lap as my father had placed them. There was a giant frog in my throat, but I conquered it as I had conquered my tears, and speaking very steadily, I said: "Good-by, Penelope—I'll not forget. Some day I will take care of you."

> She did not turn. Her eyes held right ahead, but she
> answered bravely:
> "Good-by, Davy. I'll see you soon—very soon.
> Remember—"

The rest I did not hear. A medley of hoofs, harness and wheels broke in and she was away to a new world and a new life. The brave little figure bowed suddenly, and the roses and the tulle, the precious creation of the Martinsburg modiste, were ruthlessly crushed against the sleek bulk of the man who had never had a real idea.

CHAPTER VII

That the Professor, with fear at his heels and the devils of retribution clutching at his flying coat-tails, should have plunged into silence when the bush closed around him was not strange. Every circumstance of his parting argued a long absence, a discreet obliteration of self. But Penelope left the valley in prosaic fashion, in a livery wagon, with a man as easy to find as his own bustling, pushing town; yet the dust-clouds which closed around them as they drove away shut them from my ken as the mountains had enclosed her father in their most secret hiding-places. It was the fault of Rufus Blight. He had blown beautiful bubbles to divert us in those last hours of his visit, and bubbles bursting silently into nothingness were not more fragile than his promises. To the true value of those promises I awoke slowly, as the months went by and there came no hint of their fulfilment.

I wrote to Penelope. My letters would have made volumes were their length commensurate with the pain of composition. Even the heart of Rufus Blight would have been touched could he have seen me, bent over a table, digging my teeth into my tongue and my pen into the paper as letter by letter and word by word I constructed those messages of my boyish love. But he knew only the finished gem, and not the labor of its cutting. The more I sought to break the silence, the surer I became that he, the omnipotent one, had ordained it, and I fancied him reading my letters and destroying them, a thin smile lighting his chubby face as he thought of the easy way in which I was being outwitted. I went to my mother for help. She knew nothing of my unavailing struggles, and was herself offended and heart-sick. At my entreaty she overcame her pride and wrote to Mr. Blight inquiring as to Penelope's welfare. In return her existence was recognized; hardly more than that, for the great man did not trouble himself with a personal answer. His reply was given vicariously, through one P. T. Mallencroft, his secretary, on flawless paper, three sentences in bold clear type and a Spencerian signature closing it. It was a bloodless thing. It spoke the commands of omnipotence as though carved on tablets of stone.

Mrs. Malcolm's favor of the 10th ultimo was acknowledged; Mr. Blight instructed Mr. Mallencroft to thank Mrs. Malcolm for the interest which she had shown, and to assure her that Miss Penelope was quite well.

It was perfectly polite. It was the finished bow with which Rufus Blight was backing from our presence, never to trouble us again. I knew this when I saw the sheet drop from my mother's limp fingers and, sinking to a chair, she tossed her apron over her head and rocked violently to an accompaniment of muffled sobs.

It was clear to me that Rufus Blight was not only neglectful of our claims, but had been so with purpose, and as I wandered aimlessly through the fields in the wake of James, and as in the evening I sat again with him on the barn-bridge, looking over the darkening valley, there held one enduring thought in the chaos of my brain. Looking back now, I see in my childish enmity toward Rufus Blight the impulse that set me on my course. But for that I might have stayed in the valley, dozing, as the Professor had said, like the very dogs. In Rufus Blight I was conscious of an opposing force. He had taken Penelope from me; he had cheated me with flattery and broken promises; and the dominating sense in my mind was one of conflict with him. I looked to the west. Mountains rose there, range beyond range, and beyond them, miles away, was his bustling, pushing town. To cross them and to close with him was my one desire, and though time dulled the edges of my purpose and the figures of the Professor, of Penelope and of Rufus Blight grew dim in the distance, and at last the old motive was lost beneath a host of new impelling forces, still it was Mallencroft's letter that touched the quick and aroused me from my canine slumber.

The Professor's words came back to me. The mountains seemed to echo them always. "Wake up, Davy! Do something; be somebody; get out of the valley." Here was my shibboleth. I must do something; I must be somebody; I must get out of the valley! And then I should go to Penelope Blight, and a hundred urbane, unctuous uncles could not defraud me of my right in her.

In my father I found the first mountain on the way that I had chosen, for to his mind my destiny was settled and to be envied. All that was his would some day be mine—the best farm in the county, his Pennsylvania Railroad stock, his shares in the bridge company, and his Kansas bonds. The dear soul had arranged my course so comfortably and in such detail that in me he would have been living his own life over again. And what my father said, my mother echoed. Was I too proud to follow in his footsteps? Was I, a child in years, to hold myself above the ways of my forebears?

Such arguments came too late to my rebellious spirit. I should no longer have told the Professor that I was going to be like my father. Necessity had made me more ambitious. I dreamed now of the power and fame of a Washington, a Webster, a Grant—names which stood to me as symbols of accomplishment. So what my parents at first brushed aside as the idle dreaming of a boy they soon realized to be a vague but persistent purpose which must be beaten down. They gave me a certain dignity by descending to debate. What did I want to be? How could I answer, who could not even name the vocations in which men won their way to coveted heights? My mother gave me the key which opened the world to me.

"William," she said, addressing my father, "I do believe Davy is thinking of being a minister and is kind of ashamed to own it."

I caught the softening note in my mother's voice and in her eyes a light of pride as she regarded me inquiringly. Whatever obligation lay on me to till the ancestral acres, there was a higher duty which would absolve it. This she had pointed out. My plans at once took a concrete form, and though my first faltering assent might have savored of hypocrisy, I was soon sincere in my determination. And now the opposition crumbled and my parents found pride in a son whose heart at the age of ten was stirred by the need of lost humanity. My father discovered that it had been his own early ambition to be a minister; it was as though I was to erect the edifice to which he had feared to put his strength, and it comforted him. He delighted to lay his hand upon my head in the presence of company and to announce that his David was going to do the work to which he had always believed he had himself been called. With my mother the son's gifts became a subject on which she never tired dilating, and naturally such flattery reconciled me to a calling far removed from all my old ambitions; but had it been intimated to me that I might become a plumber I should have accepted that vocation just as readily, provided that by following it I should go out of the valley, over the mountains, to Pittsburgh and the presence of Rufus Blight.

Now arose Mr. Pound to help me. Here was the crowning incongruity in a chain of incongruous events. I had never liked Mr. Pound. He had overwhelmed me too often. His sermon was the rack on which I was stretched for an hour every Sunday to endure untold agonies of restlessness; his house the temple to which too often I had to carry propitiatory offerings of vegetables and chickens. And then his persecution of my friend the Professor still rankled in me. Yet I found myself, of necessity, using him as the one known quantity in the equation over which I worked. He became my model. I fancied myself attaining a mien like his, a deep, resonant voice and a vocabulary of marvellous words. I dressed myself in material garments like his, in spreading folds of awe-inspiring black; I wrapped myself in his immaterial cloak, his dignity and goodness. I faced Rufus Blight and he quailed before a presence so imposing, and when I spoke in a voice vibrating truth my eloquence smothered his feeble, shifty protests. Always I asserted my right to Penelope and led her from her prison. And always, it seemed, with that victory I cast off my Pound-like sanctity and became as other men.

With it the great task of my ministry was accomplished, though there was a certain charm in the idea of continuing it in the hunting fields of Africa, an appeal of romance in a kraal, a cork hat, and the picture of Penelope and me setting forth with a band of faithful converts to the slaughter of elephants and lions.

Idle dreams of boyhood! Absurd, incongruous fancies! And but for them I might at this very moment be dozing in the valley; I might be another distinguished Judge Malcolm, with my little court of ministers and squires, with old Mr. Smiley as master-of-the-horse and Miss Agnes Spinner as lady-in-waiting. Instead? I did not stay in the valley. Aroused by the sense of antagonism to Rufus Blight, and spurred on by the ambition to confront and defeat him, I began my struggle to cross the mountains, and Mr. Pound became my support and guide. He never knew the real truth behind my commendable resolution. The inspiring thought in my mind, as he insisted on judging it, was born of his own teaching. As my father had planned to live his life over again in me, so Mr. Pound saw a hope of his own intellectual immortality. Were not the evidences of grace so suddenly revealed in me the reward of his own labors?

When he came to the house, summoned in consultation over my future, he placed a hand upon my head and solemnly repeated the lines of the grand old hymn: "God works in a mysterious way, His wonders to perform." There was here a gentle hint that my past had not been altogether good or full of promise, and as Mr. Pound undoubtedly believed this, it made more generous his conduct toward me. He was a narrow man, an egotist, unlearned, too, save in the cruder forms of his calling, but he was sincere. He sought to mould me to what he thought the form a man should take, and now as I look back on the five years through which he labored with me, I may smile at the memory of his mien, his pomposity, his bigotry, yet I smile too with affection. He taught me without pay. His study became my school-room, and when at times I chafed under his vigilant tutelage and wearied in my well-doing, he steeled himself with the remembrance that Job endured more than he without complaint. In my sulkiness or open rebellion he found evidences to confirm his belief in the doctrine of innate evil; he seemed to rush singing into battle with the devil that was in me.

Through this intimate association I became a little Mr. Pound. How could it have been otherwise when day after day, books in hand, I walked down to his house to recite my lesson of Latin and Greek, and with him worked through the mysteries of algebraic calculation and studied the strange habits of the right line? He pressed me into his mould. Years went by. In the valley the Professor was forgotten, and to me Penelope was but a dim figure in the past. Even the memory of Rufus Blight ceased to awaken rancor, and I could contemplate with growing cynicism my old-time hatred of him. Unconsciously new ambitions stirred within me, and they were fostered by the flattery of my elders. In that Africa of my dream-land I no longer pictured myself in a cork helmet slaying lions, but dying at the stake, a martyr to my duty and—must I add it?—being preached about afterward from a thousand pulpits.

Mr. Pound was my model of deportment, my glass of fashion. I see him now as we used to sit, vis-a-vis, at his study table. Samson's physical strength came from his hair. From the same source, it seemed to me, Mr. Pound derived that mental vigor with which he pulled down the temples of ignorance and slew the thousand devils of unorthodoxy which sprang from my doubting mind. From the top of his head a red lock flamed up, licking the air; over its sides the hair tumbled in cataracts, breaking about his ears; then the surging hair lost itself in orderly currents which flowed, waving, from his cheeks, leaving a rift from which sprang a generous nose and a round chin with many folds. His mouth was formed for the enunciation of large words and pompous phrases. From it monosyllables fell like bullets from a cannon. He seldom descended to conversation. He declaimed. He sought to impress on me the importance of using resounding sentences which he said would keep reverberating in the caverns of the mind. For this effect he had a theory that words ending in "ation" and "ention" were especially fitted. Trumpet-words, he called them, brazen notes which penetrated the deepest crevices of the brain. I must admit that in the practice of his theory he was wonderfully successful, for after thirty years I can still hear his sonorous voice filling the church with the announcement that the "Jewish congregation was a segregation for the preservation of the Jewish nation." I can see him pausing in his discourse to lubricate his vocal chords with a glass of ice-water, and then drawing himself to his full height, fix his eyes on his hushed people and cry: "What did I say the Jewish congregation was? Let me refresh your recollection." His answer must ring to-day in the caverns of many minds. Others of his phrases, I know, still echo in my own. But this is because so often in my own room I practised declaiming them, striving to enunciate them with my mentor's finish.

Was it a wonder that I became a little Mr. Pound? I suppose, too, that I became a veritable little cad. Conscious of my advantages in birth and breeding, much impressed on me by my mother, I had never been intimate with the village boys. Now I shunned them altogether. To me they were thoughtless heathen and unprofitable company. I strove for a time to correct their evil ways and to bring them to repentance. That was something which I could properly do without unnecessary association. I had for my reward only taunts. They called me "Goody" and "Miss Malcolm," and like names contemplated to shame me from the course which I had chosen, but in the martyrdom which they made me suffer I only gloried, and I could have let them stone me to death and forgiven them, provided, of course, that Mr. Pound preached about me afterward and that my name were enrolled in the company of well-known martyrs. Looking back, I realize that I was playing. There was a fine excitement in being hunted in my comings and goings through the village. It became my Africa, where any tree might hide a deadly enemy, and any fence an ambush. I discovered secret passages through backyards. I matched cunning against overwhelming force, and sometimes, when the odds were not too great against me, I remembered Joshua and another David and turned on the Philistines and smote them right manfully. At other times the hostilities lagged, but they never ceased entirely, and often they broke out suddenly with increased fury. It was a mass and class war. To the butcher's son and the blacksmith's boy and their like, the restless masses, I was indeed a bumptious Malcolm. Conscious of the superior quality of the blood of the McLaurins, and a little inflated with the pride of wealth, I had long patronized them, so there was needed only my assumption of virtue to fan the flames. But as I grew in years and knowledge, and the days of my departure from the valley drew nearer, I relied less on my fists for protection and more on a defensive armor of dignity. I became less a target for missiles and more an object of jibes. These I met with contempt, for I was going to college; I was going to McGraw University, the alma mater of Mr. Pound, and this thought alone nerved me to step out of the course of a flying stone with unconcern and to move down the street with Pound-like mien.

There never was any discussion in our family as to where I should take my collegiate training. Had there been, Mr. Pound would speedily have quelled it. McGraw was the one college of which I knew anything. The little that I could learn of others was through the sporting pages of my father's Philadelphia paper, and here the name of Mr. Pound's alma mater was strangely missing. But he drew a real picture of it for me; gave me a concrete conception which I could not form from records of touch-downs and runs and three-baggers to left field. Sometimes in the study I would rise to points of information on Harvard, Princeton, or Yale, but I was promptly declared out of order. Mr. Pound admitted that these universities were larger than McGraw, and acknowledged that in some special lines of education they might be in advance of McGraw; yet, withal, had he a son he would intrust him only to the care of Doctor John Francis Todd. As an educator and builder of character Doctor Todd had no equal in the country. Mr. Pound could prove this. He pointed to his old friend Adam Silliman, who graduated at Princeton and was to-day a struggling coal merchant in Pleasantville, and drank. With him he contrasted Sylvester Bradley, who got his degree at McGraw in exactly the same year, '73, and had been three times moderator of the Pennsylvania Synod. Of such comparisons between McGraw men who had succeeded and other university men who had failed Mr. Pound had so many at his fingers' ends as to be absolutely overwhelming. So before I had seen McGraw I was a McGraw man to the core, and my mentor, with a subtlety astonishing for him, missed no opportunity to increase my devotion. He even taught me the college yell in one of his lighter moments, and I, in turn, taught it to James that it might ring out with more volume from the barn-bridge of an evening.

You may think that I was to be disillusioned. That could not be. When first I saw McGraw she was a giantess to my eyes. The time was to come when I was to see her in a new light, to judge her from a new perspective, to realize the incongruity between her aspiration and accomplishment, to smile at her solemn adherence to academic ritual; and yet to realize that in her littleness and poverty she gave me what was good and all that was in her power. I may regret that I did not delve deeper into the mysteries of those foot-ball scores and discover, through them, the greater seats of learning. Perhaps I might have known then that not all their sons became coal-merchants and drank, and I might have gone much farther on that September day when first I set out into the world beyond the mountains. But for all that I cannot imagine the four years which I spent at that tiny college taken from my life. For all the four years that might have been I would not exchange them.

That September day? It is a tall white mile-stone on my way. I can look back and see its every detail. On its eve James and I sat for the last time on the barn-bridge and he sang of Annie Laurie and Nellie Gray. And when we heard my mother calling me, we stood together and gave the college yell.

"I s'pose, Davy," he said, as we were moving toward the house, "folks will think I'm a little peculiar, but I'm going to give that cheer every night, just for old times' sake—for your sake, Davy."

Our elders have a fashion of making like inopportune remarks when we are struggling to keep our hearts high. It seemed as though they were trying to break my spirit. My mother's white silence, my father's long prayer, James feverishly coming and going on that last morning—little things like these almost made me abandon my great plans. But pride sustained me—that same pride which sends men into battle for foolish causes. I wanted to hurry the fall of the blow. I even protested against my parents and Mr. Pound driving with me to the railroad, and they did not understand. I had to meet their last embraces under the eyes of the motley crowd who had come to the station to see the train, and under such conditions I dared not show emotion. Again they did not understand and were a little hurt by my coldness. I sprang up the car steps jauntily. To show my independence I stood by the smoker door and waved a smiling farewell to the silent, wondering three. I did not wait there, as they waited, looking after me, but turned, tossed my new bag into a rack, threw myself into a seat, and crossed my legs with the nonchalance of one who left home every day.

The river travelled with me out of the valley. I looked from the car window and saw it at my side, and together we went away. I was silent, wondering at the shadow which seemed to overcast the earth. The little river was bright in the noonday sun—a cheery fellow-traveller through the green land. I leaned from the car window in the suddenly born hope that I might see the three still figures, back there in the hot glare of the station. But the river had turned, and I saw not the roofs of Pleasantville dozing in the sun like the very dogs, nor the court-house tower and the tall steeples that pierced her shade, but a high wall of mountains. We seemed to be driving straight for their heart. The river's mood was mine. It shrank from that forbidding wall and the mysteries beyond; it swept in a wide curve into pleasant lowlands. And now I looked across it northward, to other mountains—to *my* mountains, to the friendly heights that watched over *my* valley. Closing my eyes I saw it as on that morning when Penelope and I rode in terror from the woods. I looked across it as it lay in the broad day, under the kindly eye of God, across the rolling green, checkered with the white of blossoming orchards and the brown of the fallow, past the village spires and up the long slope to the roof among the giant oaks. You've had enough, the river seemed to say; and, turning, it charged boldly into the other mountain's heart. I went with it, but my face was pressed against the pane, that those who travelled with me might not see.

CHAPTER VIII

Harlansburg, with practical sense, shields itself from northern winds by a high hill, spreading over the barren southern slope. Trade clings to the river-front, in a compact mass around the square, and from there the town rises, scattering as it climbs, and the higher it goes the larger are the houses and the more imposing, suggesting a contest in which the stronger have overtopped their weaker brethren. But the university, I suspect, was never surfeited with practical sense, else she would not have settled on the very crest of the hill, to shiver the winter through in icy winds and in the summer to bake in tropic heat. There was, indeed, a delightful lack of responsibility about the university. She had something of Micawber's nature, and was so inured to adversity that she would have been ill at ease in a position less imposing, even though less exposed. She might shiver, but she would dominate the town. She was hopefully waiting for something to turn up, and for such a purpose was well placed, for the railroad threaded the narrow valley below, and at any moment some multi-millionaire might see her from the car window, take pity and endow her. This impression of worth in honorable tatters, of virtue appealing for aid, is made on me to-day when the train swings around the jutting hill and I behold the roof of "Old Main" rising from the trees, and the smutted white dome of the observatory. But that afternoon when I first saw my alma mater, I was quite overwhelmed by her magnificence. Before that I had known McGraw only by an ancient wood-cut of Mr. Pound's, which showed a long building, supremely bare, set among military trees; with a barouche in the foreground in which was a woman holding a parasol; with wooden-looking gentlemen in beaver hats pointing canes at the windows as though they were studying the beauties of imagined tracery. The military trees had grown, and through the gaps in the foliage as I drew nearer I made out the detail of the most imposing structure I had ever seen. Not St. Peter's, nor the Colosseum, nor the Temple of the Sun have awakened in me the same thrill of admiration that shot through my veins when "Old Main" stretched its bare brick walls before me to incomprehensible distances, and rising carried my eyes to the sky itself, where the Gothic wood-work of the tower pierced it.

In the name, "Old Main," there is a suggestion of a score of collegiate Gothic quadrangles clustering about their common mother, but these existed only in the dreams of Doctor Todd, and the most tangible expression they found was in a blue-print which was hung in a conspicuous place in his study and presented his scheme of placing the different schools in that hoped-for day when the multimillionaire untied the strings of his money-bags.

"Our founder, Stephen McGraw," Doctor Todd was fond of explaining, "gave us the nucleus of a great educational institution. Our task is to build on his foundation. It is true that in fifty years not a new stone has been laid, but that must not discourage us. We shall go on hoping and working."

Dear old Doctor Todd! He still works on and hopes. He has had bitter disappointments, but they have never beaten him down. Had Stephen McGraw left his money and not his name to the university, the doctor's task would have been easier, for it is not the way of men to beautify another's monument. Once, I remember, a Western capitalist was persuaded to make a great gift to McGraw. He made it with conditions, and for a while our hopes blazed high and with exceeding fury. The collegiate Gothic quadrangles were within our reach, as near to us as the grapes to Tantalus. A half-million dollars was promised us if we raised a like sum within a year. Doctor Todd tried to effect a compromise by accepting two hundred thousand dollars outright, but the philanthropist did not believe in making beggars of institutions by surfeiting them with charity. So we cheered him right heartily and went to work to gather our share. I remember it all very well because I sang in the glee-club concert which we gave in the opera house to help the fund, and because our classroom work was very light, as the president and half of the faculty were canvassing the State for aid. We worked desperately—faculty, alumni, and students. Even Mr. Pound gave ten dollars from his meagre salary, and the Reverend Sylvester Bradley, three times moderator of the synod, a round hundred. With only a month in which to make up a deficit of four hundred thousand dollars, we did not abandon hope. Every morning in chapel the doctor prayed earnestly for a rain of manna or a visitation of ravens, which we knew to be his adroit way of covering a more mercenary petition. But heaven never opened, and a check never fluttered to earth from the only source from which it could be expected. The year ended and our would-be benefactor gave his money outright to Harvard or Yale, I forget which, for a swimming tank or a gymnasium.

Some day McGraw may get the coveted money. I know that were it in my power the collegiate Gothic quadrangles would rise on the lines of Doctor Todd's faded blue-print. I should build Todd Hall and McGraw Library, but not one brick would I add to "Old Main." There would be the only condition of my gift of millions. They might suggest oriel windows to relieve the bare facade, buttresses to break the flatness of the wall and pinnacles to beautify the roof, but I would have "Old Main" always as I saw it on that September afternoon, when I had climbed the hill, paused, set down my bag and stood with arms akimbo while I scanned the amazing length and height of the splendid pile. My heart at each remove from home had become a heavier weight until I seemed to carry within me a solid leaden load. Now it lightened mysteriously. Face to face with a new life that had its symbol in this noble breadth of wall, the cords which held me to the old snapped. That very morning seemed the part of another age, and yesterday was spent in another world. I was wide awake at last. The cheer which Mr. Pound had taught me was on my lips, and I should have given it as a paean of thanksgiving had I not been embarrassed by the scrutiny of a group of young men who loitered on the steps before me. So I picked up my bag, a feather-weight to my new energy, and went boldly on.

My impression of the splendor of college life was heightened by the first acquaintance I made in my new environment. This was Boller of '89, and today Boller of '89 holds in my mind as a true pattern of the man of the world. His was the same stuff of which was made "the perfect courtier." The difference lay solely in the degree of finish, and justly considered, true value lies in the material, not in the gloss. Boller, polished by the society of Harlansburg, appeared to my eyes quite the most delightful person I had ever met. It was the perfection of his clothes and the graciousness of his manner that awed me and won my admiration. In those days wide trousers were the fashion, and Boller was, above all, fashion's ardent devotee. His, I think, exceeded by four inches the widest in the college. Recalling him as he came forth from the group on the steps to greet me, I think of him as potted in his trousers, like a plant, so slender rose his body from his draped legs. His patent-leather shoes were almost hidden, and from his broad base he seemed to converge into a gray derby of the kind we called "the smoky city," the latest thing from Pittsburgh. Looking at him, so wonderfully garbed, I became conscious of my own rusticity, so old-fashioned did the styles of Pleasantville appear beside the resplendent garments of my new friend. I was sure that he must notice it. If he did, he gave no sign.

"I'm Boller of '89," he said, grasping my hand cordially. "What's your name?"

"Malcolm, sir—David Malcolm," I answered.

Boller clapped an arm across my shoulders in friendly fashion. "You're three days late, Malcolm, but better late than never. I suppose you were hesitating between McGraw and Harvard."

"Oh, no!" I faltered, not fathoming his pleasantry. "I had to wait until the tailor finished my new suit. It should have been done last Monday, but—"

Something in Boller's eyes checked me. He was regarding me from head to foot so gravely that I divined that I might have joined the crew of the Ark in my new clothes, judged by their cut.

"You have come here to study agriculture, I presume," he remarked most pleasantly.

So subtle a reference to my bucolic appearance was lost on my innocent mind. He seemed quite serious and as he was mistaken I wanted to set him right. I was proud of my laudable ambition. Proclaiming it had brought me only commendation, and I proclaimed it now.

"I'm going to be a minister," I said, drawing myself up a little.

"Indeed—a minister—how interesting!" returned Boller, raising his eyebrows.

Now had he laughed at me, had he called his fellows from the step to mob me, in the glory of my martyrdom I should have held fast to my purpose; or had he flattered me like Miss Spinner or Mr. Smiley, my vanity would have carried me on my chosen path. His middle course was disconcerting. He treated my ambition as though it were quite a natural one and just about as interesting as to follow dentistry or plumbing.

"I'm going to be a missionary," I said in a louder tone, hoping to arouse in him either antagonism or adulation.

"Curious," he returned. "Very curious. Why I am thinking of taking up the same line myself. It makes a man so interesting to the girls. I've a cousin who is a minister, and last year he received seventeen pairs of knit slippers from the young ladies of his congregation. That's going some—eh, Malcolm?"

What a different picture from my cherished one of cork hats and express rifles! The suggestion was horribly insidious. To be interesting to women *en masse* was to my manly view exceedingly unmanly; to labor for reward in knit slippers the depth of degradation. I was about to declare to Boller that I was not going to be his kind of a clergyman when I stopped to ask myself if I had ever known any other kind, if my own ideal were not as unattainable as to be another Ivanhoe or Captain Cook. Mr. Pound rose before me, his feet incased in the loving handiwork of Miss Spinner. From him my mind shot wide afield to the Reverend Doctor Bumpus, fresh from the dark continent, thanking our congregation for the barrel of clothing sent to his eleven children in far-off Zululand. Thoughts like these were as arrows in the heart of my noble purpose.

"I haven't absolutely made up my mind," I said suddenly.

But Boller refused to accept such a qualification. He had me firmly by the arm and brought me face to face with the loungers on the step.

> "Gentlemen," he said, "allow me to present to you the Reverend Doctor David Malcolm!"

And the loungers on the step saluted me as gravely as if I had been that friend of Mr. Pound's, the Reverend Sylvester Bradley, thrice moderator of the synod.

It was thus that I became the Reverend David Malcolm, and this was all the authority I ever had for so honorable a cognomen. So it was that by the insidious raillery of a moment, Boller shook the foundations laid by Mr. Pound in five years of labor, and it was not long before the whole structure of his building tumbled into ruins. My first violent protest against a nickname which seemed to me to savor of sacrilege served only to fasten it to me more securely. Resigning myself to it, I came to regard it lightly, and the longer I bore it in jest the less I desired to earn it in honor. It was a far cry from Mr. Pound to Boller of '89, but I doffed the vestment and donned the motley that September day, for Boller became my mentor and in all things my model. I was flattered by his condescending treatment. Before a week had passed my engrossing ambition was to wear trousers as wide as his and to crown myself with a "smoky city" derby. Having accomplished this ambition by going into debt, I realized a greater, and pinned to the lapel of my gayly checked coat, the pearl and diamond-studded pin of Gamma Theta Epsilon. That, of course, was Boller's fraternity, and I think he could have persuaded me to join whatever he asked, so wholly was I captured by his kindness.

In the study of Doctor Todd to which he led me, in the presence of the great man, he did not venture any airy presentation. Boller of '89 inside of the study door was quite a different person from the Boller without it. The bold manner fled. He was suppressed, obsequious; even his clothes seemed to shrink and grow humbly dun. We entered so quietly that the doctor, bending over his desk, did not hear us, and we had to cough apologetically to apprise him of our presence.

"David Malcolm, sir—a new freshman," Boller said.

The doctor rose. I saw a little man with a very large head covered with hair which shot in all directions in scholarly abandon. His neck seemed much too thin to carry such a weight, but that, I think, was the effect of a collar much too large, and a white tie so long that its ends trailed down over an expanse of crumpled shirt. The doctor's black clothes looked dusty; the doctor himself looked dusty, yet the smile with which he greeted me was as warm as the sunshine breaking through the mist.

"This is splendid," he cried, shaking my hand fervently. "Mr. Malcolm, you are welcome. You make the thirty-ninth new man this year—a record in our history. McGraw is growing. Have I not predicted, Mr. Boller, that McGraw would grow?"

To this Boller very readily assented, and the doctor, rubbing his hands with delight at his vindication, placed a chair for me at his side and began talking rapidly, not of me, nor of my plans, but of the university. He did mention incidentally that he had heard of me through his dear friend, Mr. Pound—a man of whom the university was proud—yet, though I was sure Mr. Pound had spoken well of me, he made no mention of it. I was of interest to him simply because by my coming I had broken the records of McGraw's freshman class. Last year it numbered thirty-eight; this year, thirty-nine. Through me the university had taken another stately step onward. He showed me the blue-print and explained it in detail. He spoke so earnestly that in a moment he had abandoned the subjunctive mood, and was describing the buildings as though they actually existed—here the new dormitory, there the chemical laboratory, the gymnasium, the chapel. So potent was his imagination that when I was dismissed and stood again on the steps, I found myself sweeping the campus in search of the beautiful structures which he had pictured for me. Not finding them, I was prey to disappointment, so small did the McGraw that was appear beside the McGraw that should be. I began to suspect that those other universities upon which Mr. Pound looked with such contempt might resemble the creation of Doctor Todd's imagination, that there might be more behind those foot-ball scores than my old mentor had cared to disclose. Distrust of him was rising in me, but I was not allowed to remain long pondering over these things, for Boller had been waiting for me and I was quickly in his possession.

Had the murmurs of rebellion risen to a point where I was planning to abandon McGraw, my new friend must have blocked me. He regarded me as his property. He installed me in the bare little room which for four years was to be my home. He took me to his own quarters and there gave me such a glimpse of my new life as to make me forget my momentary disillusionment. While he dressed, arrayed himself more impressively than ever in evening clothes, I divided my eyes between him and the pictures on the wall. Here Boller, in foot-ball clothes, sat on a fence, wonderfully dashing, with a foot-ball under his arm; there he was in base-ball toggery, erect with bat lifted, ready to strike; here holding a baton, a conspicuous figure in a group of young men, looking exceedingly conscious and uncomfortable in evening clothes—the glee club, he explained, taken on their last tour of the State. And while he dressed, he painted such a glowing picture of life at McGraw as to make it of little moment to me now whether or not Doctor Todd's dream ever came true. That I should grow to Boller's size and fashion was all I asked.

As I watched him soaping and brushing his hair, struggling a half hour with his tie and setting that hair all awry again, soaping and brushing once more and at last emerging flawless from the conflict, my own self-confidence ebbed away and the sense of my own rusticity and awkwardness oppressed me. I was to go with him to the first important social event of the year, the reception to the new students, and seeing how my friend arrayed himself for it, I wanted to crawl away to my own room and hide there. But he would not let me. He laughed at my excuses. To be sure my clothes were not the best form, but it was not to be expected that a man new to university life should be—here Boller surveyed himself in the glass and I understood the implication. So I polished my shoes, wetted and soaped my own hair to rival his and went with him. Had he been leading me into battle I could not have been colder with fright. Had he not had a fast hold on my arm I am sure that when I came face to face with the formidable array of faculty and faculty wives waiting to receive me, I should have beaten a precipitate retreat. I had never before been received; I had never before been a guest at any formal social function, and it was appalling to have to charge this battery of solemn eyes. But there was no escape. Boller pushed me into the hands of Doctor Todd, who gave another hearty handshake to the thirty-ninth and presented him to Mrs. Todd. She assured me that it was a great pleasure to meet me, a statement entirely at variance with the severity of her countenance and the promptness with which she passed me on to Professor Ruffle, who combined the chair of modern languages with the business management of the college. He with a dexterous twist consigned me to his good lady, and thus I passed from hand to hand down the dreaded line.

The ordeal was over. I had had my baptism of social fire. Fear left me, but not embarrassment. I forgot that thirty-eight other young men were being received and were undergoing numberless bewildering introductions. It seemed that the whole college was there simply to meet me, and I returned its greeting in a daze. If I lost Boller in the press, I felt the need of his supporting arm and peered longingly among the jostling crowd to find him. He was continually going and coming, but he never forgot me for any time. He was wonderfully kind about informing as to whom it was worth my while to be agreeable. . . . Don't trouble with Brown; be pleasant to Jones, but look out for Robinson, the fellow with a Kappa Iota Omega pin.

He had hardly warned me against Robinson, before that young man was addressing me with great cheerfulness. I saw nothing whatever repulsive about him; but to Boller I was evidently in danger.

"There's a young lady here who is dying to meet you," he whispered in my ear as he drew me from the sinister clutches.

Oh, subtle flattery! This was the first time I had ever had a young lady dying to meet me. Of course I understood that Boller had spoken figuratively, and yet I did not question that the young lady had seen me, and I was vain enough to hold it not at all unlikely that something in my appearance had interested her. Had not vanity overcome my embarrassment, curiosity would have done so. I wanted to see what she was like who had been so affected by the sight of me. And when I did see her, when I stood before her on shifting feet, I would have given the world to be somewhere else, yet, by a curious contradiction, nothing could have dragged me from the spot, so fair was she to look on.

"Miss Todd—Mr. Malcolm," said Boller of '89. Then he mopped his brow with a purple silk handkerchief and added that it was very warm. I said that it was very warm, and Miss Todd smiled quite the loveliest smile that I had ever seen.

I realized that this Miss Todd was the doctor's daughter, of whom I had heard Boller speak in the most extravagant terms, and now it seemed to me that his praise had quite failed to convey an adequate idea of her charms. She was very fair, very pink and white, with a Psyche knot of shimmering hair; a tall, slender girl, clad in clinging, gauzy blue. To my mind came the picture of Penelope Blight, the only girl to whom I had ever given a thought; I remembered her tanned cheeks, her brown arms, and hard little hands, and it seemed to me that even she could never grow to such loveliness as this.

I loved Miss Todd. Had she offered herself to me at that moment, I should have married her on the spot, and now there was shattered my boyish contempt for all that was weak and gentle, however beautiful. The ideas which composed my mind rattled and tumbled about like the bits of colored glass in a kaleidoscope, and in a flash they formed a softer and more harmonious design. The world was something more to me than a happy hunting-ground, life more than an exciting adventure. The world was the home of Gladys Todd; life was to win her love; happiness was to sit at her side.

And now I was sitting at her side in a seventh heaven; in one of the silent places of the seventh heaven, for we had little to say to each other. We were tyros in the art of conversing, and our promising ideas born of long mental struggles were stilled with bludgeons of assent and dissent. We knew not how to nourish and embellish them, and yet, though there were long stretches of embarrassed silence, we were not unhappy. Even Boller found his subterfuges to drag me away quite futile, and Miss Todd herself seemed content, for she met a dozen like efforts with a quiet and unpenetrable smile.

So Gladys Todd and I sat the evening through as on a calm cloud, looking down to earth and the antics of little men. They crowded close to us, laughing and talking; they called up to us and we did not hear them; they jostled one another and they jostled us, but they could not entice us into their restless social game. They offered us coffee, sandwiches and cake, and we brushed them away. The very thought of food was repulsive to me, and this was not because I had reached that point where the immeasurable yearning of the heart dwarfs all mean desire. I was really hungry, but I had no mind to spoil the impression which it was evident I had made; I had no mind to let Miss Todd see me with a half-eaten sandwich poised in one hand and scattering crumbs untidily, and in the other a cup of muddy, steaming fluid. She seemed to have a like conception of the undignity of eating, for when she declined the proffered feast it was with the air of one who never ate at all, who never knew the pangs of appetite, but lived on something infinitely higher. She even spurned the cake, and I was glad to let her deceive me. I liked to coddle myself with the belief that she never ate. I knew that she did not want me to see her eating, for then I must have classed her with the mass of women—with Mrs. Ruffle, whom I heard choking on a bit of nutshell; with her mother, who was standing near us talking in a voice muffled in food; I must have slipped off the cloud to earth.

But Gladys Todd was wise, with that innate wisdom of her sex in matters of appearance when appearance is to be considered, and we held in silence, loftily on our cloud. And looking back on that evening, my recollection is of misty, nebulous things; not of a passing flow of incident, but of a welling up of new thoughts as I sat awkwardly pulling at my fingers and caressing my collar. Yet there were incidents, too, of high importance to McGraw. Doctor Todd declared that the evening was historical. Standing in the centre of a hushed company, he announced that the year had broken all records for matriculation; McGraw was growing; McGraw could not long be contained within her present walls, and the world must soon realize that in simple justice something must be done for her. The doctor was not cast down by the fact that nothing had been done and that there was no sign of anything being done. Hope was his watchword, and so hopefully did he speak of the future that the collegiate Gothic quadrangles began to rise in the imaginations of the company as dreams almost accomplished, and so infectious was his confidence that his hearers caught the high pitch of his enthusiasm, and when he had finished Boller sprang to a chair, and, waving a coffee-cup, struck the first deep tones of "Here's to old McGraw, drink her down!" and everybody joined in as fervently as though it were a hymn. They were not satisfied with it once, but Doctor Todd himself cried, "Again," and, waving an imaginary cup, led us off once more into the bibulous and inspiring song.

I remember joining in the first bars, but not because I was unduly stirred by the love of my alma mater. It was rather to give Gladys Todd a hint of the rich depths of my voice. To make an impression on Gladys Todd had become the business of my life. I was glad that I had come to McGraw, because here I had met her. McGraw's past and future were of no moment to me; her growth was nothing. She might shrivel up until I was the only student, yet I should still be happy in my nearness to Gladys Todd. And what of Penelope? I did think of Penelope that night as I sat alone in my room, cocked on two legs of my chair, gazing blankly at the ceiling. I remembered the foolish, childish promises which I had made to her that I should never forget her. Of course I should never forget her, no more than I should forget the moon because I had beheld the sun's dazzling splendor.

But a man's ideas change, I said; his view broadens. And I remembered Penelope as I first saw her, in her tattered frock and with the faded ribbon tossing in her hair. I liked Penelope. I thought of her with brotherly affection. But I said to myself that she could never grow to the wonderful beauty of this Miss Todd.

CHAPTER IX

I was not long at McGraw University before I had attained my ambition to be like Boller of '89. I draped my legs in wide folds of shepherd's plaid; the corners of a purple silk handkerchief protruded from my top pocket; and as long as the "smoky city" was the proper form I crowned myself with one of them, and as promptly discarded it for the newer tourist's helmet, and that in turn for a yachting cap. Must I confess it?—before Boller left McGraw I had quite surpassed him as a model of fashion. But my ambition did not end here. The very conceit which had made me such an insufferable youth in my last days at home was the spur which drove me to win every honor that could come to an undergraduate. As Boller stepped out of offices I stepped into them—in presidencies and secretaryships almost innumerable, into editorships, and even captaincies. Physically timid, I endured much pain in winning these last honors. The stretch of rolling turf which we called the foot-ball field became the arena in which I suffered martyrdom daily. I hated the game. When I donned my padded toggery it was with the secret spirit I should have felt in preparing for the rack, yet I played recklessly for the *éclat* it gave me. To-day I have an occasional reminder of those struggles in a weak knee, which has a way of twisting unexpectedly and causing excruciating pain, but I consider that these twinges are fair payment for the pleasure with which I contemplated my picture years ago in the Harlansburg *Sentinel*, showing me in my foot-ball clothes, poised on a photographer's fence. The subject, the *Sentinel* explained, was Captain Malcolm of McGraw, who had made the winning touch-down in the Thanksgiving-Day game with the Northern University of Pennsylvania. The photographer's fence, you might think, was the summit of my career at McGraw, reached as it was in my last year there. To the admiring eyes of my fellows it was, but the McLaurins of Tuckapo and the Malcolms of Windy Valley were above all a practical people and to them I am indebted for a little common-sense, which told me that I could not play foot-ball all my life, nor would the heavy bass voice, so effective in the glee club, support a family, and deep in my heart I admitted the possibilities of a family. I might strive to keep that thought in the background, but it would rise when I dreamed of a home. That home was not a plain stone farm-house, hidden among giant trees. My view had broadened. I dreamed of a Queen Anne cottage, with many gables, and a flat clipped lawn, with a cement walk leading over it to an iron gate. I looked back with affectionate contempt to the art I had known in my youth, to the Rogers group, Lady Washington's ball, Lincoln and his cabinet, the lambrequin and the worsted motto. On my walls there would be a Colosseum, Rembrandt's portrait of himself, a smattering of Madonnas, a Winged Victory, and a Venus de Milo. To preside with me over such a house, to sit at the piano of an evening and play accompaniments while I sang sentimental songs, to fly with me over the country in a side-bar buggy, behind a fleet trotter, I thought only of Gladys Todd. She was accomplished, highly trained, it seemed to me, in all the finer arts of life. In our valley the women never rose above their petty household problems. They could talk, but only of recipes and church affairs, and if they left this narrow environment at all it was to fare far—to India and China, the foreign mission field. My view had broadened. Gladys Todd had her being in higher airs. She painted. Pastels of flowers and plaques adorned with ideal heads covered the walls of the Todd parlor. She wrote. Doctor Todd assured me, speaking without prejudice, that his daughter's essay on "The Immortality of the Soul," which she had written out of pure love of the labor, equalled, if it did not surpass, the best work of the senior class. She sang. Perhaps I see her now in the same wizard lights of distance that glorified the mountains in my boyhood, but I always recall her as a charming old-fashioned picture, sitting at her piano and babbling her little songs in French and German. Of the quality of her French and German I had no means of judging, but that she could use them at all was to me surpassingly enchanting.

So Gladys Todd had her part in completing the wreck of my worthy ambition. What Boller had begun, she unconsciously finished. Yesterday I had planned to make self-sacrifice the key-note of my life. To-day I could not picture her contented to move in the narrow sphere of a Mrs. Pound, cramping her talents in the little circle of the Sunday-school and the Ladies' Aid. Her influence for good must be a subtler one than this. To wield it, she must have her being in higher airs, in an atmosphere of Colosseums, of Rembrandts, and Madonnas. Remember, she was no longer the shy girl whom I had met on the first night of my university life. Then she was only in her fifteenth year. I was a junior when she produced her lauded essay on "The Immortality of the Soul," and it revealed to me the profundity of her mind. To match her, I must sit many a night driving my way through difficult pages of the classics, and often when my heart was in some smoky den with a few choice spirits, my body bent over my table and my brain wearied itself with abstruse equations.

If Gladys Todd unconsciously wrecked my early scheme of life, she unconsciously spurred me to the hard task of learning. I flattered myself that in the new calling which I had chosen I should be able to be even a greater power for good than in the old. Having attained to Boller's perfection, as I had abandoned Mr. Pound for him, I now abandoned him for ex-Judge Bundy. As Harlansburg was far above Malcolmville, so ex-Judge Bundy was above Mr. Pound. He was not the creator of Harlansburg, but he was its providence. He owned the bank and the nail works, he was a patron of its churches, the leading figure at the bar, and a man of wonderful eloquence. Every year he delivered the graduation address at the university, and mentally I modelled my future appearance on the rostrum from his benign demeanor, his forceful gestures, his rolling periods. Yet deep as was my admiration, he held views on which I differed with him. I felt that I had gone deeper than he into the logic of things. To him, for example, the high tariff was the source of all good, of life, health, food, clothes, and even morals. My view was broader. I brushed aside the beneficent local effect of any system and went on to study its relation to all mankind. He was prone to forget mankind, and yet his faults were those of his generation and he remained a heroic figure in my eyes, and it seemed to me that in setting myself to reach the mark he had made I was aiming very high indeed. Perhaps I should have gone on, striving to attain to the Bundian perfection had not the ex-judge himself been the instrument by which I was awakened and shaken out of my self-complacence. Among the benefactions which had brought him such high esteem in our college community was "the Richardson Bundy course of lectures on the activities of life." He paid for the services of orators whom Doctor Todd delighted to call "leaders in every branch of human endeavor." In my last year at McGraw we heard the Fourth Assistant Secretary of the Treasury on "Finance," the art critic of a Philadelphia paper on "Raphael," and as a fitting climax to the course we were to listen to the famous Armenian scholar and philosopher, the Reverend Valerian Harassan in a discourse on "Life." The adjective is not mine. I had never heard of the famous Armenian until Doctor Todd in chapel announced his coming, and made it clear that it was a special privilege to listen to the eloquent preacher, and that we owed a tremendous debt to our friend and benefactor, Judge Bundy.

The picture of the Reverend Valerian Harassan, which was posted on the bulletin-board, gave promise of a realization of the hopes which the good doctor had raised. It showed a man in evening clothes, impressively massive, with a clean-shaven face and Roman features, a broad, low forehead from which the hair rolled back in glistening black folds, curling around his ears to the line of his collar. The deep-set eyes seemed to look out from a mind packed with knowledge, and the firmly set mouth to hold in check a voice of marvellous power for eloquence.

In high spirits I went one evening to hear this eastern philosopher. It was cold and raining, but in those days the worst of weather could cast no shadow over me. It was a pleasure even to battle with the elements with no other weapon than an umbrella, and multiplied a hundred-fold was that pleasure when with that weapon I was battling also for Gladys Todd. Though as yet I had said nothing to her of my cherished hope, I know that when we stepped out together into the night, we both believed that we should face many another storm under the same umbrella. I was conscious that she clung more closely than usual to my arm, and, with spirits keyed high with the sense of protecting her, my feet hardly touched the dripping pavement which led from the doctor's house to the college building and the chapel. We said little on the way. We had long since passed the point where idle chatter is needed in communing. I remember that I did ruminate pleasantly on my good fortune in having found this sympathetic spirit to share with me the intellectual pleasure of a scholarly discourse, whose heart could beat quicker in time with mine at the inspiration of some fine thought. I remember that she broke the current of these meditations to ask if I had decided to make Harlansburg my home after my approaching graduation. She asked it with a tone of deep personal interest. At that moment I should have proposed to Gladys Todd had not the wind been tugging at the umbrella, and had we not come from the shadow of the trees into the glare of the college lights. So I answered affirmatively. Of course I should remain in Harlansburg. At that moment my resolution was fixed unalterably, if only for the sake of Gladys Todd; and if I had settled in my mind that I should walk in the way of Judge Bundy till, like him, I dominated the town and the county and my name was known in the farthest corners of the State, that, too, would be for the sake of this gentle, clinging girl whose nearness to me made my umbrella seem like the sheltering roof of home. But in this calculation I left out of my equation one important element—the throat of the Reverend Valerian Harassan.

The source of the Armenian's flowing eloquence would have seemed as far from affecting my life as the source and flow of the sacred Ganges, and yet it was some trivial irritation of it that kept us from hearing his philosophy that night, and, more important to me, that sent another to expound ideas far different than could ever have come from the famous thinker. All the college, all in Harlansburg who were well-to-do and wise, watched for his coming expectantly; but when the door on the chapel platform opened and Judge Bundy stepped forth, he had on his arm, not the monumental preacher of the clean-shaven face and rolling black hair, but a man who in no line met the hopes raised by the impressive picture. A murmur of disappointment ran through the hall. Doctor Todd, following the great men in the humble capacity of beadle, stilled it with a raised hand.

To Judge Bundy's mind, as he expressed it to us, there was no cause for disappointment. While the Reverend Valerian Harassan's bronchial affection was unfortunate for us and for him, yet for us it was in a way, too, a blessing, for he had sent in his place to speak to us on "Life" no other than the famous journalist and traveller Andrew Henderson. The judge paused to give time for a play of our imaginations, and such a play was needed. I do not think that a soul in the audience had ever heard of the famous journalist and traveller, but we should not have admitted it, and set ourselves to looking as though his name were a household word. It was enough that Judge Bundy declared him to be famous. It was decreed, and for Harlansburg, at least, he became a celebrity. Having given us time to imagine the deeds which had won fame for the lecturer, Judge Bundy saw no need to trouble himself with specifications. The rolling periods of his speech would have been rudely halted by facts, so he spoke in general terms of the inspiration it would give to the young men before him to see such a man face to face—a man who knew life, a man who had lived life, who had ideas on life. It seemed as though the judge himself was about to deliver the lecture on "Life," but he paused, out of breath, and Andrew Henderson, mistaking the moment of rest for the end of the introduction, rose from the chair about which he had been shifting uneasily and came to the rostrum's edge.

He came with a shambling gait. The tall, thin, loose-jointed man, resting with one hand on the pulpit at his side, in every way belied the pompous tribute which had just been paid him.

I watched him. I studied the face masked in a close-cropped gray beard. I studied the angles of the loosely hung limbs and the swinging body clad in unobtrusive brown. For a moment I doubted. Then he spoke. I heard his voice, and it seemed as though it were threaded with a sharp, shrill note of bitterness. His eyes were not turned to us. Gladys Todd must have thought them fixed on a spot in the ceiling, but to me they were watching a flake of cloud hovering just above the tall pine across the clearing. Gladys Todd must have thought me beside her, sitting upright on the very edge of my seat, but I was back in the mountains; I could feel Penelope's brown hand in mine and I could see her proud smile as she looked up at me and said: "That's father; he's studying"; I could see her father as he leaned on his hoe, beaten in his fight with the ever-charging weeds; I could see him in the murky light of the cabin, a trembling hazy figure in the gun smoke; and again, with the devils of retribution at his heels, flying for the bush. Now the worthless, shiftless man, after long years, stood before me, a professor in truth, a professor of life, and perhaps he would give belated expression to what was in his mind that day as he studied the flake of cloud.

Unrolling a portentous manuscript on the pulpit, the lecturer began to read in a mechanical voice. The restless shuffling of feet and a volley of dry coughs soon spoke the hostile attitude of the audience, a longing for the coming of Valerian Harassan. The Professor did not heed them. He read on, pompous phrases such as might have come from the lips of Mr. Pound. He was unconscious of the increasing hostility of his hearers. When he stopped suddenly, it was not because the feet in the rear of the hall were shuffling a rising chorus of protest, despite the frantic signals of Judge Bundy and Doctor Todd's upraised hand. What he saw in his own manuscript checked him, for stepping back from the desk, he frowned at it. The corners of his mouth twitched in a passing smile, and pouncing upon his handiwork, he held it at arm's length, dangling before the astonished eyes of the company.

"What rot!" he cried. "What utter rot!"

A shout from the rear of the room evidenced the approval of his younger hearers. The elders glowered at what they thought a trick to catch their attention. But trick or not, he did catch their attention, and he held it; he ceased to be the utterer of pompous platitudes; dropping his paper to show that he had done with it, he leaned across the pulpit and brought his long arms into action. He became the caustic iconoclast of the valley.

"We all agree that what I have been reading is nonsense," he said in a sharp-edged voice. "But I am here in the place of Valerian Harassan, and it seemed to me that I must give you what you were paying him for. I have been trying to say the kind of things he would have said. If you had been able to stand it a little longer, I should have told you that all the world's a stage and men and women but the players. I might even have attacked your risibles by anecdotes about my little boy at home and the southern colonel. Of course, I should have given you some inspiring thoughts, convinced you that life was a wonderful gift, something to be treasured and joyously lived, that work was a pleasure, that happiness came from accomplishing a set task. It's all here in this paper. I wrote it—and it was easy enough to do—because that is the kind of stuff you pay for. But it is one thing to write what you don't believe; quite another to speak it face to face. And yet if I am to speak the truth as I see it on such a simple little subject as life, I guess I am here on a fool's errand."

Doctor Todd and Judge Bundy seemed to be of the same mind, for they were whispering together; debating, I suspected, whether it were better to let him go on and try to talk fifty dollars' worth or to break abruptly into his discourse and end it. For so harsh a measure as the last they lacked courage, and the Professor hurled on, unconscious of the hostile stares with which they were stabbing him in the back.

Now, optimism was the foundation on which McGraw strove to build up character. Optimism permeated every part of our life there. From a narrow environment we looked out hopefully into broadening distances. Every year some confident youth told us from the college rostrum in rounded sentences that life was worth living; that sickness, poverty, disappointment, the countless evils which dog our footsteps, were nothing in the scale against the boon of opportunity. Every morning in chapel the doctor voiced our gratitude for the privilege of living and working. And now over heads that moved in such charged airs the Professor cast his pall of pessimism. He took his text from Solomon, and found that all was vanity. It mattered little whether or not what he said was true. He believed it to be true, and for the moment at least his incisive voice and long forefinger carried with them conviction. He railed at the old dictum that man was God's noblest work. The ordinary dog, he declared, was more pleasing to the eye than the ordinary man, and the life of the ordinary dog more to be envied than that of the ordinary man. Knowledge only lifted us above the animal to be more buffeted by a complexity of desires. The greatest thing in the world was self, and even the roots of our goodness burrowed down into the depths where the ego was considering its own comfort either in this world or the next. The proud man for whom the universe was made was nothing but a fragile thread of memories wrapped in soft tissue, packed away in a casket of bone, and made easily portable by a pair of levers called legs. After countless ages spent on earth seeking the true source of happiness men were still countless ages from agreement. One half sought by goodness to attain happiness in immortality; the other in Nirvana. One half found the shadow of happiness in inertia, in stupefaction, a mere satisfying of physical needs; the other in motion, joining in the mad procession which we call so boastfully Progress. By accident of birth we were of the progressive half and we paraded around and around, puffed up with pride of our little accomplishment, until we fell exhausted and another took our place.

Judge Bundy nudged Doctor Todd again. Doctor Todd shook his head and looked at the ceiling, as if to show that he found more of interest there than in the speaker's words, and he held them there defiantly as the Professor went on to controvert the optimistic philosophy which had been taught at McGraw for so many years. That knowledge was the greatest source of unhappiness was a bold dictum to hurl at a company of seekers after it, but Henderson Blight had little respect for mere persons. The ignorant animal did not exist, he argued; it was with knowledge that the plague of ignorance came to man. A draught of knowledge was like a cup of salt-water to the thirst, and the more we learned the less value we could place on the things for which we labored. A man worked a lifetime to obtain a peach-blow, and it crumbled to dust in his hands. What, then, should we strive for?

At this question Doctor Todd brought his eyes down from the ceiling and Judge Bundy lifted his from the red rug of the platform. The judge was our great authority on striving. He had qualified himself by years of successful labor. To us he was a living example of the rewards which come to endeavor, and so it was with evident self-consciousness that he now sat very erect, thinking, perhaps, that he would hear some views akin to his own.

"I was born in a narrow valley," the Professor pursued, "and perhaps I might have dozed there like the dogs, but I learned that beyond the mountains there was another valley, broader and richer. I longed to live there. One day I crossed the mountains to it and I found it all that I had heard. But it, too, had its wall of mountains and my eyes followed them, and I learned that beyond them was still another valley, broader and richer. And I went on. So it will be with you. There is a big nail factory down by the river—I saw it as I came in, and I am sure that to some of us to own that factory might be a life's ambition. How fine it would be when our work was ended to fold our hands peacefully and say: 'I have fought the good fight, I have run the race, I have made a million kegs of nails!'"

Judge Bundy half rose from his chair. Through the hall sounded a smothered murmur of applause, for it is always satisfying to hear a truth which hits another. Judge Bundy would have wholly risen from his chair, but he was checked by a hundred covert smiles and Doctor Todd laid a hand upon his quivering, indignant knee. All unconscious of the cause of this stifled mirth, and fired by it as in the old days he was fired when Stacy Shunk leered beneath the shadow of his hat, the Professor leaned far over the desk with both hands outstretched.

"I have failed utterly in my own living," he cried. "I have loafed and lagged. At times I have worked hard until I wearied myself chasing shadows. But in my failure I have learned a few things. We may live and doze in our little valley, but still we shall long for the broader and richer valley across the mountains. The yearning for that something better is born in us all. Shall we call it simply something more; shall we measure our service in kegs of nails or shall we seek for something really better? If we listen we can hear in the depths of our souls the divine drumbeat, and it is strange what cowards we are when we come to march to it. But we can march to it. We may not know why we go, nor where, but we can go straight. The country we travel may seem waste, but we cross it under God's sealed orders, given to us when we opened our eyes on life, and only when our eyes are closed again will they be opened to us."

So it was that the Professor carried me again from my little valley! The great Judge Bundy standing at the platform's edge, brusquely dismissing us, had dwindled to pygmy height. He was a mere maker of nails. Life a moment since had been very simple, very concrete, a mere game in which the stake was food and clothes, a Queen Anne house, a clipped lawn and trotting horses. Now it was a mysterious expedition into the unknown. With the Professor's last word I rose, ready to march, not knowing whither, but sure that it would not be to a conquest measured in kegs of nails. In this exalted mood Gladys Todd could have no part, for I knew that I could go faster and farther in light marching order, unhampered by impedimenta of any kind. Gladys Todd suddenly took her place with impedimenta. Her first act was to confirm this judgment of her, for as I was forcing my way down the crowded aisle, intent on reaching my old friend, she kept tugging at my sleeve and entreating me not to hurry. Her remonstrances aroused my antagonism. Inwardly I was calling down maledictions on her head, for I saw the Professor's tall form receding through the door. I would have rushed after him; there were a thousand things I wanted to know, a thousand questions I had to ask him. But I was checked. I could not abandon Gladys Todd; nor had I the courage to present myself to him after so many years in the light of a youth given to sentimental dalliance. He would remember the boy who had come to him, cold and wet, from the depths of a mountain stream, the boy who had run miles in the early morning to warn him of the approach of the terrible Lukens, the boy whom he had called his only friend. He would see me dignified by a tail coat and beautified by a mauve tie, a white waistcoat and gleaming patent-leather shoes. He would remember me as I stood by the cabin door, a strong, rugged lad. He would see me a devotee of fashion, a dawdler after a pretty face. So it was with a feeling of relief that I saw the study door close after my friend. I intended to find him, but not until I was as free as on that day when I first came upon him in the clearing.

Gladys Todd was inclined to lag. There were a dozen persons to whom she wished to speak, but with rude insistence I hurried her away. Outside the rain fell heavily. I held my umbrella at arm's length now and abandoned my fine feathers to the storm. She feigned not to notice my changed demeanor and tried to talk pleasantly, but I answered only in monosyllables, and brusquely, I fear. The interminable journey ended. From the steps of the president's house, with all the graciousness she could command, she asked me not to hurry away when we had so many things to talk over. My answer was a quick "good-night," and I ran as I had run years before to the mountains, with my heart in every stride.

When I entered the doctor's study I found him alone. Mr. Henderson, he explained, had gone to Judge Bundy's. Judge Bundy always entertained the lecturer, and he was too generous a man to make an exception even in this case. In speaking of the lecturer the doctor made a wry face. He could not understand how a man of Valerian Harassan's reputation ever allowed such a mountebank to take his place. At McGraw we believed in life; we believed in ambition, and it was terrible—terrible, sir, to have to sit in silence and hear our dearest traditions assailed by one who admitted that he was a failure. Did Mr. Malcolm hear the brutal cut at Judge Bundy? Judge Bundy, sir, was—

I did not stop to hear the eulogy, nor did I consider how I might be prejudicing myself with the president by so rudely breaking from him. But the Professor had come back to me. I cleared the college steps with a bound, and ran over the campus and down the hill into the town. I ran with all a boy's reckless waste of strength, so that when I had covered my half-mile course I had to lean for support against the iron fence which guarded the Bundy home. The great stone pile, with many turrets and a dominating cupola, with wide-spreading verandas and marble lions on the lawn, in the daylight comported itself with dignified aloofness, and now, when night exaggerated its size and a single lonely light flickered in all its vast front, it was forbidding. With something of that forced boldness with which years before I had braved the dark mountains, I made the gate ring a proper notice of my approach and groped my way about the door until I found the bell. The answer came from over my head. Stepping back and looking up, I saw framed in a lighted window a white figure, coatless and collarless, not the distinguished jurist, but a portly man who had been interrupted in the act of preparing for bed. Clothes go a long way toward making a man, and the lack of them brought the judge down to hailing distance.

"What do you want?" he demanded of me, addressing me as any disrobed plebeian might have done.

"I'm Malcolm, sir, David Malcolm," I returned apologetically. "I wish to see Mr. Henderson."

"Henderson, eh?" The judge leaned over the window-sill, and he spoke less sharply. "You'll find him at the station waiting for the night train out. I tried to persuade him to stay, but he wouldn't. How in the world, Mr. Malcolm, could Harassan have sent such a fool in his place? Did you ever hear such utter nonsense? I forgive him about the nails—that was inadvertent, but that stuff about ambition—"

I did not wait to hear the judge controvert my friend's pessimistic philosophy, but with a brusque "good-night" hurried away. The window banged behind me, a sharp commentary on my rudeness. The iron gate clanged again, and I was off down the hill, running toward the lower town.

A shrill whistle stopped me. Looking into the valley I saw a chain of lights weaving their way along the river. They wound through the gap in the mountain, and I saw them no longer. I heard the whistle again, far off now, and it seemed to mock me.

CHAPTER X

I listened to hear the divine drumbeat. I set myself to march under sealed orders.

To most of us the Professor's speech had been pessimism compact; to me it was inspiring, though wofully lacking in details. I seemed to be marking time. The duties which lay at my hand were unchanged, and I was plodding along as I had plodded before through a commonplace routine. I sought to give to my duties some of the glamour of conquests, but they soon failed to lend themselves to any simulation of romance. After all, marching to the divine drumbeat was simply to follow the precepts ingrained in me as a child, but it is much easier to make a quick charge amid the blare of bugles than to plod along day after day to the monotonous grumble of the drum. I wished that the Professor had been a little more explicit, and yet his last words were always with me. It was as though they were intended for me alone, and I coupled them with his admonition to me that day long ago in the cabin: "Get out of the valley. Do something. Be somebody." My great desire was to see him, for I believed that he could help me to set my course. I wanted help, and my father, my natural adviser, was of little service to me. To him my opportunity was the small one that lay at home. Mr. Pound had washed his hands of me that day when I was bold enough to renounce my purpose of entering the ministry, and now, when in the exultation of the moment my mind reverted to that abandoned plan, I found my own ideas too nebulous to permit me to set myself up as a teacher of divine truth. The law had taken its place with the making of nails, and I did not believe that when my race was run, when I had counted up the wills I had drawn, the bad causes I had defended, the briefs I had written in useless litigations, I could content myself with the thought that I had fought a good fight. For there is a good fight, and to the weakest of us must come a sense of futility in those moments when we awaken from our sloth and hear the distant din of the battle. I thought of medicine, of all professions in itself the most altruistic, and then I found myself face to face with that distressing commonplace, the need of money, for though my father was accounted a rich man in the valley, his wealth was proportioned to the valley standards. A commercial life alone seemed left to me, and then I remembered the million kegs of nails, and I recalled Rufus Blight's achievement of giving away a prize with every pound of tea. Here indeed was a march through waste-lands.

You will think that I was a dreamy, egotistical youth for whom not only the ways of home but the ways of the mass of his fellows were not quite good enough. Perhaps I was. But you must remember a boyhood passed in loneliness; long days when my feet followed the windings of the creek, but my eyes were turned to the distant mountains; the evenings when from the barn-bridge I watched the shadows fall and saw the valley peopled with mysterious shapes. I was ambitious, and I coddled myself with the belief that my ambition did not spring from selfishness, from what the Professor had called the yearning for something more, but from the desire for something better. I did not drag up the roots of my motives to light. Had I, the cynical philosopher must have found that they were nurtured in the same soil that nurtured the ambitions of Judge Bundy.

I had faith in the Professor and I wanted to find him. I could see the inconsistency of his practice and his preaching, but truth is truth no matter by whom uttered. I believed that he could help me, and I wrote to him in the care of Valerian Harassan. The writing of this letter was an evening's labor, for in it I had to tell him what had passed after that day when he had fled into the mountains, of the coming of Rufus Blight and the disappearance of Penelope out of my life; I had much to ask him of her and of himself, and then to lead on to my present quandary. The labor was without any reward. Weeks passed and he did not answer. I wrote to Valerian Harassan and was honored with a prompt reply—his friend Mr. Henderson had returned to San Francisco and he had forwarded my letter there. "But you had as well try to correspond with the will-o'-the-wisp," he wrote. "When last I talked with him, he spoke rather vaguely of going to China and making a trip afoot to Lhasa." Nevertheless, I wrote again, and it was a year later when both of my letters came back to me bearing the post-marks of many cities from coast to coast, to be opened at last by the dead-letter office.

The Professor was silent. Within a week of my graduation I found myself still in a quandary as to my course, and then it came about that it was set for me by the last man in the world whom at that moment I would have chosen for a pilot. This was Boller of '89.

Boller's father was the owner of a daily newspaper in a small inland city, and in the two years since he had left McGraw the son had risen to the chief editorship. His return to college that year was in the nature of a triumphal progress. He sat with the faculty in the morning chapel service, and Doctor Todd took occasion to refer to the presence of a distinguished alumnus who had made his mark in the profession of journalism. In two years Boller had matured to the wisdom and manner of fifty. He had abandoned the exaggerated clothes of his college days for careless, baggy black. His hair had grown long and was dishevelled by much combing with the fingers, and the mustache, once so carefully trimmed and curled, now drooped mournfully, and he had added a tiny goatee to his facial adornments. Drooping glasses on his nose, with a broad black ribbon suspended from them, gave him an appearance of intellectuality, so astonishing a transformation that it was hard for me to believe that this was the same Boller who had greeted me four years before on the college steps. The next morning after his reappearance Doctor Todd announced that our distinguished alumnus had been induced to speak informally to the students that evening on journalism and its appeal to young men. In the rôle of a very old man, Boller from the chapel rostrum descanted learnedly on what he termed the "greatest power for righteousness in modern times and the dynamic force through the operation of which the race is to attain its ideals." To my mind Boller's view of the power for righteousness troubled itself chiefly with the opposing political party, as was shown by the instance he cited where his own paper had exposed the corrupt Democratic ring in Pokono County and had put in its place a group of Republican patriots. Doctor Todd, however, said afterward that Boller had treated the subject in masterly fashion and that he was proud that McGraw had had its part in forming such a mind. While I had listened to Boller in all seriousness, the Professor's diatribe was too vividly in my memory for me to accept without reservation everything that our distinguished alumnus said. But he did bring to my mind the idea that here possibly was the opportunity which I sought, and long before he had finished my thoughts had wandered far from the chapel and I was picturing myself in an editorial chair and with a caustic pen attacking the devils of which poor man is possessed.

I met Boller in the hall afterward, and as he took my arm condescendingly and walked with me a little way I summoned up courage to invite him to my room and there to open my heart to him.

He lighted one of his own cigars after having declined that which I offered him, and this little evidence of his superior taste served to confirm my opinion of his importance. He crossed his legs carelessly, leaned back and watched a long spire of smoke rise ceilingward. "So you are thinking of journalism, eh, Malcolm?"

"You have set me thinking of it," I returned. "Somehow the law doesn't appeal to me any more. The truth is—" I hesitated, recalling how Boller's subtle ridicule had shaken the purpose so carefully nourished by my parents and Mr. Pound. Though his talk that night had been filled with high-flying phrases about ideals of citizenship and useful manhood, I still had lingering doubts of his entire sincerity, and I cast about for some way of expressing my thoughts without making myself ludicrous in his eyes.

"The truth is—" Boller repeated.

"That I want to take up work that means something more than bread and butter," I responded. "I don't want to be a big fish in a small pond."

"And you think that journalism offers a chance of becoming a whale in a big pond. It does, Malcolm, it does," said Boller. "Journalism is the greatest power in the country to-day. We used to call you the Reverend David. Well, if you still have any lingering desire to be a preacher, the paper is the place for you, not the pulpit. The editorial is the sermon of the future. If you would become a preacher, by all means take up journalism. If you have red blood in your veins you will be a journalist."

Having delivered this advice, Boller sat in silence, regarding me through his drooping glasses and pulling at his goatee, and at that moment I decided to be a journalist. It was the picture which Boller made that settled my mind. There was something attractive in his careless attire—the baggy clothes, the flowing tie; and the glasses with the broad ribbon gave an air of dash and intellectuality which I had never seen in the stiff uniform of the bar, even as worn by that leader, Judge Bundy. It is often such absurd impressions on our unsophisticated minds that set the course of our lives. It was so with me. I compared Boller with Doctor Todd, with Mr. Pound, and in the younger generation with Simmons of his own class, who had become principal of a high-school, and I said to myself that the profession which in two years had made him this confident, masterful man offered the opportunity that I sought.

"If you have red blood, Malcolm—" Boller went on as he polished his glasses. There was a suggestion in his careless manner that he waded in red blood set flowing by his pen. "Journalism is one long fight. If you have ideals, Malcolm—" He looked at me, and then my cheeks flushed as by an inclination of the head I confessed to the possession of ideals. "If you have ideals, you can make a fight for right. In journalism we stand aloof from the play itself, but we endeavor to make the actors perform their parts properly. You remember my description of how we exposed the Pokono County ring. It's a fight like that all the time, but you make yourself felt, you know."

Thoroughly pleased with the militant side of the profession, and having decided that I should enter it, I lost no time inquiring how I should begin. This question took some thought on Boller's part, and he combed his hair with his fingers while he gave it consideration.

"I could put you on the *Sentinel*," he said at last. "You will have to start at the bottom, as a reporter, you understand."

He evidently believed that I should jump at such a prospect, but he did not know that the Professor had filled me with the hope of bigger things. I had taken what Boller had said, and I enlarged it to a wider scale of life. I had no intention of exchanging the opportunities of Harlansburg for those of Coal City. Even the Pokono County gang would be small game for me. But before I could thank Boller for his interest and decline it, he hurried on to fix my salary and to explain the nature of my work. He nettled me, and I protested with heat that I wished to start in a broader field.

"That's all right, Malcolm," said my mentor, undisturbed by the reflection on his own city. "But you can get an invaluable experience on the *Sentinel*. If you start right for New York how are you going to get a job? On the other hand, look at Bob Carmody. He learned with us—three years—and now he has a splendid place on the New York *Record*, making forty a week—covered the Douglas murder trial. Look at Bush, James Woodbury Bush—he went to Philadelphia after two years with us, and he is literary editor of the *Gazette*—landed it easily. He has already published one book—'Anna Virumque'—a charmingly clever story of early Babylon."

The success of Bob Carmody and James Woodbury Bush, while they confirmed me in my respect for the profession of journalism and in my resolve to enter it, did not shake my purpose to waste no time in desultory skirmishing. That I decided so promptly that New York was to be my scene of action was due to Boller's casual mention of Bob Carmody's salary, which by rapid calculation I found to equal Doctor Todd's and to surpass my father's income. The figures were large. I flattered myself that I found no appeal in the money, but regarded it simply as the measure of the power and importance which Bob Carmody had attained. The value of his brain labor was nearly double the value of the foodstuff produced on my father's farm. The figures were impressive. I knew, however, that I could not argue with Boller, supported as he was by experience, and my way with him lay in an obstinate declaration of my purpose.

"It's good of you to offer me a place," I said. "But I'm not going to waste any time. A few days at home, and I am off to New York."

If Boller felt any irritation at my rejection of his offer, he did not show it. Doubtless he laid my refusal to the ignorance of youth, for he stood over me, regarding me through the drooping glasses, as my father would have regarded me had I declared to him some reckless purpose.

"You make a mistake, David," he said. He stood at the door, with one hand fumbling the knob. "Still, I wish you success. Suppose I give you a letter to Carmody. It would be a great help, you know. And I'll write for you a general recommendation—to whom it may concern—on our letterhead; it will be of service." He opened the door and stepped out. He hesitated and came back. "I might tell you, Malcolm, that I hope soon to launch into New York journalism, when I have exhausted the possibilities of Coal City. A man can't sit still, you know—that is, if he has red blood in his veins."

Boller said no more that night, but his manner in parting made it clear to me that if he came to New York it was his purpose to be of great service to me, to lift me up with him. His assumption of superiority filled me with a desire to outrun him. Vanity is a great stimulus to action, and the inspiring note of my life was forgotten as I contemplated David Malcolm in his sanctum, at a table littered with pages, every one of which would stab some devil of corruption or brighten some lonely hour, pausing at his labor to blow spires of smoke ceilingward while he gave kindly advice to the man who sat before him, respectfully erect on his chair, regarding him through drooping glasses.

The college lights were out. I moved to the window and stayed there for a long time, looking into the summer night. The street lamps checkered the slope below me, but my eyes went past them; in the depths of the valley the nail-works were glowing, piling up their tale of kegs, but I looked beyond them to the mountain which rose from the river and travelled away like a great shadow, cutting the star-lighted sky. Where mountain and sky mingled, indefinable in the night, my eyes rested, but my mind plunged on. My arms lay folded on the window-sill, and into them my head sank. I crossed mountain after mountain, and they were but shadows to my youthful strength. What a man David Malcolm became that night! He won everything that the world holds worth striving for. He won them all so easily by always doing what was right. He travelled far because he marched so straight. Then he mounted to the highest peak—a feat so rare that even his great modesty could not suppress a cry of exultation. He heard the crunching of a hoe, and, following the sound, saw the Professor battling with the ever-charging weeds. The gaunt man regarded him quietly; then said: "David, you have come far." He raised the hoe and pointed to the sky. "And I suppose they have heard of it off there—in Mars and Saturn." He turned to the ground, to an army of ants working on a pyramid of sand. "And down there—I suppose they have heard of it." David Malcolm looked about him. The world seemed waste as far as his mind could carry. The Professor saw the disappointment clouding his face, for he stepped closer to him and, laying a hand upon his shoulders, said: "Remember, David, sealed orders."

CHAPTER XI

In those last days at college, when in moments of contemplation I sketched with free imagination a long and unbroken career of success, whether I would or not, Gladys Todd was always gliding into my dreams. She had been too long a central figure in them for me to evict her easily. I knew that I had best begin my march unhampered by impedimenta of any kind, but I found it no easy task to get myself into light marching order. While I had never made a serious proposal for her hand, I had in sentimental moments said things which implied that at the proper time I should offer myself formally. That the offer would bring her prompt acquiescence I never for a moment doubted. But more embarrassing was the attitude of Doctor and Mrs. Todd. They treated me as though I were a member of the family. Mrs. Todd's eyes always beamed with a peculiarly motherly light when they rested on me, and now I recalled with something akin to terror an evening when Gladys at the piano was accompanying me as I sang "The Minute Guns at Sea." Her mother entered the parlor. It did her good, she said, to see us, for it brought back the dear days when she and Doctor Todd had sung as we were singing at that very same piano. Doctor Todd never expressed his thoughts with quite such frankness, but now I could remember many times when he had treated me with fatherly consideration. To end abruptly such a friendship seemed not alone a gross abandonment of Gladys Todd, but of Doctor Todd and Mrs. Todd. The sensible thing to do was clear to me in my saner moments. During the few days that remained to me at college I should continue the friendship, but it would be friendship and nothing more. Then I would go away, politely, as hundreds of other young men before me had left Harlansburg, with a formal parting handshake to hundreds of other young women who had played soft accompaniments while they sang "The Minute Guns at Sea"; as for Doctor and Mrs. Todd, another young man would soon be standing by that same piano awakening their cherished memories.

It was in this other hypothetical young man that I found the stumbling-block whenever my mind was settled to do the sensible thing. The trouble was that I loved Gladys Todd. When I fixed my purpose to march to the strife unhampered by any domestic ties, I felt that I was making myself a martyr to duty. I began to compromise. In a few years, when my feet were firmly set in the road and I had grown strong enough to march with impedimenta, I should come back and claim Gladys Todd, and my return would be a triumph like that of Boller of '89, only in a degree far higher, for from her hands I should receive the victor's garland.

I might have struggled on with such confused ideas as these had it not been for the hypothetical other man. He haunted me. The hypothesis became a fact. It found embodiment in Boller of '89. When after three interminable days of self-denial I presented myself one evening at the president's house, a look of annoyance with which Gladys greeted me seemed connected in some way with the presence of Boller. In my state of mind I should have suspected any octogenarian who smiled on Gladys Todd as plotting against my happiness. That she was essential to my happiness I realized as I watched her, in the shaded lamplight, her face turned to him as she listened intently to an account of his recent visit to Washington. They did not treat me as though I made a crowd. That, at least, would have given me some importance. My rôle was a younger brother's. Boller's greeting was kindly, but he made unmistakable his superiority in years and wisdom as he lapsed into an arm-chair and toyed with the broad black ribbon adorning his glasses, while I was condemned to sit upright on a spindly chair. When he addressed me it was to explain things of which he presumed that I was ignorant, and he gave no heed to my vehement protests to the contrary. When Gladys Todd addressed me it was to call attention to some peculiarly interesting feature of Boller's discourse. They did not drive me to despair, though I was sure this to be their aim. They simply aroused my fighting blood. All other thoughts for the future were forgotten, buried under the repeated vow that I would repay Gladys Todd a thousand times for this momentary coldness and would deal a stinging blow to Boller's self-complacency.

Boller announced to us in confidence that, having seen Washington, it was now his intention to go abroad. I could not understand why we were pledged to secrecy as to his plans, for the country would not be entirely upset by his departure; but it was clear to my suspicious mind that his revelations had a twofold purpose—to lift himself to greater heights of superiority over the humble college boy and to make himself a more desirable *parti* for Gladys Todd. In his words, in the quiet smile with which he was regarding her, I read his secret hope that when he went abroad she would be with him as Mrs. Boller. Restless, uncomfortable, and angry as I was, I had been at the point of leaving, but this disclosure changed my purpose. I realized that I was in no mere skirmish and I dared not give an inch of ground. I stayed. Boller talked on. The clock on the mantel struck the hour, then the half. He looked at me significantly, but I did not move. The clock struck the hour again, and Boller rose with a sigh. He suggested that I go with him, but I shook my head and stood with my hands behind my back, tearing at my fingers. He smiled and stepped to the door, with Gladys Todd following. They paused. He spoke in an undertone, and I caught but two words, "At three." He raised his voice and bade me good-night, calling me "Davy" as though I were a mere boy. Again he said, "At three," jotting the hour indelibly in his mind.

Gladys Todd from the shaded lamplight looked at me with a face clouded with displeasure. I, sitting on my spindly chair, very upright, heard the cryptic number three ringing in my brain. What was going to happen "at three"? At three to-morrow they would walk along the lane which wound around the town and down to the river. I thought of it now as "our lane," a sanctuary that would be desecrated by Boller's mere presence. The plausible theory became a fact. I must act, and act at once. For me to act was to avow my love. I must propose to Gladys Todd. In that purpose all else was forgotten—even Boller. Over and over again I declared to myself that I loved her, but the simple words halted at my lips. A thousand protestations of my undying love pushed and crowded and jostled one another until they were strangling me. Without a tremor in my voice I could have told Gladys Todd that some other man loved her to distraction, and yet, when it was so vital to my happiness that I speak for myself, the simple words halted at my lips and checked the whole onrush of passionate avowal.

Thinking that distance might have some part in my unnerving, I joggled my chair a few feet nearer, grasped a knee in each hand, and leaning forward fixed a determined gaze upon her face. I had abandoned all idea of saying those three words as they should be said for the first time. To say them at all, I must blurt them out, but I believed that with them said the floodgates would be opened and the true lover-like appeal burst forth. Gladys Todd must have thought that I was angry, for she asked me what was the matter. Some inane reply forced its way through the press of unuttered avowals. Now, I said, I will tell her what the matter really is, and I have always believed that I should have done so at that moment had not the front door banged, heralding the coming of Doctor Todd.

He entered the room, and I numbered him with Boller among the enemies of my happiness. He took the very chair which Boller had occupied, and made himself comfortable for the rest of my stay.

"Well, David, you will soon be leaving us forever," he said, bringing his hands together and smiling at me over his wide-spread fingers. In that word "forever" I saw a hidden meaning, and behind my back I clinched my hands and registered my unalterable will. "You are going out into the world to make your name, David," the doctor went on, growing grave. "I do hope that you will succeed as well as Boller of '89. Boller, David, is a man of whom McGraw is proud—a remarkable young man. He dropped into my study for a few minutes this evening and it was a pleasure to listen to him. Such a breadth of view! Such nobility of purpose! He will rise high—that young man. We shall hear much of Boller."

It had been my intention to try to sit out Doctor Todd, but I was in no mood to listen to these praises of Boller from one whom I now regarded as his confederate. I took my leave as quickly as I could, but it was with the inwardly avowed purpose of returning as quickly as I could. Then, I said, the three words would be spoken, not rudely blurted out, but spoken as they should be for the first time. The mention of Boller had brought back to my mind the haunting "three," to echo in every corridor of my brain, and before I fell asleep that night, exhausted by over-thinking, I lifted my hands into the blackness and whispered what had so long hung unuttered on my lips. To-morrow, I said, I shall say it—at two.

At two in the afternoon I found Gladys Todd in the little vine-covered veranda in the rear of the house, painting. I am sure that had I seen her for the first time as she sat there at her easel beautifying a black plaque with a bunch of tulips, every wave of her hand as she plied the brush would have struck the divine spark in my heart. Marguerite at her spinning was not more lovely. The place was ideal for my purpose. We were above the town, hidden by height from its sordidness, and we looked far into mountain-tops where white clouds loitered on the June-day peace. The fresh green of early summer was about us, and the only sound was the drum of bees in the honeysuckle. The time, too, was ideal, for it was a whole hour until "three." My position was ideal, for I placed my chair very close to her and leaned forward with one hand outstretched to support my appeal. Thus I stayed, mute, like an actor who has forgotten his lines. The three words came to my lips, only to halt there.

Fortunately Gladys Todd did not notice my embarrassment, for her eyes were on her work, and while she painted she was telling me of a game of tennis which she had played that morning with the three Miss Minnicks. To the three Miss Minnicks I laid the blame of my silence. Had she been talking of any one else or of anything else, I said, I could have uttered the vital fact which hung so reluctantly on my lips, but to break in rudely in a recitation of fifteen thirties, vantages in and vantages out, with an announcement that I loved her would be quite ridiculous. I dropped my hand and stretched back in my chair. Gladys Todd talked on and painted.

The college clock struck the half-hour, and for me the one clanging note was a solemn warning. I sat up very straight, I grasped the sides of the chair, and the words were uttered. But to me it seemed that some other David Malcolm had spoken them—mere shells of words that rattled in my ears.

"David!" The voice and tone were like my mother's. Gladys Todd stopped painting and, turning, looked at me strangely. I could not have faced that gaze of hers and said another word, but she quickly averted her eyes, abandoned brush and palette, and sat studying her clasped hands.

There was nothing now to hold back the flood of passionate avowal. Perhaps my voice was a little weak, but it grew stronger as I took heart at the sight of her listening so quietly. I told her that I had loved her that evening when we first met; that since then, in all my waking moments, she had been in my thoughts; I had never loved another woman; I never could love another woman. With my outstretched arm hovering so near to her I might have taken her unawares, taken her into my possession and throttled any rising protest; but to touch her with my little finger would have seemed to me a profanation. I expected her to sink into the embrace of that solitary arm.

But she did not. She looked up at me and said: "David, I am sorry—so sorry."

"Sorry?"

There was a ring of indignation in my voice. I was not prepared for such an enigmatic answer. Indeed, I had expected but one response, the one that was mine by right of four years of devotion, by right of those beacon-lights which I had seen so often in her eyes. Sorry? If she was sorry, why had she led me to spend so many hours in her company, why had she walked with me in "our lane," where the very air seemed to brood with sentimental thought? I doubted if I heard her rightly.

"Very, very sorry, David," she repeated. "I never dreamed that you cared for me in this way. I thought you were a good friend. I never could think of you as anything else than a good friend."

I was too much stunned to speak. For days I had been rehearsing in my mind what I should say to her when her hand was in mine, but I had not prepared for a contingency like this. I was helpless. I could only lean back in my chair and gaze at her reproachfully.

"You will forget me very soon," she said, looking up after a moment. "You are going away in a few days. You must forget me, David. Promise me you will."

She took up her brush and palette and began to touch the plaque lightly. As I remember her now, Gladys Todd's face was loveliest in profile. "Promise me," she said, tossing her head and focussing her eyes on the tulips.

Poor David Malcolm! You were young then and little learned in the ways of women. You did not know that to a woman a proposal is a thing not to be ended lightly with consent. You did not know that when the gentlest woman angles she is as any fisher who plays the game with rod and reel and delights in the rushes of the victim. You made no mad rushes. You sat stupidly quiescent. You saw the fair profile dimly as though it were receding into the mists beyond your reach. Your pride was hurt. You were angry and would have flung yourself out of her presence, but you could not endure the shame of defeat.

The college clock struck three. It aroused me from my stupor, and I did make one mad rush, in my confusion acting with more acumen than I knew.

"I never will forget you—I never can forget you," I said brokenly.

The door creaked and I arose, but it was not to face Boller. Knitting in hand, Mrs. Todd bustled out. She made no apology for her intrusion. The veranda was the coolest place in the house, and as she sank into a chair I numbered her with Boller and Doctor Todd, with the enemies of my happiness. Her round, innocent face seemed to mask a grim purpose to sit there for the rest of the afternoon. Gladys Todd talked of the three Miss Minnicks again as she plied her brush, and Mrs. Todd of Mr. Minnick and Mrs. Minnick as she worked her needles. They crushed the struggling hope I had for one moment more in which to make a last appeal. Boller did not come. The college clock struck four and still there was no sign of him. I was sure that he had some knowledge of my presence, and perhaps waited for a signal from the house announcing my departure. In that case it was useless for me to stay longer listening to idle chatter about the Minnicks, and so, utterly unhappy, smarting with the sense of defeat, humiliated, I made my departure, and fled across the campus to the college and my room.

I took no supper. The mere idea of food was nauseating. I paced the floor with my thoughts in chaos. Of consolation I had but one unsteady gleam—at least I should be burdened with no harassing financial problem. Sometimes the question of my meagre resources had been amazingly persistent, but I had fought it down as unworthy to have a place with nobler thoughts. Now it rose again, and for a moment it seemed that I had escaped a heavy burden. Then I remembered Boller. I pictured Boller sitting in the vine-clad veranda while Gladys Todd painted; Boller in the Todd parlor, standing under a bower of clematis, while Gladys Todd moved toward him in step to the wedding-march played by the eldest Miss Minnick. In the sleepless hours that followed, one purpose fixed itself in my mind. I should leave McGraw next day at the sacrifice of a useless diploma. So I wrote to Gladys Todd. I wrote many notes before I was satisfied, and the one I despatched had, I thought, a manly, sensible tone. I did not wish to spend another week in sight of her home and yet banished from it, I said; I had cherished certain hopes, and now I could not stand idle in their wreckage; I had my work to do and was away to do it, but I could not leave without a friendly good-by to her and without expressing a wish for her happiness. This last was a subtle reference to Boller. Having made it, the words which followed were astonishing, but they were born of a faint hope that after all I might not have to go. I told her that she knew best and I would forget her, and now I was going for a last walk in the lane where we had spent so many happy hours, and then to take myself to new scenes, bearing with me the memory of her as just a friend.

The afternoon found me in the lane, on a knoll where the leafage broke and gave a vista of rolling country. My eyes were turned to the hills, but my ears were quickened to catch the sound of foot-falls. In my heart I said that I should never hear them; my dismissal had been too peremptory for me to cozen myself with so absurd an idea. But the hope which had brought me there would not die. Sometimes the wind stirred the leaves and grass, and I would start and look up the lane. Time after time I was the victim of that teasing wind, and with recurring disappointments my spirits sank lower. Then when an hour remained before my train left, and I was standing undecided whether or not to keep to my vigil, I heard a sharp crackle of dry twigs behind me.

Gladys Todd had come. She was carrying her sketch-book, and dropped it in confusion when she saw me emerge from behind the trunk of a great oak. I seized it and held it as a bond against her retreat, affecting not to see the hand which she held out commanding its return. I had planned exactly what I should say did she appear in just this way, and now my well-turned phrases scattered and I stood before her, silent, regarding her. It was just as well. My solemn eyes must have said more than any wordy speech.

"I did not expect to find you here, Mr. Malcolm," she said, dropping her hand as a sign of momentary surrender.

Her tone was one of genuine surprise, and though the statement was astonishing I could not conceive a woman of her character deviating from the straight line of truth, and the hope which had soared high at her coming in answer to my subtle call now sank away. I held out the book mutely.

She did not see it. "I was on my way to the river to sketch," she said. "I had no idea—" She dropped down on the bank and began to pick vaguely at the clover. "Please go. Good-by."

The brim of her sailor hat guarded her face, so that she really did not see the book which I was holding toward her. I placed it on the grass beside her and turned to obey, intending to march away in military fashion, perhaps whistling my defiance.

"You'll promise to forget me," I heard her say.

I looked down at her, but the hat screened her face.

"Yes," I answered, with a steadiness that was surprising, for my throat was parched and my knees had become very weak, so weak that I gave up all thought of marching in military fashion and gathered strength to drag myself out of her sight. I went up the lane slowly. I looked back and saw her sitting very still, one hand on her big portfolio, the other listless on the clover. I reached the bend in the lane. Passing it, I should march on to my conquests, unhappy, wofully unhappy, but going faster because alone.

"David," she called.

I stepped back, hardly believing my ears. She was sitting very still, looking over the lane and the hills. I went nearer. She was like stone. I sat down at her side and somehow my hand touched her hand on the big portfolio, and her hand did not move. And somehow my hand closed on hers.

"David," she said, looking up, "you won't forget me, will you?"

Forget you! I swore to Gladys Todd that I had been idly boasting. I would have carried her image to the grave, burned on my heart. The memory of her would have been the only light in all my life of darkness. But now there was no darkness. For us there was only glorious day. The astonishing thing, the incomprehensible thing, was that Gladys Todd could love me; that it was really true that she loved me that first night we met; that she loved me yesterday when she sat on the vine-clad porch painting tulips so carelessly.

"But I did, David," she protested.

"Then why didn't you say so?" I returned reproachfully.

"Because I wanted to make you say so," she answered.

"But, Gladys," I cried, "I was sure you were in love with Boller."

She stared at me with eyes full of wonder.

"With Boller," I exclaimed. "Boller of '89."

"Why, David Malcolm, you poor, dear child," she cried. "How could you have been so foolish. He left yesterday—yesterday at three."

A cloud suddenly hurled itself across the brightness of my day. It seemed that after all I had hurried unnecessarily, for the financial problem forces itself even into the seventh heaven of love, and now it came like a ghoul to devour my happiness. It assumed concrete form in a picture of Doctor Todd when I went to him empty-handed, and I could not help feeling that it would have been better had I not let suspicion and jealousy hurry me to the attainment of what could have been mine a year later under less embarrassing circumstances.

My moment of abstraction was quickly noticed. Gladys Todd wanted to know my troubles. They were hers now, she said, for thenceforth we must share our burdens. I rose, for I was young. I laughed, and with my laugh the clouds were swept away, for no cloud could veil the sunshine from my heart when the big sketch-book was under my right arm and her small hand was under my left arm as we walked together down that clover-carpeted lane.

CHAPTER XII

I have travelled far in my life, travelled the seven seas by sail and steam, and on horse and camel crossed plain and desert. The Pacific, the Indies, the Arctic—I count over the coasts where my ships have cast anchor; I go back in my memory to the first foreign shores on which my eyes rested, and you perhaps will smile when I tell you that they were the Jersey meadows. I saw them from a car window on a June evening. The train had crossed the bridge at Newark, and below me in the river lay ships—tiny coasters, I know now, but then in the dusk magnified for me to the dignity of world-wanderers. In the salt vapors of the marshes I scented the sea and the far-borne aroma of the tropics, the lands of palm and spice, and I looked away to the encircling hills and their scattered lights with something of the exultation of Columbus when he spied the blazing torch which marked the New World. This was a new world to me. I had known only the inland, little valleys where life moved as placidly as the little rivers which threaded them. Now the sight of mast and spar, the salt vapors, the far-spread lights told me that I had come to a strange land, and I was eager to reach its heart and to see its mysteries. I was keyed high with the hope of conquest. With the salt marshes behind me, I left behind me, too, the Old World, the little valleys, the placid streams, and very straight I was, and very self-confident, when at last I looked across the dark river to the towering shadow of the city, pierced by its myriad stars. I felt neither fear nor loneliness. This city had been building for these hundreds of years for just this hour. It waited to receive me.

But the David Malcolm who stood bewildered in the streets was not the conqueror who had stepped ashore from the ferry-boat. The life a moment ago so precious had suddenly lost its value in the eyes of the unknowing. Yesterday he had walked through Malcolmville, and every man, woman and child in its straggling length had come out to bid him farewell. His departure was an event. His arrival in these strange streets was an event, but to him alone. His very existence was not recognized save by those churlish souls with whom his awkwardness brought him into physical contact. A belt-line car charged at him as though it mattered little if he were ground beneath its wheels. A truck hurled at him as though it were a positive blessing could the world be rid of him. Plunging to safety, he bowled over a man who made it perfectly plain that he regarded himself as just as important as Malcolm of '91. Pausing on a corner with his shining suit-case at his feet, he looked about him. Then he became in his own mind but another ant in a giant hill.

I was lonely now, but I had no fear. I watched the unceasing flow of life around me, and I said that I could move in it as boldly as any man, and perhaps a little better than most men, and if the time came when I must at last be caught beneath a belt-line car my removal from these mad activities would at least be dignified by a notice in the papers. The shrinkage to my self-importance added fire to my ambition. More carefully but resolutely I threaded my way up Cortlandt Street, and at every step my sense of my unimportance increased. Even my hotel seemed to be a hotel of no importance. Mr. Pound had stayed there in 1876, and his account of its magnitude and luxury had led me to believe that I could find it merely by asking. Three men met my simple inquiry with shakes of the head and hurried brusquely on, and yet they were respectable and intelligent-looking. The policeman at the Broadway corner had at least heard of my hostelry; he remembered having seen it when he first came on the force, but he was inclined to believe that it had long since been torn down. This was discouraging, but I did not abandon my search, for Mr. Pound had advised me to make myself known to Mr. Wemple, the head clerk, a friend of his, who would doubtless be of service to me. And now in my great loneliness I wanted to find not the hotel, but Mr. Wemple, for I knew that with him I could talk on terms of friendship, however frail. From the horse-car jogging up Broadway I watched for the corner where the policeman told me the hotel had been; I reached it and saw a tall building adorned by many golden signs, inviting me not to the comfort of bed and board but to the purchase of linens and hosiery. It was growing late. The part of the town through which I was passing had put out its lights and gone home to bed, so I had to abandon hope of finding Mr. Wemple, and turned into the first hotel I saw, an imposing place with a broad window in which sat a solemn, silent row of men gazing vacantly into the street.

Here at last I ended my journey, weary and lonely, without even Mr. Wemple to welcome me to the city where I had cast my fortunes. Before long I joined the solemn line and sat watching the street, and Broadway below Union Square at night, even in those times, was not an enlivening scene. My conquest was forgotten; my mind wandered back to the valley at home. Here I sat listlessly, in a hot, narrow canyon through which swept a thin, sluggish stream of life; above me was just a patch of sky; before me was a tall cliff of steel and stone, pierced by numberless dead windows. As I sat in the glare of electric lights, in smoke-charged air, my ears ringing with the harsh medley of the street, I fancied myself on the barn-bridge again. The moon would be rising over the ridges and the valley would lie at my feet with its checkered fields of brown and gray rolling away to the mountains, and the music of the valley would be no harsh clatter of bells and hoofs; I should hear the wind in the trees, the rustle of the ripening grain, the whippoorwill calling from the elm by the creek, and the restless bleating of sheep in the meadow. Thinking of these things, I asked myself if the life I had left was not far better than the one I had chosen; if the highest reward for my coming years of labor would not be the right to return to it. But for pride I could have abandoned all my mighty plans at that moment and gone back, even, as the Professor had said, to doze like the very dogs. I dared not. My parents' joy at my return might over-balance the loss of their high hopes for my fame, and had they alone been in my thoughts I should have taken the night train home. But I could not go back to Gladys Todd beaten before I had even come to blows with life.

The last picture I had of her was the heroic one of a woman speeding her knight to battle. Gladys had an embarrassing way of calling me "her knight." She stood on the platform of the Harlansburg station, and I leaned from a window of the moving train. Beside her was Doctor Todd waving his hat, and behind her the three Miss Minnicks with handkerchiefs fluttering. She was very straight and very still, but I knew what was in her thoughts. She had faith in my strength; when she saw me again my feet would be firmly set on the ladder by which men climb above the heads of their herded fellows. In the hours of the long journey the picture of her was very clear to me; I seemed to be wearing her colors as I went to the conflict; with her spirit watching over me, I could strike no mean blow nor use my strength in any unworthy cause.

How glad I was that she could not see me now, as I sat in the hotel window on two legs of my chair, with my feet on the brass rail, a figure of dejection. The glamour of my great adventure was gone. I had come quickly to the waste places of which the Professor had spoken. When I closed my eyes to the noisome street and the clamor, when I saw the pines on the ridge-top clear cut against the moonlit sky, when I heard the whippoorwill calling from the elm and the sheep bleating in the meadow, I believed that I was marching to barren conquests and fighting for worthless booty. But I dared not turn back.

In the morning, however, I looked at that same street with different eyes. The thin, sluggish stream of life had swollen to a mighty current. The raucous little medley of the night was lost in the thunders of the awakened city. The towering canyon was swept by the brightest of suns. I seemed to be standing idle in the midst of the conflict, and I was eager to plunge into it. So at noon that day I began my fight. I presented myself at the editorial rooms of *The Record* and asked for Mr. Carmody. In my hand I held a letter to him from Boller, recommending me in such high terms that it seemed highly improbable that he could refuse me his good offices. To support Boller's assertions as to my acquirements I had also letters from Doctor Todd and Mr. Pound. According to Doctor Todd, the journal which secured the services of David Malcolm was to be congratulated; he recited my high achievements, my graduation with honors in the largest class in the history of McGraw, my winning of the junior oratorical contest with a remarkable oration on "Sweetness and Light." Mr. Pound was less fulsome in his praises, for he was by nature a pessimistic man, but he could vouch for my honesty, though, to be frank, he had been disappointed by my abandoning my purpose to enter the ministry; yet he had known me from infancy, he had had a little part in the development of my mind, and he was confident that I needed but the opportunity to make my mark in any profession.

With such support, my air when I asked for Mr. Carmody was naturally one of assurance. The office-boy, an ancient man in the anteroom, handed my card and Boller's letter to a very young assistant, and where my eyes followed him through a door I saw a number of men seated at battered desks. Some were writing; some were reading; some merely smoking; some had their heads together and talked in low tones. All were in their shirt-sleeves; and none presented the dignified appearance of my conception of a journalist, and especially of so successful a journalist as Mr. Bob Carmody. I was confident that the very young office-boy would pass them and go to the doors beyond, which must lead to the true sanctum. No; where he stopped I saw a wide-spread paper; over the top of it a mop of flaming red hair, and bulging from the sides of it the sleeves of a very pink shirt. The curtain was lowered, disclosing a round, red face heavily blotched with shaving-powder. There was nothing of dignity in Mr. Carmody's appearance; there was nothing in his rotund features to suggest any high purpose or distinguished ambition; indeed, it seemed that he would be content to sit forever on that small chair at that battered desk.

He dropped the paper, looked at my card, and read Boller's letter. Evidently it amused him, for the half-burned cigarette in his mouth moved convulsively, and as he came toward me there sprang up in my mind doubts as to Boller's estimate of him. But he proved a good-natured young man and certainly very modest. Sitting on the ancient office-boy's desk, he addressed me in low tones, as though he feared to be overheard. He was glad to know any friend of Boller's, but evidently Boller was laboring under a misapprehension as to his importance. He disavowed having any influence. Had he the power, nothing would delight him more than to give a friend of Boller a job. I had never thought of myself hunting anything so commonplace as a job, but as I listened to him and looked past him into the editorial room my ideas of my chosen profession were rapidly readjusting themselves and I was casting about for a way in which to continue my quest without the influence on which I had counted so heavily. I protested that I had never dreamed of him giving me a job; I had come to him simply for advice, and perhaps an introduction to the real powers.

Mr. Carmody gave an uneasy glance over his shoulders to a large desk in the corner, where sat a tall, thin man who seemed absorbed in a game of checkers played with newspaper clippings. Mr. Hanks, the city editor, he explained; nothing that he could say would have any influence on Mr. Hanks. On my insisting, however, he at last consented to sound Mr. Hanks on my behalf; he approached him with something of the caution he would have used in confronting a tiger; he waved his hand to me to assure me that all was well, and when I stood by the big desk he disappeared, and it was many days before I saw him again.

There was nothing repelling in Mr. Hanks. Indeed, he seemed rather a mild man, but when he turned on me a pair of large spectacles I felt suddenly as though I were a curious insect being examined under magnifying-glasses. Mr. Hanks, with his thin, pale face and dishevelled hair, appeared more an entomologist than a militant editor. In a moment, however, I saw him in action. He shot his bare arm across the littered desk, he seemed to try to destroy his brass bell, and with every ring he shouted, "Copy—copy!" Office-boys sprang from the floor and dropped from the ceiling; they tumbled over one another in their hurry to answer the summons. He reprimanded them for being asleep. I thought that they would be ordered to bring Mr. Malcolm a chair, but instead one received from a waving hand a bunch of paper, and they retired as they had come, into the floor and the ceiling. I was under the magnifying-glasses again.

"Well, Mr. Malcolm," said Mr. Hanks, leaning back in his chair and clasping his hands behind his head, "ever done any newspaper work?"

"No, sir," I answered boldly. "I have just graduated from McGraw."

"And where in the devil is McGraw?" he asked in a slow, wondering voice.

How I wished for Doctor Todd! In five minutes this self-confident journalist would blush for his own ignorance. But Doctor Todd not being here to confound him with facts, there was nothing better for me to do than to hand him the letter. His face lighted with a smile as he read it. The effect was so good that I followed it with Mr. Pound's. The effect of Mr. Pound's was so good that I was confident that I should soon be a journalist in fact, for Mr. Hanks read it over twice.

"My boy," he began, regarding me through his spectacles benignly. At that familiar address my heart leaped. "Let me give you some advice." My heart fell. "Take those letters and lock them up to read when you are ten years older. Then start out and go from office to office until you get a place. Don't be discouraged. Some day you'll break in somewhere."

"But I want to work on *The Record*," I cried. "It's politics agree with mine—it is Republican. It is a respectable paper. It—"

Mr. Hanks was leaning over his desk. "Pile," he said, addressing the fat man who sat across from him, "that was a good beat we had on the Worthing divorce—I see all the evenings are after it hard. We must have a second-day story."

"I am ready," I said a little louder, "to begin with any kind of work."

Mr. Hanks looked up as though surprised that I was still there. "You've come at a bad time," he said brusquely. "Summer—we are letting men go every day. But don't get discouraged. I worked four months for my first job, and I didn't come from McGraw either. Keep going the rounds."

Then he seemed to forget my existence and resumed his game of checkers.

His dismissal was a terrible blow, but I had read enough of great men to know that they had to fight for their opportunities, and I was determined not to be a weakling and go down in the first skirmish. For a moment I stood bewildered at the entrance of *The Record* building, stunned by the unexpected outcome of my visit there. I was indignant at Boller for having raised my hopes so high. I was indignant at Mr. Carmody for not measuring up to Boller's estimate. I was indignant at Mr. Hanks for not making a searching inquiry into my attainments, for his ignorance of McGraw and his amusement over my precious letters. I vowed that some day Mr. Hanks should be put under my magnifying-glass, to shrivel beneath my burning gaze.

To break in somewhere proved a long task. From Miss Minion's boarding-house on Seventeenth Street, where I established myself, I went forth daily to the siege of Park Row. I was shot up to heaven to editorial rooms beneath gilded domes, and as quickly shot down again. I climbed to editorial rooms less exaltedly placed, up dark, bewildering stairways which seemed devised to make approach by them a peril. I soon knew the faces of all the city editors in town, and all the head office-boys were as familiar with mine. At the end of the first round I began to look more kindly on

Mr. Hanks and to realize the wisdom of his advice that I lock away my letters. I recalled the varied receptions they had met, and when I started on my second round they were hidden in my trunk. Repeated rebuffs had a salutary effect. My egotism was reduced to a vanishing-point, my pride was quickened, and with my pride my determination to accomplish my purpose. Even had I lacked pride, I must have been nerved to my dogged persistence by the memory of Gladys Todd with Doctor Todd and the three Miss Minnicks speeding me to my triumphs. Every evening when I came home, tired and discouraged, to Miss Minion's, I found a letter addressed to me in a tall, angular hand—a very fat letter which seemed to promise a wealth of news and encouragement. But Gladys Todd could say less on more paper than I had believed possible. Encouragement she gave me, but never news. News would have spoiled the graceful flow of her sentences. Yet she was wonderfully good in the way she received my accounts of my disappointments. She was prouder than ever of "her knight"; her faith in him was firmer than ever; as she sat in the evening, in the soft light of the lamp, she was thinking of me with lance couched charging again and again against the embattled world.

At first in my replies I found a certain satisfaction in recounting my defeats; for in fighting on I seemed to be proving my superior worth and strength, and I became almost boastful of my repeated failures. But the glamour of defeat wears off as the cause for which one fights becomes more hopeless, and after a month I seemed farther than ever from attaining my desire. I became depressed in the tone of my letters, but as my spirits sank Gladys Todd's seemed to soar.

One particularly fat epistle I found on my bureau on an evening when I was so discouraged that I was beginning to consider heeding my father's appeal that I return home and study for the Middle County bar. I opened it with dread. I wanted no comfort, but here in my hands were twenty pages of Gladys Todd's faith in me and her pride in me. She was sure that I should have the opportunity which I sought, and, having it, would mount to the dizziest heights. She likened me to a crusader who wore her colors and was charging single-handed against the gates of the Holy City and shouting his defiance of the infidels who held it. It was an exalted idea, but I remembered my tilt that afternoon with the ancient office-boy of *The Record*, and his refusal to take my seventh card to Mr. Hanks. The comparison was so absurd that I laughed as I had not laughed in many days, and with the sudden up-welling of my mirth, lonely mirth though it was, the blood which had grown sluggish quickened, the drooping courage rose, I saw the world through clearer eyes. The next afternoon when I faced the ancient office-boy the remembrance of Gladys Todd's metaphor made me smile, and so overcome was he by this unusual geniality that he did take in my card to Mr. Hanks.

"Again," said Mr. Hanks, leaning back in his chair and surveying me through his magnifying-glasses. "Young man, are you never going to give me a rest?"

"Never," said I, smiling. "You advised me to go the rounds and not to be discouraged."

"Have you got your letters with you?" he asked mildly.

"They are locked away in my trunk," said I.

"You certainly have taken my advice with a vengeance," said he. "I suppose I shall have to do something to protect myself."

He leaned over his desk and became absorbed in his everlasting game of checkers. The smile left my face, for I thought that he had forgotten my presence, as he had forgotten it so many times before. But after a moment he slanted his head, focussed one microscope on me, and said: "Do you think you could cover Abraham Weinberg's funeral this afternoon?"

So it was that Gladys Todd's crusader at last broke down the gates of the Holy City. But I fear that it was to become one of the defending infidels. Doctor Todd, in his letter to whom it might concern, announced that David Malcolm was about to launch himself into journalism. And now, after long waiting, David Malcolm was launched. Just when he was despairing of ever leaving the ways he had shot down them suddenly into the Temple Emanu-El and the funeral of Abraham Weinberg.

CHAPTER XIII

You can well understand the elation with which I announced my success to Gladys Todd. It was magnified by the month of disappointment, and to her I felt that I owed a debt. Though I had come to look with irony on her high-flown expressions of faith in me, I realized that the fear of her equally high-flown scorn had more than once kept me from abandoning my project. With pride I enclosed in my letter my account of the funeral of Mr. Weinberg, though I refrained from marring the trophy with an explanation that this first public production of my pen had been allowed to attain the length of a column because his store covered half a block and his advertisements many pages of *The Record*. As a trophy Gladys Todd received it. Declaring that she lacked words in which to express her pride in her knight, she flew to greater heights than ever before. She had placed my first journalistic effort in a scrap-book, and all that I wrote was to be preserved in like manner. I must send her every published line that came from my pen. Her knight had triumphed in his first real passage at arms, and she sent to me a chaplet of victory. It came—not a wreath, but a cushion worked with her own hands, mauve and white, the colors of McGraw, with '91 in black on one side and on the other the word "Excelsior."

The scrap-book grew rapidly to alarming proportions, for having now my opportunity I worked hard, and Mr. Hanks was fond of telling me that I was rapidly outgrowing the reputation Doctor Todd and Mr. Pound had made for me on Park Row. Accounts of murders, suicides, yacht-races, robberies, public meetings, railroad accidents—all the varied events which make up a day's news—followed the funeral into Gladys Todd's archives. You can readily imagine that my views of life soon underwent a change. They became rather distorted, as I see them now; and was it a wonder when my day began at noon and ended in the small hours of the morning, carried me through hospitals, police-stations, and courts, from the darkest slums to the stateliest houses on the Avenue, from the sweatshop to the offices of the greatest financiers. To me all men were simply makers of news, and by their news value I judged them. A man's greatness I measured by the probable length of his obituary notice. Indeed, greatness itself was but the costume of a puppet, so often did I see the sawdust stuffing oozing from the gashes in the cloth. When I met one bank cashier simply because he had stolen, I forgot the thousands of others who were plodding away through lives of dull honesty. Because one Sunday-school superintendent sinned, I classed all his kind as sinners. Becoming versed in the devious ways of statesmen, I began to doubt the virtues of my old heroes whose speeches I had often declaimed with so much unction. I became a cynic. At twenty-two my thoughts matched the epigrams of Rochefoucauld and my philosophy that of Schopenhauer. All my old ideas as to the importance of the work I had chosen and of my own value to the world were quickly dissipated. Often I had cause to remember the Professor and his argument that even of our good actions selfishness was the main-spring, and accepting it as true, and laying bare the roots of my own motives and of those around me, I should have moved confusedly in the darkness had I not come to see more clearly what he meant by marching under sealed orders and to realize that I had a duty and that it was to live by the light I had. I did try to do this. I had a conscience, and though I might believe that it was but a group of conceptions as to the nature of right and wrong poured into my mind by my early instruction, it protested as strongly against abuse as did my digestive organs. Sometimes I had to effect strange compromises with it. Sometimes, in my never ceasing search for facts, I found myself causing pain and trouble to those who were innocently brought under the shadow of crime and scandal, but I justified myself by the theory that they suffered for the good of the many. To me the old dictum that the end justifies the means became a useful balm.

You might think that, with so radical a change in my ideas, I should see Gladys Todd in another light than that of my college days. Indeed, looking back, those college days did seem of another age and another world, but in them Gladys Todd had become linked to me by ties as indissoluble as those which bound me to my father and mother. To what I deemed my broader view of life, their ways of living and their ways of thinking were certainly exceedingly narrow, but none the less I thought of them only with reverence and affection. So it was with Gladys Todd. That mirthful outburst over her effusion about the crusader was followed by many of its kind as her daily letters came to me, but this meant simply that I was growing older than she, and she to my mind became a child, but was none the less lovely for her unsophistication. In the turmoil of my daily work, in the unlovely clatter of Miss Minion's boarding-house, I often recalled the vine-clad veranda and our walks in the grass-grown lane, looked back to them regretfully, looked forward yearningly to the renewal of such hours.

Sometimes when my evening was free from my routine duty, and I was working harder than ever I had worked in my college days, I would forget my task to dream of the time when Miss Tucker's piano would no longer be clattering beneath me, and I should be no more disturbed by Mrs. Kittle, who had a habit of jumping her chair around the room next to mine, when somewhere in the city's outskirts I should have a house of my own, a little house in a bit of green, where I could find quiet and peace and Gladys Todd. For the realization of that dream all that I needed was money. By the lack of it I was condemned to Miss Minion's. Even when I had attained to the munificent salary of Mr. Carmody, a figure which Boller had announced to me with so much awe, I was still far from having an income to keep two in the simplest comfort. It was difficult to make this clear to Gladys Todd. Her father and mother had married on eight hundred dollars a year, and even now my salary equalled the doctor's as president of the college. To her my salary read affluence, and in my letters I began to have difficulty to convince her that I had not grown exceedingly worldly and was not putting material comfort in the balance against unselfish and uncomplaining love. On my third biannual visit to Harlansburg I went armed with facts and figures as to house rents and flat rents, the prices of meats per pound, the cost of fuel, light, and clothing. Having in my pocket such a tabulated statement which showed for incidentals a balance of but fifty dollars, I could not but smile ironically at the manner in which Doctor Todd presented me to his friends. Boller was forgotten. Boller's achievements were outshone by those of David Malcolm. Malcolm's success demonstrated the high character of McGraw's system of training. Malcolm was already being heard from!

Malcolm, with the problem which confronted him, was inwardly gauging his success by his bank account, and even the pride of Gladys Todd was a little clouded when she was called upon to use the same measure.

Sitting in the very chair in the shaded lamplight from which she had looked so admiringly on Boller two years before, she now studied the prospectus of our contemplated venture. She was very lovely, but I remember noticing what I had never before noticed, the wisps of hair which floated a little untidily about her ears. And I did what I had never done before—I compared her with another woman, with Miss Tucker, whose piano had so often disturbed my evening labors. Miss Tucker taught mathematics in an uptown girls' school. She was not as pretty as Gladys Todd, but I remembered how wonderfully neat she was, with never a hair blowing loose, and I remembered too that, though she had disturbed me with her music, I never complained of it, for the sake of the picture which she made every morning when she descended the stoop beneath my window, going to her work as cheerfully and daintily as many of her sisters would to a dinner or a dance.

"We shall only have a hundred dollars left for doctor's bills and car-fare then, David," said Gladys Todd, looking up from the paper. There were tears in her eyes, but they did not affect me as much as her way of doing her hair. How I longed for the courage to tell her that it was decidedly bad form!

"But we shall only have to wait a little longer, Gladys," said I, and I moved my chair beside her chair.

"I know," she returned more bravely, putting her hand in mine. "But you don't realize how lonely I am without you. I want to be with you, helping you—to be at your side comforting you when you are tired, cheering you when you are discouraged."

For that moment I forgot the stray wisps and the Langtry knot.

> "But it is only a little while longer," I pleaded. "Let us say in June. I shall come for you in June. You will wait for me till June?"

Her hand was on my shoulder, and I forgot all about Miss Tucker. For that moment I was the happiest of men.

"Wait for you till June?" she cried. "Why, David, I'd wait for you to eternity."

"You need not," I replied, laughing. "In June I am coming to take you to a little house on a green hill, with a veranda where we can sit on my holidays, you painting tulips on black plaques, and I—well, I with you, just thinking how wonderful it all is and—"

"How wonderful it will be in June!" said Gladys Todd.

CHAPTER XIV

Fifth Avenue was in those days a favorite resort of mine. Every morning I plunged into the rush downtown I dived from the elevated railway station into the tatterdemalion life of Park Row, and when I raised my head above that ragged human maelstrom and climbed to the editorial room of *The Record* it seemed as though I lifted my body out of a little muddy stream and plunged my mind into a Charybdis which embraced the whole world. Its centre was the same desk which I had so often approached with trembling in the days when I was breaking spears with the ancient office-boy and Mr. Hanks. I was fixed now in a chair opposite Mr. Hanks. I had become an editor. But I was not hurling my spears against the devils that possess poor man. My principal daily task was to read the newspapers with a microscopic eye, to glean from them every hint of news to come and to be covered, to present the clippings to Mr. Hanks ready for his easy perusal, and though in our province we had to do only with events of a local character, the life of the city was so interwoven with that of the whole world that to me our desk seemed a high lookout tower from which we kept an eye on the very corners of the globe. Did I look from the smutted window at my side, it was into the struggling throng on the pavement below or, over the line of push-carts displaying tawdry wares, into the park where the riff-raff seemed to reign, because the riffraff was always there, dozing on the benches. Did I look to the other hand, it was through the great murky room, through air charged with tobacco smoke and laden heavily with the fumes of ink, molten lead, and paper which filtered from the floors below through every open door. In a distant corner, a gloomy figure in the light of a single lamp, I could see the keeper of the "morgue" cutting his way through piles of papers, filing away his printed references to Brown, or Jones, or Robinson, against that day when Brown might die, Jones commit some crime, or Robinson, perchance, do something virtuous. I could see, in nearer prospect, the rows of little desks and the reporters at them, some writing, some reading, some smoking wearily; some young men fresh from college and keyed high with ambition; some old men shabbily dressed and carelessly groomed who had spent their lives at those little desks and asked nothing more than the privilege of ending them there; some of more corpulent minds, like the great Bob Carmody, who were happy in the attainment of a life's ambition to become authorities on base-ball, foot-ball, or rowing. Wherever I looked I seemed to see nothing but the titanic tread-mill and to hear the clatter of its cogs: within, where the presses rumbled deep in the ground below me, where the telegraph clicked in the adjoining room and overhead the typesetting-machines rattled incessantly; without, in the medley of the street, the cries of the hawkers, the clang of car gongs, and the never-ending shuffle of feet. Uptown life seemed on its surface to be lighter, and the curse of Adam to rest more easily on the shoulders of his children.

Of Fifth Avenue this was especially true. It was not a canyon of brick and stone in those days. Trade had just begun its invasion and had gained a foothold only in the few blocks above and below Twenty-third Street, and for the rest it was still a street of homes, where people moved in a more leisurely fashion than in the crowded thoroughfares downtown. The very air was charged with a healthier life, and here amid the opulence one could forget the near presence of the squalid alley. So it had become a habit of mine always to begin my day with a walk uptown, as a gentle tonic for my body and to give my mind a brief but more cheerful outlook than through the smutted office windows. I never tired of the life which I saw about me. And it was about me and I not of it, for though I might pause at a tailor's to examine his fabrics, it was always through his plate-glass window; beyond the window I could afford to go only in the cheaper Nassau Street; and I might stop in front of a picture-shop, but only to o select prints for that dream-land house on the hill, set on the bit of green. Smart carriages rolled by me, manned by immaculate, haughty servants, drawn by horses stepping high in time with the jingle of their harness. At one time I had planned an equipage such as these for myself; but now, computing, from past experience, my future possibilities in finance, I saw them fascinating as ever, yet as far from me as though they dashed through some Martian city, and their occupants as removed from my ken as the inhabitants of the farthest planets. Indeed, even in the commoner throng about me I knew no one. It was seldom that I was called on to doff my hat, and then to some of the queer old women who were moulding away in the corners of Miss Minion's boarding-house or to Miss Tucker hurrying to her school.

One morning in May, as was my custom, I set out for work by my circuitous route, with the intention of walking to Fifty-eighth Street and taking an elevated train downtown. The day was one of the loveliest of spring. The brightest of suns swept the Avenue. In Madison Square the fresh green had burst from the trees overnight, and I should have liked to drop down on one of the benches there, to look upward through the branches into the clouds and forget the enclosing wall of buildings and the tumultuous streets. But I was late, and I had no mind to hurry on such a day. The languor of the spring was in my veins, and I strolled on, almost unconscious of the life about me. Ahead, at the crest of Murray Hill, the city seemed to end, and I to look through a great gate-way into the blue sky, and I fancied myself standing there in that gate-way, with the valley lying at my feet, my valley awakened from its winter's sleep, its hill-sides decked with blossoming orchards, its mountains carpeted with the soft shadows of the clouds. I saw the ridge, its green slope slashed by the white winding road which crossed it. That was the same road up which I had climbed on a May morning long ago, when I hurried to the Professor's aid, and I followed it now to the clearing; I saw the clearing with the Professor leaning on his hoe studying a fleck of cloud, and Penelope watching him silently, fearing to disturb his important meditations. In these busy years Penelope had been rarely in my thoughts; if at all, it was as a little girl with a blue ribbon in her hair, the companion of a few brief weeks of my boyhood. I dared not picture her as growing up, for I had no faith in the influence of Rufus Blight, whom I had always associated with packages of tea and prizes. Penelope grown, I feared, might have become fat and florid, might speak with a twang and wear gaudy hats and gowns. My life in New York, even though I was but a quiet observer, had made me critical of women, and when I could brood unhappily over Gladys Todd's stray wisps of hair I could have little sympathy with the type of the imaginary Penelope Blight. But this morning, when the far-borne freshness of the woods and fields was in the air, and I longed to feel the soft earth beneath my feet, to break from the enclosing walls and to stride over the open fields, I recalled days like this when the wine of spring was in my veins and I had run through the meadows in a wasteful riot of energy; and then a particular day like this when Penelope and I had ridden out of the woods, had come to the ridge-top and looked over the smiling valley. I seemed to feel Penelope's arms drawn tightly around me as I pointed across the friendly land and promised to take care of her. I had had no fear then that she would ever grow corpulent and florid, and now I found myself asking if my boyish intuition might not have been right, and she fulfilled entirely the promise of her girlhood, defying the insidious generosity of time and the vulgar influence of Rufus Blight. Should I ever know? Should I ever see her?

I must have been looking at the clouds as I asked myself these questions, for I walked right into an elderly woman, a tall, buxom woman who carried in her arms a tiny Pomeranian. The force of our collision made her drop her pet, and for an instant he hung suspended by the leash and choking. I apologized humbly, bowing; but my victim—for such she seemed to think herself—the victim of my premeditated brutality, lifted the frightened dog back to the refuge of her arms, glared at me, turned, and swept on to a modiste's door. Her haughtiness angered me. I held the fault as much hers as mine, for the pavement was not crowded and she seemed to have risen from it just to obstruct my passage. I looked about me to discover whence she had come so suddenly, and in a carriage standing at the curb I found an explanation. I said to myself that if she had emerged from so smart an equipage I had indeed committed *lèse-majesté*, for it was such a turnout as I had dreamed of in my days of opulent dreaming; it was such a turnout as a poor poet could have used without offending his sense of the beauty of simplicity. The high-headed horses with their shining harness, the smart brougham, so spotless that it was hard to imagine its wheels ever touching the street, the men in their unobtrusive livery, spoke of unostentation in its most perfect and most expensive form. The woman of the Pomeranian, I said to myself, must be surely some *grande-dame*, a leader in that mysterious circle which I knew only by its name "society." My view of that circle in those days was tinged with the cynicism of one who knew nothing of it; and though at the boarding-house table I was prone to rail at it, secretly I had to admit that my raillery was born of envy. So now it was with a mind filled half with awe and half with envy that I turned to look after the imposing woman with the dog.

For the first time I noticed that she had a companion. First, the companion was but a slender figure in black, smartly clad. I could see only her back, and yet as I carried my eye from the dainty boot which rested on the lowest step to the small gloved hand on the railing, to the small black hat with its blue wings airily poised, I found myself making comparisons between this daintiness and the untidy loveliness of Gladys Todd. I was almost angry with Gladys Todd because she did not dress with such simplicity, not knowing that all her wardrobe cost hardly as much as this unobtrusive gown, this masterpiece of a tailor's art.

Gladys Todd was not long in my mind. It was as though the memory of her was swept away by the turn of the blue wings on which my eyes rested. They moved with a majesty that sent my thoughts hurling down into the past to match them. I matched them with a bit of blue ribbon. It had moved as majestically as they. I almost laughed outright. It was absurd to compare the forlorn child of the clearing with this smartly groomed young woman, and remembering Nathan, the white mule, I looked again to the perfectly turned-out carriage at the curb. You must suspect that there was in my mind, born of a wild hope, a suspicion that I was seeing Penelope Blight. True. But from Nathan, the white mule, to this perfect carriage with the haughty footman at the door was so far a cry that I was about to go on. The girl had turned also, and I found myself halted and staring at her. I was sure that she had been studying my back at that moment when I was looking at the carriage, but being discovered in such interest she gave a start, recovered herself, and with an angry toss of her head sprang up the steps and through the door.

In that moment when our eyes met I was sure that I was face to face with Penelope Blight.

The old Florentine writer, Firenzuola, commends nut-brown as the loveliest color for a woman's eyes, declaring that it gives to them a soft, bright, clear and kindly gaze and lends to their movement a mysteriously alluring charm. These eyes were blue, but in that fraction of an instant when I looked into them, their light was soft and bright, clear and kindly; I was sure that they were the same mysteriously alluring eyes that I had first known years before when I had crawled, wet and cold, from the depths of the mountain brook. Knowing no more I should have spoken her name, my hand was rising to my hat, but the soft and kindly light changed suddenly to hostility, and she was gone.

I hesitated, not knowing what step to take next. With hesitation doubt came. I began to argue. The hostile flash of her eyes angered me. She had tacitly charged me with impertinence, with the manners of a common Broadway lounger. Then I said, had this really been Penelope she must have recognized me, for twelve years could not have obliterated all outward traces of the boy whom she had once known as her only friend. Remembering that time, remembering the forlorn cabin in the mountains and the brown, barefooted girl, remembering the promise of later days given by the sleek vulgarity of Rufus Blight, I said that she could not have grown to this faultless picture of young womanhood. Yet the forlorn hope that I might be mistaken would have held me there awaiting her return had it not been for the haughty footman by the carriage door. He had been a silent observer of what had passed, and seeing me now loitering, staring at the modiste's shop, he cast off his expressionless mask and assumed a very threatening and scowling appearance. Evidently he, too, thought me a street lounger who, not satisfied with nearly killing madam, was bent on thrusting his impertinent attentions on the young mistress. I could not explain to him that I had known the young mistress years ago when she lived in a log hut in a mountain valley. His own perfection as a servant made such an explanation the more incredible; and though loath to abandon the opportunity to convince myself that I was mistaken, I saw nothing left for me but to go my way downtown.

As I sat at my desk I was so distrait that Mr. Hanks accused me of being in love, speaking as though I were the victim of a mental derangement which unfitted me for serious labor. After the way of men, I boldly denied his charge. He paid no attention to my protest, but expressed himself freely on the unwisdom of a man allowing himself to fall under the influence of delusions which cost him his mental poise and might disarrange his whole life. Hearing Mr. Hanks, it was difficult for me to believe that he had ever been in love himself. Watching him at his work, with his sharp, restless eyes always alert, and listening to his voice as incisive as his shears, he seemed a man whose whole mind was possessed by the pursuit of news, a man whose brain and body worked with such machine-like accuracy that he could never fall into the puerile errors of his fellows. Now when he was misusing his authority to browbeat me into what he termed sanity, I found comfort in recalling that after all he had once in a moment of forgetfulness confessed to having a home at Mentone Park, with a wife and four daughters of whose accomplishments he spoke almost with boasting. So I troubled no longer with denials, but sat listening to him with a smiling face. Whereupon he brought his fist down on the desk and called me a soft-brained idiot.

"Of course, Malcolm," he said, "I don't know who she is, but my advice to you is, whoever she is and whatever she is, get her out of your mind."

At that very moment Malcolm's mind was occupied with just these questions: Who was she? What was she?

With a sense of duty to Gladys Todd I strove hard to put Penelope Blight out of my thoughts, but I could not. Sometimes I would recall the face of the girl whom I had seen in the morning, and every feature would bring back the child of the mountains. Then I went to directories and searched them for the name of Rufus Blight, but I could get no trace of him. I evolved a theory that Penelope was the guest of the woman with the Pomeranian. The carriage must belong to either the elder or the younger woman. Granting that the younger was Penelope, then the elder could not be her mother. As I had examined many directories and found none that gave her uncle's name as living in the city, I had to conclude that the owner of the Pomeranian was her hostess and that I was the victim of a trick of fate which had allowed her to flash across my path and disappear, which had allowed me to have but this tantalizing glimpse. Then I found consolation in the thought that after all a glimpse was enough for my peace of mind. Indeed, if this really were Penelope, then it had been best that I had never seen her at all, grown to such loveliness.

Considering myself as I sat in my shirt-sleeves amid grimy workaday surroundings, remembering the frayed environment of my life uptown, this Penelope, stepping, daintily booted and gloved, out of that perfect equipage, was indeed a being who moved in higher airs than I. Here was an insuperable difficulty. In the valley, David Malcolm, with the blood of the McLaurins in his veins, might look with contempt on the Blights and their kind. But we were no longer in the valley, and a Blight driving down the Avenue in a brougham, drawn by high-headed horses and manned by haughty servants, would see me not as the head of a wealthy patrician house, but as a young man on his way from his boarding-house to labor for a petty wage. Such a reversal of our relative conditions was so incredible that I found myself arguing that I could not have seen Penelope Blight, and I tried to return to loyal devotion to Gladys Todd.

We were to be married in June. There was no reason why we should not be married in June if we were content to begin our venture in a modest five-room flat in Harlem, abandoning for a while the house on the bit of green. Gladys was not only contented but was enthusiastic over the prospect. In my pocket was her last night's letter asking if I had yet rented the apartment. She had already planned it in her mind—here the piano on which she would play soft accompaniments while I sang "The Minute Guns at Sea"; there by the window her easel, and near it the table where her brilliant husband was to sit at night writing novels and plays and poems which would carry us not only to the green hill but to the Parnassian heights. When in the quiet of my room I had first read her letter, I had been lifted on the wave of her ardor, but now, struggle though I might to look forward to June with contentment, down in my heart I had to confess a strange uneasiness. It seemed to me that we were rushing into matrimony. With my mind revolving such problems over and over, was it a wonder that Mr. Hanks noticed my distraction and pounded the desk and spoke cuttingly of the effect of love on a man's mental balance! All that day I neglected my tasks for the study of my own engrossing business, but when evening came and I started home I was able to say to myself that I had reached a definite and unchanging conclusion—I loved Gladys Todd; like all of us, she had her peccadilloes, and yet I was not worthy of her, but I would try to be; the girl with the blue wings bobbing so majestically in her hat was not Penelope Blight.

Having reached this unchangeable decision, the very next morning, and every morning after that, I walked up Fifth Avenue with but one thought in my mind, and this was to see again a small black hat with blue wings. I became argus-eyed. I peered boldly into passing carriages, watched the foot traffic on both sides of the street, scanned the windows of dwelling-houses, and even developed a habit of looking behind me at fixed intervals that my vigilance might be still more effective. One day I went boldly into the shop which I had seen the stranger enter that day with the woman of the Pomeranian, and asked if I could have Miss Blight's address. A saleswoman, a very blond and very sinuous person who was standing by the door revolving a large hat about on one hand while she caressed its plumes daintily, replied that no Miss Blight was known there. I described her hat with the blue wings, her companion with the Pomeranian, the very hour of her visit, but my persistence brought only the information that hundreds of the shop's patronesses wore blue wings and thousands carried Pomeranians. The sinuous young woman became so cold and biting in her tone that I was sure that she believed that I had been fascinated by her own charms and was using a ruse for the pleasure of this brief interview, so I made a hasty retreat. My only clew to the owner of the blue-winged hat had failed me, and all that was left to me was to patrol the Avenue day after day, forever hoping and forever being disappointed.

June came. The five-room flat was still unrented. My daily letter from Harlansburg breathed devotion and happiness over the approach of a day as yet unset—unset because I had been rather procrastinating about arranging leave of absence from the office. Doctor and Mrs. Todd had wanted a college wedding in the chapel. They had even gone so far as to suggest appropriate music by the glee club and the seniors as ushers, but when that proposal was made to me I had found to my distress that I could not leave New York before the summer vacation had begun. June brought me, too, the very last good fortune I should have asked at that moment, an unexpected increase in my salary, and unless I lowered myself by an act of despicable cunning I could not withhold news of such good import from the future companion of my joys and sorrows. So I went uptown one night struggling hard to imagine myself supremely happy. I knew my duty—it was to be supremely happy. I should write that night to Gladys Todd and announce my coming on the 29th; to-morrow I should find the flat; the next day I should order new clothes and look at diamond pins.

I opened Miss Minion's front door with my pass-key, and as I climbed to my room I seemed to emphasize with my feet the fact that I loved Gladys Todd and was in an ecstasy of happiness. I slammed my hat down on the bureau as I vowed again that I loved Gladys Todd. Then I drew back and stared at my pin-cushion. The usual corpulent letter was not leaning there; its place had been taken by an emaciated telegram.

"Do not rent flat. Have written explanation." Such was the message to me that day.

At that moment I loved Gladys Todd, and I did not have to stamp the floor to prove it. I was sure that I had lost her, and it was the sense of my loss that made my love well up from unfathomable depths to overwhelm me. I was angry. My pride was hurt. I counted over the years of my untiring devotion to her, and they seemed to sum up the best years of my life. That the telegram foreran a more explicit statement there could be no doubt. After all she had written about the flat, her instructions that the furniture which she had inherited from her aunt must fit in, that my table must be near her easel—after all these evidences of her thought—her command could mean only that our romance was at an end and our dreams dissipated into air. There was some other man, I thought—perhaps Boller of '89—and remembering him, his picturesque garb and ridiculous pose, my own vanity was deeply cut. Until late that night I sat smoking violently and turning over in my mind the problem and all its dreadful possibilities. In bed, Sleep, the friend of woe, was long coming with her kindly ministrations, and yet held me so long under her beneficent influence that when I awoke I found lying beside my bed, tossed there through a crack in the door, the corpulent letter addressed in the tall, angular hand.

The first line reassured me. Strangely enough, being reassured, knowing that all the night's fears were silly phantasies born of a jealous mind, I fell back on my pillow and, holding the letter above my eyes, read as I had read a hundred of its fellows. Strangely enough, I said over and over to myself with grim determination that I loved Gladys Todd. From what she had written it was evident that I need have no fear that her love was not altogether mine. She believed that where two persons loved as we did, two persons who possessed each other in such perfect happiness, it was our duty to sacrifice ourselves a little for those less blessed than we were. As we gave so we received, and in giving up our summer of happiness for the happiness of others our winter would be doubly bright. I must confess that while I agreed with her as to the duty of self-sacrifice I was a little irritated when I found that our happiness must be deferred for Judge Bundy's sake. He was the last person in the world whom I had expected could have any influence on a matter so personal as the date of my marriage. Now Gladys called to my mind the recent death of his wife, and she spoke of his being ill, inconsolable, and miserably lonely. His life was at stake unless he could have a change of air and scene. His physicians had ordered for him three months' travel abroad, and he simply would not go unless Doctor and Mrs. Todd went with him. Unfortunately, Doctor and Mrs. Todd could not go without their daughter. Surely David, always self-denying, would understand. On one side was her own happiness; on the other her duty to her parents to whom had come this opportunity to see Europe, their life dream, as guests of this generous friend. It was very hard for her to have to choose. David knew, of course, what she would say were she really free to choose, but, after all, it was only for four months, and all that time I should know that, though she was far away, her eyes were turned over-sea.

I did not read the last five pages. They fluttered to the floor from my listless fingers, and I turned again to my pillow and sought the friend of woe, and again Sleep came to me with her kindly ministrations. And again I walked the Avenue, and by a modiste's door I saw a slender figure, a little, spotless, booted foot upon the step, a little, spotless, gloved hand on the rail, and a small black hat with long blue wings moving majestically.

y since we went fishing in the meadow. Mrs. Banniste back alone—will you, Mrs. Bannister?"

lid mind it very much. She was, I learned afterward, ght to the right people, and it was a violation of her Blight to allow his niece to walk in the public eye with a be the kind of a person Miss Blight should be seen with hole future depended on her following the narrow way ocial heaven. Of course she would not mind driving hat about the hats? Mr. Malcolm would pardon her mate domestic matters, but Miss Blight had been away not a hat of any kind fit to be seen in.

!" said Miss Blight.

on her chaperon's arm and pushed her gently into the ster made feeble protests. Penelope was the most wilful n and knew perfectly well that she had not a thing to ea; if she had to go home she objected to being arrested d into a prison van. The last was hurled at us as the the door, and when Mrs. Bannister fell back in the seat, Pomeranian projected his head from the window and

is a good soul," Penelope said when, side by side, hat wonderful walk uptown. "She has to be properly I should be her slave. Her husband was a broker, or and died during a panic, and as she was in straitened me to us. You see, she knows everybody, and is awfully must be very nice to her, David."

avid as naturally as though it really had been yesterday in the meadow. My heart beat quicker. I laughed aloud ving in the same world with her. I vowed that I should to Mrs. Bannister. Had Penelope asked me to be very edusa I should have given her my pledge. Subtly, by her l conveyed to me the promise that this walk was to be y walks, the rambles of our childhood over again, but ser and more sedate. Under what other circumstances rs. Bannister?

my line of conduct toward the martial woman with the n my account of the years missing in our friendship. It

CHAPTER XV

"Penelope!" I exclaimed, holding out both hands as though her joy at the meeting must match mine and she would spring forward to seize them. Then I checked my ardor, for it was the highest presumption for me to address so familiarly this woman grown, even though in years gone by she had raced with me over the fields and had ridden behind me on such a poor charger as Nathan, the white mule. "Miss Blight," I added, with a formal bow.

"I beg your pardon," she returned, implying that she had not the remotest idea who the man could be who had so boldly spoken, halted her, barred her passage from the brougham to the modiste's door.

"Don't you remember David Malcolm?" I said.

The frown fled from her face. She regarded me a moment with wide eyes. "Of course I remember David Malcolm," she cried, and, smiling, she held out a small gloved hand. "And I have seen you before at this very spot—I was sure it was you. But why didn't you speak to me then?"

"Because I was not sure," I returned, laughing aloud for the joy of this meeting. "You have changed since I saw you last, Penelope. It is hard even now to believe—"

Again I checked myself. I was looking past Penelope to the woman with the Pomeranian. Disapproval of me was so plainly evident in her eyes, she seemed in herself so far removed from mountain cabins, and if Penelope had grown worthy of such distinguished company, discretion bade me be silent.

Penelope divined my thoughts. "And it is equally hard for me to believe that this tall man is the boy I pulled out of the water." Half turning, she addressed her companion. "This is David Malcolm, Mrs. Bannister—an old, old friend of mine."

Mrs. Bannister probably had her own ideas of Penelope's old, old friends, but she was fair enough to examine me from head to foot before she condemned me with the mass of them, and then finding that, to the eyes at least, I presented no glaring crudities, she accepted me on sufferance, inclining her head and parting her lips.

"But tell me, David," said Penelope eagerly, "where have you been all these years and how do you happen to be here?"

Had I told Penelope the truth I should have replied that I happened to be there because for four long months I had been looking for her, whenever I could, walking the streets with eyes alert, even on midsummer days when I had as well searched the Sahara as the deserted town. Perhaps in thus surrendering to the hope that, after all, I should find her, I had laid myself open to a self-accusation of disloyalty to Gladys Todd; but she was far away in those months, and the daily letter had become a weekly and then a semimonthly budget, and though their tone was none the less ardent I had begun to suspect that Europe was a more attractive abiding-place than the little flat with the easel by the window. In one letter she spoke of her longing to be home; she knew that there would be music in every beat of the ship's propeller which carried her nearer me. In her next she announced her parents' decision to prolong their stay abroad on Judge Bundy's account and her regret that she could not leave them. There was something contradictory in these statements, and yet I accepted them complacently. Then postcards supplanted the semimonthly budget, and only by them was I able to follow the movements of the travellers all that autumn. One letter did come in October. It covered many sheets, but said little more than that it had been simply impossible to write oftener, but she would soon be following her heart homeward. Enclosed was a photograph of the party posed on camels with the pyramids in the background, and I noticed with a twinge of jealousy that Judge Bundy's camel had posted himself beside the beast on which Gladys was enthroned, while Doctor and Mrs. Todd had less conspicuous positions to the left and rear. Studying the judge, I laughed at my twinge of jealousy, for knowing him I could not doubt that Doctor and Mrs. Todd kept always to the left and rear, which was but right considering the generosity with which he treated them; but he looked so little the dashing Bedouin in his great derby and his frock-coat, so hot and uncomfortable that even the burning sands, the pyramids, and the curious beast which he straddled could not make of him a romantic figure.

Young Tom Marshall, who honored Miss Minion's with his presence, studying the photograph on my bureau one evening, asked me who was "the beauty with the pugree." And when I replied with pride that she was my *fiancée* he slapped my back in congratulation.

CHAPTER XV

"Penelope!" I exclaimed, holding out both hands as though her joy at the meeting must match mine and she would spring forward to seize them. Then I checked my ardor, for it was the highest presumption for me to address so familiarly this woman grown, even though in years gone by she had raced with me over the fields and had ridden behind me on such a poor charger as Nathan, the white mule. "Miss Blight," I added, with a formal bow.

"I beg your pardon," she returned, implying that she had not the remotest idea who the man could be who had so boldly spoken, halted her, barred her passage from the brougham to the modiste's door.

"Don't you remember David Malcolm?" I said.

The frown fled from her face. She regarded me a moment with wide eyes. "Of course I remember David Malcolm," she cried, and, smiling, she held out a small gloved hand. "And I have seen you before at this very spot—I was sure it was you. But why didn't you speak to me then?"

"Because I was not sure," I returned, laughing aloud for the joy of this meeting. "You have changed since I saw you last, Penelope. It is hard even now to believe—"

Again I checked myself. I was looking past Penelope to the woman with the Pomeranian. Disapproval of me was so plainly evident in her eyes, she seemed in herself so far removed from mountain cabins, and if Penelope had grown worthy of such distinguished company, discretion bade me be silent.

Penelope divined my thoughts. "And it is equally hard for me to believe that this tall man is the boy I pulled out of the water." Half turning, she addressed her companion. "This is David Malcolm, Mrs. Bannister—an old, old friend of mine."

Mrs. Bannister probably had her own ideas of Penelope's old, old friends, but she was fair enough to examine me from head to foot before she condemned me with the mass of them, and then finding that, to the eyes at least, I presented no glaring crudities, she accepted me on sufferance, inclining her head and parting her lips.

"But tell me, David," said Penelope eagerly, "where have you been all these years and how do you happen to be here?"

Had I told Penelope the truth I should have replied that I happened to be there because for four long months I had been looking for her, whenever I could, walking the streets with eyes alert, even on midsummer days when I had as well searched the Sahara as the deserted town. Perhaps in thus surrendering to the hope that, after all, I should find her, I had laid myself open to a self-accusation of disloyalty to Gladys Todd; but she was far away in those months, and the daily letter had become a weekly and then a semimonthly budget, and though their tone was none the less ardent I had begun to suspect that Europe was a more attractive abiding-place than the little flat with the easel by the window. In one letter she spoke of her longing to be home; she knew that there would be music in every beat of the ship's propeller which carried her nearer me. In her next she announced her parents' decision to prolong their stay abroad on Judge Bundy's account and her regret that she could not leave them. There was something contradictory in these statements, and yet I accepted them complacently. Then postcards supplanted the semimonthly budget, and only by them was I able to follow the movements of the travellers all that autumn. One letter did come in October. It covered many sheets, but said little more than that it had been simply impossible to write oftener, but she would soon be following her heart homeward. Enclosed was a photograph of the party posed on camels with the pyramids in the background, and I noticed with a twinge of jealousy that Judge Bundy's camel had posted himself beside the beast on which Gladys was enthroned, while Doctor and Mrs. Todd had less conspicuous positions to the left and rear. Studying the judge, I laughed at my twinge of jealousy, for knowing him I could not doubt that Doctor and Mrs. Todd kept always to the left and rear, which was but right considering the generosity with which he treated them; but he looked so little the dashing Bedouin in his great derby and his frock-coat, so hot and uncomfortable that even the burning sands, the pyramids, and the curious beast which he straddled could not make of him a romantic figure.

Young Tom Marshall, who honored Miss Minion's with his presence, studying the photograph on my bureau one evening, asked me who was "the beauty with the pugree." And when I replied with pride that she was my *fiancée* he slapped my back in congratulation.

"And Julius Caesar," he went on—"Caesar visiting his African dominions is, I suppose, her father, and the little fellow in the top-hat his favorite American slave, and—"

With great dignity I explained to young Marshall the relations of the members of this Oriental group. At his suggestion that I had best take the first steamer for Egypt I laughed. The implication was so absurd that I even told Gladys Todd about it in my next letter to her, for I still sat down every Saturday night and wrote to her voluminously of all that I had been doing. Yet I was growing conscious of a sense of her unreality. I seemed to be corresponding with the inhabitant of another planet, and when I looked at the girl on the camel, with the strange pugree flowing from her hat, and the pyramids in the background, it seemed that she could not be the same simple girl who had painted tulips on black plaques.

Penelope Blight was a much more concrete figure. At any moment as I walked the Avenue she might come around the corner, or step from a brougham, or be looking at me from the windows of a brown-stone mansion. Was it a wonder that my eyes were always alert? One morning three lines in a newspaper convinced me at last that the girl with the blue feathers was Penelope Blight. They announced that Rufus Blight, the Pittsburgh steel magnate, had bought a house on Fifth Avenue and would thereafter make New York his home. That night the city seemed more my own home than ever before and the future to hold for me more than the past had promised. The drawn curtains of this house might be hiding Penelope from me; she might be in the dark corner of that smart carriage flying northward; even the slender figure coming toward me through the yellow gloom, with her muff pressed against her face to guard it from the November wind, might be she. And when on the next afternoon—by chance, it seemed, as by chance it seems all our lives are ordered—when at last by the same modiste's shop the same smart brougham drew up at the curb, the same haughty footman opened the door, and I saw the very same blue wings, I knew that I had found Penelope at last and I spoke without fear.

She asked me what I had been doing all these years. I laughed joyfully, but I did not tell her. For all these years I had been working for this moment!

"What have I been doing?" I said. "Why, Penelope, it would take me forever to tell you."

"You must begin telling me right now," she returned quickly. "You must walk home with me to tea and I can hear all about it as we go. To me it seems just yesterday since we went fishing in the meadow. Mrs. Bannister won't mind driving back alone—will you, Mrs. Bannister?"

Mrs. Bannister did mind it very much. She was, I learned afterward, introducing Miss Blight to the right people, and it was a violation of her contract with Rufus Blight to allow his niece to walk in the public eye with a man who might not be the kind of a person Miss Blight should be seen with at a time when her whole future depended on her following the narrow way which leads to the social heaven. Of course she would not mind driving home alone, but what about the hats? Mr. Malcolm would pardon her mentioning such intimate domestic matters, but Miss Blight had been away all summer and had not a hat of any kind fit to be seen in.

"Bother the hats!" said Miss Blight.

She laid a hand on her chaperon's arm and pushed her gently into the carriage. Mrs. Bannister made feeble protests. Penelope was the most wilful girl she had ever seen and knew perfectly well that she had not a thing to wear to the Perkins tea; if she had to go home she objected to being arrested this way and clapped into a prison van. The last was hurled at us as the footman was closing the door, and when Mrs. Bannister fell back in the seat, angry and silent, the Pomeranian projected his head from the window and snapped at us.

"Mrs. Bannister is a good soul," Penelope said when, side by side, we were away on that wonderful walk uptown. "She has to be properly handled though or I should be her slave. Her husband was a broker, or something like that, and died during a panic, and as she was in straitened circumstances she came to us. You see, she knows everybody, and is awfully well connected. You must be very nice to her, David."

She called me David as naturally as though it really had been yesterday that we went fishing in the meadow. My heart beat quicker. I laughed aloud for the sheer joy of living in the same world with her. I vowed that I should be very nice indeed to Mrs. Bannister. Had Penelope asked me to be very nice to her friend Medusa I should have given her my pledge. Subtly, by her admonition, she had conveyed to me the promise that this walk was to be but the first of many walks, the rambles of our childhood over again, but grown older and wiser and more sedate. Under what other circumstances could I be nice to Mrs. Bannister?

Having settled my line of conduct toward the martial woman with the Pomeranian, I began my account of the years missing in our friendship. It was very brief. It is astonishing in how few words a man can sum up his life's accomplishment if he holds to the essential facts. Since that day when she had left the farm with Rufus Blight I had studied under Mr. Pound, spent four years in college and three years working on a newspaper. Was I successful in my work? she asked. Fairly so, I answered modestly. I might have told her that I had gone ahead a little faster than my fellows, but even then seemed to advance at a snail's pace to petty conquests, for if at the end of years I attained to Hanks's place, I was beginning to doubt that it was worth the pains which I was taking to win it. I did not tell her of the ambitions which had led me into my profession, nor how all my fine ideas had been early dissipated and I had settled down to a struggle for mere existence. On one essential fact, too, was I silent. It arose to my mind as I told my brief story and it spread like a cloud darkening this brightest of my days. You know what the shadow was. By her absence, by her remoteness, Gladys Todd had for me a shadow's unreality. At this moment the tie between us was so attenuated that it was hard for me to believe that it existed at all. I knew that it did exist, but I could not surrender myself to be bound by so frail a thread. I was silent. Childlike, I wished the clouds away. Royally, I commanded the sea to stand back.

"And you—what have you been doing all these years?" I asked, turning suddenly to Penelope.

"Just growing up," she answered, laughing. "It's very easy to grow up when one has such a kind uncle as mine. You remember the poverty in which he found me. I was a mere charity child, and he took me—"

"To his lively, pushing town," said I.

"Yes," Penelope went on, "to a big stone house with a green lawn about it dotted with queer figures in iron and marble. They were the most beautiful things I had ever seen—those statues. Now they are all stored in the stable, for we grew up, uncle and I, even in matters of art. But it was like heaven to me then, after the mountains and the smoky cabin, after the clearing and the weeds—"

"After our farm," I broke in with a touch of irony, "and to ride behind the fast trotters compared with our farm wagon—"

"David," returned Penelope in a voice of reproach, "I have never forgotten the mountains, or the cabin, or the farm. In the first days away from them I was terribly homesick for them all. My uncle suffered for it. His patience and his kindness were unfailing, and he softened me at last. There is nothing in the world that I have wanted that he has not given me."

I was silent. The old boyish dislike of Rufus Blight had never died. I could think of him only as a sleek, vulgar man who by the force of his money had taken Penelope from me. His money had raised her far above my reach, and even the cloud which shadowed this day which might have been my brightest seemed to have had its birth in vapors of his gold-giving furnaces. That I had forgotten Penelope and entangled myself in the cords of a foolish sentimentality I charged to him, and Penelope, seeing how I walked, silent, with eyes grimly set ahead, divined that I still nourished the aversion to which in my childish petulance I had given vent so long ago.

"You are still prejudiced against poor Uncle Rufus, I see," she said, smiling. "I remember how badly you treated him that day when he came to take me away."

"Yes, I never have forgiven him," I snapped out. "He may have reason, and justice, and saintliness on his side, yet I never can forgive him."

"Oh, yes, you can," said Penelope with an indulgent laugh. "You will when you come to know him as I do. You must, for my sake."

"Perhaps, for your sake," said I, relenting a little.

"I knew you would for my sake, David," said Penelope. "Why, I owe everything I have in the world to him. Since he has retired, sold his works to a trust, I think they call it, his whole life seems to be to look after me. Pittsburgh isn't much of a place for a man who has no business; so we thought we should try New York for a while, and we bought the house last spring and spent the summer in Bar Harbor. Now we are just settling down."

I was hardly listening as she spoke, for my mind was occupied by Rufus Blight. He had reason and justice on his side. That much I surrendered to him, but I clung obstinately to my dislike. I thought of the Professor flying over the clearing to the hiding of the mountains; I remembered him in the college hall, with his bitter words pointing the way from which his own weakness held him back, the man whose imagination ranged so far while his hands were idle. I pictured his brother grown fat and happy at the trough of gold at which he fed, and even had I not felt a personal feud with Rufus Blight, my sympathy for the under-dog must have aroused my antipathy. But I hated him for my own sake. For every foolish step that I had taken since that day when he had carried Penelope away the fault seemed to have been his as much as mine, and yet I was wise enough to see that if I would hold Penelope's regard it would be very rash to show by word or deed that I nursed any resentment.

"For your sake I will, Penelope," I said.

So soft and satisfied was the smile with which she rewarded me that I vowed to myself that I really would forgive my old archenemy. A moment before it had been on my lips to speak of my confiscated letters, for I had no doubt that Rufus Blight had intercepted them. Now I realized that in them was a mine which I might fire only to shatter our new-found friendship. That treachery, too, I said, I should forgive. When Penelope set the light to the fuse, I with rare presence of mind stamped out the flames and prevented a disaster.

We had passed Fiftieth Street, and I was telling her of my last visit home, of my father and mother, of Mr. Pound, and of all the friends of our younger days, when she suddenly turned to me. It was as though the question had for some time been hanging on her lips. "David, why did you never answer the letters I wrote you?"

"Because." I was playing for time. To carry out my plan of silence, it seemed that I must deceive her, and I hesitated to tell her an untruth.

"Because why?" she insisted.

"Because I never received them," I answered, cheered by the thought that thus far I could tell her the truth. "Did you really write to me?"

"Many times," she said; "until I got tired of writing and receiving no answer. You made me very angry."

"The letters must have been lost in the mail," said I, bent on keeping this disagreeable subject in the background. "Country post-offices are very careless in the way they handle things, and mine to you—my letters—must have gone astray too."

"Then you did write to me as you promised, David?" she exclaimed.

"Until I got tired of receiving no answer," I returned, laughing. "But of course it is too late to complain to the government now."

Penelope was not satisfied. Her brows were knitted. I believed that there lurked in her mind a suspicion that not the government alone was concerned in the interruption of that early correspondence, but I was determined to ignore a subject which, if too closely pressed, might bring about unpleasant consequences. The easiest way was to turn the trend of her thought with a bold question, which had been hanging on my lips through many blocks of the walk. And so, as casually as though I inquired of her about some distant friend or relative, I spoke of her father.

Penelope stopped short and laid a hand upon my arm. Then as suddenly she strode ahead.

"I know nothing of him, David," she said in a voice almost harsh. "I have not seen him since that dreadful day in the clearing. Once I heard from him—a few lines—but that was so long ago that at times I almost forget that I ever had a father."

"What did he write to you, Penelope?"

She seemed not to hear my question, for she was walking very fast, with her eyes set straight ahead of her. "He might pass me at this minute, David, and I should not know him. That might be he, standing by that window, and I should be none the wiser, yet the fault is his. I try always to think of him as I should, but at times it seems as though he had disowned me, abandoned me on his brother's doorstep and then run away. You ask of the letter. It came to me soon after I left the farm. He said that it was best that my uncle should have me, better than to condemn me to shift about the world with him; he said that he had been a lazy, worthless creature, but he was going to do something, to be somebody—those were his words; and some day, when I could be proud of him, he would come back and claim me, and, David, he has never come. Will he ever come, do you think?"

"I think he will," I answered. "For I have seen him."

"You have seen him!" The hand was on my arm again, and, forgetful of the hurrying crowd around us, we stood there face to face, while I told her of the brief glimpse I had had of him four years before. She listened, breathless, and, when I had finished, walked on in silence.

We were crossing the Plaza when she spoke again, half to me, half ruminating. "Poor father! He must have tried and failed. He was going to Tibet, David, you told me; that was four years ago. Where can he be now? Wandering around the world alone, in want, perhaps, and I have everything. Do you suppose he believes that I have forgotten him—as if I could forget those evenings when we sat together and painted pictures of the times when we should be rich! He called me the princess and planned great houses in which we should live, and he would talk of our travels and the wonderful places we should see together. Even then I had faith that our dreams would come true, though it did seem that we were getting poorer and poorer all the time, and father doing nothing to help our plight. The dreams came true, David—for me. Why doesn't he come and share them with me, with me and Uncle Rufus? That is what troubles me; that is what I can never understand."

I said to myself that Rufus Blight, were he so minded, could clear the mystery away. I thought of him as a selfish, arrogant man, who was, perhaps, too well satisfied not to have an undesirable third person in his household to undertake any sincere search for his brother. But these thoughts I concealed. There was something behind it all that we two could not understand, I said, and Penelope looked up to me with clouded eyes.

"But we will find him, Penelope!" My stick hit the pavement as I registered a vow. "We will find him—you and I."

"How like the little David you are," she cried, and then smiling light broke through the clouded eyes. "We shall try to find him, anyway, shall we not—to bring father home. For look, David!" She had halted. The small gloved hand was lifted, and the blue wings in her hat moved with an old-time majesty. "There is the palace we dreamed of!"

CHAPTER XVI

Penelope and I were standing before a great gray-stone house. I carried my eyes from the doors of iron grill-work over the severe breadth of wall, broken only by rank above rank of windows so heavily curtained that one might have suspected those within to live in darkness, fearing even to face the sunlight. I laughed. When I had been searching for the girl with the blue feathers in her hat, I had never given this house more than a passing glance, deeming it altogether too palatial in its size and too severe in its aspect to shield a man of so garish a mind as I attributed to Rufus Blight, judging him from memory alone. I should have placed him rather next door to it, behind the over-ornate Moorish front and had him look out on the world through curtains of elaborately figured lace. But within, I now said to myself, I shall find the expression of the man in a riot of color in walls and hangings and in ill-assorted mobs of furniture. Here again I was wrong. We passed the grilled doors into a place so gray and cold that it might have led us to a cloister. We mounted broad stairs, our footfalls muffled by a heavy carpeting of so unobtrusive a color that I cannot name it. We crossed a white panelled hall, so sparsely furnished that the untutored might have thought that the family were just moving in or just moving out. Penelope pushed through heavy portières and we stood at last in a room that seemed designed for human habitation. But it was the design of an alien mind, not of the owner. The owner had not been allowed to fit it to himself as he would his clothes. The alien mind had said: You do not know; you must allow me to arrange your habitat. Here I have placed the wonderful old fireplace which I bought for you in France, and above it the Reynolds for which you paid forty thousand dollars; here in the centre is the carved table which I got for you in Florence, and geometrically arranged about its corners are books of travel; with its back to it, a great divan covered with most expensive leather, so that you can lounge in its depths and watch the fire. Around it I have arranged sundry other chairs done in deep-green velour to tone in with the walls, and along the walls are bookcases, fronted with diamond panes and filled with leather-bound volumes—for this, sir, is your library.

The room was so perfect that Mrs. Bannister, seated before the fire, brewing herself a lonely cup of tea, seemed a jarring note. She would have been as much in place in a corner of the *Galerie-de-Glace* at Versailles, and but for her presence and her domestic occupation I might have said to myself after a languid survey, "So, this is where the king lounged"—then waited to be led on.

Mrs. Bannister was expecting us. She spoke as though in having tea waiting she had acted in the forlorn hope that some time we might return, and as though for hours she had been a prey to the gravest apprehensions, for Penelope's safety. In bringing Penelope back at all I had in some degree allayed the hostility with which she at first regarded me, but though she was now outwardly quite cordial, I was conscious that over the top of her cup she was studying me closely as I sat on the divan stirring my tea and striving to be thoroughly at home. Her subtle scrutiny made me very uncomfortable. She asked me questions with an obvious purpose of putting me at my ease, and I answered in embarrassed monosyllables. Whether I would or no, I seemed constantly to slide to the perilous edge of my seat, and no matter what care I used, I strewed crumbs over the rug until it seemed to me that my bit of cake had a demoniacal power of multiplying itself.

I was angry—this hour, this formal passage of inane conversation, was so different from what I had pictured my first meeting with Penelope to be. I was angry at my weakness in letting this perfect room overpower me, and this woman of the world, with no other weapon than the knowledge of the people one should know, transfix me, silence me, transform me into a dull, bucolic boor. Penelope was annoyed. I knew that she was chagrined at my lack of *savoir faire*, for in one of the long pauses following an abrupt response of mine I caught a glance of mute despair. She seemed to accuse me of falling short of her expectations by my lamentable lack of the social graces.

I was for flight then. I rose to go. I paused to dispute in my mind whether I must say farewell first to the older or the younger woman, and from the hopelessness of ever solving the question I might have stood there for an hour pulling at my hands had not the portières opened and Rufus Blight come in.

I should not have known him as Rufus Blight but for Penelope's joyous hail. I had expected to see him as I saw him that day when he came to the farm to take Penelope away—a short, fat, pompous man with a bristling red mustache and a hand that moved interminably; a sleek man in spotless, creaseless clothes who might have stood in his own show-window to inspire his fellows to sartorial perfection. I saw, instead, a small man, rather thin, and slightly bald. The bristling red mustache had turned to gray and drooped. His whole figure drooped. His black clothes hung in many careless creases, and as he came forward it was not with his old quick, all-conquering step, but haltingly, as though Mrs. Bannister owned the room and he doubted if he were welcome. I lost my embarrassment in wonder. I recalled my old fond pictures of Rufus Blight when he should have grown older and fatter, more pompous and more all-commanding. I watched the little dusty man draw Penelope's head down to him and kiss her. I looked around the room, at the great fireplace, at the Reynolds, at the carved table and the costly empty spaces, and I lost myself in the marvel that he should have attained them.

"Uncle Rufus," Penelope said, drawing him toward me, "here is some one you will be glad to see. It's David Malcolm, my old friend David Malcolm."

"Why, David Malcolm—my old friend, too," cried Mr. Blight, his face lighting genially as he took my hand. "The boy who wouldn't let me have Penelope. Upon my word, David, I didn't blame you."

He laughed and shook my hand again and again. He asked after my father and mother as though they were his dearest friends, and I contrasted his cordial mention of them with his once cavalier treatment, but when he made me sit beside him on the divan and meet and answer a rapid fire of questions as to myself and my occupation, the old prejudices began to disappear before his simple, unaffected kindness. Penelope was on his other side, and her hand was in his. I forgave him. I forgot the neglect of long ago. I forgot even the mystery of the letters. I forgot the fat, pompous, all-commanding man. This was a meeting of three rare old friends. Mrs. Bannister, too, had gone from my thoughts. If she still regarded me over the top of her cup, I was unconscious of it, for I was telling how I had come to meet Penelope again, and he was recalling the day when, as a small boy, I had resisted him so vigorously.

"It has all turned out well, eh, David?" Rufus Blight said, laying a hand upon my knee. "Here we are—the three of us—just as if we had never quarrelled—good friends; and it is good to find old friends. We haven't many old friends, Penelope and I. Indeed, but for Mrs. Bannister"—he bowed to the majestic woman—"we should have few new ones. An old one recovered is too precious to lose; and we are not going to lose you again—are we, Penelope?"

The color shot high on Penelope's cheeks as she laughingly assented, and I flattered myself that she had forgotten the boor who a few moments before had shown to such disadvantage under Mrs. Bannister's critical eye.

"You must come to us often," Rufus Blight pursued. "I shall be glad to see you any time. It is good to have an old friend about when time hangs so heavily on one's hands as it does on mine. Never go out of business, David. Take warning from me, and don't let yourself be stranded, with nothing to do but to play golf. Golf is a poor occupation. I was out to-day—couldn't find a soul around the club—had to take on the professional—spoiled my score by getting into the brook on the tenth hole, and came home utterly miserable and dissatisfied with life. But when you get well wetted you appreciate the kitchen stove, as old Bill Hansen, in our town, used to say—eh, Mrs. Bannister?"

From this I surmised that Mr. Blight as well as the ball had gone into the brook, and in the homely aphorism I divined a subtle purpose to bait Mrs. Bannister, which showed an astonishing courage in so mild-mannered a little man. Such was the awe in which I held Mrs. Bannister that I could have loved any one who dared in her presence to acknowledge an acquaintance with old Bill Hansen. If Mrs. Bannister did disapprove, she was careful not to show it. Her lips parted in a half smile and she observed to me that Mr. Blight had a jovial way of quoting Mr. Hansen, as though Mr. Hansen were his dearest friend.

"He is," declared Mr. Blight. "To be sure, I haven't seen him for years, but I always remember him as the wisest man I ever knew. Why, if it wasn't for Penelope I should go back to the valley, just to be near him. It would be better than golf—to sit with him on the store porch on a sunny day listening to the mill rumbling by the creek and the killdee whistling in the meadow, to watch the shadows crawl along the mountains, and now and then to hear Bill Hansen say something. That would be living—eh, David?"

Rufus Blight touched a train of thought which had been often in my mind. Here was a man who had won in the great fight and he seemed to be camping now on the field which he had taken. About him were the spoils—the Reynolds, the fireplace, the perfectly bound books, and the costly spaces of the great room. Yet he was voicing the same longing that I, whose fight was just beginning, had often felt—the longing to step aside from the struggle for vain things, the longing to turn from the smoke and grime of the conflict to the quiet and peace of the valley. Now I voiced that longing too, forgetting Mrs. Bannister and her evident creed that man's chief end was to know the right people.

"It would be living, indeed," I said with enthusiasm. "More than once I have been on the point of going back to stay. I don't suppose you ever knew my old friend Stacy Shunk, did you? When it comes to real wisdom I'd rather talk to Stacy Shunk than—"

Mrs. Bannister had half risen—I thought in horror. It was really the butler who had brought my eulogy of Stacy Shunk to a sudden close, for, appearing in half-drawn portières, he announced: "Mr. Talcott."

The mere entrance of Mr. Talcott carried us far from the valley and such rude associates as old Bill Hansen and his kind. I think that even Rufus Blight would have been too discreet to refer to them in his presence—for Penelope's sake, if nothing else. He was a slender young man of medium height, clean-shaven, perfectly groomed, and perfectly mannered. He was as much at ease as I had been ill at ease, and I envied him for it. He declined tea because he had just come from the club, and I envied him this delightful way of avoiding cake and embarrassing crumbs. Mrs. Bannister addressed him as Herbert, and I knew at once that he was Edward Herbert Talcott, whose name I had often seen in my paper-reading task. His claim to distinction was descent from the man whose name he bore, a member of the cabinet of one of our early presidents. A dead statesman in a family is always a valuable asset, and the longer dead the better. Statesmen, like wines, must be hidden away in vaults long years to be properly mellowed for social uses. I think that Mr. Secretary Talcott would have been astonished, indeed, could he have measured his influence after a century by the numbers, collateral and direct, who were proud to use his name. There were Talcott Joneses, and Talcott Robinsons, and Talcott Browns by the score in town, but one and all they acknowledged the primacy of this Edward Herbert Talcott, and never lost an opportunity of speaking of him as their cousin. He had written, I learned afterward, a monograph on his great-grandfather, which had given him a certain literary distinction in his own set, and it was generally understood that, while he might easily have earned a livelihood by his pen, he had been relieved of the necessity of doing it by his ancestors' investments in Harlem real estate.

Talcott looked perfectly inoffensive, and yet he had hardly been seated before I conceived a profound aversion to him. Mrs. Bannister's treatment of him did much to arouse it. Here, she seemed to say, is a human being, a sentient creature with ideas in his head, a finished man with an appreciation of the finer things of life. She asked him if he was going to the Martin dance.

Mr. Talcott did not know—he might—he hadn't made up his mind.

"There will probably be a rather mixed crowd," he said, with his lips twitching into a cynical smile.

Rufus Blight, who had moved to a chair by the fire, shook his head in disapproval of mixed crowds, and Mrs. Bannister said that, nevertheless, the Martins were getting along and certainly would get in.

"And sometimes, you know, mixed crowds are rather fun," said Talcott; and turning to Penelope: "I suppose you are not going?"

"I certainly am," Penelope answered heartily. "I love dancing so."

"Well, I shall, then," said Talcott. "You see, I was up awfully late at the Coles's last night—three o'clock when I left. Why did you go so early? I looked for you everywhere. I rather thought I should lay off to-night and rest up for a dinner, the opera, and the Grants to-morrow evening. But I'll go to-night anyway. We'll get up a little crowd of our own for supper. That's the thing about mixed crowds: at least you can have your own little set for supper."

Having settled this problem and taken possession of Penelope for that evening, Talcott went on to outline a jolly little plan of his to take possession of her for an entire day in the near future—as soon as there was skating at Tuxedo. Quite a large party were going up, Bobby This and Willie That, to all of which Penelope assented, while Mrs. Bannister laughed merrily. She understood that Bobby This was not going anywhere this year. Between them they drove me quite mad. A moment ago I had been so much at home; now I should have been more at ease in a company of astronomers talking of the stars, though I knew nothing of the heavens. I could only smile vaguely in a pretence of entering into all that they were saying; and when Talcott looked at me, when he pronounced his dictum that mixed crowds were a bore, I gave a feeble assent. When, to make my presence felt, I boldly asserted that I had never been to Tuxedo, Talcott replied that some time I must go there—I should like it—he was sure that I should like it, though the crowd was getting rather mixed. Having thus quieted me, he reverted to Bar Harbor and the summer, to various persons and events concerning which I was supremely ignorant. I left abruptly perhaps. I had forgotten the problem as to whom I should say my farewell last. Penelope said that I must come again and often. Mrs. Bannister gave me a pleasant but, I thought, a condescending smile, and Rufus Blight followed me down the stairs, talking platitudes about the weather while he called a man to bring my coat and hat.

The grilled door closed behind me, and I walked down the darkening street. I had found Penelope grown lovelier than the loveliest figure of my boyish dreams. Yet it was as though I had found her in another world than mine, and moving among another race. She might remember the boy whom she had dragged from the mountain stream, the boy whom she had carried to the desolation of her humble home; could she long remember the awkward man who sat on the edge of his chair and scattered crumbs, who when he talked could talk only of old Bill Hansen and Stacy Shunk? The longing for the valley was gone. Had the world been mine I would have given it for a card to the dance that night, however mixed the crowd, for then I should be near her. If I would be near her, then her friends must be my friends, and, whether they would or no, I swore that day they should be.

The hall of Miss Minion's house smelled terribly of cooking that night as I passed through it. Standing at last in my own narrow room, I brought my clinched fist down on my table as I registered my vow that I would attain to her world. Then I sank down and covered my face with my hands, for out of the little frame Gladys Todd was looking at me.

CHAPTER XVII

When I sat again on the great divan, I said to myself that, after all, the alien mind who designed this room had worked with cunning; he must have seen in his fancy the very picture that was now so delightful to my eyes—the gray old fireplace with its tall columns wound with vines whose delicate leaves quivered as the firelight fanned them; before it Penelope, a slender figure, softly drawn in the evening's shadow, bent over the low tea-table as she worked with the rebellious lamp; from above, looking down kindly, half smiling, Reynolds's majestic lady, frilled and furbelowed; at her feet a giant white bear, its long claws gripping the polished floor, its jaws distended fiercely as though it stood guard, ready to spring at him who dared to cross the charmed circle drawn by the glowing coals. I sat in the half-darkness, for it was late in the day, and but a single shaded lamp burned in a distant corner. What was new in the room grew old under the wizard touch of shadows. The mahogany bookcases stretched away on either hand, and there were cobwebs on the diamond panes and dust on the ancient tomes. Penelope was in her home! A hundred years ago that majestic lady in frills and furbelows sat by this same fireplace, in that same old carved chair, making tea, and now she smiled with great content as from her frame she looked down on this child of her blood and bone. And the ancestor who had gathered those dusty volumes—what of him? Two hundred years it was, perhaps, since he had burrowed among the cobwebs, now caressing his rare old Horace, now turning the yellow pages of his learned treatise on astrology. He was a distinguished figure in his wig, his velvet coat and smallclothes, and something of his features, refined by intellectual pursuit, I read in the face that now was turned to mine. For blood does tell. Father Time is a reckless artist, clipping and cutting and recasting incessantly, and producing an appalling number of failures; but now and then it would seem that he did take some pains and, studying his models, combine the broad, low brow of this one with another's straight and finely chiselled nose, and still another's smoothly rounded cheek; and sometimes, in his cynical way, he will spoil it all with a pair of coarse hands borrowed from one of his rustic figures or the large, flat feet of some study of peasant life, which we should have thought cast away and forgotten. In Penelope we were offended by none of these grotesque fragments. They must have been long since cleared out of her ancestral line. When she raised herself after her battle with the rebellious lamp, it was with the grace of unconscious pride, with the majesty of the lady in the frame, but finer drawn, thanks to the thin old gentleman of the books, who had overfed his mind and bequeathed to his descendants a legacy of nerves.

This Penelope Blight, daintily clothed in soft black webs woven for her by a hundred toiling human spiders, was not even the Penelope Blight of my wildest boyish dreams. Our dreams are circumscribed by our experience, and in those days it had been inconceivable to me that she should grow more lovely than Miss Mincer, the butcher's daughter, and I had pictured myself walking proudly through the streets of Malcolmville at the side of a tall, slender girl, her head crowned by a glazed black hat, her body incased in a tight-fitting jersey. This Penelope Blight in the carved chair where generations of her grandmothers had made tea before her, by the stately fireplace at which her forebears had warmed their hands and hearts, could have no kin with the barefooted girl who had stood with me at the edge of the clearing and, pointing over the weeds to the forlorn cabin, called it home.

Was it a wonder that my tone was formal; that, overcome by a sense of estrangement, I talked of the weather as I sipped my tea; that I asked her if she had enjoyed last night's dance, speaking as though dancing were my own favorite amusement; that when I pronounced her name it was in a halting, embarrassed undertone? Even speaking, it thus seemed gross presumption. How unlikely, then, that I should refer to by-gone days in her presence when it was incredible that there had ever been days like those! In all probability she would draw herself up and reply that I must be thinking of some other Penelope Blight, that to her I was nothing more than a formal creature whom she had met somewhere, where she could not remember, a man like hundreds of others whom she knew, lay figures for the tailor's art, who spoke only a language limited to the last dance and the one to come. Believing this, I finished my tea, and, putting down my cup, I abandoned my one resource when conversation lagged. Why had I come at all?

I had come to sit with Penelope, just as we were sitting now, in the shadows, in the firelight. At home we had often sat together on the back steps, in the shadows of the valley, in the firelight of the clouds glowing in the last sun flames. Now we should be, as then, good comrades, and freely as I had talked to her then as from our humble perch we watched the departing day, so freely could I talk to her now in the statelier environment. In that short walk uptown I had left a thousand things unsaid. But one special thing I had left unsaid, one vital fact in my life unrevealed, that was of paramount importance. In the excitement of our first meeting my silence had been discretion, but discretion became deception as time passed, and every day was adding to its sum. Sometimes I could forget the vital fact. Sometimes at night in my room, sitting with my book at my side neglected, I would stare vacantly at the wall and treat myself to a feast of dreams, contentedly munch the most delicate morsels of the past and present. And by right of that past and present it was almost fore-ordained that Penelope and I were to go down the years together. Then I would remember. I would start from my chair with a despairing laugh and pace up and down my narrow room, restless and unhappy. I knew that I could not long delay revealing to Penelope the paramount fact, and in revealing it to her I seemed to say that after all she was only a casual friend, that all my life's interest was bound up in Gladys Todd, and my life's ambition expressed in a room with an easel by the window, a bird's-eye-maple mantel, and around the walls a rack for odd lots of china and black-framed prints. It was hard to tell her that, but I knew that I must, and I said that I should talk freely as in the old days of brotherly confidence, as though of all others she would be happiest in hearing of my good fortune. With my mind made up to face boldly this bad situation, I could not crush the consoling hope that in hearing she would give some sign of the pain of the wound that I was making. What a fatuous illusion! In her presence, in an environment which made that which I planned for myself seem so narrow and commonplace, she became a spirit thoroughly alien. I could as easily have talked to some foreign princess of the blood of Mr. Pound or Stacy Shunk. I could as easily have announced to Mrs. Bannister that I was engaged to Gladys Todd. And I must have gone away, fled ignominiously after one cup of tea, had not Penelope, with a sudden impatient movement, turned her chair and leaned forward with her chin cupped in her hands, as she used to sit in the old days on the back steps, with her eyes fixed on mine.

"David," she said, "did you really come here to talk to me about the weather or to tell me things I really want to know—of Mr. Pound, of Miss Spinner and Stacy Shunk. Who drives the stage now?"

I was on the edge of the divan, my hands playing an imaginary game of cat's-cradle when she spoke, and now I pushed back into the comfortable depths and stared at her in surprise. I was amazed at hearing this princess of the blood descend to an interest in such plebeians. She, seeing that I was silent, leaned back too, each small hand gripping an arm of that throne-like chair.

"Well?" she said; and when still I was silent she repeated more insistently: "Well, David?" Then raising her voice a little to a tone of command: "I asked you who drives the stage."

I forgot the carved chair and Reynolds's majestic lady. I forgot the imposing fireplace and the old gentleman in wig and smallclothes. I laughed with the sheer joy of being with Penelope again. I forgot even the great divan and made a futile effort to jump it nearer her in my burst of enthusiasm for our new-born friendship.

"Why, Joe Hicks," I said. "You remember Joe Hicks, Penelope?"

"Joe Hicks," she said, pronouncing the name as though it were that of some dear friend suddenly dragged out of the by-gone years. "Surely not the same Joe Hicks who used to let us ride with him sometimes from Malcolmville out to the farm?"

"The same Joe Hicks," said I, and with a strange disregard for forms and effects I gave way to a natural desire of hunger and dived at the curate's delight, forgetting entirely the crumb-begetting habits of cake. "Try one of those," I went on, indicating the topmost plate, and to my delight she helped herself, almost with avidity. "You remember, Penelope, how we used to loiter near the kitchen when we smelled cake in the oven?"

Then Penelope laughed as though in the sheer joy of casting years away and living over her childhood.

"Indeed I do," she returned. "But we were speaking of Joe Hicks. You surprised me. He was an old man when we knew him."

"He was seventy then. He is still seventy," I returned. "Stage-driving, you know, is conducive—"

"I used to think I'd like to be a stage-driver when I grew up," she interrupted. "You would see so much of the world with so little trouble, just holding the reins as the horses ambled along. How our ideas change, David!"

It was on the old and unchanged ideas that I wanted to dwell. The new would bring me back all too quickly to ancestral portraits, to imposing fireplaces and costly bear-skin rugs. I assented readily to her self-evident proposition and brushed it aside for the most interesting matter of Joseph Hicks.

"You used to love to drive," I said. "I can see you now wheedling Joe into letting you have the reins. Don't you remember his telling you that no self-respecting woman was ever seen driving more than one horse?"

"How shocked he would be could he see how I handle four," she said.

Should we never get out of the shadow of costly things, out of the clutch of changed ideas? For a moment I had a picture of Penelope on the box of a coach, ribbons and whip in hand, with four smart cobs stepping to the music of jingling harness, with bandy-legged grooms on the boot, and beside her some perfectly tailored creature in a glistening top-hat. It was a gallant picture, and one in which there was no part for me. Metaphorically I hurled at it a missile of the common clay of which, after all, we were both made. Surely fishing was a subject on which her ideas could not change.

"Do you remember the great expeditions we used to have along the creek?" I said.

"Remember them? Why, David, I never could forget such days as those." She leaned forward, with her hands clasped in her lap, as though to bring herself into closer touch with the kindred spirit on the divan. "I often laugh over the time I caught the big turtle on my hook. You remember—we were on the bridge at the end of the meadow, and I thought I had captured a whale, and when I saw it I was so astonished that I went head-first into the water."

"And I dived after you," I cried excitedly, "into two feet of water and three feet of mud."

"And we both ran home soaking wet and covered with green slime," she went on rapidly. "Will you ever forget her look when mother—"

"Mother?" There was in my exclamation a note of surprise in which was almost lost the delight I felt in her use of that word.

She caught the surprise alone, and spoke now as though offended at what she thought my protest. "Yes, mother. Why, David, don't you remember I always called her mother? And she was the only mother I ever knew—even if only for a brief summer."

"I was glad, Penelope," I said. "Yet you surprised me just a little, because I feared that so much had come into your life you might have forgotten—"

"Forgotten?" she returned with a gesture of impatience. "You do not grant me much heart if you think I could ever forget those who took me in when I was homeless, the mother who tucked me into bed every night, who taught me the first prayer I ever uttered." She paused for a moment, and sat with her eyes fixed on her clasped hands. I, too, was silent. Suddenly she looked up. "You are right, David; I had forgotten. I was ungrateful, too; but seeing you again and talking with you has brought those days very near to me. When I have thought of your father and mother it was as though they lived in another world, as though, if I would, I could never see them, they were so far away." She leaned back in her chair and broke into a little laugh. "How foolish of me! Why, David, we shall go to see them—you and I and Uncle Rufus. We shall go very soon, David." Her slender figure was clear-cut in the firelight and a hand was held out to me in invitation.

Had the world been mine to give, how gladly would I have lost it for the right to answer her as she asked; to go with her and to walk by the creek to that deep sea of our childhood where she had caught the turtle; to ride with her again over the mountain road where we had careered so madly on the white mule; to sit with her on the humble back steps and watch the sun sink into the mountains, and listen to the sheep in the meadow, the night-hawk in the sky, the rustle of the wind in the trees—to the valley's lullaby. From this I was held by the vital fact still unrevealed. I folded my arms and looked at the floor, to shut from my eyes the idle vision of the days to which Penelope would lead me, to shut from them Penelope herself sitting very straight, with head high, so that I had fancied the blue bow tossing there.

"We'll go in May," she said with a sweep of a small hand, as though our great adventure were settled. "We will go when the orchards are in blossom, David. The valley is loveliest then."

To go in May! To go when the hills were clad in the pink and white! To sit with her on the grassy barn-bridge in the evening as we had sat in the old days watching the mountains sink into the night, listening to the last faint echoes of the valley as she turned to restful sleep. Had the universe been mine to give, I would have bartered it for the power to answer her as she asked. Such joys as these I dared not even dream of now, but still I had not the strength to cut myself forever from the last faint hope of them. I looked up into her face aglow with prospect of a return to those simple, kindly days; into her eyes, kindled with that same light that glowed in them in the old time when she would slip her hands so trustingly in mine as we trudged together over the fields. I could say nothing.

"Why, David!" she cried, and again a hand was held out
to me in appeal.
"Don't you want to go with us?"

I laughed. And what a struggle I had to force into that laugh a note of happy gayety! I sat on the edge of the divan, very erect, pulling at my fingers, for I was no longer David Malcolm, a dreaming boy; I was a man with a vital fact to meet. Meeting it, I must become to her as any other man she knew—a formal creature, a lay figure for the barber's and tailor's art, with a gift of talking inanities.

"It's not because I don't want to go," I said. I was glad that I was in the shadow, for though my voice was steady I felt the blood leave my face. "But you see—there is something I have been wanting to tell you. I'm to be married."

"Oh!" she exclaimed.

If I had hoped to hear more of a cry of pain than that one exclamation of surprise, I must have been disappointed. But I cherished no such hope now. I was utterly miserable. I was awkward and ill at ease. The Penelope Blight I had known lived in another world, and this Penelope Blight who was regarding me so quietly, meeting my covert glance with a friendly smile, could, after all, never be more than a casual acquaintance.

"How splendid!" she said. Mrs. Bannister, I think, would have spoken in that same way, as though the news were quite the most delightful that she had ever heard. "Who to? Quick—I must hear all about it."

"To a Miss Todd," I answered, and, though I struggled against it, I cleared my throat dryly. "A Miss Gladys Todd."

The name sounded harshly in my ears. I was conscious that I had used it in the manner of the select circles of Harlansburg, and I was angry that, though knowing better, I had let myself lapse into the ways of a manikin. When I had spoken of Joe Hicks it was from my heart; I had forgotten my hands, and Penelope and I had laughed together. When I spoke of Gladys Todd my voice was tainted with apology. Inwardly I was calling myself a cad, for it mattered little whether or not I loved her. I had won her trust, and my first duty was to speak her name with pride. But I had had that brief glimpse of Penelope Blight, the companion of my boyhood; I had walked with her, grown lovelier than my dreams, through visionary woods and fields. She was before me, a dainty woman of the world; behind her the firelight fanned the leaves carved for her long ago by the old Italian artist; from above Reynolds's majestic lady looked down at her kindly, at me with a haughty stare, as if she read presumption in my mind. Never could I imagine her photographed on a camel's back by the side of ex-Judge Bundy. For this alone, it seemed to me as though I were unfolding to her the love story of a Darby and Joan, adorned with a chaos of easels and camels, bird's-eye-maple mantels and gayly painted plaques; as though I had come to tell the great lady of it, because she had always taken a kindly interest in my affairs.

Against this absurd humiliation I was fighting when again I coughed dryly and said: "She is the daughter of Doctor Todd, the president of McGraw."

"Oh, I see," returned Penelope brightly. "She must be very learned, David. But of course I knew that you would marry a clever woman." To this gentle flattery I raised my hand and shook my head in protest. "And I see, too, how it all came about—at college. How romantic! Just like you, David. And yet I can hardly think of you as a married man. It was only yesterday that I pulled you out of the creek; to-morrow you are to marry a charming woman—an accomplished woman, I know. She must sing and play the piano and do all kinds of things like that. How proud you should be!"

"I am," said I in a sepulchral tone, much as I might have answered to my name at roll-call.

"When she comes to town you must let me know—I shall call on her." There was no note but one of kindliness in Penelope's easily modulated voice, nothing but friendliness in the smile which parted her lips. As she leaned forward again, grasping the carved arms of her chair, she was speaking with queenly condescension, and it nettled me to find myself reduced to the level of the herd.

So there was in my voice a faint ring of pride when I said: "Gladys is abroad now." At least in this august presence a fiancée abroad sounded more impressive than a fiancée in Harlansburg, and I wanted it known that mine was a woman of the world and not simply the accomplished daughter of a small country town.

I think that the point struck home, for a hopeful "Oh!" escaped from Penelope's lips, as though she were giving vent to bottled-up doubts as to whether or not she could ever more than call on Gladys Todd. I think that she divined what I wanted her to understand—that though Gladys Todd had painted tulips on black plaques, she had acquired the dignity that comes with travel and the grace of a widened view.

"You must both come and dine with me when she gets home," Penelope said, with a manner of increased interest. "I suppose she is studying, David, music or painting."

"Travelling," I answered, encouraged to nonchalance by the impression I was making, for to travel merely sounded much more prosperous than to be working at the rudiments of an art. "She has been over since last May—just travelling around."

"And gathering together a trousseau—how delightful! You must be counting the days till she comes home, David?"

I nodded. I tried my best to look as though at that very moment I was busy with the fond calculation.

"And who is with her—some friend?" Penelope asked.

"Her father and mother," I answered. That sounded still more prosperous: the family of three—the learned doctor, his wife and accomplished daughter—wandering where they willed about the world. I should have stopped there, but I am one of those unfortunate persons who in telling anything must tell it all. My better judgment made me hesitate. My habit carried me on. "And Judge Bundy," I added.

"Judge who?" she exclaimed.

I fancied that I detected a strange note in her voice.

"Bundy—Judge Bundy," I replied, my own voice rising to a pitch of irritation.

Would she go on and make me spell the name that sounded so strangely when spoken in her presence? I was angry. It was at myself for my uncalled-for frankness. For one brief moment I had almost raised myself again to the level of the dainty creature in the old carved chair, to the approval even of the majestic lady above the great fireplace; speaking so nonchalantly of my friends who could wander where they willed over the face of the globe, I had almost made myself one with those for whom Italian sculptors drove the chisel and Reynolds plied his brush. But that name, so unwisely given, called to my mind the figure on the camel, and I was sure that by some strange freak of conjury Penelope must see it too; and worse, that other, the girl in the pugree, and behind them, discreetly placed, Doctor Todd, uncomfortably balancing on his giant beast, and Mrs. Todd taken inopportunely as she was mopping her brow. Well might Penelope look at me with quizzical eyes. I had tumbled again among the common herd. In my desperation I might have gone on to the whole truth recklessly; told her what an absurd man Judge Bundy really was, and how the Todds were being dragged over Europe on a glorified Cook's tour, captives at the wheels of his chariot; told her how I appreciated her sweet condescension in offering to call on the woman I loved. The woman I loved? For that moment I think I did love Gladys Todd, for I was standing to her defence against the crushing weight of millions of money and the bluest of blood. Yes, I am sure that I should have gone on and told her all, but Fate, wiser than I, intervened, and the butler announced Mr. Talcott.

As usual, Mr. Talcott did not wish tea—he had just come from the club, but he could not see why we were sitting in utter darkness. With Penelope's assent, he turned a button, showing thereby an exasperating familiarity with the room, and, seating himself comfortably before her, expressed his wonder that he had not seen her last night; he had hunted for her everywhere to join his party at supper. And now the lights were on and I a mere spectator at the play; I was having a glimpse of the stage on which I could never move. The lights burned high; they swept the dust and cobwebs from the diamond panes; they drove the flames to hiding in the ashes; their touch turned the leaves of the fireplace to dead stone. But Penelope they could not change. In the soft black webs, woven for her by a hundred toiling human spiders, she held still the heritage of the proud woman in frills and furbelows and the fine old man in wig and smallclothes. She was more radiant, as though her blood ran quicker in the joy of the part she played. Enter the butler. Enter Mr. Grant, a tall young man in business clothes, a good-natured fellow who laughed joyously at nothing. He had just dropped in on his way home after a beastly day downtown—a horrible day—a new attack on the trusts and a smash in the market. He fixed himself close to the curate's delight and beginning at the bottom worked upward, fortifying himself, as he explained, for a late dinner. Talcott thought that he had heard Grant say that he was going to the opera. Grant had never said any such thing. Didn't Mr. Malcolm agree with him that more than one act of opera was a bore? Mr. Malcolm quite agreed. Mr. Talcott wondered if Miss Blight had heard that Jerry White was engaged. Miss Blight was at once dying to know to whom. Mr. Talcott admonished her to think. Mr. Grant wanted to know if Mr. Malcolm had heard. But Mr. Malcolm had a strange unappreciation of important news. He moved in another world than this and he wanted to flee from it. He was homesick for familiar scenes and faces, for Miss Minion's and the long table in the basement to which the wizened old women would soon be crawling down for their evening nourishment, for Miss Tucker and his neighbor, Mr. Bunce, who by day made tooth-powder and by night talked Pater. He rose and held out his hand to the princess of the blood. Graciously she rose from her throne.

Graciously she said: "Good-by, David. It was good of you to drop in."

And graciously she added, as he backed awkwardly away: "Remember, you must let me know when Miss Todd comes. I shall call."

CHAPTER XVIII

I dined with the Blights. It had been a month since the afternoon when I talked with Penelope, and this evening in December I went to the house with hope high that in seeing her again I might have an opportunity of regaining a little of our lost friendship. The invitation had come from her, over the telephone, to dine with them most informally, and though she cleared herself of any charge of interest in the matter by adding that Mr. Blight wished to see me, I flattered myself with the hope that she might be speaking more personally than she cared to admit. How soon was that illusion wrecked! I entered the great library. Mrs. Bannister was standing by the fireplace, her eyes fixed on the opposite wall, her mind occupied with a struggle to suppress a yawn of boredom. Rufus Blight was reading a newspaper, but when I was announced he came forward and greeted me cordially. With his arm in mine he led me to Mrs. Bannister, and she allowed me to raise her hand and drop it. She said something, made some conventional remark on the great pleasure it gave her to see me; the yawn almost forced itself into view, but she set her lips firmly and drove it back. As I made my response to these friendly expressions of welcome my eyes swept the room and rested at last on the door through which I had come. There they held expectantly.

Mrs. Bannister read my thoughts. "Penelope is so distressed that she cannot see you to-night," she said, drawing her scarf across her bared and massive shoulders, so that I wondered if my entrance had suddenly chilled the air. "She had expected to be here, but this afternoon the Ruyters called up and insisted that she dine with them and go to the opera. It's 'Tristan.' She is mad about 'Tristan.'"

So faded the last vain hope! Had Penelope spent hours in devising a way of making it plain to me that the link between the past and the present was broken, she could not have been more adroit. Had David Malcolm, the boy, been coming to dine that night I know that she would have been standing there at Mrs. Bannister's side, her own eyes fixed expectantly on the door. But between the company of such excellent folk as these Ruyters, with the glorious music of "Tristan," and this awkward man whose people were not her people, who found content in the lodges of the Todds and

Bundys, there could be but one choice. I was humiliated. The good-natured grace with which I expressed my disappointment to Mrs. Bannister belied my angry mind, and as we moved toward the dining-room, she chattering incessantly, she must have believed that I was entirely satisfied with just her company. Fortunately I had only to smile my responses, while my thoughts were busy with the cavalier way in which I had been treated. I was incensed at Penelope, but had it been any balm to my wounds to make her feel the weight of my anger, I knew well enough that she was far beyond the reach of my reproaches. But hopelessly I repeated over and over to myself that I never could forgive her. Then, by a sudden weak reversal, I did forgive her and let my anger evaporate into a silent protest against the unkind fate which had decreed that her people should no longer be my people.

It was when I saw her that I forgave her. As we three sat at dinner, Mrs. Bannister chattering on, Rufus Blight meditative but offering a monosyllable now and then as evidence that he listened, I smiling responsively, Penelope came in. How could I not forgive her when I saw her thus, gowned in the daintiest art of the Rue de la Paix, cloaked in soft white fur, capped with a scarf of filmy lace, and one small hand held out to mine.

The fault, I said, was my own, mine and the Fates which had ordered that the orbits in which we moved should meet but rarely. The fault, too, lay with my forebears, who, had they considered me, would have settled on the shores of the Hudson instead of pushing westward so recklessly. Then I might now be going to the Ruyters', to sit at dinner at her side, to sit behind her in the shadow of an opera-box and whisper in her ear the ten thousand things which I had to say. I forgave Penelope. I called down maledictions on the robust Malcolms and McLaurins who had carried me out of her world and abandoned me to the garrulous Mrs. Bannister and the taciturn Rufus Blight.

Penelope was exceedingly sorry to be going out, but she knew that David would understand and would come some other night. David understood thoroughly; there was no reason for her to apologize, and, of course, he would come again. Penelope was immensely relieved to find him so complacent; she even wished he were to be of the company to which she was going. She had just come in to have a glimpse of him, and now she must be hurrying. And so she went away to take her bright place in that social firmament of which the abandoned Mr. Malcolm thought with so much envy and longing while he dallied again with sweetbreads and peas.

"It was very late when I got home," said Mrs. Bannister, taking up the thread of her narrative, "and who should I find here, as usual, but Herbert Talcott!"

The emphasis which she put on the words "as usual" aroused Mr. Blight from his placid interest in his glass of claret. "And who," said he, "is Talcott, anyway? What does he do?"

"Herbert Talcott is a remarkable man," replied Mrs. Bannister. "He does nothing."

It should have mattered little to me that Herbert Talcott refused tea from Penelope's hands every day of the week because he had just come from the club. Had Mrs. Bannister announced that he was calling daily on Gladys Todd, then I should very properly have been startled. Yet I sat up straight now as though she had named an archenemy of my happiness and my ears were keen to hear every word.

"He does absolutely nothing," she continued. "He has absolutely nothing, in spite of the reports that he is quite well off. I know positively that his father left him only ten thousand a year, and yet he knows everybody and goes everywhere. He is undeniably clever and was a great favorite at Harvard."

"Doesn't he work at all?" said Mr. Blight with a rising inflection of astonishment.

"Why, no," replied Mrs. Bannister. She saw the disapproval in my host's face and was quick to bring herself into sympathy. "That is what I can't understand. Now, there is Bob Grant, who is very rich in his own right, and yet goes religiously down to the Stock Exchange every day because he feels an obligation to be of some use in the world. But of the two men, Herbert Talcott is the more sought after."

"Sought after?" said my host inquiringly.

"Yes, sought after," repeated Mrs. Bannister. "He is asked everywhere. I suppose his name has something to do with it, but in these days, when name counts for so little and money for so much, it is remarkable."

"It is remarkable," said Rufus Blight, with a return to the spirit of the day when I had known him as a bustling, pompous man. "It is remarkable that he can be happy doing nothing. Look how restless I am with nothing to do but to play golf and read magazines. I can't understand him. And yet he seems a decent young man."

"But, you must remember, he is going out all the time," said Mrs. Bannister. "A man simply couldn't go out as he does and do anything. He is always in demand. Why, I know a dozen families into which he would be heartily welcomed. Last year it was reported that he was engaged to marry Jane Carmody, the mine man's daughter; but she was rather plain—to be truthful, very plain—and I will say for Herbert Talcott that he is not the kind who would marry solely for money."

Mrs. Bannister went on chattering her praise of Herbert Talcott, with a subtle purpose, I suspected, of impressing on me the utter absurdity of my entering the lists with him and of bringing Rufus Blight to a keener appreciation of the man whom he might be called on any day to welcome into his own family. With me her efforts were quite unneeded. With Rufus Blight the impression which she seemed to create was alone one of astonishment that any man could be happy doing nothing. Again and again he interrupted her to express his doubt on that point, and when dinner was over and Mrs. Bannister had retired, and we were smoking in the room which he called his den, he unmasked to me a mind weary of working over nothing. He should never have sold out to the trust, he said; in the mills he had been happy; every hour had its task and every day its victories in orders for rails and armor-plate. Now in a single day every month he could cut coupons and attend to dividends, and the others he must pass with golf and magazines.

His den? How quickly does this bourgeois phrase call up before us a hodgepodge room, an atmosphere of stale tobacco smoke, a table covered with pipes, books and magazines, littered with tobacco, walls burdened with hideous prints, a mantel adorned with objects dear to their owner from their associations, to the visitor hideous. The alien mind which had conceived the great library had evidently been held at bay when Rufus Blight was fitting himself into this den, his real home.

Over the fireplace was a great steel plate of the regretted mills, a world covered with immaculate smokeless buildings and cut with streets in which women were taking the air in barouches as though in a park; before the fireplace two patent rockers, and behind them a table littered with magazines and novels; in the corners golf sticks of innumerable designs, and wherever the eye turned it met coldly colored prints showing trotting horses in action. I had one of the rocking-chairs and Rufus Blight the other, and he was looking up at the mills when he spoke so regretfully of them. He referred again to Talcott.

"I can't understand it—a man happy doing nothing. I suppose I am a sort of machine—I must have work fed into me. Here I am at fifty-five and not a wheel moving. It was the power of the mills that kept me running. Now I have lost that." For a moment he was silent. Then he leaned toward me and said in a wistful voice: "David, you remember my brother. He could be happy just sitting thinking. Now if my energy could have been combined with his mentality, what—"

I finished the sentence. From the past came the picture of the Professor at the bare table in the cabin, pointing a long finger at me.

"What a man we would have made."

Rufus Blight's eyes opened wide. "How did you read my thoughts so well!" he exclaimed.

"The conclusion was simple," said I. "Years ago I heard your brother say the same thing."

"Oh! Well it does express the case exactly. Henderson was always a wonderful man for thinking, David. In his young days he was perfectly happy with a book. There were not many books in our valley, but he read them all and it was very interesting to hear the ideas he formed from them. He was a wonderful talker." Rufus Blight nodded his head reminiscently. "A wonderful talker. But when it came to practical things he was quite helpless. It wasn't that he was lazy. If there had been at hand anything big to do, anything that appealed to him, he would have done it. What he needed was an opportunity. He really never had half a chance. He did try working in the store with me—and he tried hard, but a mind like his could not be happy measuring out sugar and counting eggs. Such work seemed to lead to nothing—I know it did to me. But I had a different kind of a mind. I had to feed it, like a machine, with figures and facts. But to him it was of no importance that butter had gone up a cent a pound. He would say that the ants weren't worried about it, nor the birds, nor the people of other planets. Do you know, David, I really used to envy Hendry his way of seeing things."

For a few moments Rufus Blight was silent, and my eyes were on the picture of the great mills to which the counting of sugar and eggs had led. From the mills they wandered to what they had given the man who built them, from the golf sticks to the prints of trotting horses and to the litter on the table. This den measured the true extent of his conquest. I looked at him. With a movement of weariness he stretched his feet toward the fire and leaned back and gazed at the ceiling, with a whimsical smile playing around the corners of his mouth.

"I had to work, David," he went on. "Hendry could earn a living teaching school, but I hadn't the brains, so I toiled away in the store from early morning until late at night. Teaching school was easier. He used to say that if the sluggard did actually go to the ant he would probably find him a most uninteresting creature to talk to. I guess Hendry was right. I do know that he had little of the virtue of the ant, but he was one of the most interesting men I ever heard talk. When I was behind the counter it was my main pleasure to listen to him, perched on a chair in front of it." Rufus

Blight laughed. "Really, David, in those days I was proud of having such a distinguished brother. I had always looked up to him. He was older than I, four years, and he was my protector against the assaults of other lads—my ready compendium of universal knowledge. I never dreamed but that if I prospered he would prosper; and if he, then I. Why, David, I can feel him now clapping me on the back and calling me his grub-worm. 'Some day,' he would say, 'I'll come and ask a bed in your garret.' And I would laugh at him and talk of the time when we—I always said 'we'—when we should have a pair of fine trotters, and should go skimming over the country together instead of crawling along behind our blind mare." Rufus Blight paused. The whimsical smile was gone and he was looking at me through narrowed eyes. "Then the break came." And quickly, as he said it, he turned from me and began to smoke very hard.

"The break?" said I in a questioning tone; for I believed that at last I was to know the mystery which lay behind the Professor's conduct if only I could lead him on.

"Yes," said he in an even voice, "the break. The break came and I had to leave the valley. I wouldn't stay after that, David. There was nothing left for me there, but I had my work; I could go on weighing butter and counting eggs." Rufus Blight's voice was low and he spoke rapidly. He seemed to have it in his mind that I knew the story of those early days, had heard it, perhaps, from the lips of his brother or from common report, for men are prone to think their fellows well informed of the conspicuous facts of their lives. I dared not interrupt again for an explanation, lest my question should betray me to him as nothing more than a curious stranger. I know the story now in all its detail, but it came to me only from Rufus Blight, and from him in a few scattered threads, dropped for me to weave while in his den that night; feeling that he had found one whom he could trust, he unburdened his heart. Doubtless he had no such thought when he led me into the room, but there might have been in my eyes, when he spoke of the valley, some light of sympathy. And when he turned from that great hall, from his heavy table and his liveried servants, to speak of counting eggs and weighing butter, I had not even smiled at the incongruity. Then the dam broke, and memories backed up in years of silence broke forth in a quick and troubled flood.

"It was my fault, David, as much as his. I was a grub—a dull, toiling grub. But those long hours that I was toiling came to be good hours for me when it was for her sake. Why, it seemed that every pound of sugar I sold, that every little profit I made, was for her. I planned the finest house in the country as I stood all day at the counter, and it was for her. She was to have it all, and I only asked to be allowed to grub away—for her. She didn't understand me, David. She used to taunt me with being sordid, and said that I stayed at the store early and late because I loved a dollar most. I didn't understand women. I guess at least I should have closed up the store for an evening or two a week, and yet"—Rufus Blight hesitated—"and yet it wouldn't have made any difference. Hendry was a tall fellow. I was short and rather fat. Hendry could talk in a wonderful way. I was always silent except when it came to a trade. It had to be as it was, David, but it was hard—very hard. I don't think I said any more than most men would have said to him—perhaps less, because I never was a talker. And, after all, I couldn't blame them. Why, I remember, as I was leaving the valley, I said to him that if they ever needed a home they must come to me. He was offended. He drew himself up and said proudly that when I needed help I must come to them. Poor Hendry! It wasn't long before he did need help; but could you imagine him taking it from any one? He lost the school—he had become not quite orthodox in his ideas and was inclined to rail at church doctrine. He never was intended for manual labor; he worked hard when he could get work, but everything seemed against him. Then Penelope came, and he was left alone with her, and it made him bitter. I tried to get him to come to me; but could you imagine a man as proud as he, David—a man of his mind—coming to me after what had happened! Why, he called my offer charity. Then he left the valley, too, and I wrote to him from Pittsburgh, where I had bought a little mill. I wanted them to come to me—him and Penelope—for I was lonely. I had nothing but the mill; why, only in the mill was I happy. But could you imagine a man as proud as he, David, taking help from me? He answered rather curtly; said that some day I should see what he was worth; that he was not the idler he seemed. He said that again to me face to face, that once when I have seen him in all the years since the break."

Rufus Blight left his chair and stood by the fireplace, a hand on the mantel, his eyes watching the flames.

"Could I have done more, David? That night when I saw him I had come in from the mills late, and the servants would not let him wait for me even in the hall. He told me how he had shot the constable. He feared he had killed him, but he did not know, not daring to turn back to find out. He had walked the whole way, travelling day and night. I wanted him to stay, but he said that in Mary he had taken from me everything I had ever had; he could take no more. He had come not to beg, but to give me Penelope; and when he came again it would not be as a brother who could be turned from my door by the servants; when he came again it would be as a father of whom Penelope could feel no shame. I could not move him. I did my best, David, but he laughed and slapped me on the back and called me his old grub; said that some day I should really see what was in him. Then he went away—God only knows where."

"To the West," said I. "To the East, to Tibet."

"Yes," said Rufus Blight. He was standing before me, his hands clasped behind him, his eyes intent on the ceiling.

"And you came to us for Penelope," I said. The last trace of my antipathy to this man, once to me so fat and pompous, was gone.

He looked at me with a faint smile of embarrassment. "And what an ungrateful brute I was!" he exclaimed. "David, did you remember the promises I made that day?"

"I used to remember them," I answered, "and to wonder."

"You had the right," he said. "But remember what I was—just a lonely grub. Till Penelope came to me I had nothing but the mills. Having her, I wanted her entirely." He held out his hand. "She was only that high, David, and I was getting gray. I never looked at her but there came into my mind another just that high who had a desk in school in front of mine, and sometimes I seemed to be looking again over the top of my spelling-book at the same bright hair and the same bobbing bit of ribbon. Can't you see what she meant to me, David? She hated me at first—she spoke always of her father and of you—and I was jealous."

"I understand," said I.

He had not spoken of the letters. There was no need of it. I knew that they were in his mind and that he was perfectly conscious of the pettiness of his action. But for me his simple confession had absolved him.

"I wanted her entirely," he went on, throwing himself into a chair at my side. "I wanted something to live for beside the mills. In Penelope I found it. What the mills gave me was for her. Every hour I worked was happier because it was for her good. Sometimes I have to fight against a dread that Hendry will come back and take her from me, and yet when I think of him, tumbling around the world alone, I want him too—want him in that very chair you are sitting in. It would be so good just to hear him talk, and it wouldn't make any difference to us now if he did just talk." Rufus Blight brought a fist down on the arm of his chair. "David, I must find him!"

"He went to Tibet," said I.

"To the South Seas, to the Arctic, to Tibet—everywhere, David. His trail has led me all over the world. I can never catch up to him. The Philadelphia man you told me of—Harassan—dead three years. My secretary, Mallencroft, has found that in San Francisco a man named Henderson worked on *The*

Press there, but only two men remembered him. They said he was erratic, always in trouble by writing things contrary to the paper's policy, and gave up in disgust, to ship as supercargo on a vessel trading in the South Seas. He wrote a book after that, but the publishers failed, and Mallencroft couldn't even find a copy of it. That must have been about the time you saw him—when he lectured on 'Life.' Poor old Hendry! It's his pride, his confounded pride—that's the trouble."

I had risen. Rufus Blight came to me and laid a hand on each of my shoulders. What a change since that day long ago! He had to reach up to me, and I looked down into his face.

"You'll think me a strange fellow, David. I didn't mean to tell you so much, but it just would come out when I saw that you understood. We must find him—you and I. We may find him any day; at this very minute he may be going by the Old Grub's door. Watch for him."

I promised. I must come often, he said; it was good to have such a friend as I was, one who could understand, to whom he could talk of old days in the valley. He had never really been at home since he left the valley. He had lived in strange places, among strange people. We must all go back—back to the valley, he and Penelope and I—we should go in May—Penelope had talked of it—in May, when the orchards were in blossom.

Rufus Blight laughed at the joyous prospect. And I? I closed my eyes to it. I turned away, through the great hall, but he, with unwelcome kindness, followed me to the stairs. What a great expedition it would be—to the valley—just he and I and Penelope! I laughed ironically—at myself. I plunged down the deep-carpeted steps. The grilled door closed behind me. I paused a moment to turn up my collar against the cold, to button my gloves and collect my scattered thoughts. How the wind bit!

Across the Avenue a dark figure leaned against the wall of the park. As I stepped over the pavement the man seemed to think that I was moving toward him, for he roused himself quickly and walked rapidly up the street. I laughed at his fright and turned on my way downtown, for I was thinking of myself and of what I had lost, and I had no care for shivering tramps. I reached the corner. Rufus Blight's words came back to me. Had that man been watching the Old Grub's door? I turned sharply, but I saw nothing, no sign of a living thing save the lights of a retreating cab.

CHAPTER XIX

I have spoken casually, in this rambling story of mine, of young Marshall, a fellow-lodger at Miss Minion's. He was the Brummel of the boarding-house. The fact that he occupied the smallest rear hall-bedroom, with the minimum of daylight, in no way affected his standing, for everybody knew that he went out in society. Indeed, for him more spacious quarters were hardly needed, as he was seldom at home except to dress and to sleep. By day he hurried about Wall Street, buying and selling bonds. On the winter evenings he stepped forth from his cell a splendid figure, realizing, as nearly as possible, those spotless and creaseless young men whom the illustrators draw with so much unction. Then we might have imagined that he would step on, into his brougham, to be whirled away to some smart dinner. Alas! his equipage was not even a cab. His pair of prancing blacks were only his galoches, and his protection against the weather a long ulster, a chest-protector of thickly padded satin, and an opera-hat. The great trouble which Marshall had on these nightly expeditions was getting home. I do not mean to insinuate that it was to find Miss Minion's door. It was to pass Miss Minion's door. There were several absent-minded old gentlemen living in the house who had a way of forgetting that they were not its sole occupants. Coming in from their weekly or monthly trip to the theatre, the hour would to them seem horribly late and they would catch the chain. Occasionally I was myself their victim, and had to stand shivering outside, ringing the bell with one hand and with the other playing a tattoo on the panels. More generally it was Marshall, for, though I was frequently held very late at my work downtown, he was abroad at his pleasures even later. The lateness with which he pursued these pleasures was no evidence against their innocence. Tom Marshall was one of the most innocent men that I have ever known. He was not a New Yorker. He came, as he told me, of the Marshalls of Pogatuck, in Maine. The way that he said it made me understand that there was no bluer blood in the land than that running in the veins of the Pogatuck Marshalls, and it explained why the Knickerbockers were so willing to meet him as an equal. He had come from Pogatuck by way of Harvard, and one advantage which his education had given him was an acquaintance that he could turn to use, inasmuch as his great ambition was to "go out." To him a card to the Ruyters would have been an olive-wreath of victory. It was a trophy that he hoped to win, and to that end he worked patiently, selling bonds all day, and at night as patiently setting forth in his galoches, his ulster, and his opera-hat to storm the outer works of society. He belonged to innumerable dancing-classes. Indeed, it seemed to me that he kept himself poor meeting their dues, for I remember more than one occasion when he appealed to me in distress because he had to send fifteen dollars to the treasurer of the Tuesdays or the Fridays and the pater had forgotten to remit his allowance. Tom Marshall's father was the most forgetful of men.

I liked him. You could not help liking him. He was so thoroughly good-natured and affable. His conversation was by no means instructive, but there was an airiness about his views and ambitions which was restful to one who was taking life as seriously as was I in those days. I got to know him by having constantly to let him in. Of all the lodgers in the house, I was the most likely to be up late, and if one of the forgetful old gentlemen fastened the door-chain, to me would fall the duty of answering the signals of distress from the stoop.

Tom Marshall has played but a small part in my life. Like that of Boller of '89, his place in the cast is a minor one. He is one of those who fall in near the end of the line when the company joins hands to sidle across the stage, bowing and smiling, after the second act. Yet without him I wonder sometimes how my own play would have ended. It seems to me now as though he must have been born in Pogatuck, as though his whole life had been ordered, his love of going out developed, so that at the proper moment he might enter the stage where I was playing the hero to an empty house. He entered it at one o'clock in the morning. The door was chained. At the moment I was sitting in my room, on my one comfortable chair, my book on the floor at my side, my pipe in my mouth, and I was smoking very hard. What countless pipes I had smoked in this same way since the night, a month before, when I had dined with Rufus Blight! What countless nights I had sat in this same way, in this same month, with my book on the floor and my mind revolving ceaselessly in a circle! This night I had come to that part of the circle where I thought of Penelope, the lovely, the formal, the distant Penelope, when down in the depths of the house I heard the muffled clatter of the bell and faint rat-tats upon the front door. I went to the window and put out my head, to see on the stoop the muffled black figure of Tom Marshall.

"It was old Ransome again, I'll bet you," he said, when I had unchained the door and we stood in the dimly lighted hall. "This is the third time this month that he has locked me out, confound him!"

I raised my finger to my lips, cautioning Marshall not to arouse the whole house. But he would not be silenced—it was early yet, anyway—he had been to a Friday cotillon and it was a beastly bore—even the supper was poor—he wanted something to eat. His foot was on the stairs when he discovered that he was hungry. He discovered at the same time that he was indebted to me for having let him in, not alone this time but many others, and he insisted on showing his appreciation by taking me out to a late supper. I demurred. Marshall talked louder. I insinuated that he had been drinking, to which he replied that the Fridays never served anything but weak punch. I should have protested further, but Mrs. Markham's door opened at the head of the stairs and I heard her breathing indignantly. For the sake of quiet I consented, and so it happened that at one o'clock in the morning I found myself in the street, with my arm tucked under Marshall's and our faces set toward O'Corrigan's chop-house.

O'Corrigan's has been torn down these many years, but you can see a score of replicas of it on upper Sixth Avenue and Broadway. Its plate-glass windows were adorned with set pieces of lobsters and oysters, celery and apples, and you entered through a revolving door into an atmosphere laden heavily with kitchen fumes, into a room which multiplied itself in many mirrors. When you went there for the first time the man who took you, if he knew his New York, would tell you of O'Corrigan's rise from waiting at a downtown lunch-counter to the ownership of these glittering halls.

Of course, Tom Marshall knew O'Corrigan. He hailed him cordially, and it seemed to me that he had no little pride in the privilege. He even nodded to the bartender as we passed him, leading me to the archway whence we could survey the adjoining room to see what was going on there. But nothing was going on there. These late-night restaurants are at their best in colored pictures. There they seem to own an atmosphere of light and joy. There lovely women sip champagne, that gayest of wines, from dainty glasses, and gallant men seem to say to us that if you would have health and wealth and happiness you would never go home until morning, but would live with them in this bright world of wine and women and song. Really, they are melancholy places, especially in their gayest hours. If vice really were attractive, how vicious most of us would be! I do not say that O'Corrigan's was a vicious place. At certain hours its patronage was of the dullest respectability from the suburbs. Dull respectability is not supposed to be abroad in the early hours of the morning, but it does seek at times to hover on the edge of disrespectability with something of the roguish curiosity of childhood. And now the respectables and the unrespectables, a motley gathering in that garish room, amid the ugly debris of their feasting, made an unattractive picture from which I turned with a sense of relief to the quieter place behind us.

As we moved to a table in a secluded corner, I saw Talcott and Bob Grant sitting with their heads close together over a litter of plates and glasses. Grant spoke to me. As he rose and offered his hand, I noticed in his eyes that watery brightness which comes in certain stages of conviviality. The effusiveness of his greeting might have flattered me had I not realized that his heart was unduly expanded by alcohol. To see such a great, good-natured animal as young Grant thus exhilarated was not surprising to me, but with Talcott it was different. I had known him only as a quiet, self-possessed man who, from policy if nothing else, I believed must be as circumspect in his life as in his clothes. Now he spoke to me. His greeting was perfunctory. In his eyes was that watery dulness which comes with the later stages of conviviality. His hair was tousled, his collar crushed, his tie awry; for whiskey muddles the clothes as well as the brain. He nodded to me; he wondered what I was doing out so late; he snapped his fingers and called loudly for Andrew. The summons to the waiter was for me a hint to be gone.

Tom Marshall was greatly impressed by the fact that I knew Talcott and Grant. When I rejoined him he seemed to treat me with greater respect than hitherto, for he had been rather patronizing. It was surprising to him, always so busy storming the outer works, to know that I, the drudge of the fourth floor front, who never "went out," was so intimate with these gallant cadets who lived in the citadel. He had come to give me beer. Now in a faltering voice he suggested champagne, rubbing his hands and smiling as he named it, as though it were his habit to indulge nightly in so expensive a beverage. Remembering that he had owed me five dollars for many months, I deemed it unwise to make an unnecessary inroad into his pocket-book. With my refusal he grew insistent, and at last consented, only with reluctance, to a modest repast of welsh-rabbit and beer.

"And the beer at once," he commanded the waiter.

Then, unfolding his napkin on his knees and lighting a cigarette, he looked over my shoulder to the distant table where the two heads were close together over the litter of plates and glasses. "So you know Talcott and Grant," he went on. "I'm sorry you didn't introduce me, Malcolm. I've seen them around, of course, but, strangely, have never met them. They are a great pair—stacks of money—Grant especially. Talcott was in Harvard with me—was rather a snob and went with the rich crowd—very smart now. He was one of Willie Ruyter's ushers."

I smiled with compassion at this broken discourse. It brought to my mind Mrs. Bannister. Tom Marshall and Mrs. Bannister looked at life from the same view-point and I from one entirely different. To my mind there was nothing very remarkable in having my existence acknowledged by two very muddled young men, who in their present state acknowledged also their brotherhood with the *roué* whom I had seen in the next room or the cabman sitting outside on his box in a half-stupor. I might envy the good fortune which allowed them to move in the same world as Penelope Blight, but to disavow intimacy with them, even to one so strangely ambitious as Tom Marshall, called for no loss of pride. With some show of temper I avowed that I hardly knew them. I had only met them once or twice at the house of friends. But the sincerity with which I disowned them served only to heighten the new-born respect with which Marshall treated me. He did not know that I "went out." Laughing, I retorted that I never did go out. He said that I must; that he would take me out; he would present me to the right people. He launched into the delights of going out and the necessity of going out if a man was to be anybody at all; then suddenly stopped at the thought that the beer ordered at once was very slow in coming.

"That waiter is always confoundedly slow," he said. "I should have insisted on having Andrew. I apologize, Malcolm—I should have thought of Andrew. You would have enjoyed Andrew."

"Andrew?" I repeated, questioning.

"Yes, Andrew," replied Marshall. "Here's the beer. Now, George, hurry those rabbits—I'm famished. Andrew," he went on, lighting a fresh cigarette, "is a remarkable character. He is full of philosophy. He quoted Herbert Spencer to me the other night. He has a sly way—and a somewhat disconcerting one—when you order a drink, of trying to induce you to take mineral water, and if he can, and O'Corrigan is not within hearing, he serves a temperance lecture with every Scotch and soda." Marshall tapped his forehead. "A little queer," he said sagely, "but shrewd. By Jove, there he is now arguing with Bob Grant—a temperance lecture, I'll bet—trying to persuade him to take plain soda."

I looked over my shoulder to see this philosophic waiter who served temperance lectures with whiskey. His back was to me. I saw only a tall, loose-jointed figure clad in a waiter's jacket, a long, black arm outstretched, a napkin draped over it, a long, thin hand clutching a bill-of-fare, and a head of dark hair shot with white. The bill-of-fare struck the table in emphasis, the napkin waved like a flag of battle, both arms were stretched out wide in appeal. Grant laughed again—uproariously.

"I'll bet he is trying to uplift those fellows," said Marshall. "He has a good chance to get in a word, as O'Corrigan is in the next room."

I turned to my companion. At that moment I was more interested in the non-arrival of the welsh-rabbit than in the scene behind me, for waiters are by nature inclined to be voluble when the opportunity is given them, and to me there was nothing particularly amusing in the picture of young Grant, with that graciousness which comes with too much drink, condescending to argue with this crack-brained fellow who moved with his head in the clouds while his weary feet shuffled in and out of O'Corrigan's kitchen. At the moment there was nothing familiar to me in the tall, thin figure, nothing more than I should have seen in any other lank, shambling waiter waving a napkin and a bill-of-fare. I was growing tired. I was regretting that I had even allowed Tom Marshall to inveigle me out so late, to breathe heavy air and to eat heavy food at this hour, when I should be refreshing my body with sleep.

But Tom Marshall's spirits grew higher as the night grew older. He was immensely comfortable with his beer and cigarettes, immensely amused at the argument which was going on behind my back.

"You really must meet Andrew. You will enjoy him, Malcolm," he said. "I'll call him over when he is through with those men. He is a character worth knowing."

"You speak of him as if you had known him for a long time," I returned, and I think my lips must have curled a little; but if I was unappreciative of the hospitality which I was enjoying, my excuse was my great weariness.

"Oh dear, no," he demurred; "I've been coming here for years—late at night, you understand, for a bite occasionally. I never saw him until last fall—got talking to him—I always like to talk to waiters, to get their ideas. I found him a curious chap, better educated than most of them and surprisingly well informed—surprisingly. He seemed to have knocked around a good deal."

"Had been a waiter in Hoboken, I suppose," said I, "and in Philadelphia—"

"In Hoboken!" My sarcasm nettled Marshall. "He told me that he had never been a waiter at all until he came here; he was simply looking for an opportunity to find something really congenial. He was fresh from Canton. In Hoboken!" Tom Marshall leaned toward me aggressively. "Why, man, he has been everywhere—through the South Seas, in—"

There *was* something familiar in the tall, thin figure, something that even the waiter's jacket and the waving napkin could not hide.

"What's up now?" Marshall cried.

I had half risen from my chair and turned. Talcott and Grant were leaning over their table, elbows resting there, heads close together. And behind Talcott's chair the black figure was bent until the hands could touch the floor. He was brushing up scattered crumbs. As I looked, he raised his head, and it seemed to me that he had forgotten his menial task, had forgotten his menial place, for he was very still. He was no longer dusting. The napkin fell from his outstretched hand. He was listening to the muttered, maudlin conversation as though from the chaos of it he gathered some sober words of truth.

I looked at my companion. "In the South Seas, you said, Marshall. Has he spoken of San Francisco? Do you know his name?"

Marshall sprang from his chair. I was up too, and it was to see the Professor with a hand on Talcott's collar, shaking him, holding him at arm's length as he shook him, as though this man were some contemptible thing that he would touch as little as he could and yet must hold to and shake until it was cleansed of its vileness.

CHAPTER XX

For myself I should have chosen the hut where I first met the Professor above the home to which he led me in the early morning. If the old was tumble-down, dark and ill-furnished, its air was the pure air of the mountains and the way to it through things green and lovely. To the new we went through squalid streets, westward, toward the river; we turned into a dilapidated tenement; we climbed three flights of rickety stairs into a room which compared to mine as mine to the house of Rufus Blight. The lighted gas revealed hardly more than a narrow cell, with dirty, torn paper on the walls, a narrow bed, a cheap table, and a single chair. Giving me the chair, my host seated himself upon the bed, so close to me, of necessity, that our knees touched. To my eyes he was little older than that day fifteen years before when we had met. He was old then to my youthful view. Thinner he could not have been, and now only the scattered white hairs and the deepened lines of his face marked his increased years. He had laid aside his overcoat, and sat before me clad in his waiter's clothes, but the waiter's mien was gone. With his legs crossed, his hands clasped over one knee, his head drawn down between his shoulders, he seemed the languid, weary man of the store-porch, whose eyes quickened only at the trumpet-call to debate. Clearly his attitude toward me was one of antagonism. This I saw in his quiet gaze and in the restless twitching of fingers, impatient for the cut and thrust of argument.

On our way from O'Corrigan's to his squalid room, the Professor had spoken little. For the most part, as he plodded along at my side, he had contented himself in expressing opinions not complimentary to Herbert Talcott, in voicing his regret that he had not thrashed him instead of merely shaking him. That he had not thrashed Talcott was hardly evidence of the mildness of his attack. It was rather because I had interposed; and then O'Corrigan, in the character of the outraged proprietor of a highly respectable restaurant, had intruded himself into the quarrel, even going so far as to threaten to call the police. But I was first in the *mêlée,* and on me fell the blame of saving Talcott from merited chastisement. For this the Professor upbraided me. He spoke as though Talcott had been the aggressor. Had not Talcott struck him a blow under the eye? Yes, but it was feebly given. But the sting of it was to the Professor's pride, and he would regret to his dying day that I had withheld him from giving the young scoundrel his just deserts.

Poor Talcott! I confessed to myself that it would have given me pleasure to have had some part in his chastisement, and as we plodded westward through the empty streets I pictured him driving home in a hansom, trying to gather his scattered wits and to discover some reason why a quiet, respectful waiter should have assailed him without cause. Poor muddled Talcott! He did not know that his betrayer had been distilled in far-off Scotland, and had lain away in vats a score of years awaiting that very moment to make him speak his honest thought just as the quiet, respectful waiter was bending behind him to pick up crumbs. Perhaps he could not even remember what he was saying when he was stopped by the long fingers which were thrust down the back of his neck. Did he remember, what he was saying could be none of the waiter's affair, anyway. It could matter nothing to that humble creature if he did speak of Rufus Blight as a vulgar little brute and of Penelope as "a bit raw, but worth marrying for her money alone." "A woman's millions never grow *passé*," was an aphorism which fitted the lips of the half-drunken cynic. To be sure, the things which he had said were not such as a man would give expression to were he cold sober, even if he thought them, and much less would he apply them to particular persons, yet when you are sitting late at night with such a good fellow as Bob Grant over your fifth Scotch and soda, you are likely to be a little unguarded. For who would think of a waiter objecting? Poor, muddled, drunken Talcott! He did not know that he really had given the first blow, had changed the obsequious waiter into a fury by striking him in the heart of his pride. And to such a fury had the Professor been wrought, and so firmly did anger hold his mind, that my own sudden interference was received by him as quite in the ordinary, though he protested against my good offices. He remonstrated indignantly when I acquiesced in O'Corrigan's assertion that my humble friend must be demented, a plea which opened a way out of the predicament. Fortunately, the Professor's own wisdom in refusing an explanation of an apparently unprovoked assault gave color to this theory, and as Talcott's one clear thought was to escape without any unpleasant notoriety, O'Corrigan satisfied his ire by ordering his mad employee out of the place.

So the Professor came into my charge. Had we met after a separation of only a day, his treatment of me could not have been more casual. He consented to my accompanying him home, but this seemed less from a desire to see me again than to protest against my having publicly humiliated him by treating him as demented. He had always thought that David Malcolm would understand him under every circumstance; that whatever his condition and whatever mine, when we met again it would be with mutual esteem. Yet David Malcolm had judged him by his clothes, had given him a waiter's heart and mind with a waiter's garb! He was bent on proving to me that, however low he might have fallen in the world's eye, he was as sane as he ever had been, and that in accepting O'Corrigan's opinion so readily I had done him a wrong.

Now when we were sitting in his room, so close that our knees touched, he seemed by his silence to tell me that he had spoken, and that my part was to excuse and to explain what he deemed a reflection on himself. I saw him in his shabby waiter's garb. This was the uniform in which he marched, moved night after night with shuffling feet and eyes alert lest he break the dishes—marched to the divine drumbeat, marched under God's sealed orders. His own high-flowing phrases came back to me, and I could have laughed, seeing him, but I remembered that those phrases had been the sabre cuts which drove me into action, that but for them I might be dozing like the very dogs, dozing with the unhappy restlessness of enforced inaction. Perhaps I was moving to barren conquests, but barren conquests are better than defeat. He had moved to defeat, and I pitied him. He asked of me excuse and explanation. I, having none to give, was silent. But I think he must have seen in my eyes something of the same light which he found in them that morning in the smoky cabin. Then he had reached down, taken me in his arms and called me his only friend. Now with a sudden movement he held out his hand to mine. Anger was gone. He had forgotten Talcott. He had forgotten the stranger who seized his arm and thwarted his fury. He saw only the boy who yesterday had stood at his side when every man's hand was against him.

"Davy—Davy," he cried, "you have come again to help me."

"Yes—to take you home," said I, "to your brother and Penelope."

He made a gesture of dissent and his eyes narrowed. "No," he returned with sharpness. "That cannot be. Don't you suppose that I should have gone to them of my own accord had it been possible?"

"But it is possible," I said. "They want you. I have it from their own lips."

"I know—I know," he replied. "Rufus would give me a home. Rufus would give me money—all I need a hundred times over. But is that what I really need? I want to do something myself, David—to be somebody myself. I have it in me. All I ask is an opportunity." He brought his fist down on his knee. "And by heaven, I will find it! I will show them I'm not the worthless fellow I seem."

"But they don't think you worthless, Professor," said I, addressing him as I might have, had we been in the cabin again. "They have been searching for you everywhere—"

"But never expecting to find me as I am now," he interrupted, spreading wide his arms and inviting me to behold him as he was, a shabby waiter. "Rufus, who has made what the world calls a success, would be proud of me; and Penelope, who has learned to think with the rest of the world, would be proud of me—proud to present me to her friends—to splendid fellows like Talcott and his muddle-headed companion." He leaned forward and tapped me on the knee with his long forefinger, and his face broke into a bitter smile as he spoke more quietly. "David, I have seen Penelope. I came to New York just to be near her, and many a night I have stood for hours across the street from her house only to get a glimpse of her. And sometimes as I see her stepping in or out of her carriage I say to myself that she cannot be my daughter; and if I spoke to her how high she would toss her head! Why, she would lose less caste by walking with Talcott drunk than with me as I am now."

"But she need not see you as you are now," I protested, half smiling at the incongruous picture which he had drawn of Penelope walking down the avenue by the side of this shabby waiter. "They need not even know—"

I paused to grasp at some inoffensive phrase in which to describe his forlorn condition.

"That I have fallen so low," he exclaimed. He had been quick to see my predicament, and laughed. "I know what you are thinking of, David. You saw me an obsequious, tip-grasping fellow, with a spirit as heavy as his feet. You think me broken and down and out." The hands spread wide again. "I—down and out? Why, Davy, I've been like this a score of times, and I am still game. You must not think that because of a little temporary embarrassment I am in prime condition to go crawling to Rufus and tell him that I have failed and need his help. I told Rufus that I would come back and claim Penelope when she could be proud to own me as her father." He brought his fist down on his knee again. "She couldn't be very proud now, but I'll show them!"

It was hard to combat so overwhelming a pride as this, a pride which seemed to thrive in the ashes of hope. I tried to break it by speaking of his brother and daughter, giving him an account of my renewed acquaintance with them and of their talk of him. The effect was to set him smoking a very black pipe. Rising and leaning over the foot-rail of the bed, much as in the old days he leaned lazily over the store counter, he held his eyes fixed on mine, and smoked while I argued. He was a patient listener. My own story was interwoven with his, and that he might understand my relations with his brother and Penelope, I told him briefly all that had occurred with me since that day when we parted in the clearing. When I came to the college lecture, and my efforts to see him then, and to find him, he made a motion as though to interrupt. I paused. He commanded me to go on, and the smile which came to his face at my mention of his discourse on "Life" held there until I had finished. But my story, intended to give force to my arguments for him to surrender his pride, only served to put him in a reminiscent mood.

"That was a lecture, wasn't it, David?" he said, laughing. "Why, do you know that when I talked that night I almost imagined that I was a success in life. It was the introduction that did it—distinguished traveller—famous journalist. And you, I suppose, accepted it all as truth. Still, you may be thankful you didn't have to hear Harassan—a gigantic windbag, if there ever was one. I fell in with him one day in a smoking-car and got to talking about my travels. He was preparing a lecture on China, and as he had never been there, I was useful, so he took me into his house until he had pumped me dry. I substituted for him that night at your college for half the fee—was to read his lecture, but when I got started on it I couldn't stand it. An astonishing man, Harassan! When he died he left a modest fortune made in spouting buncombe; and yet—" The Professor held out a hand in appeal. "How many men are called great because they succeed in talking buncombe and selling rubbish! That is what discourages me so; and doesn't it make you a little bitter when you meet men surrounded by every material evidence of success and go fishing in their brains and can't hook up a single original idea of any kind? Why, I've met hundreds of them, Davy. Now that night Harassan would have hurled at you a lot of pompous commonplaces, and you would have hailed him as a great and wise man. I broke from the beaten path. I told you plain truth. Was I ever asked to lecture again? People won't pay to hear plain truth, Davy. I suspect that I should have done better had I not been trying all my life to drive plain truth into unwilling ears."

"I suspect so, too," said I mildly.

He laughed at my ready acquiescence. "I started wrong at home," he went on. "Had I listened to Rufus and plodded along in his humdrum way, I suppose I'd be rich now. But I couldn't. After I left the valley I went to Kansas and really settled down, got a school to teach, and for a time I was quite in the way of becoming a successful educator—principal of a high-school, perhaps. I might even have become president of a college, but to die the head of a fresh-water college did not seem a very glorious end; nor did teaching a lot of foolish young men to live what are held successful lives seem very inspiring living. So I went on west to San Francisco and tried newspaper work. It seemed just the vocation for me. Here I could use my sword against the dragons of untruth and corruption. The beast stalks forth brazenly enough, and without considering the moral side at all, it is sport to attack him. To get myself into a position to attack him, I had to serve an apprenticeship. You know what that means—the daily digging for ephemeral facts. But I stuck to it. I saw the day when I should be the most feared man on the coast, wielding a pen as efficacious as a surgeon's knife. Unfortunately, my knife first struck a politician named Mulligan, who owned some stock in the paper. You know the result. I could direct my caustic pen against O'Connor or Einstein, but from Mulligan came my living. I took to the sea to breathe purer air, sailing as supercargo on a trading vessel. For two years I knocked about the South Sea Islands and along the coast of Asia, and it seemed that I was gathering a vast amount of information which would be of service to the race if preserved in a book. How I worked over that book! When I got back to San Francisco I saw my fame and fortune about to be made by it. At last the power to do something worth while was in my reach."

The Professor paused. He spread wide his arms in a gesture to express futility. "I had as well stood on the highest peak of the Rockies and read my manuscript to space. The distinguished traveller and author!" With a hand upon his heart, he bowed gravely. "The author of one thousand volumes of uncut leaves. Useless! Well, I suppose Harassan found the one I gave him of some service, for he got most of his famous Chinese lecture out of it. There was some pretty good stuff in that book, too, but Harassan was the only man I ever heard of who agreed with me; and he—well, he was a successful idiot."

"And of course you never shared the benefits he reaped," said I.

"Benefits from Harassan?" The Professor laughed. "Why, David, you might have thought that I had ruined Harassan from the way he talked when he received a letter from Todd, that president of yours. Todd said that I would subvert the morals of the country. So the Reverend Valerian and I parted with words—he to go to China in his mind, I to work my way there in the body." The Professor rested himself on the bed, and between puffs at his pipe continued: "I had an idea of going to Tibet. That seemed to be really doing something—to go to Lhasa and unveil its mysteries to the world. I started from Peking, afoot mostly, and so you see I didn't make very rapid progress, and while walking I had plenty of time to think. When I was about half-way to the border, the absurdity of the thing came to me—spending years to get into Tibet, only to find there a filthy land ruled by a mad religion. I got almost to Shen-si, and turned back. Somehow China suited me. I fell into the Chinese way of thinking, and might have gone on satisfied with a daily dole of rice and fish had it not been for Penelope. I never could forget

Penelope. Always, it seemed to me, she must be waiting for me to come back with my promises fulfilled, to return a man she could be proud to own her father. It looked pretty black for me then, David. China isn't a place to accomplish much, and I might as well have gone on to Lhasa as to do what I did—work three years in the consulate at Che-Foo as interpreter and useful man, eyes, arms, and brains for a politician from Missouri. But my one purpose was to get home, to see Penelope, to see her a woman grown, and perhaps—I would say to myself sometimes—to speak to her."

"And you have found her a woman grown," said I. "Now you have only to speak to her."

He shook his head. "I've been here three months now, David, and I have seen her perhaps a score of times; and when I see her, sometimes entering that great house, sometimes driving in her carriage, always the very picture of the ideal princess, she seems a creature of another world than mine, and I laugh at myself for trying to believe that there ever was a time when she sat on my knees and talked of days to come when we should have a house like that and drive in such a carriage! Would she understand me now? Would temporary necessity condone my descending to this uniform? I tried to do better when I came here, but I couldn't. I tried even your profession, but they wanted young men. I came to this only to be near her. But I am away again, David. I must be up and doing." He had risen, and was speaking rapidly as he paced the narrow limits of the room. "Money is what I need and I will have it. Money has always seemed to me a paltry thing to work for, but now it is for Penelope's sake. There has been a plan in my mind for some time, David, only I have delayed starting on it—for Penelope's sake, you understand. I'm going to Argentina. There was a man on my ship coming out from Yokohama who was bound for Argentina, and he told me—"

The Professor launched into a glowing account of the promise of the southern country. To his mind, he had only to reach it to acquire the wealth which he wanted. The man who had failed in every undertaking, who had turned back from every goal to which he had set his eyes, would win there in a few years that for which men in other parts of the world strove a lifetime. I pointed out that the opportunity lay right at his hand, and his answer was to spread wide his arms that I might see the waiter's jacket. He had the better of the argument, but the reason lay in his own character. Then I had recourse to pleading, and my plea was made not for his sake, but for Penelope's, for only when I spoke of her would he listen. I tried to show him Penelope's danger, as it had been revealed to us that very night in Talcott's drunken talk. His reply was a laugh. He had so idealized Penelope that it was inconceivable that she should fall a victim to the attentions of such a vapid creature. He had not seen, as I had, Talcott sober and correct in deportment. He had not fallen, as I had, under the spell of Talcott's easy manner when he had just dropped in from the club to talk of last night's dance and to-morrow's opera. He did not know, as I did, that the whole company from whom Penelope might choose a mate were to the outward eye just such commonplace men whose power of fascination lay in commonplace deeds and words. The Professor, whose whole life had been spent pursuing shadows, was naturally of a romantic turn of mind, and it was even difficult for him to conceive of Penelope marrying at all. That she could be inveigled into so grave a step with a man whose sole claim to merit was well-cut clothes and a command of social *patois* was quite beyond his comprehension. In vain I argued that most women married just such men, and perhaps it was because the sex had attained wisdom with experience, had discovered that a brilliant mind on parade might be amusing, but that, like its duller fellows, it retired to barracks and found contentment in the same humdrum existence as they. The birth of eternal, enduring love was but a matter of propinquity. Sitting on the front doorstep of an afternoon talking and strolling down to the drugstore every evening for soda-water, Darby and Joan discovered that existence apart was worse than death. And so might Joan's richer sister in the old carved chair, under the eyes of Reynolds's majestic lady, grow accustomed to the coming and going of Darby's richer brother, confirm herself in the habit of taking narcotic conversation, talk of last night's dinner and to-morrow's dance, until he seemed to become essential to her existence. All this I explained to the Professor. He retorted that I had grown cynical. Perhaps I had grown cynical, but my cynicism was born of experience—bitter experience, I called it then. Perhaps, imbittered by my own thwarted hopes, I exaggerated the danger in which Penelope stood. Perhaps, in my own vanity and jealousy, I magnified Talcott's sins, knowing well enough that, after all, he was no worse than most of his brothers. Yet there was a danger, and its avoidance was simple could I only induce the man before me to abandon his foolish pride. At least, said I, his brother should know of the night's occurrence.

"Know that, after all my boasts, I had come to waiting in a restaurant and quarrelling with drunken boys?" he cried, shaking his head and waving an arm to deny my demand. "Of course, if there were any possibility of Penelope marrying that fool it would be different. But, David, I know Rufus. He is not brilliant, but he is shrewd, and I'll trust him to find out if anybody is after his money. And Penelope? Haven't I seen Penelope many a night stepping into her carriage—don't you think I can trust her to look higher than that?"

I could not change him, though we argued until dawn came. Then we walked together, in the gray of the early morning, from the poor quarter where he lived to Miss Minion's, a house that had grown in my eyes, by contrast, palatial. The street was still deserted, and standing by my door I made a last appeal. But he shook his head.

"Davy, can't you understand?" he said, as he took my hand in parting. "I admit that I have been a failure up to date, but Rufus and Penelope are the last people in the world that I want to know it, and I'll trust you to be discreet. Some day it may be best to tell them, but at present, no. Silence, David; I have your promise. I'm to have one more chance in Argentina, and if I fail you have your way; but I won't fail."

He turned from me and stood very straight. His overcoat collar was buttoned to the neck, hiding the uniform of his adversity. For a moment, as I watched him, he seemed to be in the gulch again; we looked over the towering walls of brick and stone, and to me they were the ridge-side, dark and sombre in the gray light; we looked beyond the crest of it, beyond the chimneys, the tall pines which pierced the sky-line, and our eyes rested on a flake of cloud. I think it must have been there. I felt the pressure of his hand.

"I'll not be gone long, Davy," he said. "I'm coming back very soon, and till then you will take care of Penelope; won't you, boy?"

CHAPTER XXI

Spring came and with it the Todds. All that winter they had been so far from me, often so far from my thoughts even, that the remembrance of them would bring a shock like a sudden consciousness of sin or the recollection of a duty left undone. My fiancée's communication with me had dwindled to a weekly post-card. At first these had carried to me some little hint of affection, but latterly Gladys had contented herself with commonplace scrawls announcing that this was where they were staying for a few days or that the window in the hotel marked with a cross was hers. And my replies, so conscientiously written every Saturday night, had become rather brief and formal statements of facts. I had long since ceased to take Miss Minion's stairs two steps at a time in my eagerness to secure the portly epistle from abroad; the post-card which had filled its place I regarded with languid interest. You can imagine, then, that it was with surprise that I found, one evening in May, a fat letter directed to me in the tall, angular hand. The reading of it was like a blow which restored me to my senses. I had awakened to find myself not only engaged but on the verge of marriage. The Todds were coming home!

If my fiancée had neglected me for many months, she now overwhelmed me with sixty closely written pages of devotion. It was as though on coming face to face with steamer tickets she, too, had awakened from a dream and found herself engaged. It might well be true that the few weeks in London before embarking on the homeward stage had been her first opportunity to sit down with pen and paper to have what she called "a talk" with me. A year before that talk would have been highly gratifying and flattering, but now I read with a critical eye, and while I could find no fault with the sentiments expressed, the form of the expression irritated me. It was natural that the sentiment pent up in those months of hurried sight-seeing should break forth in this moment of leisure, but to me, grown practical, the form would have been more effective if direct and simple. In those days Penelope was so distant from me, so cold and implacable, that I might have turned to Gladys Todd with a thought that here at last was peace, an end of absurd and inordinate ambition, and perhaps content. Had she written to me simply that she was coming home, I might have soothed myself with the idea that I, too, was going home, back to the simple ways to which I was born, back, after all, to my own people. But Gladys Todd, grown more cultured than ever in the grand tour and revealing her mind in poetical phrases, was as much a being of another world than mine as was Penelope set in her frame of costly simplicity. I should go to the pier to meet her, I said. I knew that it could not be gladly, but I was bound by a sense of honor, by the remembrance of four years through which she had waited for me so patiently, always cheerful and firm in her faith in my power to win a home for us both. Because I was so bound, I vowed that she should never know the change in me, and then if I set myself to the task I might fan into flame the dead embers of my boyish infatuation.

So I stood on the pier that May morning when the Todds came home. So grim was my determination that I might have stood there with a smiling, expectant face had I not in that very hour seen Penelope. I had held to that cherished custom of mine to begin my day with a walk up-town, for always there was a bare chance that I might have a glimpse of her. There was poor consolation in her passing bow; but I could not let her go altogether out of my existence, and even her distant greeting served to keep me in the number of her acquaintances. This day I wanted to take a formal farewell, as if in doffing my hat I renounced all my claims, abandoned all my idle dreams, and set myself to the right path. Of course, I met her, and for a time I had cause to regret that I had not taken the direct way to the pier, for Penelope that morning, as she drove by me rapidly down the avenue, was the embodiment of loveliness, a loveliness beyond the reach of him whom fortune held to the sidewalk. Her horses seemed to step with pride at being a part of such a perfect turnout, and the men on the box to have turned to statues by the congealing of their self-importance. Seeing her, erect, a slender, quiet figure in filmy black, with a white-gloved hand on her parasol, you forgave the horses for lifting their feet so mincingly and the men for staring before them with such hauteur. She whirled by me in all that costly simplicity. I doffed my hat. She saw me and, strangely enough, smiled at me more kindly than in many days. I watched until even the men's tall hats were lost in the maze at Twenty-third Street, and as I watched I said my silent farewell to Penelope Blight.

On the pier, in the cheering, expectant throng that watched the steamer turning into her dock, I leaned on my cane and fixed my eyes with resolution on the ship which was bringing me a life of happiness. But I was silent as I pondered over the radiant smile with which I had been greeted as the carriage swept by. A week ago Penelope had given her head just a tilt of recognition; this morning she had seemed genuinely glad to see me, as though it were a pleasure to know that I lived in the same world. This afternoon, I said forgetfully, I would call upon her again—I had not called for so long. Then I heard my name. I came back to the pier and the cheering crowd, and, looking up, saw Gladys Todd.

Beside me there was a young man who brandished his cane to the peril of his neighbors' heads while he shouted again and again to his inamorata. My duty was to evince just such joy, but when I tried to call her name my lips refused to form it, and I only raised my hat and smiled. Gladys, standing by the ship's rail, waved her hand at me. Then she seemed to forget me entirely, and turned to a youngish-looking, stout man at her side.

The stout man began to interest me, because Gladys had written to me that she would be on deck this day straining her eyes to the shore where her knight would be waiting. Now it seemed as though a brief glance at her knight was sufficient, and that she found more charm in this portly fellow traveller.

Ex-Judge Bundy had small side-whiskers, and always wore a large derby and a frock coat, sometimes black, sometimes pale gray. This youngish-looking stout man was clean shaven, and he had the ruddy skin of the out-of-doors. His hat was brown felt, with its crown wound around with a white pugree—a rather affected hat, but it harmonized with his rough gray tweeds. His appearance was English; he might be, I thought, the governor of some island colony. But when he raised himself from the rail on which he had been leaning, slipped one hand into the breast of his coat, and turned to address Doctor Todd, speaking as though he were Jupiter and the doctor Mercury disguised in dingy clerical clothes, I recognized the patron of my alma mater.

They came down the gangway one by one, the ex-judge leading; then Gladys Todd, rather mannish in a straight-cut English suit and a sailor hat, slung from her shoulder a camera, and nestling in one arm a Yorkshire terrier; then Doctor Todd, unchanged, in the same clothes in which he had sailed, for he was one of those men who could go twice around the world and collect nothing but statistics and postcards; then Mrs. Todd with her two greatest acquisitions in bold evidence, a lorgnette and a caged paroquet.

For a moment I felt that I had come solely to welcome ex-Judge Bundy home. He was first to get my hand, and he held it while he told me how kind it was of me to take so much trouble; it was good to be home; he was always glad to get back to America—speaking as though these expeditions were annual events. He might have gone on and presented me to his friends the Todds had I not disengaged myself and turned to my fiancée with a hand outstretched.

"Look out for Blossom," she warned me, hardly more than touching my finger-tips. "Blossom always snaps at strangers."

Blossom justified the statement by barking viciously at me.

"I am so glad to have you back again, Gladys," I said, speaking in a low voice, for I had an instinctive feeling that ex-Judge Bundy had turned his head, though ostensibly he was busy with porters.

"And it's so nice to see you," she replied, and her gaze wandered vaguely about the pier. She had written that it would be so good just to let her eyes rest on me, but now their appetite was quickly satisfied, and it nettled me.

I spoke to her again, louder, reiterating my delight, and she raised her eyebrows and answered that she was glad that I was pleased. Doctor Todd and Mrs. Todd, however, were not so casual in their greeting. The doctor took both of my hands and declared that this was a happy family reunion. Mrs. Todd kissed me on both cheeks and gave me the paroquet to carry. As we made our way through the crowd, she asked me if I did not think that Gladys had improved, but to myself, as I watched her striding ahead of us in her mannish clothes, I said that she certainly looked quite trim and smart, and I found myself wondering if she still painted tulips on black plaques or would deign to sing "Douglas, tender and true"? Perhaps, to her mind, broadened by a year of travel, I was but a provincial fellow, whose musical education had not gone beyond "The Minute Guns at Sea," who, never having seen the galleries of Europe, could have no appreciation of art.

I was irritated. I wanted to set myself right in her mind, to show her that I, too, had grown broader and wiser. But there was no opportunity. She was busy either with the trunks or in keeping Blossom quiet. During the drive to the hotel the situation was little better. We were in an ancient barouche, piled high with luggage, Mrs. Todd, Gladys, and I, ex-Judge Bundy having tactfully suggested that he take the doctor with him in a hansom.

Mrs. Todd was voluble. She was artfully sentimental. She spoke of the day when, as a young girl, she had left home for six weeks, and she recalled her emotions as she came back to find the doctor waiting for her at the station. They were married shortly afterward. How history repeats itself! But Gladys was not impressed by the coincidence. She merely said that she was glad to have Blossom ashore again, for at times the dog had been fearfully sea-sick. I could have strangled Blossom. Nothing is more humiliating to a man than to discover that a woman's love for him is waning.

Here is a reflection on his power of fascination. But it is doubly humiliating to find himself supplanted by a little woolly dog, to see the caresses which he would claim as his showered with ostentation on a diminutive animal. At that moment it seemed that Blossom had supplanted me. He nestled in her arm, and when for the tenth time I expressed my delight in having her home, she turned from me and stroked the creature's silky back. Time and again I, striving to do my duty, charged against the steel points of her indifference. Even Mrs. Todd noticed my plight. As we were leaving the carriage at the Broadway hotel whither Judge Bundy had led the way she whispered to me that evidently three was a crowd, and acting on that belief, she contrived to leave the two of us alone in the great parlor of the hotel while the doctor and the Judge held a colloquy with the clerk.

This Gladys Todd, sitting amid the faded grandeur of the hotel parlor, this handsome mannish woman in a tweed suit, with a snappy dog in her arm, was not the same girl beside whom I had sat ages ago, watching her paint tulips and sprays of wisteria, not the same whose voice had joined with mine in the sentimental strains of "Annie Laurie." But I felt that I had a duty, and I sat down on the sofa and held out my hand and in a voice of pleading asked her again if she was not glad to see me.

"No, David," she said, turning her eyes downward to Blossom.

I was quite unprepared for such a frank admission, and it came like a blow. In all my thought of Gladys Todd I had quite accustomed myself to the confession that I did not look with pleasure to her home-coming, but that she might regard me in the same light never occurred to me. This knowledge was humiliating. I had been holding myself to the strict line of duty and honor, but I had never suspected that she might be impelled by exactly the same motives. Now I was hurt. As I sat staring at her I cast about for the reason of the change. In my case it was another woman, but a superlatively wonderful woman. In hers it might be another man, a superlatively wonderful man. The idea was not pleasant. In my case there was at least the excuse of old acquaintance. In hers the change must have come in a single week at sea, where miles of walking on the deck and hours leaning on the rail with elbows close together might have revealed some kindred spirit. There flashed to me her action in turning from me, the watcher on the pier, to ex-Judge Bundy, and in him losing all thought of me. But ex-Judge Bundy was not a superlatively wonderful man. He was only a rich widower with two married daughters, and was old enough to be her father. My estimate of my own worth was not so modest that I could conceive of my interests ever being seriously jeopardized by this pompous maker of nails. It was pleasanter to think that the fault lay rather in my own unworthiness than in another's worth, and my pride urged me to combat her, to prove that while I might not be all that a woman of her ideals could ask, yet my shortcomings were those of my fellows in mass and not of the individual.

"I do not understand, Gladys," I said, and I held out my hand to take hers and to reassert my old ascendancy, but I was foiled by Blossom, who darted at me with such fierceness as to compel me to draw back.

"David, I'm so sorry," she said. She looked me in the eyes and spoke with the even voice of one who had entire command of herself. "The plain truth is that I have made a great mistake. I really thought I cared for you."

"And now you think you don't," I said, brushing aside such an absurdity with a wave of my hand. "Nonsense! After four years, you can not tell me that you have suddenly discovered that you never cared for me. I can not give you up for some absurd whim."

She shook her head. "It is not a whim. I see clearly now. We were very young when we became engaged, and I didn't understand how serious the step really was. In the last week at sea I have had time to think it all over, and now I know it best that after this we be just friends—nothing more. You will forget me. You will find another woman worthier of you."

Little as I knew of women, I realized that while these last two statements might be perfectly true, to accept them as true would sever the last strand of the cord which bound us. At that moment I did not want to lose Gladys Todd. She was very lovely as she sat there, with her eyes downcast, caressing her dog. She was the promised reward of my years of work. For her I had labored, scrimped and saved, cramped myself in a narrow room in a boarding-house, and almost shunned my fellows, to realize our dream of the little house on the bit of green. At that moment the dream was very dear to me and I could not see it wrecked for some whim. I grew belligerent. I reached out my hand again, as though by mere physical power I would prove my unchanging mind, but again Blossom was on guard.

"I shall not forget you," I said, and I folded my arms with grim determination and fixed my eyes on her face to break her by mere will-power. And then to what untruth did pride drive me? "I have not changed.

I shall never change, Gladys. I love you now more than ever, and I will not give you up."

The light in her eyes was not quite so cold, nor was her voice so even and at her command. "I am sorry, David, but you must."

"But I won't," I returned.

"Oh, why do you drive me to it?" she cried with a gesture of despair.
"Can't you see, David, that there is some one else to be considered?"

"Some one else?" I exclaimed.

"I didn't think you would be so ungenerous—so selfish," she said in a low voice, while her hands played rapidly over Blossom's head. "I have tried to be honorable and fair to you. But he was so kind, so good—he is so lonely—"

"He—who is he?" I demanded, in my anger abandoning all effort to hold to the honorable course to which I had set myself.

"You should not ask me," she replied, her voice growing hard. "After I had come to know him, to know how fine he was, I really tried to keep on caring for you, David, but I simply couldn't. I am fond of you, of course, but not in the way I thought. You are too young. It is a mistake for a woman to marry a man of her own age. She should marry one whom she can look up to, honor and respect. Love in a cottage is well enough to read of, I suppose, but enduring love must be built on something more."

I wanted to laugh at myself for the fool I had been. I arose. It was useless to sit longer with folded arms and determined eyes fixed on her face, to break her will by hypnotic power. I knew that I was defeated, and however better defeat might be than victory, judged in wisdom, it was not pleasant to a man of spirit. I stood before her pulling on a glove and she looked up at me with a suggestion of defiance. I was not heart-broken. I felt that I should be, but I knew that I was suffering only in my pride. I wanted to sit down again in friendly fashion and tell her how hard I had tried to do my duty, that I too loved another, and that now she had made the way easy for me, but I refrained from such petty revenge.

I held out my hand. "I wish you all happiness, Gladys," I said. "You must not trouble about me. No doubt you have chosen wisely."

"You are a dear, good boy, David," she said, rising and addressing me in a motherly tone as though she had suddenly attained twice my years.

"You will find another woman more worthy of you—I know you will. And when you come to Harlansburg you must bring her to see us. We shall be such good friends."

To Harlansburg? The whole story was clear in my mind. I remembered the Egyptian picture, the pyramids, the camels, and young Marshall's warning. And I had been so blind that a moment since I was saying that if another man had wrought this changed mind in Gladys Todd he must be a superlatively wonderful man. After all, the superlatively wonderful man was ex-Judge Bundy. Now the blow to my pride was fairly crushing. It did seem that I had a few natural qualities which should have weighed in the scales against such a rival. But if I had youth, he had wealth; if I had promise, he had the same promise of youth fulfilled in giant nail works; if I offered a vine-clad cottage on a bit of green, he could give the big gray-stone house with many turrets, the lawn with the marble lions and perfect terraces sloping down to the ornate fence. The very absurdity of the situation saved me from regret.

Gladys Todd was looking at me with narrowed eyes. I think she expected some outburst of emotion. Perhaps she felt sorry for the pain that she had caused me. But as I looked at her and remembered the past, as I thought of the judge, the house, and the marble lions, even my wounded pride was forgotten. I checked the smile which was threading my lips. I took my congé as a man should, gravely, with head bowed under the crushing blow, with eyes downcast as though they would never again look up into the joyous sunlight. I turned and left the room.

By the rule, I should have looked back, hesitated, and gone on. But my mind was filled with the fear of meeting Doctor Todd or Mrs. Todd, or worse, Judge Bundy. How to treat Judge Bundy, did I meet him, was not clear—whether to pass him with a haughty stare, or to stop and congratulate him, or even thank him. Discreetly I followed the dark windings of the hall and left the hotel by a private entrance. In the street I looked up into the sunshine. I was free. I could not dissemble with myself any longer, and I turned to the avenue with a quick and joyous step. A new life had opened to me and I was stepping into it unburdened, and with a prize to fight for. In those few moments Gladys Todd had gone into the past. She was hardly more than a shadow to me now, hardly more real than Mr. Pound or Miss Spinner or any other of the dim figures in my memory. Before me was Penelope—the future and Penelope. Her world was not my world, but I vowed that I would make it mine.

Perhaps, I said, I shall see her again this very morning and perhaps she will greet me again with that same kindly, glorious smile. And surely she would smile did she know that I was free from the yoke to which I had bent myself in a moment of forgetfulness. My duty had been to Penelope since that day when we rode from the clearing, and from that day my heart had always been with her. Reading from the past, her destiny and mine were written before me in clear, bold letters. How good the world was! How bright the day! How quick my step as I turned up-town!

And I saw Penelope. She bowed to me from a hansom, and I answered, beaming. I halted. Herbert Talcott was sitting at her side. He stared at me, tipped his hat brusquely, then turned to her and made some laughing remark.

I stood looking after the receding hansom until it disappeared in the maze of traffic. I took my congé as a man does sometimes, with my head bowed under the crushing blow, and my eyes downcast, knowing in my heart that for me the sunshine could nevermore be joyous.

CHAPTER XXII

There was no doubt in my mind that Penelope Blight was engaged to marry Talcott. They announced the fact when they rode the length of the Avenue together in a hansom. But had I questioned the meaning of their appearing thus in public I could not long have cheered myself with vain hope, for the papers next morning blazoned the news to all the world. That they printed it under great staring head-lines was not surprising to me, for to me this fact transcended all others in importance. Beside it the rumblings of war in the Balkans, the devastating flood in China, or the earthquake which wrecked a southern city were trifles. So to my distorted view the papers were filled with the announcement of my overwhelming misfortune. Only by the greatest effort could I drag myself from reading and rereading to my humdrum task. Before me in black and white was the last chapter in my own story, the story which had begun that day when I went fishing. Every line of it, couched in the hackneyed phrases of the business, was a cutting blow, and yet I must return again and again to the beating. Had Rufus Blight been a poor man, a worthy man whose sole claim to consideration lay in his having discovered some balm for human ills, then a paragraph would have sufficed for the announcement of his niece's engagement. But he was a millionaire; he lived in one of the largest houses in town, and his niece was the greatest catch of the day, measured in dollars; therefore, the coming marriage was worthy of columns. The existence of Herbert Talcott became also of prime importance, not because he had ever done anything, but because he was to marry the heiress of the Blight fortune. How many a worthy Jones or a poor but noble Robinson has to descend to an advertisement to make his happiness known to the careless world? How many a lovely Joan goes to her wedding unread-of because her forebears were lacking, not in those qualities which open the gates of heaven, but in acquisitiveness?

To the public it could matter little that Rufus Blight was a simple, kindly soul who was as contented years ago when he stood behind his counter as to-day when he sought on the golf-links that sense of action which is necessary to a man's happiness. The vital fact was that the trust had paid him millions for his steel-works; not that Penelope was a simple, lovely woman like thousands of her sisters, but that her wedding-gifts would be worthy of the daughter of Maecenas. Accustomed though I had become in the routine of my work to just such a judgment of vital facts, now that the story told was my own last chapter I made a silent protest against the manner of the telling.

I thought of Rufus Blight as a quiet man, happiest not in the stately library, but in his den surrounded by a medley of homely things. Thinking of Penelope I turned to those vagrant dreams, now forbidden. In them Penelope and I were to go back to the valley, to ride again over the mountain road, to stand again as we had stood that day when she led me over the tangled trail into the sunlit clearing. Those were joys in which millions had no part. But as I read of the Blight millions, and of that blue-blooded Talcott line which traced back a hundred years to a member of the cabinet, it was hard for me to believe that I knew these exalted beings, that I had sat with Rufus Blight and talked of days in the valley, that Penelope and I had galloped over the country astride the same white mule, that I even had engaged with one so distinguished as Herbert Talcott in a brawl in a restaurant. Gilded by those who report the comings and goings of those whom one should know, as Mrs. Bannister might put it, they seemed aliens, manikins that moved in a stage world. As such I tried to think of them, for it was best, but I had as well set myself to efface my memory.

The last chapter of my own story was written by unknown hands. The epilogue remained, in which I was to go on seeking what contentment I could find in action. But my whole story was not written on these flimsy pages. It was before me always and always I was turning to it, always asking myself how it would have run had this not happened or had that occurred. Studying it over and over again in my room at night and on my long walks up-town, I found that I could not think of Penelope Blight as an alien creature for whose happiness I had no longer any care. What of her story which was in the writing? Did she know this Talcott whom she had chosen to fill its last pages? She knew him as I knew him first, as a quiet, gentlemanly man with pleasant manners. Was it not her right to know him as I knew him now, as a drunken brawler, who in his cups had betrayed the unworthy motive of his devotion? These questions troubled me for many days. I was not a prude. I knew that all men have their foibles, that many great men have over-indulged in liquor, that a man's whole character is not to be damned by a single slip. I knew that did all women see the men whom they choose for marriage as others see them we should have a plague of spinsters. But I feared for Penelope Blight. This was not because Talcott was worse than the mass of his fellows, but because the best of his fellows was none too good for her. But how could I go to her and declare that Talcott when drunk had avowed a purpose to marry her for her millions? It seemed the part of a tattler. The world would say that I acted from jealousy. Indeed, it was hard at times to convince myself that jealousy was not the basis of my fear for her. Yet I felt that I must save her from a disillusionment which might come too late. Were her father here that disillusionment would be speedy; but he was far away, and always his last words were with me, as he spoke them that night in the street: "You will take care of Penelope, won't you, boy?"

I had promised that. It was simply repeating my boyhood promise. And now I kept asking myself if I was not forgetting that trust when I kept silent because I feared in my pride to place myself in the light of an intermeddler, a bearer of scandalous tales; I would remember that morning when we had stood by the cabin door and I told her not to be afraid for I was guarding her. Was I guarding her?

For two weeks I kept puzzling over my course of action. I felt that the knowledge I held was hers by right, and hers, not mine, to judge of its triviality. Yet I could not bring myself to face her with it. Then came the time when I had to speak at once if I was to speak at all.

Mr. Hanks sent for me. As I stood before him, he studied me through his spectacles with his cold eyes, as he had studied me in those days when I was trying to persuade him to give me work, and I began counting my sins, wondering if in the cataclysm of ill luck which had overtaken me, I was to lose my position also.

After a moment he asked, as casually as he might have assigned me to an expedition to Harlem a few years before: "Malcolm, how soon can you leave for London?"

"At once," I said, and I spoke as casually as he, though my heart leaped at the mention of London, for here I sensed an opportunity beyond my wildest hopes.

"At once," he laughed and rubbed his hands with satisfaction. "I told the old man you would say that. He said that you were too young to fill Colt's shoes. Colt is ill, Malcolm; has to come home for a year's rest and I have backed you to do his work awhile. Of course, you won't do it as well as he, but you will do it fairly well, I think."

"I will do my best," said I, smiling.

"That is the way to talk," he returned. "I need hardly tell you to keep your head and work hard, and perhaps you will pull through till Colt gets back. He will be a little hurt when he sees his substitute. He has been there twenty years and feels himself quite a figure in the world, but as he has cabled for relief at once, he can't complain if we send him the one man who is always ready to go anywhere at once. Really, you have three days; you sail on Saturday."

I could have gone that day, had Hanks commanded it. The trust which he imposed in me was my reward for always having obeyed him without question, and in my state of mind that morning, between walking from his office to the steamer for years of absence and staying as I was, I should have chosen the former alternative. I wanted to get away. The only place where I could find even the shadow of contentment was at my desk. There imperative tasks filled a mind at other times occupied with unwholesome brooding. I seemed to move through waste places, with no object to catch the eye and thought and to drive away the consciousness of my unhappiness. Even my walk on Fifth Avenue had been abandoned lest at any moment Penelope might pass me with Talcott at her side; Miss Minion's had become a place of terror, for by ill chance Tom Marshall had been introduced to Talcott and he had developed a habit of dropping in on me and telling me what he had said to Bert Talcott and what Bert Talcott had said to him. He seemed to think that Talcott had conferred knighthood on him by knowing him. There were times, even, when I had gravely considered abandoning my chosen career and retiring to a bucolic life of loneliness in the valley. And at other times, into such depths of despondency was I plunged that I could seriously consider abandoning self entirely and devoting the remainder of my wrecked life to doing good, though just what trend my saintliness would take I never determined. In monkish days, I suppose, I should have gone into a cloister. But Hanks aroused me. Of course he did not know my thoughts. With his clear eyes he did not see that my life was a ruin. He regarded me rather as a fortunate man to whom opportunities were opening wonderfully well, and I accepted his view; though I was sure that I was taking a road which led to nowhere, yet travelling was better than sitting still. Looking at Hanks, I forgot that he had a wife and four accomplished daughters over in Jersey, and I said that I should take life as he took it, with a cynical interest in the game, with all thought on the run of the cards and little for personal winnings.

When I had cleared my desk for my successor and had bidden good-by to my old known tasks, I found myself turning to the new and unknown with more interest than I had believed myself capable of showing. So much was to be done in those three days that I had little time for self-condolence. One day had to be taken for a farewell to my parents; and what a day it was, with my father and mother driving down to Pleasantville in the late night to meet me that they might not lose one moment of my visit! Only when I slept were they from my side, for my mother's mind was filled with all the stories of shipwreck that she had ever read, and my father had doubts as to whether or not the moral environment of London was such as he would ask for his son. My father never had much faith in my moral strength. Then Mr. Pound came up to see me, having, as usual, commandeered Mr. Smiley's comfortable phaeton for the transport of himself and Mrs. Pound. His hair was white now, and he bent a little, and his voice had lost some of its pompous roll, but his phrases were as round as ever. He insisted that I owned the paper. He placed his hand on my head and for the information of Miss Agnes Spinner named my good points much as a jockey would those of a favorite horse. He congratulated himself on the success of his method of training and called on Judge Malcolm to admit that his effort to have his son go to Princeton had been based on a misconception of the underlying merits of the McGraw system of education.

The Pounds stayed to supper, much to my mother's suppressed indignation, for she had invited them, never thinking that under such unusual circumstances they would accept so promptly, so that by the time they drove away I had begun to feel that I must have made this hurried journey just to say good-by to my old mentor. In the hour, all too brief, that remained to me my mother broached the subject of my broken engagement, for in that she saw the reason of my melancholy, which I had been at pains to conceal. It could not be hidden from her quick eyes. She was convinced that Gladys Todd was not in her right mind; no woman in her right mind would deliberately refuse to marry such a man as her son. Was it a question of blood? Surely there was none better in the land than that which flowed in the veins of the McLaurins. Was it money? There was no finer farm in all the valley than the one which some day would be mine, with the bridge stock and the Kansas bonds. Was it character? Recalling the Sunday afternoons when she and I had worked together so patiently over the catechism and Bible lessons, she was sure that she had done her duty toward me and could never dream of my having failed in mine. So, to my mother's thinking, the loss was Gladys Todd's, a consoling view of my plight which she endeavored to make me take, and she sought to cheer me with a highly uncomplimentary estimate of the frivolous character of my quondam fiancée. It could serve no purpose for me to enlighten her as to the real truth, for did she know the truth she might be haunted by the dread spectre of self-destruction. So her last words as we parted were an admonition to me not to think that all women were as blind and as faithless as Gladys Todd.

Her arms were around my neck and she whispered in my ear, that even my father might not hear her: "Davy, take Penelope. We McLaurins always looked down on the Blights, but that makes no difference, Davy—take Penelope."

CHAPTER XXIII

But one day was left to me before I went to my new life, and yet I was still asking myself if I was taking care of Penelope. I had set myself to go through life alone, regarding all women with cynical indifference. But of her I could not think with cynical indifference. Her one act which might have fed my cynicism was her choice of a man of the character of Herbert Talcott. Then, after all, I reflected, she did not know his true character. And yet did I? Was it my place to become a bearer of tales? Over and over I asked myself the question, and I could find no other answer than that of affirmation, for it was her right to know what had occurred between her father and Talcott. And she should know it, I said at last decisively; she should know it, not from me, but from Rufus Blight. And, telling it, I must give up my last hope of her.

So I went to Rufus Blight on the afternoon before I sailed, and I went not without misgivings as to the part that I was playing. Many times in the walk up the Avenue I turned back, doubting, and then I would repeat my old-time promise to Penelope and the Professor's injunction given to me that early morning as we stood together on the street. And so at last I found myself before the great house, and the grilled door closed behind me, leaving no retreat.

Mr. Blight was in his "den," resting after his day's golf in a deep chair by an open window, and he rose from a litter of evening papers to greet me.

"Well, David, we thought that you had forgotten us," he said. "Penelope remarked just this morning that it was high time you appeared to offer your congratulations."

"I have been very busy," I returned. "To-morrow I start abroad for a year at least, and I came to say good-by and to tell you—"

In my eagerness to have my story over I should have plunged right into it, but he interrupted me.

"Abroad, eh? Well, we may see you after the wedding. We are all going over after the wedding."

The calm way in which Mr. Blight spoke of the wedding chilled me. It was so absolutely settled that there was to be a wedding that in me there seemed to be embodied that mythical person who is commanded so sternly to speak or forever hold his peace. For a time I did hold my peace, but it was only because Rufus Blight evinced such a lively interest in my affairs that I had no opportunity to speak of those matters which touched him so intimately.

"Well, we certainly shall hunt you up in London in September," he said. "We shall be over in September. The wedding is to be in July at Newport. We have taken a house there, or rather Mrs. Bannister has for us." He saw that I could not restrain a smile at the mention of Mrs. Bannister, and he laughed heartily. "I don't know how we should get along without Mrs. Bannister. You see, David, all I know anything about is the steel trade, and being out of that I have to have a general manager for this social business. She certainly does manage. Why, if it wasn't for her I doubt if we could arrange a wedding. Indeed, I sometimes even doubt if there would be an engagement."

This same doubt had been tenaciously present in my own mind for some days, and much as I should have liked to express it with heat and to join to it my opinion of the masterful woman's manoeuvres, I simply laughed formally and said, "Indeed!"

"I can talk to you confidentially, David," Rufus Blight went on, leaning toward me with his cigar poised in the air. "It is good to have an old friend to whom you can unburden your mind, and it has been on my mind that Mrs. Bannister has had too large a finger in this matrimonial pie—not, of course, that I am not pleased. I am getting old, and it is a relief to think of Penelope settled in life with a thoroughly respectable, steady young man like Talcott; but, do you know, I suspect sometimes that Mrs. Bannister had more to do with Penelope making up her mind than is altogether wise? She has talked about him continually, and between his coming to the house continually and Mrs. Bannister talking of him continually, Penelope didn't have a fair chance."

Rufus Blight smoked thoughtfully, and I remarked that I had no doubt that Penelope knew her own mind.

"Oh, yes," he returned. "Understand that I have nothing whatever against Talcott. She might fare far worse. He is unapproachable as far as character goes, but sometimes he seems to me rather dull. I suppose that is because he doesn't do anything, and I wonder how long Penelope will be satisfied with a man who doesn't do anything but what Mrs. Bannister calls 'go everywhere.' Will she not soon weary of going everywhere? I couldn't stand it myself. The other night I had to go to Talcott's uncle's to dine, and how I wished that I was home! The uncle is a respectable old man, too, who has never done anything either, and all he talked about was terrapin and gout. When he had finished with them in the smoking-room, his mind seemed exhausted, and he left me to the mercy of another man who tried to pump me about International Steel common. Is that pleasure?" Rufus Blight waved his cigar with a gesture of contempt. "I suppose Penelope would be perfectly safe with such people if anything happened to me; but would she be happy? Mrs. Bannister says that I should be satisfied to have her marry into a family so eminently respectable, and I suppose I should."

He looked at me, asking my opinion.

"Undoubtedly the Talcotts are highly respectable," said I. "They are one of the few old families who have succeeded in maintaining their position in New York."

"That is just what Mrs. Bannister says," he returned. "They are certainly very kindly, and could not have treated Penelope better than they have. Talcott's aunt has Penelope with her all the time. I suppose I should be satisfied." He hesitated a moment. "But, confound it, David, don't you see, I am not? Sometimes I think it must be because I am jealous, and I try to put that feeling away and to look impartially at Penelope's happiness. Then I must agree with Mrs. Bannister. Here is Talcott, a young man of good family, of exemplary conduct. The only thing against him is an idle life; but if he doesn't have to work, why should he? Yet it seems to me that Penelope is not the kind of woman who would be satisfied with a husband who sat around the house all day and found his main interest in terrapin and gout. Can't you see my predicament, David?"

He rose and paced the room. Twice he circled the table, while I sat in silence watching him. Then he halted at the fireplace and stood there, forgetfully warming his hands at an imaginary blaze. After a moment he faced me. "I know about making steel, David, but in matters like this I am utterly lost. How I wish Hendry were here to advise me!"

My opportunity had come more easily than I had expected. "I can help you, perhaps," said I, "for I have seen him."

"You have seen him?" cried Rufus Blight, and he crossed the room to me in great excitement. "When, David, and where?"

"Here in New York."

"Splendid! And he is coming to us, eh? I know he is at last."

"In two years. He has promised to come home in two years."

Rufus Blight sat down in his old chair and stared at me. "In two years? Why, David, we need him now. He must come now. We will bring him home—you and I."

"But we can't," said I. "He is far from here now; he went away last winter."

"You saw him and did not bring him home!" Rufus Blight's voice rose to a pitch of indignation. "I don't understand. Did you tell him how we wanted him—Penelope and I—how we had searched for him everywhere?" I nodded. "You told him that and he would not come?" He leaned toward me angrily. "Well, why didn't you let me know about him?"

"Because it could have done no good," I answered. "I had to promise him that I would not, yet because he feared that I should break my promise, he slipped away. I saw him but once. When I went to see him again he was gone—to Argentina."

"I see," said Rufus Blight more gently. "You must pardon my losing my temper, but it was hard to think that he was near us and yet we never knew it; strange that you did not tell us of it earlier."

"I should not tell you now were there not certain circumstances connected with my meeting with your brother that it is best that you know," I returned.

I went on with my story very quietly, as if it were one in which I had little personal concern. I knew that Rufus Blight was not quick to catch the hidden meaning of a word or tone, so that it was not from any fear of him discovering my biassed mind that I made my statement so unimpassioned. It was because I wanted to satisfy myself that I was acting alone for Penelope's good and disclosing the truth, uncolored, for her to judge. Slowly I told it all, in a dry, unvarnished sequence of facts. I told him of my visit to O'Corrigan's; of the fight and my interference; of my hours with his brother and his account of his wanderings and trials; of my vain plea to bring him back to Penelope and his refusal to surrender his search for that chimerical prize for which he had struggled so futilely. To me the vital part of my story had to do with Herbert Talcott. But for its apparent effect on Rufus Blight I had as well discovered his brother thrashing Tom Marshall. To him that incident was trivial. What he wanted to know was how Henderson looked. Was he well? Was he in absolute poverty? Did he speak as though he really meant to come home in two years? When I had finished he asked me these questions again and again. He thrashed the whole story over, all but the essential part. He leaned back in his chair and stared at the ceiling. Henderson in want? To think of his brother in want and he so willing to share with him the fruits of his enormous prosperity. Henderson going afoot to Tibet? What a man he was! That was just the kind of thing he would do—some wild chase like that. And the South Seas? How I should like to hear him tell about them, David! He will come back—he has promised—in two years. He will fail. Poor old Hendry always fails, but it will be good to have him—he in that chair, I in this—and to hear him talk of it all.

So always was the essential fact missed. I was angry with Rufus Blight. I wanted to shake him, to shout into his ear, to drive into his dull brain the real purpose of my story. But I held my temper and reverted to the fight with quiet but meaning emphasis.

"Hendry was always a handy man with his fists, David," said Rufus Blight. "In his younger days he was hard to arouse, but get him angry and he was the devil himself. He wasn't afraid of anything. It was just like him to start alone to Lhasa—just like him, David."

I had begun to suspect that Rufus Blight was not so obtuse as I judged him, but was passing over that part of my story which had to do with Talcott, because he really liked Talcott and was inclined to lighten the shadow which his conduct that night had thrown on his exemplary character. I had told him all. I had repeated the exact words which the Professor had given me as the cause of the assault, and now in his brother's mind they were lost in a rapt interest in his adventures. If with design, then my mission had been futile, and it was wisdom to retreat. If without design, I could not bring myself to the rôle of a prosecutor, and to argue was to tread on dangerous ground. I had done what I believed right. I had kept my promise. So I rose to go. I must have given Rufus Blight a strange look as I held out my hand. I was furious at him for his obtuseness or his cunning, and I must have shown it, for he returned my gaze with a puzzled stare. Then a gleam of light filtered into that brain, so competent to deal with steel-works, so hopelessly dull on other matters.

> "David," he said, "you have delayed a long time in
> telling me this.
> Now, why?"

I answered him, speaking no longer in cold, business-like tones. I held out my hands wide apart and took a step toward him to bring my eyes nearer his, for every nerve was set to drive the truth into him.

"I tell you now because your brother's last words to me were, 'Take care of Penelope.' How can I take care of Penelope? She has gone far from me. It is for you that his words have meaning. Can't you see?"

His hands were groping vaguely in the air behind him. He found the arms of his chair and sat down weakly, and with his head thrown back he looked up at me with an expression of wonder on his face.

"I leave to-morrow," said I. "It will be a long time before I see you again. Will you say good-by to Penelope for me?"

"I see, David," he exclaimed. His voice snapped, as I fancy it did sometimes when affairs in the steelworks were awry. "I was so interested in Hendry I forgot all about that fellow Talcott. Now, tell me this—did he—"

"I have told you everything," said I. "There is nothing left for me to say except good-by."

Far, indeed, had Penelope gone from me. So I had said to Rufus Blight—almost my last word to him. So I said to myself as I stood by the steamer's rail and looked back to the towering mass of the lower city. That very morning I had seen her: she driving down the Avenue, alone, sitting very straight and still in her victoria; I on the pavement, taking my last walk up-town in the never failing hope to have a glimpse of her. Now, what would I have given not to have yielded to that temptation? She had seen me. I halted sharply and raised my hat, thinking that she might stop to say good-by, for she knew that I was going away. She did see me. She looked straight at me, coldly, and not even by a tremor of her eyebrows did she give a sign that to her I was other than any stranger loitering on the curb.

CHAPTER XXIV

Time, the philosopher said, takes no account of humanity. "The activest man sets around mostly," I once heard Stacy Shunk remark as he sat curled up on the store-porch, nursing a bare foot and viewing the world through the top of his hat. Did the most active man calmly and without egotism dissect the sum of his useful accomplishment, he would be highly discouraged, for time is a relentless destroyer. But a man can not take so disdainful a measure of his own value. He must live. To superior minds like the philosopher's or Stacy Shunk's he may be living his tale of years happy in constantly hoodwinking himself with the idea that he is an important factor in some great purpose. Now in certain moods I might attain to the lofty view of the philosopher and Stacy Shunk. Then I would be confronted by my friend the Professor, who would have been dissatisfied had he been the author of Plato's dialogues or the victor of Waterloo. Then it seemed to me that the wise man would allow himself to be hoodwinked, and would walk hard and fast without too critical an eye on the results of his journey. It is when he sits around that Stacy Shunk's active man is discontented, and this is not because he accomplishes much when working, but because he accomplishes less when idle. Here I had the example of Rufus Blight, brought at last to expending his restless energy in chopping golf-balls out of bunkers. So work became to me the panacea for my ills. I plunged into the struggle harder than ever, and in working found that self-forgetfulness which is akin to contentment. It was indeed marching under sealed orders.

Those nights at sea the Professor's words were often in my mind. I was terribly lonely, and I could stand by the hour at the ship's rail looking into the heavens, and beyond them into the limitless spaces where our vulgar minds have placed the home of the Great Spirit whose mysterious purposes we fulfil. How infinitesimal seemed my own part in that purpose, though I played it as best I could. I turned in vain to those limitless spaces to ask why and for what I lived? Did I ask how I should live, the answer came from the limitless spaces within me as clearly as though written on this page. My mother had written it there, unscientifically yet indelibly, in my boyhood days, and Mr. Pound had added his few words, almost hidden beneath a mass of verbiage about Ahasuerus, and before them my forebears had every one of them left imprinted some sage injunction gained from their experience in living. So I gathered my strength to do my best. But there was a lack of definiteness in my purpose. There was no goal at which I aimed. In my younger days I had had instilled into me the necessity of aspiring to a particular height, to something concrete, to become a leader at the bar, in politics or commerce, a Webster, a Clay, or a Girard. But now I cared little if I never owned the paper for which I worked. The task at hand alone interested me, and to that I bent every energy.

One task lay at my hand that year when I was in London, beside the routine of my office, and now I undertook its completion for the personal pleasure which it gave me to gather into concise form the result of some years of study and patient digging for facts in forgotten volumes and manuscripts. The result was surprising. The book, offered to a publisher with diffident apology, raised a storm of discussion in a half-dozen languages. To me it had been only a pleasant intellectual exercise to trace "the habit of war" back to the simple animal instincts of our ancestors; to follow the changing methods of fighting from the days when men assailed one another with stone axes to the modern expression of fighting intelligence in the battleship; to show how, with every step which we had taken to eradicate disease and alleviate suffering, we had taken two in refining and organizing our power of destruction. I had facts and figures to mark the steps in this twofold human progress, and to show the cost to the race of a single century not only of warring, but of following the sage injunction to be prepared for war in times of peace. Had I closed my labor there, the book would have been lost on the shop-shelves; but writing ironically, I went on to argue on the benefits of war and of the necessity of the race continuing in the exercise of this elemental passion. I had always abhorred preaching, and here to preach I used a method of inversion, peppering my argument with platitudes on war as a needed discipline for the spiritual in man by its lessons in fortitude and self-sacrifice, and on the softening influences of peace. But what I had intended as subtle irony was discovered by a great conservative journal to be an unassailable argument, supported by facts and figures, demonstrating the futility of the movements for international amity. I was hailed as a bold, clear thinker who had pricked the bubble of unintelligent altruism, who at a time when philanthropists were preaching disarmament had proved that men could never disarm as long as they were born with arms, legs and healthy senses.

So David Malcolm was quite unexpectedly raised to some eminence by a conservative English journal which was clamoring for increased naval expenditure; and once discovered, he found himself not without honor in his own country, for he was assailed from the platform of Carnegie Hall by the advocates of a gentle life, and in Congress his work was used as a text-book by those who were fighting for a larger military establishment. The *Morgen-Anzeiger*, in Berlin, printed a translation with the purpose of quelling the opposition to army service, while the reading of a chapter in the French Chamber resulted in an appropriation for experiments in submarines. Such was the effect of my well-intended irony. To-day, of course, the true purport of the facts, figures and argument are better known, but then I had the chagrin of seeing my projectile explode in the wrong camp, and I did not try to right myself, because I feared that to explain the error might nullify the ultimate effect of the explosion. To my mother alone did I trouble to point out my real meaning, and then because she had been shocked to see me assailed in her favorite journal, the *Presbyterian Searchlight*, as a notable example of the result of philosophy unwarmed by religion.

That I should have to make my peace with my mother was not surprising, but my old professional mentor, Mr. Hanks, loved a paradox; if he wanted to call a man a fool, he praised him for his wisdom; if he wished to disprove a proposition, he argued for it, adroitly exposing its weakness, and yet he wrote to me indignantly.

"I can not understand how from the mass of facts you have gathered you could calmly advance to so cruel an argument," he said. "Your own figures protest against your bloodthirsty philosophy. Machiavelli's Prince is a mollycoddle beside your ideal modern statesman. And yet, Malcolm, you could as easily have produced a work which would have stood for years as a reproach to the diplomacy of our time."

Dear old Hanks! It was from his suburban heart that he spoke thus, as the father of four accomplished daughters, and not as the sceptic of the office who was always quick to prick the bubbles of pretence. But it was not long before he had an opportunity to turn ironical himself, and I could fancy the grim smile with which he wrote the despatch which sent me from the academic discussion of war to the study of war at first hand.

"Join the Turks at once."

It was laconic. To me it said more. It was addressed to David Malcolm, suddenly become known as an advocate of wholesale human butchery, and told him to follow the camp and see how suffering benefits the race, to stand by the guns and watch them take the toll that nations pay for their aggrandizement. To-day, when the book is understood, when peace conferences invite me to address them and navy leagues condemn me in resolutions, Hanks wonders why I accepted his commission with such hearty acquiescence. He deems me inconsistent.

The truth was that my heart leaped at this opportunity for real adventure. I was years older than in the days when I dreamed of wearing a cork helmet and carrying the Gospel and an elephant gun into darkest Africa; but few of us, when we become men, really put away childish things. Here was my boyhood's dream come true and glorified. And what a week I had buying my toys! The cork helmet became a reality, and with it I equipped myself with smartly fitting khaki, and in the quiet of my lodgings viewed myself with ineffable satisfaction. I bought equipment enough to have lasted me through a three years' campaign, as I have since learned from experience, for the exigencies of transport made me abandon most of it at the very outset of my new career. But the loss was more than compensated by the delight which I had in the brief possession of so much warlike paraphernalia.

For two years after that I lived in the midst of armies. It was action, and to me inaction was a dreadful sickness. Even when we lay in camps for weeks and months there was the never-ending preparation for the struggles which lay ahead, and though there were hours as quiet as Broadway in mid-August, days could not be dull when you could see the smoke of hostile fires on distant mountains or a wild scout hovering on the fringe of the desert. For me the happiest days were when I could ride with the marching columns, when the distant barking of the guns called me to a hard gallop, when at night by the scant light of a candle I sat in my tent cross-legged, with my pad on my knee and my pencil in hand.

In war man strips himself of the unessential things which make up the museum of superfluities that he calls his home. At home he has countless troubles. Here he has few, but though they are simple, they are vital. I faced these elemental problems for the first time when with my little caravan I set out to join the Turkish army where it lay camped near the Greek frontier. As I rode my vagrant thoughts might turn back to home, and in my heart I might feel the old dull pain and longing, but when a pack-horse was running away with half my commissariat on his back such moody meditations had to be broken short. Some days the question of mere bread for a crying stomach became vital, or a flask of water for a parched throat. There were nights when I should have given all I possessed, not for the folding-bed long since abandoned, but for a blanket in which to wrap myself as I slept in a trench. Within a week it was hard for me to believe that I had not spent all my life in the wake of an advancing army. London, New York—they were of another age. Home to me was a tent pitched by the Thessalian roadside, with my shaggy horses picketed about and my shaggier attendants chattering their strange jargon. This was luxury to one who had slept the night before in the rain, or worse, perhaps, in some shamble in a filthy Greek village. This was hardship, but I came to love it for the action and the forgetfulness. In the brief weeks of an opera-bouffe war I had my first taste of great adventure, and once knowing the joy of it I forgot for a time my academic ideas on the absurdity of international quarrels, and was happy only when I rode with the marching columns.

I came even to love the Turks, and I rode almost a Turk at heart over the plain of Thessaly. For they were strong men, these sturdy brown fellows who slouched as they marched, but always went forward, never faltering when the bullets snapped around them and the red fezzes of their comrades were dropping in the dust. It angered me to see my fellow-Christians shoot them down and then run toward Athens and the protecting skirts of the powers, for I knew that the powers would render their battles futile and their conquests empty and send them back with ranks depleted to their distant hills. They fought, most of them, hardly knowing why, save that in some mysterious way it was for their faith. They were dirty and ragged, but they were patient and brave. Ill-fed and ill-clothed, they could march all day in the scorching sun, uncomplaining, shiver all night in chilling winds, and then shamble on in the face of death.

The Greeks fought a little and ran. They would stand and fight a little again—then run. I thought that we should chase them to Athens. I had visions of riding into the city in the wake of Edhem Pasha and pitching my ragged camp by the Acropolis. But I never passed Pharsala.

It was there that I met the Professor again.

He lay at the foot of a roadside shrine which had been wrecked by a shell and hardly cast a shadow. But he had been dragged out of the noonday heat into that bit of shadow by some kindly enemy and there left to die. The war had finished with him and had swung on. He was hardly worth even an enemy's glance.

Riding by with my eyes intent on the moving fight ahead, I should have passed him but for my dragoman. To Asaf there was nothing unusual in the pitiful figure by the roadside, propped against a stone, with the head fallen on an outstretched arm and a still hand clutching an empty water-flask. It was the clothes that called a second glance. Save the cartridge belt around the waist there was nothing to mark the man as a soldier. The kindly hand which had placed him there had drawn over his face a soiled gray hat; his suit was a worn blue serge, dyed now with dark stains, and his feet were encased in patent-leather shoes, cracked and almost soleless. The plain ahead was filled with the clamor of battle; a pack-train clattered by me, hurrying to the front, and but for these and for Asaf, the ragged Turk at my side, pointing mutely to the still dark heap, I might have thought myself at home, in my own valley, come suddenly on a mountain tragedy. And now I dismounted, and, raising the hat, looked into the thin brown face that I had first seen years ago so wistfully watching the little flake of cloud which hovered over the ridges.

CHAPTER XXV

I had thought this morning that at last I was to see a pitched battle, for the Greek army was well intrenched in the hills north of Pharsala and made some show of a stand there. At noon I stood on the crest of the same hills watching the usual retreat. A few miles away, its gray houses blotched against the mountains which guard southern Thessaly, was the town, and in the valley, drawing in toward it, the Greeks, with the enemy on their rear and flanks enclosing them in a narrowing semicircle of fire. Before me stretched the road, a white band across the undulating green of the plain. In that road, a mile away, I saw the rear-guard as it retired swiftly but steadily, facing again and again to deliver its volleys into the lines of the advancing foe. Once before I had seen that same small company fighting bravely as they were now, checking the advance of a whole division. I knew them for the Foreign Legion. Little black patches were left in the road as they fell back, and it made me sick at heart to think of these men throwing away their lives in so futile a cause. That little black patch had been perhaps a student filled with fervor for Pan-Hellenism, a college boy out for an adventurous holiday, or perhaps a soldier of fortune who held his life cheaply and was ready to give it for the brief joy of a battle. Now I stood by one of those little black patches, by the first still outpost which marked the fight down the road.

Had the horse which I had bought from a dealer in Ellasona been four or five years younger, I might never have noticed my friend as he lay there by the ruined shrine. In the ride out from Larissa, on the day before, I had found the animal a very unsteady framework on which to load two hundred pounds. At the first gallop I put him to he went down on his knees and rolled over on me, so that thereafter I had to content myself with going more cautiously, keeping as close as I could to the cloud of dust raised by the general staff. So it happened that I was ambling along at a gait regulated only by my beast's vagrant will, when Asaf's exclamation checked me.

I stood now, gazing stupidly at the figure beneath me. He lay so still that I thought him dead. Then his fingers tightened on the water-flask and his arm trembled as he tried to draw it to him.

This was no time to stand idly by, wondering how and why he had come to this useless sacrifice. It was enough that he was here and living. I knelt at his side, and though my surgery was rough, it stopped the flow in which his life was draining away; his parched lips drank the proffered water, and when his head was on my knees he turned his face from the light and clasped his hands almost with contentment. He seemed to know that a friend was with him. The friend who had bound his wound and given him drink would find him a better bed than these rough stones and a kinder shelter than this bit of shadow, swept by the dust of endless pack-trains.

In such a place a friend could avail little. We carried him back from the turmoil of the road into the trampled wheat and there made him a rude tent of my blanket and a pillow of my saddle. Then I looked about me for help. The pack-trains clattered along the road and through them wounded men were threading their way, painfully hobbling to the field-hospital, miles away. Of ambulances there were none. I knew that when night came they would stagger back from the fighting front with their loads of wounded, and that so few were they in numbers the chance of finding a place in them was of the smallest. The Turk does not trouble much with the wounded. When a man is hit and he can hobble miles to the hospital, then Allah be praised! If not, he lies where he falls till night comes and his comrades find him and tie him like a bag of grain on a pony's back and send him on a journey that would be death to any Christian. If a surgeon finds him he is lucky. Remembering this, I looked back over the road by which I had come, measuring the miles we must cross before we reached help, and then at the Professor lying at my feet hardly breathing. I knew that we stayed where we were. Then I looked to the front. There was help there. There were surgeons working in that wide-spread wreath of smoke. I pointed over the plain and called to Asaf to hurry and bring me a surgeon. He demurred, for he was always chary about entering the zone of fire. I promised him a hundred pounds, a farm, a horse, a flock of sheep, if only he would go and bring me a surgeon. Malcolm Bey was mad, he said; no surgeon would come at such a time, miles for a single wounded man. I knew that he was right, but I could not sit idly watching my friend's life ebb away. I doubled the prize, and with a shrug of the shoulders Asaf mounted and galloped off.

I sat by the wounded man and waited. It was for hours. To me it seemed days. Thousands passed by—the men of the trains, stragglers, wounded, troops of the reserve. There were among them hands willing enough to help, were there any help to be given, but between them and me there was the inseparable gulf of language. One officer, a tall Albanian, rode over, and in French asked if he could be of any assistance; the man was a Greek; it made no difference, if he was a friend of Malcolm Bey; he could spare a pony and men to take him back to Larissa. I pleaded for a surgeon and an ambulance, pointing over the plain as though there they could be had for the asking. He bowed gravely—my request was a simple one; he would send them at once. And he rode forward toward the smoke and the clamor.

I sat watching. My hand held the Professor's. My eyes were turned down the road to catch the first sign of Asaf and help.

"Davy!"

He was looking up at me from beneath half-raised lids. How long he had been watching me I did not know. His voice was very low, but in it there was no note of surprise. To him it was quite right that I should be there. That was enough. His sickened mind could not trouble itself with wherefores.

"I am here, Professor," I said. The old nickname of the valley sounded strangely, but I could not call him Mr. Blight when he lay this way, looking up at me with eyes that seemed to smile with contentment despite his pain.

"You will be all right, Professor, but you must lie here quietly till the surgeon comes."

"I will be all right," he repeated slowly, and closed his eyes.

I looked over the plain. Would Asaf never return? The dusk was gathering and the wide-spread wreath of smoke mingled with it and was lost. I could see the flash of the Greek guns as they made their last stand to hold back the enemy till night came with its chance of escape. Even the near-by road had its moments of quiet and the moving figures grew blurred. Every clatter of hoofs might be Asaf coming, every rumble of wheels the ambulance. But Asaf did not come.

"Davy!"

I looked down. He was indistinct in the shadow of the rough tent. He had brought his other hand to cover mine.

"It was a good fight, wasn't it, Davy?"

"It was a grand fight," said I.

"And you'll tell them at home, Davy?"

"Yes, you and I will tell them together," I said with forced cheerfulness. "But you must be quiet till the surgeon comes."

It was growing dark. Over the plain the bark of heavy guns and the crackle of rifles had stopped. Camp-fires were lighting, a circle of them hemming in the town. Even the near-by road had grown quite quiet, like any country road where the stillness is broken by the rare clatter of hoofs or the curses of some stumbling pedestrian.

His hands were pulling at mine and I leaned down over him in the darkness. He could only whisper those last few words.

One hand slipped from mine; from the other life seemed to have gone, it was so still and listless.

I leaned so close over the dark form that my face touched his. I knew that he was going from me, and I wanted to hold him back. It was so terrible for him to die this way, in this lonely field with no wise hand to help him. My useless hands would have shaken him to arouse his life again, but I stayed them.

I knew that it was futile to speak, that my voice was falling on dulled ears, but what else could I do to stir him to fight for life?

"I'll tell them—we will tell them together," I cried. "We will go home to Penelope, you and I, and they shall know how you fought. And they will be proud of you, Professor; I know they will. And how glad they will be to see you—how glad Penelope will be! Can't you hear me?"

I looked up, straining my ears for the sound of hoofs, but the road was as quiet as any country lane before dawn. I leaned over the dark form and listened, and I knew that his march was ended.

CHAPTER XXVI

Through what quiet lanes of trivial circumstance do we move toward the momentous events of our lives? We go our way, whistling thoughtlessly; we turn a corner and stand face to face with the all-important. In my boyhood I went fishing and tumbled into a mountain stream; I overheard Boller of '89 speaking to Gladys Todd; I walked the Avenue at half past three in the afternoon and met Penelope Blight. How finely spun is the thread which holds together my story! A firmer foothold on the bank, an ear less quick to catch an undertone, a moment's delay before setting out on my daily airing, and there might have been no story to tell you; the valley might have been all the world I know and the wall of mountains my mind's horizon.

Then I come to the matter of Philip Bennett's motor. It was always breaking down. The delays that it caused as we journeyed north from Naples were annoying, but at the time these were trivial events, as we usually found a comfortable inn where we could wait while Bennett's man lay in the dust and peered up into the vitals of the machine. It was an adventurous thing to trust one's self to the mercy of the Italian highway in the untrustworthy little cars of those days, but Stephen Bennett insisted on our joining his brother, and as I was travelling back to England with him after a hard year in the Sudan I consented.

Bennett's brother met us at Naples, where we landed from the steamer, and, after pointing out to us the marvels of his self-propelling vehicle, put us into it, and took us puffing and rattling northward. We broke down twice a day, but we did not mind it, for after the trip from Khartum, the saddle over the desert, and the uncomfortable Egyptian rail, this new invention was to us the height of luxury in travel.

Stephen Bennett was in the Egyptian army, in the camel corps. I had ridden many a long march with him, and was beside him at Omdurman when he was struck through the body by a Remington. We got in a nasty corner that morning on the heights of Kerreri, and were so hard pressed by the dervishes in the retreat that the wounded were saved with the greatest difficulty. Bennett was so badly hurt that it took two of us to hold him on my horse; but we got him back to the river and the hospital, and after Khartum fell I picked him up at Fort Atbara. To Cairo by rail, a week at sea, and in the October days we were rattling northward and homeward over the white Italian roads. We reached Rome. I had one day in the Eternal City while François replaced a broken gear, and then we went on to Foligno, where we paced the Corso for an afternoon and the Frenchman fixed up his brakes. Late that night at Perugia we broke down at the foot of the hill and we had to climb to our hotel. At this last mishap Bennett began to show annoyance, for he had not as yet recovered his full strength, and the next morning, over our coffee and rolls, he proposed that we go by rail to Florence, where he knew people, and wait there until the car caught up with us. To Bennett's brother this suggestion was a reflection on the power of his beloved machine. He resented it, and I, not wishing to inject myself into a fraternal argument of some heat, went out to see the town, promising to return when they had amicably settled our plans.

From the rampart, where I paused that morning, as I strolled out so carelessly, leaning over the wall and looking over the Umbrian plain, there is a fair prospect—the fairest, I think, that I have ever seen, save one—and I hung there drinking in its peace and ruminating. Across that plain, and I should take another step toward home. But it was my boyhood's home alone, and yet I was going happily to sit again on the horse-hair sofa in the parlor, with my father on one hand and my mother on the other, and before me, perhaps, Mr. Pound, giving me his blessing. I saw it all: the valley clad white in snow, the house on the hill amid the bare oaks, the windows bright with potted plants, and down the path my father and mother running to meet me. I thought, with love in my heart, of that boyhood home and of my coming to it. Yet in that same heart there was a longing unfulfilled. Where was my manhood's home? Once I had had a tantalizing glimpse of it. That was when I sat at Penelope's side by the carved mantel, under the eyes of Reynolds's majestic lady. That for which I yearned so vainly was the spot which she made sweeter by her presence. Were she here at my side, looking with me over the Umbrian plain, this would be home. But wherever I travelled, east or west, north or south, my journey could have no such satisfying ending. Even in the valley, in the presence of familiar, homely things, I knew that I should look away vaguely, as I looked now, at distant mountains, wondering where Penelope was and how the world went with her.

After two years of absence from her and utter silence, I could drag out of my memory no pictures of her save old ones, and one by one I brought them forth, my favorite portraits, and saw her sitting in the carved chair pouring tea or driving down the Avenue, very still and very straight in her victoria. She must be in New York, I said, for in late October she would be hurrying back to town for the old futile routine. I went on, recklessly fancying Penelope leading that life, dancing, dining and driving, as though this were all in the world she could possibly be doing. I knew that she had not married Talcott. I had learned this much of her from a stray newspaper which announced the breaking of the engagement. I knew that it could make no difference to me if she had married some one else. That was highly possible, yet it was not a possibility on which I cared to dwell in my moments of rumination. This day my mind dwelt on it, whether I would or not. Over the plain, just beyond the mountains, I saw Penelope in my visionary eye, and I asked myself if I should find another in that coveted place from which I was barred. A bit of land, a bit of sea, and there was home. In a few hours the same sun would be smiling on it. At that moment I dreaded to go on. It was my duty, yet, could I, I would have turned back to the Sudan, to ride again over the yellow sands in the dust of marching regiments. I wanted action. Poor, pitiful action it was to walk, but with every fall of my feet and every click of my cane I could say to myself that I was going home, to my boyhood's home, and it mattered little if I had no other. The clatter of the Corso jarred on me. My mood demanded quiet places. The little streets called to me from their stillness, and I answered them. They led me higher and higher to the summit of the town. I crossed a deserted piazza, and by a gentle slope was carried down to the terrace of the Porta Sola.

There was in this secluded spot a soothing shade and silence. Old palaces, ghosts of another age, cast their shadows over it. Steps wound from its quiet, down the hill into the clatter of the lower town. A rampart guarded the sheer cliff, and with elbows resting there and chin cupped in my hands I looked away to the Apennines. Below me two arms of the town stretched out into the plain, but their mingling discords rose to my ear like the drum of insects. Beyond them, in the nearer prospect, the land seemed topsy-turvy, a maze of little hills and valleys. A pink villa flamed against the brown, and its flat, squat tower, glowing in the sunlight, called to its gaunt neighbor, rising from a deserted monastery, to cheer up and be merry with it. Distance levelled the land. It became broad plain, studded with gray villages and slashed by the Tiber; it rose to higher hills; then lifted sharply, the brown fading into the whiteness of massed mountain peaks.

This is my fairest prospect. And yet at that moment it offered me no peace. I was so infinitely lonely. With Penelope at my side, I said, I could stand here for hours feasting my eyes on so lovely a picture. To me, alone, it gave nothing. I should be happier with the Bennetts, forgetting self and self's vague longings in a plunge into the fraternal dispute.

I turned away into a narrow alley, but I was unaccustomed to Perugian streets and had not solved the mystery of their windings. Suddenly, passing a corner, I found myself again in the deserted piazza, and, looking down the slope, saw the same picture framed by palace walls. First my eyes grasped the panorama of plain and mountain. Then I saw only the terrace.

It was not mine any longer to hold in loneliness. I brushed my hand across my eyes to sweep away the taunting image. But she held there by the wall, leaning over it, her chin resting in her hands, wrapped in contemplation. Her face was turned from me, but there was no mistaking that still, black figure. If she heard my footfalls and the click of my cane, she gave no sign of being aware of my approach, but looked straight out over the plain. I checked an impulse to call her name and stood for a moment watching her. Would she greet me, I asked, with that same chilling stare with which she had said good-by? I feared it. But I tiptoed down the slope to the wall, and, leaning over it in silence, enjoyed the stolen pleasure of her presence. Whether she would or not, we looked together over the fair land. And what a prospect it was with Penelope at my side!

"David!" she said.

She took a step back, and stood there, very straight, surveying me, as though she were not quite sure that it could be. I searched her eyes for a hostile gleam, but found none, and when her hand met mine it was with a friendly and firm grasp.

"Penelope," said I, "as I came down the hill there and saw you, I thought that I dreamed."

"And I," said she, "when I turned and found David Malcolm beside me. I had heard that you were in the Sudan."

"Much as I should have liked to bury myself in the Sudan, there were calls from home," I returned.

"From Miss Dodd—what are you laughing at, David? From Miss Todd, I mean. How could you talk of burying yourself when you have such happiness before you? But, David, why do you laugh?"

With this reproof she tilted her head. That did not trouble me. I had so often seen her tilt her head in the same scornful way in the old days. And I laughed on joyfully at her calm assurance that I was going back to Gladys Todd.

"Gladys Todd is now Mrs. Bundy," I said.

"Oh!" Penelope exclaimed, and her voice changed to one of sympathy. "I am sorry, David. I see now what you meant by the Sudan."

"Didn't you know that Gladys Todd had jilted me years ago?" I asked.

"Why, no," she answered. "How should I? You never told me."

"I was on my way to tell you one day," said I. "And then—"

I stopped. Remembering why I had not told Penelope, I deemed it wiser to be evasive. I remembered, too, that in my joy at seeing her again I had been taking it for granted that she was still Penelope Blight. The gulf between us, which had been closing so fast, yawned again. "Tell me," said I in undisguised eagerness, "are you married, Penelope?"

Then she laughed, and in the gay ring of her laughter, I read her answer. She stepped back to a stone bench and seated herself, and I took a place beside her, watching as she made circles in the sand with the point of her parasol. There were a thousand commonplace questions that I might have asked her, but I was contented with the silence. It mattered little to me how she came there. It was enough that she was at my side. It mattered little to me that Bennett and his brother might have settled their dispute long since and be hunting for me, for I had made my farewell to them. I was home. I intended to stay at home. So I, too, fell to making circles in the sand, with my stick.

Then Penelope looked up and asked me: "David, how do you come to be here, in this out-of-the-way Italian town? I thought you were in the Sudan. Uncle Rufus told me that you were in the Sudan. That is how I happened to hear it. He always insists on reading to me everything of yours he can find—rather bores me, in fact, sometimes—not, of course, that I haven't been interested in what you were doing."

She spoke so coldly that I feared that, after all, I had best go my way with Bennett and his brother. I told her how I had travelled with them, and how the motor had broken down, and how my finding her was by the barest chance, for in a few hours I should have been on my way to Florence.

"It's strange," she said. "Our motor broke down, too, last night—just as we reached the gates; but this afternoon we hope to be off again to Rome."

"We?" I questioned.

"Uncle Rufus and I," she said.

"And Mrs. Bannister?"

"Married a year ago to a rich broker," she answered, laughing.

"How long I have been away!" I exclaimed.

I glanced covertly at Penelope. Despite the tone of formality in which she addressed me she seemed quite content to sit here weaving hieroglyphics with the point of her parasol, for I noticed that she was smiling, unconscious, perhaps, that I was studying her face. A while ago I had stood a little in awe of Penelope, but it was an awe inspired by her surroundings rather than by her. Going from Miss Minion's to face the critical eye of her pompous English butler was itself an ordeal; to Mrs. Bannister I was a poor young man whom it was a form of charity to patronize; the great library, the carved mantel, the portrait, the heavy silver on the tea-table, these were emblems of another world than mine. But here in this piazzetta, with the broad Italian landscape before us, those days of awkward constraint were in the far past. This quiet Penelope at my side contentedly tracing circles in the sand was, after all, the simple, kindly Penelope of the days in the valley. I had no fear of her. If she tossed her head disdainfully, I could fancy the blue ribbon bobbing there again and smile to myself as I recalled the morning when we had galloped together out of the mountains on the mule. There were questions which I wanted answered, and I dared to ask them.

"Penelope," I said, "I am glad to hear that Mrs. Bannister is happily married. Now tell me of my friend Talcott—what of him?"

Penelope sat up very straight and her head tossed. "David, I should think that one subject which you would avoid."

"I confess myself consumed with merely idle curiosity," I returned. "Talcott once made a great deal of trouble for me. Don't you remember the day on the Avenue when you cut me?"

"And if I had met you here a year ago, David, I should not have known you," she said severely. "A woman resents being made a fool of, nor can she easily forgive one who exposes the sham in which she has a part. The fault was mine and Mrs. Bannister's, and back of it there was something else."

"Something else?" I questioned.

Penelope did not answer. She had turned from me to the parasol and the sand. I repeated the question.

"Herbert Talcott is married—a year now," she said in a measured tone. "His wife was a Miss Carmody—the daughter of Dennis Carmody, who owns the Sagamore—or something like that—mine." A pause. Her head tossed. "He recovered very quickly."

"But the something else?" I insisted.

"There are some things which you will never understand," she answered carelessly.

"There are some things which you must understand," I cried. "The hardest task that ever I had was to go to your uncle as I did, like a bearer of idle gossip. It would have been easier to let you go on as you were going, ignorant and blind. I knew that it meant an end of our friendship. That day when I spoke I believed that I was going out of your life forever. I was not surprised when, on the Avenue, you looked at me as though I were beneath your notice." I rose and stood before her. "Had I to do it over again, I would, a thousand times, for your sake. And didn't I prove that it was for your sake, when I banished myself and gave up all claim to you?"

"Claim to me?" Penelope's lips curled defiantly. "I should have thought that you would have been occupied making good your claim to Miss Dodd, or Bodd, or whatever her name was. I suppose you did right, but none the less it was unpleasant. I thank you. You see I forgive you, or we should not be here now talking." She raised her parasol as though about to rise. "We must go. My uncle is waiting for me, and if you care to, you may come with me and see him before we start for Rome."

She did not rise; but the matter-of-fact tone in which she made the threat chilled me, and for a moment I stood silent, looking down at the black figure. The brim of her hat hid her face from me, but she was making circles in the sand. I asked myself if this was the time for me to speak of that claim, to speak my whole heart to her.

> She looked up. "David," she said, "you need not stand
> there so long.
> It might be bad for your wound."

"My wound?" I asked, and I took my old place at her side.

"Why, yes," she said. "Were you not wounded in the Sudan? Uncle Rufus told me that you were. He read about it in the papers. A Major Bennett, or somebody, ran out under a heavy fire and pulled you out of the hands of a lot of Arabs and saved your life."

I laughed. I would have given all I owned in the world to have had at that moment an interesting and conspicuous wound, for I knew how sympathy formed love, and how to a woman's mind a wound added interest to a man. A few weeks ago, though unwounded, I had at least been very thin and brown; but even of those mild attractions I had thoughtlessly allowed myself to be robbed by too high living and a kinder sun than the desert's. How I envied Bennett with his sunken eyes and tottering gait!

"The telegraph evidently mixed the names," I said. "It was Bennett who was shot."

"And you saved his life!" Penelope cried, forgetting herself.

However modest the man may be who hides his light under a bushel, it is always pleasing to him to have another lift the basket. As a matter of fact, on that morning at Omdurman it was almost as uncomfortable in the disordered and retreating ranks as it was in our rear, where Bennett lay crushed in the sand under his dead camel. If I did run back to him in the face of the oncoming horde of dervishes, a half-dozen of his own black troopers ran with me and helped to drag him to safety. It was an ordinary incident of the heat of battle, yet I did wish that Bennett were here to tell her about it, with his grateful exaggeration. To me fell the hard task not only of hiding my light, but of blowing it out.

"We got him away," I returned carelessly, accenting the pronoun as though the whole corps were concerned. "A lot of his men ran back to him and put him on my horse. I simply led him out of danger."

"Oh!" Penelope exclaimed in a tone of disappointment.

She looked over the plain; and I beside her, with my stick bent across my knee, studied her face, trying to read in it some promise of kindness and hope. But I found none. She seemed lost in the fair prospect. She had met an old friend and had spoken to him. That was enough. Now it mattered little whether he went away or stayed. It came to me then to try an old, old ruse to test the quality of her indifference.

"We had best be going," I said, rising.

To my consternation she rose, too, and began to move off carelessly, as though she expected me to follow her to the hotel to see Rufus Blight and then to bid her a casual farewell. I did not follow. Indifferent she might be, but my mind was made up that she should hear me. There was no longer any gulf between us. There was only the barrier of cool indifference which she had raised, and I would fight to break it down.

"Penelope," I said, "there are other things that you and I must speak of before we go."

"What?" she asked, looking back over her shoulder.

"Of your father," I answered, stepping to the wall and leaning on it.

I think that she saw reproof in my eyes. She hesitated, stirring the sand with her parasol, and then came to the wall beside me.

"Is there anything that I do not know of him?" she asked, as she stood with her chin in her hands, looking over the plain. "You wrote so fully—to my uncle. You might have written to me, David—but still you wrote to my uncle." There was no hard note in Penelope's voice. "You cared for him, David, and he died in your arms. It was for that I forgave you—everything."

"Everything? What do you mean by everything?"

"There are some things that you will never understand."

"But you speak as though I had done much that needed forgiveness."

"We have been to Thessaly, David," she went on, as though she had not heard me. "We found the very shrine where he died and the place where you buried him, and we marked it. It seemed best that he should lie there where he had fought so bravely—his last fight—as though he would have it that way. How could I help forgiving you after that—everything?"

"Everything? Penelope, I do not understand."

She laid a hand lightly on my arm. "Tell me, David, what were my father's last words to you?"

"I wrote them to you," I answered.

"To Uncle Rufus—not to me."

"How could I write to you after that day on the Avenue?"

"That was a small thing, and I was foolish. Now I want to hear it from you myself."

I looked straight before me as I repeated the words which her father had said that night as he lay dying on the plain of Thessaly. "Tell them at home—it was a good fight."

I felt her hand lightly on my arm again. I heard her quiet
voice ask:
"Was that all?"

"The rest I could not write," I answered, turning to her, and she looked from me to the mountains. "He said to me: 'David, take care of Penelope.'"

For a moment Penelope was very still. It was as though she had not heard me. Then she half-raised herself from the wall. One hand rested there; the other was held out to me in reproof.

"And how have you done it, David? With a year of silence."

"But that day on the Avenue?" I said.

"There were other days on the Avenue which you could have remembered," she returned. "There was that day when we met—after long years. And that day I remembered the valley and the boy who had come into the mountains to help me; I remembered my father's last words to us, and for a little while I was foolish enough to think that it must be for that that I had found you again."

I would have taken the outstretched hand, but she drew it away quickly and stepped back.

"And do you think I had forgotten the mountains that day?" I said. "Why, Penelope, I loved you that day as I love you now, as I have from the morning when you and I rode into the valley together."

I took a step toward her, but she moved from me, and stood with her hands clasped behind her back and her head tilted proudly as she looked up at me.

"It sounds well," she said, her lips curling in disdain. "But how about Miss Dodd, or Miss Todd?"

"Why will you be forever casting that up at me?" I protested. "For a time I did forget. I was a plain fool. But, Penelope—"

"I must be going," she said; but though she pointed toward the slope down which I had come from the little piazza, she really went again to the wall and stood there where I first found her, as though held spellbound by the view.

I was beside her. "Penelope," I said firmly, "there are some things which you and I must straighten out here and now."

"There is nothing to straighten out," she said. "Everything is settled. We are friends." Lifting a hand, she pointed over the plain. "What does that remind you of, David?"

"A little of the valley," I answered. Then I raised my hand too. "There are the mountains, Penelope, and just before them the ridge over which we rode that morning. Do you remember it? Do you remember how Nathan ran away over the trail, how you clung to me and called to me to save you? Home should be down there where you see the village. Do you remember—"

Penelope was looking from me, as though at the stone house, its roof just showing in the green of giant oaks.

Again she raised her hand. "And the barn, David—the big white barn—there!" she cried. Then she checked herself. She was very straight and very still. "I was forgetting," she said.

A step closer and I said: "You do remember, Penelope!"

"I must be going," she returned in a low voice, but she did not move.

I feared to speak now lest I should awaken her from the revery in which she seemed to have suddenly forgotten my existence.

"I must be going," she said again, and still she did not move.

She was looking across our valley! I knew that she saw it as on the morning when we rode in terror from the woods and it lay beneath us, a friendly land, in the broad day, under the kindly eye of God. Then I bent nearer her, an arm resting on the wall, my eyes on her averted face, patiently waiting until she should speak. And I could wait patiently now, for I believed that in the silence the memory of that day was fighting for me.

After a long time Penelope spoke. "David, do you remember—" She paused. Her voice fell to a whisper. "What was it that you said to me that morning—don't you remember?—don't cry, little one!"

In all the world there is no fairer prospect than that on which I looked from the little terrace in Perugia. For I saw not alone the lovely Umbrian plain. Before me stretched a fair life itself, into the unending years, from that moment when Penelope spoke, turning as she spoke and looking up at me with a smiling face. What a blind, blundering creature I had been! The black-gloved hand was close to mine on the wall, and I took it. Then I leaned down to her and said: "I remember, Penelope, and I will—I will take care of you always."

CHAPTER XXVII

"Yesterday, Harry, your mother laid a hand upon my arm, and, turning to me with a curious, far-away light in her eyes, said: 'How time flies, David!'"

And I looked down at her proudly, as though this were another of the innumerable new and clever ideas which she has a way of discovering and expressing so concisely.

"What made you think of that, Penelope?"

She pointed over the tangled briers to the woods, to the very spot where the path breaks through the bushes and leads to the brook.

"Yesterday, David—it seems but yesterday—I dragged you out of the deep pool, and to-day—a moment ago—I heard Harry there, shouting."

"He has probably caught a trout," said I as I lighted a cigar. "A small boy always shouts when he lands a fish."

Penelope laughed.

"And if," I went on, between critical puffs—"if he falls in, James is with him and James will pull him out. You must not think that these woods are full of small girls with blue ribbons in their hair who are watching for an opportunity to rescue drowning boys."

"How stupid you are, David!" said Penelope, "And yet at times you have been monstrously stupid. Of course, I know that Harry is perfectly safe with James; but what I meant was that it seems only yesterday—"

"Since you pulled me out of the brook?" I said.

Then I tucked her hand beneath my arm, and, standing there in the deep weeds and briers, we looked about the clearing. Even the Professor's care had long been missing. The roof of the cabin had fallen in years ago, and the end of a single log, poking through a mass of green, marked the stable from which the white mule had regarded me so critically. Yet the mountains rose above us, the same mountains; the same ridge sloped upward to the south, and above it was the same blue sky and a white cloud hovering in it. A crow cawed from the pines. It might have been the same crow that in other days called to me, now cawing his welcome. It did seem but yesterday. How fast the weeds and briers had grown, defying the Professor's languid hoe! How suddenly had the timbers snapped which held the roof! And doubtless Nathan's home went down in a gust of wind.

"Yesterday, Penelope," I said, "you led me out of the woods, dripping wet—don't you remember? from my tumble into the pool. Right there your father stood, looking at that very cloud, wistfully."

"And yesterday," Penelope said, pointing over the clearing, "in the morning early, father and I were sitting by that very door, when we heard a shout and, looking, saw you running toward us through the brush. Don't you remember, David? You fell down out there—why, a juniper tree has grown up there since yesterday."

Then Penelope was very quiet. I saw her glance to the bushes, and her hand gripped mine. I knew what was in her mind. I saw the same picture; I could almost hear the brush crackling under the Professor's flying feet, and leaning down over her I said: "Don't cry, little one; I'll take care of you."

That was really yesterday, Harry, and really yesterday Penelope and I rode again over the trail along which the white mule had carried us at such a terrible pace. We climbed the ridge, and at its crest Penelope reined in her horse and pointed over the valley. I followed her raised hand over the land, over the green of the fields and the white of blossoming orchards, to the great barn, gleaming cheerfully in the noonday sun, and to the dark roof nestling in the foliage of giant oaks.

Penelope turned to me with smiling eyes and said: "It's
all right,
David. Yon's our home!"